Books by B. \

STAR FORCE SERIES
Swarm
Extinction
Rebellion
Conquest
Battle Station
Empire
Annihilation
Storm Assault
The Dead Sun
Outcast
Exile
Gauntlet
Demon Star

REBEL FLEET SERIES
Rebel Fleet
Orion Fleet
Alpha Fleet
Earth Fleet

Visit BVLarson.com for more information.

Clone World

(Undying Mercenaries Series #12)
by
B. V. Larson

Undying Mercenaries Series:

Illustration © Tom Edwards
TomEdwardsDesign.com

Copyright © 2019 by Iron Tower Press.

ISBN-13: 978-1693634079
BISAC: Fiction / Science Fiction / Military

"Do not fear an army of lions led by a sheep. Fear an army of sheep led by a lion."
—Alexander the Great, 326 BC

-1-

It was early spring in the swamps of southern Georgia. That's a nice time to be off-duty in Waycross, just ask anybody.

The sky overhead was blue with white clouds splashed across it in streaks. The water trickling in the swamp behind my shack was fresher than usual, having lost the cold sluggish quality of winter. Springtime always made the world smell better.

I stood in the midst of my family land, squinting in the sun and smiling like a fool. The ground around my shack had transformed, becoming a vibrant green with wild flowers blooming everyplace. The blossoms sprinkled the land with welcome dots of color.

It had been more than a year now since I'd been called up to serve Legion Varus as an active-duty centurion. The truth was I'd grown a little soft, having enjoyed my time of relative leisure. We still had mandatory meetings every month at the local Chapter House, but they didn't amount to much. As an officer, I led those meetings, but they were little more than excuses to check on troop-readiness and drink a lot afterward.

1

Every three months, I had to report to Central for a situational briefing. That was boring, too. Other than that, my time was my own.

Unfortunately, money was starting to run thin. My daughter Etta had taken an internship up at Central, and she was getting paid... sort of... but it wasn't enough. Not to live up in the big city. They were rebuilding everything about that place, and the old neighborhoods with cheap rent had been demolished by the Skay. For some reason, everything they built new came with a much higher price tag than before.

Etta was living the independent life she wanted, but it was still an illusion. She had a job in the depths of Central, and she lived in a nice apartment with a real live cat. In order to keep her afloat, I had to make a giant deposit into her bank account every month or so.

When you're off-duty in the legions you get about one-third the pay you get while you're on active-duty. That doesn't sound like much, and it isn't. Still, as an officer I would have been doing fine if it wasn't for Etta's expenses.

"You should just let that girl borrow for school like everyone else," my dad suggested one morning when I wandered into the house late to see what was left over from breakfast.

"No way," I told him. "My daughter isn't going to end up indentured to Hegemony Financial forever."

He snorted. "Maybe not, but you'll be instead if you keep giving her top dollar."

My mom came in next, and she didn't look at me. I knew what that meant. She avoided my eyes when she wanted to argue.

"Poppa's right, James," she said as she put a fresh auto-pot of coffee on the table between us.

"No he's not," I said stubbornly. "Etta isn't gonna kick off her life owing millions to some bank."

The little coffee robot weaved its way between the dishes, examined each cup and topped it off as needed. The thing was kind of annoying, but at least this new model didn't make whining electric motor noises all the time like the old one did.

"But you're spending down all your savings, boy," my dad insisted.

Dipping my head, I hunched low over my coffee cup. The eager auto-pot wormed its way toward me again, but I shooed it away. It always screwed up the mixture of sugar and cream in my cup by adding more hot coffee, which pissed me off.

"Listen here, I'm not doing it," I said with finality. "I won't leave her high and dry. She'll be done with her schooling in only one more year. After that, she can handle her own money."

Far from being completely happy, they at least fell silent, which was fine by me. I ate some leftover eggs and toast.

I began to relax. It was never good to kick-off the morning with an argument. I began to hope this fine spring day could still be enjoyable.

Dad cleared his throat and moved around restlessly. After living with anyone for decades, you get to know the signs: he wasn't done yet.

"James..." he said, "we got a notice."

I looked up. They both met my gaze. Their lips were downturned at the corners—another bad sign.

"Uh... what notice?"

"I didn't mean to open it," my mom said. "But it was right there on the family's official email screen."

I frowned. "What notice?"

My mom looked at my dad, who shifted uncomfortably. "It seems like you bought a tram for Etta... they're going to repossess it. In fact, they probably already have."

My eyes blinked once, then twice. I nodded. I hadn't made the last payment or three. I'd gotten some colorful messages on my tapper, but I'd ignored them. Apparently, the bank had tracked down the family address and tried to contact me that way.

"She'll have to ride the city-skimmers like everyone else, I guess," I said.

"Those things aren't safe," Momma fretted. "Maybe we should lend her our tram."

My dad looked alarmed. "Are you crazy, woman? What the hell are we supposed to drive then?"

3

My mom walked out, pissed off. We let her go. The idea, after all, was insane. When you lived in a swamp, you had to have personal transportation. Owning a tram was just one more expensive luxury in the city. Clearly, I couldn't afford to keep Etta in that kind of state forever.

A full minute of silence followed while I polished off every scrap of food my parents had.

"I'm sorry," I said at last. "I know I'm spoiling the girl. I just didn't want to saddle her up with money troubles right from day one."

"Everyone owes the bank, James," my dad told me. "At some point, it'll happen to her, too. You came out of your education a million credits low, and you didn't even finish."

"Yeah…" I said thoughtfully. "Hell, the real problem isn't on Earth, it's upstairs." I pointed vaguely at the heavens above. "Things have been too peaceful among the stars lately. The big name legions have gotten cushy assignments, but not my old warhorse, Legion Varus. Ever since we saved the Pegs, we've been on ice."

"Hmm…" my dad said, frowning. He slapped the squirming auto-pot away from his coffee cup, the same as I had. It was really something my mom was into.

After I finished my coffee, I stepped back outside under that glorious sky and went for a walk. I thought about a lot of things as I wandered the back lot, eyeing bald cypress trees that had stood on this land for centuries. Some of them had lived here for a thousand years or more.

Heaving a sigh, I made a tough decision. I logged into Central on my tapper, and I selected a menu option I'd never touched before: *experimental contracts.*

Now, one thing that every second-year regular in the legions has burned into his brain is this: in military service, you *never* volunteer for anything. Not for one damned thing. Not ever.

But I did it anyway. What's more, I volunteered myself for the darkest of assignments. For the real guinea-pig stuff that no one even knows about until it bites them in the ass.

A few seconds later, my tapper buzzed. Then it buzzed again.

I had new orders. That fast, I'd been selected and given a slot. Bonus money was coming my way—lots of it.

The ACCEPT button popped up and glowed on my forearm, big and green. I stared at it, thinking hard.

The universe had immediately called my bluff. My heart rate accelerated as I looked at that button and hesitated. I was signing up to die, and I knew it.

What kind of shitty abuse had I volunteered myself for? I had no idea. That was part of the fun. It was certain to be some kind of shady-as-fuck, black ops, commando thing, I knew that much. Teleportation was likely involved, as I had extensive experience with that particular method of self-destruction.

Lots of people talk a good game about being willing to die for their kids, but for a Varus man like me, it was more than just talk. It was an easily selected option.

Finally, squinching my eyes up tight, I tapped on the accept button, then tapped yes to confirm.

Follow-up screens came at me. I agreed to report up at Central by morning, and I closed the windows. I didn't bother to read anything else because the details weren't going to help.

Looking around at the pretty green growth surrounding me, I managed to smile again. I picked a few wildflowers. I'd miss them, no matter where I was headed next.

-2-

Central was a black-glass pyramid a thousand stories high. It loomed in the midst of Central City, by far the tallest and most impressive structure in sight. Surrounding this manmade mountain, the new sleek buildings of the rebuilt city looked like toys.

The sky train banked and glided down in a spiral. It landed at the station, and I stepped onto the platform.

Wearing fatigues and carrying my ruck, I looked like any of another dozen military types that drifted around the place. Only the red crests of a centurion on my shoulders marked me as an officer.

It was enough to gain the attention of a pair of enlisted security hogs on patrol. They seemed to be eyeing everyone who disembarked from my train.

"You there, Varus!" called one hog.

I thought about ignoring him, but I didn't want to cause a scene. After all, I'd only been back in town for about ninety seconds. Besides, I was still in a good mood after my long vacation at home.

I turned to see what this pair had to say and gave them a tight smile. They walked up to me, each with one hand on their truncheons. They were shock-rods, actually. Devices built to stun the nerves and make limbs useless on contact.

"What's up, boys? You trawling for dates?"

The hogs blinked, and their faces darkened a notch, but they weren't enraged. Not yet. After all, I hadn't called them hogs or anything. For my own part, I felt like a diplomat on a streak. Meeting up with two patrolmen without friction was something of an accomplishment for me.

"Uh… Centurion? Are you James McGill?"

It was my turn to blink in surprise.

"That's right," I said. "Did someone send you out here? I'm not even late yet."

"Sorry sir. We're here to escort you to Central."

"I'm not lost, you know."

"Um… it was mentioned that you tended to wander off. Their words, not mine, sir."

I felt a pang of irritation, but I shoved that right back down. After all, this mission was classified and very lucrative. I didn't want to blow it and lose my paycheck without a damned good reason.

Forcing myself to relax, I took a deep breath and nodded. "All right. Take me in."

They looked relieved, and their hands slid away from their shock-rods. Apparently, they'd heard a thing or two about me. Sometimes, events took a bad turn when I was arrested or escorted in what I considered to be a disrespectful manner.

Following my hogs, I regretfully noted several eateries and bars along the promenade.

"You boys mind if I stop to get some breakfast?" I asked.

"No time. Sorry, sir. There will be some refreshments at the meeting."

"What meeting?"

They glanced at one another. "Uh… we don't know, Centurion."

"Right… you don't know a damned thing. I get it."

They loaded my ass into the back of an air car and zoomed over the city toward Central. We didn't land on the roof, though, not this time. We landed on a small side-platform, which stuck out like a shelf from the side of the massive structure.

"I don't remember this birdhouse," I remarked as we entered a modular structure that bulged like a wart on the side of Central's hide.

"It's probably new, sir," one of the hogs explained. "Lots of new stuff has been built since the Skay bombed us."

We passed through a security scanner and all of us lost our guns. The hogs were allowed to keep their shock-rods and I was left with my combat knife. It was stupid, to my way of thinking, to disarm loyal troops at the door. But I wasn't in charge of Hegemony's military policies.

They led me down, down, down through the building and underneath it. Down below Central… things got a little strange. The complex reached at least five hundred levels deep under the Earth, but no one seemed to know for sure how far down the digging had gone. Reportedly, after the attack by the Skay, they'd dug deeper. There could be a thousand levels by now— there was no way for a legion man like me to know for sure.

The hogs walked me to an unmarked door and waited. No one said anything, or knocked on the door, or tapped at their tappers. I figured we were being scanned and identified automatically.

After about thirty seconds, when I was just about to ask what the hell was holding things up, the door opened. It did so silently, with no one behind it pushing it open.

The hogs didn't move, so I stepped forward and entered the dim interior.

"Good luck, Centurion," said one of the men behind me.

A note in his voice made me half-turn, frowning. Was that a hint of sincerity? Of actual regret? Of pity, maybe?

The door closed behind me before I could land my eyes on his, and the moment was gone.

There were red arrows on the floor. They lit up, and I followed them. It was almost automatic. Red arrows were for combat soldiers, drop-ship splats on their way to their doom. I'd been in that classification of service for decades now.

The arrows led down dim passages. At one point, the passage went past a large door covered with all sorts of danger symbols and warning signs.

Curious, I stopped and pushed on it. The door opened, and I stepped off the trail of red arrows into a circular chamber. In the midst of the chamber was a spinning blob of light. I don't know how else to describe it.

Squinting in the silent, flickering, bluish glare, my mouth sagged open.

"What the hell is this...?" I asked aloud, but no one answered.

I heard murmuring voices on the far side of the blob. The room was spherical, I realized, with a dip in the middle that held that spinning light like a flame in a fire pit. Around the light was a flat ring of metal which provided a catwalk to safely circuit the weird light. The whole room was maybe fifty meters across and the path around it was about three meters wide.

I circled the blob of twisting energy, sticking to the metal pathway. I didn't dare get too close to whatever nightmare of physics I was circling. Staying as far away as possible, I ran my hand along the curved, crystalline walls.

Coming to the other side, I met up with a band of scientists. Floramel headed the committee. She glanced at me, but she didn't even reward me with a smile.

That was a kind of a shocker. After all, we'd had a number of nice nights together in the past. It had been years... but still.

"Floramel?" I asked.

She put a single long, thin finger to her lips, silencing me. I walked closer and peered over her shoulder and the shoulders of her two assistants.

"It's still not stable," one of the assistants said. "It's reacting to something."

"Give it time," Floramel told her. They were all females, all Rogue World near-humans. "It will settle down. This is a nonlinear continuity. The algorithm has to learn all the anomalous patterns."

"Uh..." I said, leaning over their shoulders and staring at a control console they were tapping on. Formulas and trend-line graphics were jumping all over the screens. I couldn't make heads or tails of it. "What's this thing doing? Is it dangerous?"

Floramel glanced back at me. She looked slightly uncomfortable, as did the others. That was because I was standing kind of close to them, but I wasn't touching them. You didn't touch a Rogue Worlder unless you meant business.

"It's an open rift," she told me. "A new transportation technology. Essentially, we've removed the need for suits and gateway posts. We're trying to take matter-transmission to a new level of efficiency."

"Ah…" I said. "I get it. You want good old James McGill to be your first guinea pig."

"Not exactly. There have been dozens before you."

"Oh…"

That didn't sound too hopeful. Looking around, I saw no sign of these "dozens" of other volunteers. Where could they have gone?

My eyes drifted to the blue-white blob of twisting light. The thing looked like an insane ghost that was trying to escape that circular pit. Sub-blobs flashed out bulbous pods, like the beginning of an explosion, but always they were turned back and forced into the center again. Whatever this stuff was, it was like lightning in a bottle.

Just then, another door opened. It was as silent and automated as the rest.

A figure in a lab coat walked through the door and approached. I knew in an instant who she was.

She was blondish, like her daddy. She was almost as tall as the Rogue Worlder women, but thicker of bone and more rounded in the face. She didn't wear makeup, but she didn't really need any. She had a natural beauty of her own.

Her face had always reminded me of her mama, Della.

"Daddy?" she said, shocked. "What are you doing here?"

"Playing lab rat, I guess," I told her.

I forced a smile, but she didn't return it. Instead, her mouth quivered at the corners.

Could this assignment really be that bad? I didn't ask aloud, because I already knew the answer.

-3-

"You shouldn't be here, Dad," Etta said, stepping forward and putting a hand on my wrist. "It's not safe."

"I know that honey," I told her. "That's about all I do know."

"They haven't briefed you yet?"

"Nope. They're having some kind of trouble with the containment field."

Etta stared at the blob of light while shaking her head. "We're nowhere near ready for human trials. It's not right."

"They'll just print out a new one of me if something goes wrong."

She looked at me and shook her head. "No, they'll do that if things go *right*. You see, it's a transportation system that doesn't require a preprogrammed suit, or a set of gateway posts at each end. We can send a subject literally anywhere."

I eyed the blob with new respect. "That is pretty cool."

"Not really... because we can't get them back."

"Uh... what good is it, then? One-way bombing missions?"

She shook her head again. "No, more like spying missions. At least, that's the first application they're testing. You see, the latest improvements allow the portal to stay open to the subject for a while. We can listen in, record scratchy transmissions, that kind of thing. That's the big update they did last month."

"I get it. The perfect spy-machine. What happens to the guy you send out there?"

Etta shrugged. "We watch, we record. If the connection doesn't break, and we witness the subject's death, we can print out a new man. But that isn't guaranteed."

Suddenly, I got it, and I found the truth chilling. If the spy they'd sent hadn't died by the time the connection faded, they couldn't be *certain* he wasn't captured or otherwise still alive. That meant the poor bastard was as good as permed.

"Hmmm…" I said, thinking it over.

"That's right. This is a perma-death machine. We shouldn't even be using it until we improve the links to the subjects after transmission. But Central Command wants to deploy it immediately to spy on our rivals."

Suddenly, the massive payment I'd signed up for didn't look so tempting. The bonus wasn't to reward you for just suffering and dying—this project went further than that. What they were doing down here was playing with a man's very existence.

"How many have you lost?" I asked.

"Seven. That's out of twenty-nine."

"But the odds are improving, right?"

Etta looked alarmed. She squeezed my bicep. "Don't do it, Daddy. Just turn around and go home. It's not worth it."

"Orders are orders, honey," I lied in a cheerful tone. There was no way I could tell her I was doing this to pay for her lifestyle. The truth wasn't going to make anyone happy.

"They're *making* you do this?" she demanded. "They can't do that!"

I shrugged helplessly. "There are a hundred good reasons why old James McGill shouldn't be standing in front of you and breathing canned air. I should have been permed any number of times by now. Sometimes, a man has to atone."

"You owe them for reviving you after… questionable events?" she asked.

I nodded. That part was true, after all.

Etta heaved a sigh. "The latest tests have gone better. But they keep pushing, reaching out farther. It's making the whole thing unstable. Focusing over hundreds of lightyears... the math alone is almost impossible."

"Uh... hundreds of...? What are we spying on, the Core Worlds?"

Etta looked evasive. "Floramel will have to tell you about that."

The trio of Rogue Worlders at the console had finally broken up. Floramel approached me.

"Ah James," she said, "I see you've discovered my assistant. Etta's surprisingly capable. At first, I was at a loss to understand it—but then I researched her genetics. She's related to the best minds on Dust World. In a sense, she's like a Rogue World scientist, but without the directed modifications."

"She's a smart one, you got that right!" I said, putting my arm around Etta, who looked embarrassed. "A good, old-fashioned homegrown genius."

"Yes... At times, chance can provide statistically anomalous results."

I wasn't certain if I was being insulted or not, but I decided to take her statements in the best possible light. Accordingly, I grinned and released Etta after giving her a final squeeze.

Floramel watched me the way a researcher watches a lab rat. She was an odd one, and she wasn't always as cold as she seemed now. I could tell stories... but that would be rude.

"When do we start?" I asked.

"You've volunteered to be cast?"

"Uh... cast?"

"That's the term we're using. This technology transmits matter to a remote destination without—"

"Yeah, yeah, I got all that from Etta."

Floramel nodded. "You are aware of the risks?"

"Something like a one-in-ten chance of getting permed, right?"

"More like a twenty-four percent chance."

My face fell. Not even I liked those odds.

"Uh..."

"Don't do it, Daddy," Etta said.

Floramel looked at her sternly, but she didn't say anything.

"Where would I be going?" I asked. "What would I be doing out there? Just testing the equipment?"

Floramel shook her head. "Follow me. It's time to prepare."

I gave Etta a kiss on the top of her head and left her hugging a tablet computer to her chest. She didn't look happy, she looked worried. She approached the console and began rechecking all the parameters again.

In the dim-lit passages, Floramel stopped and turned to look up at me.

"James... you can't do this. Your daughter would be devastated if you don't come back."

"I get that," I said.

"I don't think you do. She would blame herself. She's done some of the calculations on the containment fields. They're far from perfect. If you're lost..."

"Look," I said, "is this the briefing? I'll listen, and I'll make my own choices."

She sighed. "Yes... you always do." Then her eyes narrowed with suspicion. "Wait a minute, you haven't been briefed yet?"

"Well, no. I stepped off the path with the red arrows, see..."

"Come with me," she said resignedly, rolling her eyes.

Without further arguments, she led me to a rather normal-looking conference room. I found a frowning group of officials waiting for me. One of them was Primus Graves. Another, Praetor Drusus, was leading the pack.

"McGill," Drusus said. "Here at last. When are you going to learn to respect other people's time?"

"I'm way ahead of you, sir," I said. "I've been into the transmission chamber already. I know all about it."

Drusus lowered his frown, transforming it into a glare. "Another breach of security? This place is like a sieve."

Taking a seat, I smiled at the group. Floramel sat at the far end, and a few others encircled the table with us quietly.

"Here's the deal," Drusus said. "We want a volunteer to travel out to Rigel, gather intel, then self-destruct. We'll revive the volunteer upon their demise."

"Rigel? Damn, that's a long way out."

14

"About eight hundred lightyears, yes."

I knew that wouldn't be a fun trip. Teleporting wasn't really instantaneous. It took something like a perceived second for each lightyear traveled. During that time, you felt like you were suffocating.

"How long is eight hundred seconds, exactly?" I asked.

"Approximately thirteen minutes," Floramel said promptly.

"Ouch..."

"Are you seriously backing out over a bit of discomfort?" Graves demanded. "You're shaming Legion Varus right now."

"No, no, not at all, Primus. I was more concerned with the details of my return. As I understand it, you've lost contact with twenty-four percent of your prior volunteers."

Graves blinked, then he turned on Floramel. "Why didn't you just give him all the containment math on a chip?" he asked. "Then he could sell it all to Claver or something."

It wasn't like Graves to be sarcastic, and Floramel wasn't good at understanding any kind of humor.

"Because that would be a violation of classified data," she said, taking the question at face value.

Drusus lifted a hand, and the group fell silent again. He turned back to me and sighed. "We need data on Rigel. They've been quiet along the frontier between us for years, but the word is their fleets are moving again."

"So... I'm going to pop out there and bomb them?"

"Negatory," Drusus said. "This mission is clandestine. You can't take a bomb with you using this tech, anyway. You can't even get all the way to their planet with any known transmission effect. They've built some kind of planetary force field to prevent it."

"We don't have anything like that... do we?"

They shook their heads.

"Shit..." I said. "If they figure out how to use this new teleportation tech, they might throw more than spies at us. They might learn how to drop an antimatter bomb right on top of us."

"Right," Drusus said, "they might appear in the midst of Central with such a weapon. This city would be devastated

15

instantly and permanently if that happened today. We have no defense against it, while they do."

I stared at the table. They all watched me. No one spoke for several seconds.

"I'll do it," I said at last.

Graves smiled, but the rest of them still looked grim. "I knew you'd take the chance, McGill," he said. "All you have to do is walk into the enemy lair, look around and stay alive for at least ten minutes. You'll be transmitting the whole time."

"And after ten minutes?"

"Then… you die."

"Uh… any special method I should use for that?"

"No," Graves said. "We'll leave that completely up to you. Just don't take too long. We have to get a recorded death, so we can revive you without committing a crime. After twenty minutes, the connection will fade, and we won't be able to witness the death."

"Stay alive for ten minutes and be dead by the end of twenty…" I said thoughtfully. "That's precise timing in a spy mission. Is there anything special I'm looking for?"

"With luck, you'll appear on a portal entry point in orbit over their planet. Sniff around, try not to let anyone notice you. We're trying to find a way through their planetary defense screens to get down to their home world. If you can accomplish that, you've hit the jackpot."

"I'll do my best, sir. One more thing… what happened to the other guys? The ones you lost, I mean?"

Graves glanced at the tech team, and he shrugged. "They're lost, that's all. They never came back into focus—at least we can't verify that they did. We didn't get a transmission from them confirming life or death… so we couldn't revive them back here."

"Huh…"

That was it. They took me into another room and wired me up like a Christmas tree. Then they marched my ass toward the unstable ball of light in the central chamber.

Without much of a send-off, they watched me walk into that glowy ball of unstable light. The last thing I saw when

16

glancing over my shoulder was Etta—could she be crying? That wasn't like her...

Before I could say anything about it, I was transported someplace else.

-4-

The trip was a weird one as such things go. I've been transmitted from place to place for up to five minutes at a time. That doesn't sound like much, but you should try holding your breath for that long before you talk big.

The worst part was there was no way to breathe. I had no lungs. I had no body, really. I was just a collection of cells and instructions for reorganizing them into a pattern. Still, I felt the need to breathe. It wasn't intense, and I wasn't blacking out, but there was a definite panicky sense of suffocation.

That unpleasant sensation went on and on. A less experienced man might have lost it—but I'd done this sort of thing so often I didn't get too worried.

I was more concerned, in fact, about the technology itself. The tech crew never had specified why the other guys were lost—maybe that was because there wasn't anything I could do if it happened.

Could you get lost during the transmission process itself? I imagined traveling forever in hyperspace, a sliver of consciousness, unattached to any kind of reality... How long could that go on, if they missed their target?

I tried to get my mind to change the subject. To stop worrying about spending eternity as a lost cloud of thought—but once considered, it was hard to think about anything else.

Then, my reality flickered. A hole was ahead like a swirling drain—no, it was more like a maelstrom growing stronger each second. A silver-white brilliance that grew until it enveloped me.

Feeling as if I'd stepped out of the grave, I coalesced into matter again. I took a few gasping, wheezy breaths and put my hands on my knees, gulping hot air.

The air was moist and more than warm. It clung to my face, and I felt an urge to wave it away.

That was when I noticed several things. My hands, for instance, were touching the bare skin of my knees. The armor I'd worn out from Earth was gone. I was, in fact, buck-naked.

"Shit..." I said, staring down with hands uplifted, fingers splayed. James McGill was in his birthday suit. At least all my parts seemed to be present and accounted for.

"They sent me through with nothing..." I muttered aloud.

Next I noticed a glow. A white glimmer that looked just like the portal I'd traveled through—it still hovered around me, obscuring my vision at range. That was their trick, I realized. Part of the gateway was still attached to my hide. That must be how they could see what I saw, how they could monitor my actions and spy on the enemy.

Taking experimental steps, I found the glow dimmed, and I was able to make out my surroundings. I appeared to be on a ship of some kind—or maybe a station.

The walls were slanted downward from the ceiling, and the gravity was low, but it was enough to allow me to move around easily. The temperature was hotter than I liked it, but comfortable enough when you were bare-assed.

Walking was almost like bounding. I had to take easy steps, or I'd launch and hit the ceiling. Fortunately, I'm no stranger to low-G environments. In seconds, I'd adjusted and was making good time.

I came to an airlock. There was a small octagonal window in the center. Peeping through, I saw a far door and another tiny window. Beyond that was outer space with the disk of a planet spreading wide a filling the porthole with light—it had to be their homeworld.

19

"Can you see this?" I asked in a whisper. "Looks like their planet, outside this station—or whatever it is."

Getting bored fast, I reminded myself I only had a few minutes to spare. I moved on, but I marked the airlock as a possible source of self-destruction when the time came.

Another door nearly straight across was a dead-end. Beyond that there was a door to a larger passageway on the far side. I saw movement, but now wasn't the time to be cautious. Taking a breath, I threw it open.

Stepping out into the open, I saw I was in a huge chamber. My mouth fell open, and I gaped at my surroundings.

"I hope you guys are getting this…" I said aloud.

I was standing on a balcony overlooking what I could only describe as an orbital city. Overhead, a crystalline dome enclosed maybe twenty square kilometers of space. Beyond the glass was a black field dotted with stars to my right, and the glowing crescent of a vast, blue-brown planet to my left. Perhaps a thousand meters below my perch, spread out in gorgeous detail, was a city of motion and light. There were people down there of several different species. Air cars and ground trams whirred this way and that. Drones hovered and whizzed around.

And the people… most of them were from Rigel. Little bear-like dudes with tufts of nasty-looking hair growing over most of their small bodies.

My lips curled up in distaste. I knew these people pretty well by now. They were a vicious, arrogant and cruel race. They subjugated everyone they could reach and abused their vassals liberally.

"A city," I said, figuring they might be able to hear my report back home. "An orbital city. This is really something. We've got nothing like it back home."

One of the whirring drones took notice of me then. It banked sharply, coming around to investigate. A moment later I was nose-to-nose with a row of tiny, twitching tubes that had to be cameras. They studied me with interest.

Grinning, I waved my hand at it. "James McGill!" I called out. "Nice to meet you."

The thing hovered closer. I had no doubt it was calling for back up.

I kept grinning and waving like an idiot. It drifted closer. The moment it was within reach, I snatched it out of the air and smashed it on the deck. It burst into a hundred clattering pieces.

"Ha!" I laughed, and I looked down on the city again.

There were some special spots of interest. A pavilion floated over the city itself like a luxury yacht. What looked like a party, or a ceremony, was taking place aboard that fancy-looking platform. The thing reminded me of the deck of an old sailing ship, but without any obvious means of propulsion or lift.

"That's cool…" I said, watching it glide over the rest of the bustling metropolis.

The sounds drifting up from the city were full of echoes, and I found them entrancing. It was like leaning out over a Manhattan penthouse balcony. Now and then, I caught a sharp sound among the general background murmur. Sounds like the clashing of plates or the sudden grinding of machinery.

Breaking the spell, an air car bounced up into my view. Two bears sat inside—Rigellians. They had no windshield or anything. The car was open to the air like a convertible coupe. The bears were armed, and they aimed their weapons at me.

"Uh-oh," I said, and I checked my tapper. The timer running there said eleven minutes had passed. I grinned. "Time's up!"

Climbing onto the short railing that encircled the balcony I'd been perching upon, I moved to jump.

"Stop!" one of the bears said. The rattling, underwater voice effect was from his translation device. Serving like tappers, every Rigel citizen I'd ever met had a looped set of snake-bones that hung across their shoulder and chest diagonally.

I took no notice of the bear's order, and I dropped off into space. A thousand meter fall, even in low-gravity—I figured it should do the trick.

The air car surged forward and downward. It slid under me, and I landed on the hood.

"Ah now, you shouldn't have done that," I told the bears.

"You will stand down, creature."

"No, I don't think so."

One of the bastards moved to shoot me. Now, you'd think I'd welcome that, but I wasn't sure what kind of weapons they were using, it could have been a stun-gun. The last thing any legionnaire wants is to be captured on a hostile alien world.

Twisting, I caught the shot on the left side. Sure enough, it didn't hurt, it numbed me. A stunner of some kind. A nerve inhibitor.

Roaring, I reached for the bear with the gun. The other one fought his instruments, trying to keep his air car from flipping over under my shifting weight.

Now, you have to understand that even though these bear-dudes are only about a meter tall, they're plenty strong. In fact, any one of them was probably as strong as I was.

The trouble they had, however, was leverage. Sometimes it paid to be bigger than the other guy.

I grabbed the tube of the weapon. It went off again, but I managed to duck the worst of it. My right ear and my right eye were gone. They were numb. No sound, no sight came to my brain from either of them. My mouth sagged too, and my lips slobbered and drooled as I couldn't control my whole face any longer.

Still roaring, I tugged on that gun. The bear hung on. He came right out of his seat, and due to his shorter stature, he found himself lifted into open space. With a savage heave, I threw him out into nothingness. He went spinning away—still holding onto his gun and squalling in fear.

That made me laugh. Slobber flew everywhere, I must have looked demented.

I reached for the other bear. My blood was up, and I felt like killing both of them.

The driver saw my intent, and he took his paws off the controls. The air car lurched, but he steadied it and aimed his gun at me.

I pitched forward, almost falling onto his head.

22

But then, the nerve-gun went off again. I felt it in my balls—or rather, I didn't feel anything at all from the middle of my body.

That pretty much finished the fight. My hips no longer held my weight. My legs were rubber. My Johnson was nonexistent, as far as I could tell.

Falling sideways, I tipped and began the long drop to the glowing city streets.

Damn.

Chance rather than design provided me with a reprieve. My hands flung wide and clutched automatically at whatever I could cling onto. This happened to be one of the control sticks for the air car.

Heaving over, the car began spiraling downward. Every few seconds it crashed into the wall of the space station, screeching and sending a cascade of orange sparks into my hair and face.

"Human, you are a mad-thing. Help me regain control, and you might be allowed to live."

I laughed at the bear as he fought with his controls. He bit my hand, taking a finger with him, but still I hung on. In fact, I managed to get my other hand on the stick. I angled our flight toward a busy-looking area below.

"If you live," I shouted, "tell Squanto that James McGill is still looking for him! I want a wrestling rematch!"

We hit a few seconds after that, and I didn't remember anything else, not even when they showed me the fireball later on.

-5-

For once, I came out of the revival machine with a smile on my face. In fact, I started laughing when I thought about the look on the face of that last bear-dude when I rammed him into the ground.

Unfortunately, my laughter turned into a coughing fit. That didn't get any better when rough hands grabbed me by my bare shoulders and gave me a shaking.

"What the fuck did you do, McGill?" Graves demanded.

My eyes didn't work yet, so I could recognize his voice but not his face. Oddly, the coffee-breath was strongly overwhelming too. Just my vision was bleary.

"I made some road-kill," I said, still amused. "Did you see it, Graves?"

He let go of me with a shove. I almost slid off the table, but I caught myself. Another rumbling, coughing, laugh came out of me. "You should have seen his expression. It was priceless."

"McGill," Graves said in a tone that told me his teeth were clenched. "You were supposed to be discreet. You were sent in as a spy, not a saboteur!"

"What's the difference? We're at war with these little bastard bears."

"The difference is they now know we're capable of infiltrating their orbital city, and they'll be looking for all our future agents."

"Yeah? What did the last guy do?"

He got into my face again. The coffee breath was back, and the face was still just as blurry.

"I'll tell you what they didn't do: they didn't make a fire-fall spectacle in the middle of the enemy habitat. They didn't announce their names, or their intentions."

"What did they do? Squat in that tunnel?"

He let go of me. "For the most part, yes. We've been methodically exploring rarely used portions of the station. This is supposed to be an incremental experiment."

"So, all they did was poke around in passages then space themselves after a few minutes? What a disappointing way to go out. I'm just not that kind of man, sir."

Graves heaved a sigh. "I made a mistake. You don't send an ape to do the job of a ballerina."

"I'm certainly the ape in that match-up, sir," I admitted.

"All right," Graves said, starting to pace. "Get off that table and get dressed. We're going downstairs."

"Don't you mean upstairs, sir? Isn't there a debriefing in order?"

He didn't really listen to me. He began talking to himself as much as to me. "There's no more point in subtlety. We're going to have to send in fighters from now on. We'll have to accelerate all the timetables before they figure out a way to block us."

I grinned weakly and clapped my hands. One loud popping clap rang out in the revival chamber, making all the bio-people wince. "In that case, I'm your man!"

Grumbling, Graves walked out. I staggered to a rack of uniforms, selected one that didn't quite fit, and followed him. Tottering down the corridor, I felt the smart-straps stretching and slapping over my back. They were trying to reach one another and cover my skin completely.

I could see pretty well by now, and due to my unnaturally long legs, I'd almost caught up to him by the time we reached the elevators.

"Uh…" I said. "Where exactly are we going, Primus?"

"We have to refocus the anomaly. We've been using that same spot as an insertion point for the last seven jumps. Each

25

time, we got there without a hitch and got back some useful data. Each time, the agent in question offed himself with that airlock—as ordered. You *did* see the airlock mentioned in the briefing? Am I right McGill?"

"Oh yes, sir. Very handy. Spacing myself there was my original plan."

"Until you went out onto the balcony and mooned an entire city full of the enemy, hmm?"

"Uh… that's about right, sir."

Graves turned away from me and rattled the elevator call buttons again. He cursed. The elevators always took a long time at Central. After all, the building was so tall it penetrated the cloud-cover on most days, and that was only counting the part that was above ground.

"What am I supposed to do now?" I asked conversationally.

Graves gave me a hard look. I could make out his expressions now. My eyes were working at near-capacity.

"Since you like wrecking things so much, maybe we'll send you after a harder target. Something that *needs* destroying."

I brightened visibly. "What would that be, sir?"

"We'll see what the nerds downstairs have come up with for a list of viable targets."

The elevator dinged and pulled to a stop. Blinking, I turned around and saw the doors open. To my surprise, we were at the lobby. Graves all but booted me out of the elevator.

"Come on!" he ordered. He walked across the lobby, and I followed.

We headed to the back of the main promenade. Suddenly, I figured out where we were heading.

"We're going back underground? Back down to the labs right now?"

"You're a regular Sherlock Holmes today, McGill."

My jovial mood vanished. I glanced at the glass door exits wistfully. I'd kind of planned on taking the rest of the day off and downing a few beers. Maybe I'd look up an old girlfriend or two, if they were still in town.

Sadly, my workday wasn't done yet. I followed Graves dejectedly. I didn't like the labs. They were cold, silent vaults far below the Earth. Whatever had possessed my daughter Etta to want to work down here had certainly never made any sense to me.

After going down a few hundred floors, we switched elevators and went through additional security. The floors were no longer numbered down here. Instead, they had "zones" like "zone echo" or "zone bravo". At least, that's what the signs said.

We were deeper than the last time I'd come down and gone for a jaunt through the anomaly. I could tell that much.

For one thing, the air pressure felt oppressive down here. The chambers were cold in the bravo zone... but echo... it was hot down that far. I could feel it, as if I was down so deep I could feel Earth's mantle crawling around restlessly under my boots.

We stopped at "zone echo". We walked down lonely, echoing passages. The air itself was thick, maybe even a little steamy.

"This is a weird place," I complained. "I don't like it down here."

"I don't think anyone does. Here, put your hand on this plate."

We both were scanned excessively. There was no staff down here to do it, just machines. Finally, a section of the wall slid away, one black slab moving apart from the rest. An opening yawned wide behind it.

Graves walked inside, and I followed.

In the chamber beyond, a tech team surrounded another one of those white blobs—that's what I thought it was at first, anyway. Then I realized it was a holo-globe replaying someone's trip into the anomaly.

It was freaky. I could see through the agent's eyes. I could hear him breathe. Everyone else watched intently. They ignored us, and we stood in the back.

"There it is," one of the nerds said. "Right at the deep alcove over that apartment."

"But how could anyone climb into that? It's too high off the floor."

"I'll do it," I said loudly.

They turned to look at me. "That's not my vid, is it?" I asked. "Who took that trip?"

"Ferguson," Graves said next to me.

I turned to him in surprise. "Really? The hog guy? He's all right. Haven't seen him for years, though. How did he do?"

"He's permed," Graves said without pity or even inflection in his voice. "Now, take a look again, McGill. You really think you could crawl over that hot pipe and squeeze into that narrow slot?"

"Uh…" I said, regretting my earlier statements. "Did he get permed on this mission? The one we're watching now?"

"Yes," said the tech from the front of the team. "He took too long. We never saw him die. After about twenty minutes, sometimes as little as seventeen, the connection breaks. After that, there's no proof of death possible."

"Hmm…"

"Are you turning chicken, McGill?" Graves demanded.

"Nope. I said I'll do it. I can climb that, easy. Ferguson, though… his arms and legs probably weren't long enough to get a good grip."

Graves snorted. "All right. We'll send you then. Is this the best target you have? The closest thing we've seen to the reactor?"

"That's right, Primus."

"Reactor?" I asked feeling a fresh concern.

Graves looked at me. "Of course. I said we were switching the agenda from one of spying to sabotage. You're going after their reactors."

"Did you make that clear before?"

"I am now. Your mission is to travel out there, damage critical systems, and visually demonstrate it's been done. With any luck, this will disrupt the enemy shielding and let us reach all the way down to their home planet. Can you do it or not?"

"Uh… I can't carry an explosive, can I?"

"No. You'll have to improvise."

"Well… all right. If Ferguson got that far, I'll do the rest."

Graves slammed his glove into my back. "Great. I knew you were our man. Team? Lock those coordinates. Power up the device. We'll fire McGill back at them at 10 am tomorrow."

Happily surprised, I looked around at the team. I'd half-expected to be shipped right back at the enemy on the spot. Instead, they broke up and kicked me back upstairs to the lobby.

Graves went his own way, and I headed out into the streets. It was time to see if this new version of Central City had better bars than the last one did.

-6-

Someone was waiting for me the second I hit the streets outside. It was twilight, but I'd recognize that muscular, red-headed, rat-eyed guy anywhere. It was Ferguson, a hog non-com I'd met long ago in the early days of Earth's war with the Cephalopods.

"Ferguson?" I asked, stopping dead on the wide marble steps outside Central.

He grinned. "Hi McGill. You're an easy man to find, you know that?"

"Aren't you supposed to be… like… permed or something?"

It was a rude thing to ask. People didn't go around talking about perma-death with someone who wasn't a tight friend. But today, these were special circumstances.

His face faltered, but he didn't look angry.

"You heard about that, did you?"

"I sure did. What's the story?"

"It was all a big mistake. Come on, I'll buy you a beer and tell you about it."

Accepting his invitation, I walked with him across the street and two blocks down to the south. When we got to an "under-construction" zone I began to frown.

"Aren't the bars the other way?" I asked. "I mean, this area isn't even—"

30

Ferguson didn't seem to be looking at me. He stared this way and that, as if looking for someone or something else.

Now, as a long-term starman from Legion Varus, the most notorious outfit in Earth's military, I'm easily alerted. Something wasn't right here, and I stopped taking long strides into a part of town that was full of nothing but chain-link fence, scaffolding and silent hulking construction drones.

Halting, I stared at Ferguson with suspicious eyes. "What's up, hog?" I asked.

I'd thrown in the insult to see how he would react. He didn't even seem to care. In fact, he wasn't even looking at me.

Getting pissed, I reached for him. My hands—they seemed to sink right into those big shoulders. There was barely any real meat to the man below a haze of holographic trickery.

That's when something hard jabbed me in the kidneys. It wasn't a gun barrel, but it buzzed, and I felt my lower body seize up. A shock-rod. Frig, everyone seemed to want to stun old McGill today.

My hands gripped the neck under the hazy disguise. It wasn't as thick as Ferguson's would have been, but it was substantial anyway. Squeezing and growling, I tried to throttle this imposter—but I couldn't do it.

Whoever was behind me was zapping me in the ass over and over with that shock-rod. At last, I slumped on the ground between my two assailants, gasping for breath.

The man who'd been working my spine into numbness stooped and put his hands on his knees. He laughed, it was an evil sound.

"Good old monkey-brains McGill," Claver said. "You know, it's been years since I've killed you, but just beating on you a little feels *good*."

I had to suck in two breaths before I managed to wheeze out a single word. "Same…"

"Listen-up, moron," Claver said, leaning over me, "you might be wondering what all this fuss is about. It's nothing big, really. I'm just here to warn you off. To let you know that you'd best stop annoying the good folks from Rigel. They haven't been coming to Earth, after all, to shit in your backyard, have they? No, no, they haven't."

My lungs seemed to be full of cement. It was a struggle to take each breath. Claver had overdosed me with his shock-rod, and my diaphragm barely worked anymore.

Still, I managed to flick my eyes toward the fake Ferguson. "Who..?" I grunted out.

Claver looked up. "Oh… him? I'm surprised you haven't figured that out yet. Doesn't one dummy always know another? Switch off your box, dummy."

The Ferguson look-alike reached to his belt. There was a tiny, audible click.

Instantly, the holographic field that had surrounded him vanished. Instead of Ferguson, I found myself staring at another Claver.

This man, however, wasn't one of their intellectual giants. He was a Claver-2, a second-rate unit, cloned to work as a specialist. He wasn't a genius or a powerhouse. He stared at me with a blank expression.

"Happy?" Claver asked me.

I grunted and burbled, unable to speak.

"I can see that you are," Claver continued. "All right, well, that about wraps up this little get-together—"

He stopped as my hand snapped out, gripping his ankle and locking him in place.

Instantly, the Claver-2 began methodically kicking me in the ribs. His nostrils flared and his eyes widened so I could see the whites all the way around. Apparently, he'd been conditioned to protect Claver Primes just like all his brothers.

Thunk, thunk, thunk!

The boot-tip crunched into my side over and over again. My whole body shivered and jerked—but I didn't let go of Claver's ankle.

"Why…?" I asked.

Claver lifted a hand and tapped his brother's shoulder. "Thank you, that'll be enough for now."

The man stopped breaking my bones but continued to stare at me with insane eyes. The lesser Clavers had a protective instinct built into them when it came to their masters.

"Seriously, McGill?" the prime asked. "You still haven't managed to squeeze a tiny glimmer of understanding out of

32

that dim mind of yours? I swear boy, if you put your brain into a chicken skull, it would fit with room to spare—and the chicken would walk backwards."

I could feel the sick oozing of internal hemorrhaging now. It was a familiar, if unwelcome, sensation—but I still held onto his ankle.

"Why...?" I croaked out again.

"Because you pissed off Rigel, that's why, you sorry excuse for a retard! I'm operating as... shall we say... one of their representatives today. They told me to give you a mild warning. Next time, your family might be involved. I hear your daughter is working here at Central these days. That makes her a fair target in my book."

There aren't many things that get my blood pumping, but threats toward my family were definitely on the list. Rage flared up on my face.

Claver smiled down at me. "I see you got the message. Good. Now that I've delivered it, I'll be on my way. You have a nice night, McGill."

He tried to walk off, but I still had his ankle in a death-grip. He cursed and tugged, but he couldn't escape.

Waving to his side-kick, he indicated my offending hand.

The second-class Claver went into instant action. I could tell he'd been eagerly awaiting a signal to work on me again.

Lifting his boot high, he brought his heel down like a hammer onto my thick wrist and forearm. With each stomp, his face reddened and his teeth grew more and more exposed. Soon, a feral grin split his face.

It took six hard blows, but at last, my hand couldn't stay closed any longer. Claver was able to wrench himself free and stagger away.

"You have a nice night now, McGill!" he called over his shoulder.

Sucking in a breath, I rolled up onto one elbow.

Claver glanced back, and he frowned. He stopped walking away.

At his side, his sidekick began to breathe harder again, like he was aroused or something. His nostrils whistled like those of a clogged-up old man. His fingers clenched and unclenched, gripping the night air.

Grunting and moaning, I heaved myself to my feet. I began to shamble toward my two assailants.

The dumb one looked excited. He kept casting anxious glances at his master, like an attack-dog waiting for the signal to charge.

But the other man was older and wiser… he didn't look eager at all. He looked concerned.

"You never did know what was best for you, did you, boy?" he asked me when I got close.

A beamer appeared in his hand. A red, pencil-thin tube of light flared. The crimson light seemed bright in the growing darkness.

The beam sent up wisps of steam and punched a hole in my ruined chest—but it didn't put me down.

My right foot wasn't operating below the ankle, but the leg held me up. My left side worked pretty well. Better with each step, if the truth be told. Beginning to hope, my left hand came up, shaped like a claw.

Claver shot me again and again with increasing frequency, stumbling backward.

Finally, I toppled and went down.

"Fucking animal…" he grumbled, aiming the weapon at my face.

I stared at him, and I mouthed breathless curses.

He shot me one more time in the face, and my body stopped functioning at last.

Sometimes death was a relief, and this was one of those times.

-7-

In the morning, I was revived in Central again. I awakened expecting to find a pissed-off Graves presiding over the procedure, but instead, a prettier face greeted my blurry vision.

"Galina?" I asked.

"Call me Tribune, you idiot," she said.

Galina was a highly ranked officer and one of the best-looking women I'd ever slept with—but she was also the most evil of the lot.

"Why are you here… sir?"

"Graves is sick of you. He's asking Drusus to reject your pay-voucher and send you home."

"What? Why?"

"Because you can't even go a single night without getting into trouble. We realized at 10 am that our commando was AWOL. Imagine our lack of surprise, given your history."

"Aw, now, come on, sir. I was attacked."

"Of course you were. You're always attacked everywhere you go. Did you ever consider, James, that it might be *you* who's the problem? Hmm?"

My bleary eyes were functioning better now. She looked good. How long had it been since we'd been together? A year, maybe?

I made a mental resolution to make another play for her, first chance I got.

35

"—are you even listening? Are you a bad grow, or something?"

"Huh? No sir. I heard it all. I'm just a little fuzzy, that's all."

"Good. Get your kit on, and get your ass upstairs to the transport chamber."

Frowning, I sat up on the table, staring at the puff-crete floor.

"Well?" she demanded. "Are you interested in getting that paycheck or not?"

"I'm thinking," I said.

She paused and lifted her chin. She stepped closer, eyeing me. If there was anyone in the legions who knew me better, I wasn't sure who it might be.

The bio people were hovering around, taking measurements and tapping in readings and approvals. Galina ordered them all out of the room. Seeing as she was a tribune, they fled.

"James?" she asked me.

"What?"

"What's going on?"

I thought it over, and I decided to tell her the truth. That wasn't a thing that comes natural to old James McGill, but I figured the situation warranted a break with tradition.

She listened carefully, and put her hands on her shapely hips. By the time I was done describing my death at the hands of a pair of Clavers, she was strutting around the room, deep in thought.

"This is alarming," she said. "Claver is back—that's bad enough. We haven't heard from him for years. But what's upsetting me more is this business of him being in the employ of Rigel."

"Well, I guess he found greener pastures out there in Frontier 928. After all, it's a big galaxy."

She frowned up at me. She wasn't a tall woman, and even though I was sitting on a gurney, I was still taller than she was.

"You hit Rigel's space-station, and we scared them," she said. "Scared them enough that they've sent Claver out to warn us off... This is good news, really. If that's all they can do—we'll crush them."

36

I looked at her, uncertain. She seemed alight with excitement. The wheels in her little head were turning fast, that much I could tell you.

"What do you mean, sir?"

"Don't you see, James? They didn't come to the Hegemony Council and make demands. They didn't offer peace. Instead, they went directly to you and threatened you and your family. That's a sign of weakness."

"Weakness?"

"Yes. It was a very weak countermove. A joke, really. The fact is we don't even need you to continue attacking them. If you want out now, I'll arrange it."

For the first time, I looked her right in the eye. The blurry residue obscuring my vision had cleared somewhat.

Galina knew my family, and I knew she understood I couldn't allow them to come under fire due to my actions.

"Uh..." I said, chewing over her offer. "Would I still get paid?"

She rolled her eyes. "Money? You're in this for the money, really? I thought you'd just gotten bored sitting around in that Georgia swamp."

"No, I need the money."

She nodded. "Okay. Your choice, then. Are you in or out?"

Forcing a smile, I climbed off the table and reached for a uniform. My foot slipped a little in a puddle of something nasty, and I threw out a hand.

Galina braced herself and caught my big arm. It was kind of absurd, really, as I was around three times her weight. But she held on, and I regained my balance.

"Thanks," I said, smiling.

"You're welcome," she grunted out. "Now, get your big ape-arm off me."

I moved away toward the uniform rack and selected one. To my surprise, it fit perfectly.

"I had them provide you with your usual size—a long series of Xs."

We both smiled, and after cleaning up, I exited the chamber in her wake.

Following her to the lifts, I began to entertain certain thoughts. That was due to having a fine view of her hindquarters in motion, of course. They were hypnotic to most men—me most of all, I guessed.

Galina led me down to the anomaly chamber again. Graves showed up a few minutes later, and he looked annoyed.

"McGill? Fancy seeing you here." He turned to Galina. "Tribune, I thought we'd scrubbed this no-show from the mission roles."

"Have you got someone better in mind?" Galina asked him.

Graves shrugged. "I've got plenty of men who know how to avoid fighting in the streets every night."

"Your call," Galina said. "He's standing here and he's ready. Does he go, or not?"

Graves twisted up his face. "Fire up the rift. McGill, try to remember your instructions this time. There's an opening above the…"

I wasn't looking at him. I wasn't listening to him, either. Instead, I eyed the whorl of light and color that I was about to step into. Automatically, I had begun to take deep breaths, like a swimmer about to go for a long dive.

Deep breathing wouldn't actually help, of course. The suffocating feeling wasn't physical, it was psychological. The mind felt it needed to breathe, even though it didn't. The panic would set in again once I wasn't able to draw a breath for so many long, long minutes.

A few seconds later, I felt a tiny jolt in the ass. I looked over my shoulder.

Galina stood there, looking up at me angrily. She'd just kicked me in the ass. I blinked at her in confusion.

"I told you this was a mistake," Graves said. His arms were crossed.

"Get *in* there!" Galina insisted. "The rift is up, and the timer is running!"

Nodding, I waved at her and stepped into the brilliant void once again.

-8-

This time, I didn't appear inside a side passage high up above the city. Instead, I stepped into what looked like the narrowest alleyway I'd ever seen.

It was clean, surrounded by flanged metal, and narrow enough to reach out and touch both walls. Walking forward, the noise and the smells hit me—I was on the ground floor in bear-land. I was right in the middle of the city I'd seen before from high above.

I guessed this placement made sense. Sure, it was going to be difficult to sneak around, but the bears probably had the other spot staked out now. Knowing the Rigel mindset, I bet they'd filled the place with automated turrets and mines. They weren't the most cordial hosts under the best of circumstances.

Edging forward, I peeked out and had a look around. Sure enough, I was located between two metal, modular structures. They were crisscrossed with rivets and supporting metal bands. Outside my shadowy alleyway, I saw the open city.

"Shit," I whispered—feeling exposed to say the least.

There wasn't any easy way to cross what served this city for a "street". The trouble was an overload of traffic. There were lots of aliens here, it was mostly those little bears from Rigel, but not all of them. A number of centipede-like Vulbites and even a few Cephalopods wandered the pathways.

Withdrawing into the alley again, I went the other way. A few times I nicked myself on the metal flanges, which stuck out uncovered and blade-like. I cursed under my breath and bled on the deck. Walking around buck-naked in an enemy city wasn't ideal.

After making my way to the other end of the alley, which was only about fifty meters long, I poked my nose out again.

Ah... there it was. I guess I'd gotten turned around. I saw the wall I was supposed to climb and the ventilation shaft above it. All I had to do was cross three lanes of busy traffic, climb a metal wall, and go into that shaft.

God only knew what I'd discover in there, but as I didn't see any way to do this quietly in the few short minutes I had left, I decided just to go for it.

The look on the faces of the bear-folks was amusing. There I was, a giant hairless ape from their point of view, sprinting right past them. I launched myself onto the wall, and I climbed. The flanges cut my hands, and I bled freely.

I paid no attention to that. After all, I was only supposed to live for a few more minutes anyway. If they captured me and I bled out—well, that would be a stroke of luck.

The bears started hissing something awful after they got over their initial surprise. Behind me, I heard a wild scrabbling sound.

Looking down, I saw a shocking number of angry, snarling bear-dudes. It seemed like every Rigellian citizen in the vicinity had raced after me, giving instant chase.

At first, I was surprised, but their reaction made good sense when I thought about it for a half-second. After all, this was a race of apex predators. They weren't omnivores who ate fruit on their off-days, they were pretty serious meat-eaters, and they knew when they spotted a naked lunch streaking by right in front of them.

They weren't armed, fortunately, but it was only a matter of time until someone with a weapon showed up.

Climbing higher, I kept out of their reach for now. Ten seconds of scrabbling, bleeding and cursing got me up onto the wall. I never could have made it if the gravity hadn't been about half that of Earth.

The ventilation port was open and exhaling a fog into my face. A steamy scent, it... it smelled almost *human*. And not in a good way, either. Like a mix of sweat, excrement, halitosis and God knew what else.

Forcing myself to crawl inside, I wrinkled my nose and squinted my eyes. Persistence paid off, and I was inside.

What I found there left me with a wide-open mouth. My jaw sagged all the way down to my chest, I swear it.

The chamber was big, and in the dead center was the reactor I was supposed to disable. None of that was a surprise, however. What had caught my eye and shocked me were the guards surrounding the reactor.

They were Clavers. About a dozen of them. Not the smart kind, either. These fellows were Third-class Clavers, dullards left on guard duty.

"Damnation..." I said aloud as they drew sidearms and encircled me. "What the hell are you guys doing here guarding stuff for Rigel?"

None of them spoke, nor did I expect them too. With creepy unity, they all curled their lips up. They looked like a dozen humanoid dogs all about to snarl at once.

"Hold on," I said loudly. "I'm here looking for the Prime."

They paused, all of them, mid-step. None of them spoke, but several blinked.

"That's right," I said in what I hoped was a soothing tone. "I'm here to see the Prime. Where is the real Claver that you all report to? I've been sent here from the homeworld to find him."

Blinking, wavering. The weapons came up and aimed at me with precision, but none of them fired.

"Where's the Prime?" I demanded loudly, putting my hands on my naked hips. I could feel a trickle of blood run down my thighs from my mangled arms, but I ignored it.

Walking slowly forward and throwing out my chest, I acted like I belonged in their midst. This seemed to confuse them, and they broke ranks, allowing me to advance.

I was, naturally, trying to get close to the reactor. If I could discombobulate that thing somehow, my mission would be complete. They could tear me apart like a pack of wolves after that. I wouldn't even complain.

Suddenly, as if hearing a silent whistle, they all advanced at once and reached for me.

Now, I'm a big man, and I'm deadly—even when bare-handed and bare-assed. But I couldn't take twelve of them. One for sure, two maybe, three if I got real, real lucky... but not twelve.

Accordingly, I knew I had to step up my bluff.

"Claver-X sent me," I said loudly. "He has a message for a Claver Prime—any Claver Prime. Take me to him!"

That slowed them down. They paused uncertainly. These guys weren't geniuses. They were vicious and instinctually protective—but they were easily confused by any complex situation.

"Claver-X?" one of them asked. A man off to my right.

I whirled in his direction, and the others flinched. Their fists clenched and unclenched. Their muscled arms and shoulders pulsed with restrained power.

I knew that look. It was something they did sometimes, like a dog snarling and working his way up to charge in and bite.

Focusing on the man who'd answered, I smiled at him.

"That's right," I said. "I'm talking about Claver-X. You know about him, don't you? You've got special instructions regarding him. Well, I can help you catch him if you'll just take me to your Prime."

They shuffled around and looked uncertain.

"Claver-X is the wrong-prime," said the one that had spoken up before. "He's a must-die."

"That's him," I said gently. "Now, where's your Claver-Prime? Come on, fellows, I don't have all day."

"You will be taken to the Prime. You will be restrained."

Instantly, a dozen strong hands reached out and clasped me. They grabbed my arms mostly, and I let them. I stayed relaxed, giving them no hint of my real strength.

"Good idea," I said. "Take me there."

A few of them let go—but not all. One stood holding onto each arm. A third marched close behind me. The rest withdrew a few paces and milled around me like hungry sharks.

I took this all good-naturedly. The group walked past the reactor, within a few meters of an open glowing maw, and I knew it was time to put up or shut up.

I'd seen this kind of reactor before. It amounted to a region of frozen fire inside a loose cage of sorts. These reactors always contained a sustained reaction. They were inherently unstable, but with the right field formed around them, they could provide light and heat for thousands.

Sucking in a breath, I made my move.

First off, I snaked a foot to my left, hooking it around one ankle of the man who had that side. He stumbled and pitched forward.

"Oh, damn!" I said loudly. "I'm real sorry about that, let me help you up."

Reaching for him, I felt the other Claver, the one on my right, tighten his grip.

That was what I'd been waiting for. With a practiced judo move, I bent my legs, got my hip under his, and lifted him off his feet. Then, I threw him into the furnace.

He made a big flash, I'll tell you that. Then, everything got a little crazy.

The reactor sputtered and flashed intermittently. It made an awful sound—or rather, the Claver did as he was being consumed by radiation and sort of a glowy nonexistence.

"You boys sure are clumsy," I said, tsking.

At least three sets of hands grabbed me. They weren't fooling around this time. Two pistols were placed against my head.

I knew instinctively I didn't have long to live. Unfortunately, I couldn't yet be certain the reactor was going to die. My mission might not be complete.

The light inside the reactor was sputtering like a candle set in a window. It was also brightening each time it had one of these coughing fits.

It reminded me of a garbage disposal that grinds and jams temporarily on a chicken bone. The Claver I'd thrown in there was already a nasty mix of ash and blackened bone. He was pretty much gone. The damned thing was choking down its dinner.

43

"Don't kill him," said an accented voice I'd never expected to hear again.

It wasn't a Claver Prime. It wasn't even Claver-X, that mysterious renegade that helped me out now and then.

Instead, it was none other than Tribune Maurice Armel.

-9-

Stunned, I grinned at him. A dozen grunting Clavers pulled me to my feet.

"Well I'll be damned!" I said. "What are you doing here, Maurice?"

His mouth twisted, lifting the mustache that rode his upper lip on the left side. He never liked it when I used his first name. Most brass didn't.

"McGill..." he said. He walked over and inspected the fried Claver-moron in the generator. He made tsking sounds and shook his head. "Everywhere you go, you bring destruction. Even sporting clueless nudity, you are a one-man demolition crew."

"Do you smell bacon?" I asked, looking over his shoulder. "Clavers smell like bacon when they cook, it's the strangest thing."

Armel squinted at me. "Why would you be doing this damage? Why did Central send you?"

"Uh... because we're at war with Rigel? Didn't you get the memo? What are you doing out here, anyway?"

He turned around and gave me a condescending stare. "Are you serious? Are you simply playing the buffoon again today, or has your limited intellect truly met its match with this puzzle?"

"I told you why I'm here. It's your turn to talk."

Armel shrugged. "Fair enough. I will educate your unfortunate brain. I'm working, you see. I'm a tribune of the First Legion. We've been engaged to protect this facility."

He waved his hands broadly to indicate the whole station. My mouth hung open again as I absorbed this information, and my eyes ran over the assembly of retarded Clavers.

"Seriously? You're commanding an army of Clavers? And you're working for Rigel?"

"Yes, you fool."

"Wow… That's worse that becoming a hog. Why would any Legion man want to work for Claver?"

Armel pursed his lips. "I'll take your query at face-value. I'll assume you really want to know. The answer is simple enough in any case: the pay is excellent, and there is great freedom involved, but most importantly I have no overlord."

I blinked at him in confusion. "You mean there's no council of Claver-primes overseeing your performance?"

He made a dismissive gesture with his gloved fingers. "There's very little oversight. Far less than Hegemony, the Mogwa, or even the Skay would demand. I am my own man, and I serve no one other than he who pays for my services."

"A mercenary," I said.

"Yes… just like you. But with fewer masters to please."

I frowned, thinking it over. "Honestly, it doesn't sound that bad. The trouble I'd have is the part about fighting a war with Earth."

"You've done that before on several occasions."

"Hmm… you wouldn't be trying to recruit me, would you?"

Armel walked around me, hands clasped behind his back, head bowed in thought.

"It's not impossible to think you could work for New Earth. But I would not want to speak for the Council."

"The Council? Would that be a committee of Claver Primes?"

"Of course."

A pulsing light caught my attention. I looked past Armel. "Huh… do you smell something now? Besides the bacon, I mean?"

We both looked at the generator. It was sputtering now. The uneven spinning plasma reaction inside had been rotating along all the while we spoke—but now it looked more off-kilter than before. The fried body of the Claver burning inside was just ash by this time, so that couldn't be it.

Armel looked concerned. He walked to the spinning flame and touched a control panel.

"The reaction has become unstable. Hopefully, it will right itself."

Turning away from me, he made a quick call on his tapper. Soon, some Beta-Clavers showed up. These guys had more brains than the third class goons that still held me in their grips, but they were no less obedient. They worked as bio people and techs on Claver's planet full of clones.

"The containment field is breaking down," one of them pronounced at last. "The process is irreversible. Shall we inform the Rigellian techs?"

"*Merde...*" Armel said, putting his hands on his hips and clenching his teeth.

"Ha!" I boomed. "Mission accomplished! I've never seen anyone so shit-off gullible as you, Maurice!"

The Frenchman's eyes darkened and his slid his gaze back toward me. "What are you talking about?"

"I just brought down this whole station. This sky-city operates just like the one back on Dark World. Remember when that orbital factory smashed into the planet?"

He looked alarmed and pissed. "You intended this sabotage? Such a mindless act."

"I sure did! What's more, I told Squanto you put me up to it. That's the kicker, see. He wouldn't have—"

Armel moved suddenly. A blade appeared in his hand. It was too long to call a knife, but too short to call a sword. Whatever it was, the point of it now dimpled my Adam's apple. Warm blood ran down the blade and my neck.

"You spout nonsense? Even in this moment? Do you have any idea how close you are to nonexistence, McGill? Dying here, now, will almost certainly lead to perma-death. Can't you realize that?"

"Uh... just perm me, then. Get it over with."

The truth was, I *wanted* him to kill me. I'd been working hard toward that goal. If he didn't do it soon, I'd be out of time. I knew the nerd-patrol back at Central was still attached to me, still watching me, but the clock was ticking. I had to die and get out of here *fast*.

Armel's eyes narrowed. He was smelling a two-meter tall rat.

"Why...?" he began, but then the plasma flickered.

A gush of white fire came out and consumed one of the Claver techs. He didn't even scream. He just sort of melted, like a wax candlestick struck by a blowtorch. Gushing heat and smoke, the lower half of his body slid down and smoldered at our feet.

At almost the same moment, the space city shivered. It canted a few degrees toward the planet, then drifted back upward again. Metal groaned and shivered all around us, a familiar noise on a gargantuan scale. It was like listening to the calls of dying dinosaurs.

"You have killed us all, you imbecile!" Armel shouted, coming at me with a snarl. He put the tip of his blade up against my sternum, ready to cut out my heart.

"Just do it..." I gasped. My windpipe was being squeezed by the Clavers. "Do it now, you French poodle!"

Armel's eyes blazed with rage—and he did it. He plunged his blade deep into my chest. I felt my heart shiver around it. My second favorite muscle was pierced, bleeding... ruined.

"Thanks," I whispered, and I slumped.

The Clavers didn't let me hit the floor. They still held me up. Beyond them, I saw another white flash. The generator was going critical.

"Why would you thank me?" Armel roared shoving his bristling face into mine. "There can be no rescue for your sorry existence! I have *permed* you, James McGill!"

"I'll explain everything..." I wheezed out, "the next time we meet..."

He stabbed me again and again, but I didn't really feel it. By the time he finished venting his rage, I was stone dead.

48

-10-

Sometimes, revivals can come as a relief. This was one of those times.

"Is this heaven?" I asked the bio-girl who birthed me. "Or am I going to have to go to work again?"

She released a puff of laughter. "You're funny," she said. "Just like they said—and I'm sorry, you're going to have to go back to work."

"Damn... I kind of liked being dead this time around. It was restful."

She ran instruments over my slimy skin and shined lights in every opening she could find. At last, she let me off the table and sent me staggering down the hallway.

No one came to greet old McGill this time. It was the kind of thing that might have made me feel bad in the past, seeing as no one cared enough to personally welcome me back to the world of the living.

But I didn't much care. Today, I was all grins. I'd beaten the Devil again, and I was back on Earth to boot.

My tapper caught up with me before I reached lobby-level. I had a good eatery all picked out, on the south side—but it was not to be.

"McGill?" Graves asked from the screen on my forearm. "Why aren't you back in Drusus' office?"

"I'm taking a much needed and long overdue break, sir," I said.

"Forget it."

"Aw come on, sir," I said. "Are you really going to send me out to die a third time in a row?"

"No, that's not it at all. We've received a deep-link transmission from Rigel. They want to talk."

Among all the things Graves might have said right then, this one was unexpected. It was also an effective motivator. I wanted to know what the furry little bastards had to say.

"Sounds like I got their attention, sir," I said with a hint of pride.

"That you did. Be in the praetor's office in ten minutes. Graves out."

My forearm darkened, and I did a U-turn. I sighed. It was back to the elevators and up to the top floors for old McGill.

Whistling a tune I rode the elevators up and up into the sky, cracking my ears twice as the pressure changed. When the elevator doors slid open, I was two kilometers above the lobby level.

When I stepped off the elevator, I was in for a surprise. Two hogs were there, waiting for me. Both were noncoms, and they were fresh out of smiles today.

"Can I help you two gentlemen?" I asked, beginning to frown.

"James McGill?" asked the one on the left. He was the bigger of the two.

"That's right, hog."

They didn't react to the insult other than to twitch their faces a notch tighter than before.

"We're here to escort you to Praetor Drusus' office, sir."

I stared at them for a few seconds. I kind of wanted to give them some shit, but I didn't see any easy excuse for it. Nodding and sucking a breath through my nostrils, I stepped out of the elevator and marched right through them.

They stepped aside, and I was happy to see they looked just a hair nervous as I got close and passed by. After all, I had something of a reputation. You didn't just go around arresting McGill—or any Legion Varus man—without good cause.

But these two were smarter than your average hogs. They hadn't given me any kind of cause to abuse them, so I went along with it.

I took some small pleasure in walking too fast, however. The Lord saw fit to give me legs like a giraffe, so I employed them now to good effect. Each sweeping stride took me farther than a normal fellow could step, and I forced them to jog in order to keep up.

I led them on a ground-eating march to Drusus' door. In fact, I beat them both by several seconds. Straight-arming the door, I strode inside the reception area with a false smile on my face.

Drusus was there, standing near his secretary's desk. He looked up, eyebrows riding high, then his expression quickly transformed into a frown.

"McGill? Don't tell me you—" but he broke off, seeing two panting hogs appear in the doorway behind me.

They were puffing a little and looked annoyed. I ignored them.

"Praetor!" I boomed. "I hear there's good news! Do those squatty little bears from Rigel really want to talk?"

Drusus gave me a flickering smile. "Yes. Yes they do. Let's go inside—you two stay here. You're not much good if you can't even keep up with him."

The hogs exchanged glances. They looked crestfallen, and it did my heart good to see their shame.

Whistling again, I followed Drusus into his office. The place was far from empty. Graves was there, as was Turov. Even Tribune Deech had made an appearance.

Hmm…

My mind couldn't help thinking up some bad thoughts. This was quite a line-up of brass. In fact, going up the chain of command, it was practically everyone who was above me, all in one room. I tried to think of how this could be a positive sign, but my mind drew a blank.

Then I had it. My face split into an honest grin. "Is this some kind of award ceremony?" I asked loudly. "I've already got the Dawn Star, but I'm sure there must be more medals where that came from!"

51

No one met my eye except for Deech. She stared at me like I was dog meat—or dog shit, maybe. She'd never liked me much.

"James," Drusus said, "you will probably earn a medal today, it's true. But it might be a posthumous one."

"Uh... that doesn't sound good at all."

"No, I'm afraid not. We're here today to ask for a tremendous sacrifice."

My eyes ran over the group. Still, most of them weren't quite up to looking at me. Galina did once or twice, but she mostly stared at the carpet, looking troubled. Even Graves seemed disturbed and unhappy.

Shit. If Graves was upset, I knew something truly heinous in nature was about to be delivered unto poor old James McGill.

"Uh... Did something go wrong with the mission?"

"Far from it," Drusus said. He turned toward Galina and made a spinning motion with one finger. "Play it."

Galina leaned over the praetor's vast desk, stretching her shapely body to touch an icon. It was the virtual play button.

I stepped up so I could get a better view—both of Galina's butt and the video playing on the desk.

I'd half-expected to see Squanto himself, listing his demands for peace. Instead, I was treated to a long shot of a large orbital structure. It was shaped like a conch shell made of titanium and other reflective metals.

Below it was a large blue-brown planet, the homeworld of the Rigellians. In the distance on the left side, lighting up both the planet and the orbital, was a massive red star. It smoldered and rippled with a fierce light.

"Look at that thing!" I exclaimed. "Is that Rigel?"

"Yes," Drusus said. "An ancient red giant."

"I never got to see it in perspective when I was there. Quite a sight."

Drusus nodded his head absently. "Notice, James, that the orbital is dipping now... just a little on the port side."

My eyes drifted back to the orbital. I could see what Drusus was talking about now. The orbital was tilting, wobbling one way then the other.

"At first, its orbit was unstable after the generators went down—"

"But I only messed with one of them. There are other stations projecting their screen, right?"

"Yes, but a chain reaction overloaded all of them. Watch."

Beginning to frown, I saw the orbital city twitch, then—well, it kind of crinkled.

"Hmmm… am I looking at fissures?" I asked.

Galina reached out a hand, she traced a fine finger over the white vapor trails. "The dome has cracked. The whole thing is losing integrity. She's beginning to break up."

"Break up?" I asked. My jaw drooped.

"Yes, keep watching," Drusus said.

The lovely sky city twisted and sagged. At last, it began drifting downward.

Tiny ships fled the disaster. Dozens of them. But there was no way they all could've escaped. I doubted, in fact, that more than few hundred had made it to safety before the orbital touched the atmosphere.

A long streak of orange fire erupted then from the lowest cage-like struts. The whole platform was burning, crumbling. Eventually, it broke up and dropped into the soupy skies of the homeworld.

My hand was on my mouth by this time. I stared in a mixture of shock and awe. The rest of them seemed as dumbfounded as I was.

"This looks kind of bad…" I said at last.

That was it for Deech. She wheeled on me, baring her teeth.

"That's all you've got say? You're a war-criminal, McGill! A mass-murderer of millions."

"Now, hold on just a minute!" I said. "This whole thing wasn't my idea. I was sent on a mission to sabotage that station. I did exactly as ordered."

"You certainly did," Deech said, turning away from me. "And I hope you're proud of your handiwork."

"Wow…" I said, stepping up to the screen and leaning my big hands on the bezel. "I wonder how Armel made out? He probably couldn't have seen this coming."

"Armel?" Drusus asked, stepping up to my side. "What are you talking about?"

It was my turn to be surprised. "Didn't you see that part? That's who killed me—Tribune Maurice Armel."

"That's an obvious lie," Deech said, snorting.

"No one has seen him since we fought the Skay..." Galina said thoughtfully. "But what would that rodent be doing out at Rigel?"

"He said he was running a legion of clones—for Claver. He's gone free-lance. You guys did see the Claver patrol that was protecting that generator, didn't you?"

Deech stepped up, scoffing. "Of course we did, and we also saw how easily you brushed them aside."

She turned dramatically toward the other officers. "Gentlemen, this is a setup. McGill is in on it. If we keep listening to him, we're never going to resolve the truce offer."

"Truce offer?" I asked. I turned toward Drusus with real interest. "Is she on the level? Does Squanto want to sue for peace?"

On the desktop screen, the video had continued playing. The orbital city was half-gone now, the lower portion of it scraping the atmosphere and burning with bright orange plumes of plasma.

"McGill, Rigel does want to sue for peace. We've accepted their offer."

"Why all the long faces, then? This is great news for Earth!"

"It certainly is," Graves said, "but not for you. Squanto has offered peace in exchange for your perma-death."

"Oh…" I said, not liking the sound of that. "Well…" I said, brightening after a few moment's thought. "I guess you could print out a stillborn McGill and ship him out there. He'll never know the difference."

Graves shook his head. "He's not that stupid. He demands that we report your perming, with a full DNA sample, back to the Skay and the Mogwa. If you're ever found alive again…"

"Then Earth will be permed in your place," Deech said. "We're not going to allow that—not even the faintest threat at that level can be entertained. In short, we can't revive you once you've been delivered to the enemy."

I looked around the group again, squinting my eyes. Now I understood the long faces. Only Deech seemed happy about the situation.

"Uh…" I said, chewing things over. "Is this where you ask me to volunteer for another special duty?"

"That would be the easiest way, McGill," Drusus said quietly.

"You'd volunteer?" Deech asked, relaxing and taking a step back. "That would be… most honorable. I'd be the first to recommend another citation. It would have to be awarded posthumously, of course."

"Of course…" Galina echoed with a hint of sarcasm. She didn't look happy. We had our differences, but we'd been off-again on-again lovers for years. I supposed that moments like this really showed a man who his true friends were.

Deech eyed me thoughtfully. "So… you're really willing to sacrifice yourself for Earth? It would be best if we could deliver a live specimen. Are you willing to be transported to the enemy at a place and time of their choosing?"

There was an odd light in her eyes. Torture, that's what she was thinking about—torment and imprisonment. Whatever version of McGill got airmailed out to those bears was going to be a very sad puppy indeed—and I could tell that thought made some part of her happy.

Sucking in a breath and nodding, I put my hands on my hips. "That's right," I said. "I'm willing to give it all up. Tell Squanto he's got a hot date tonight."

All of them seemed relieved, if not happy. Except for Deech, that was. She was about to break into a grin.

That's when my finger quietly unsnapped my sidearm. I'd placed my hands on my hips to get them that much closer to my real goal.

My gun came up, and I fired a single shot.

Deech gargled in surprise, flopped onto the desktop screen with a spray of blood, then sagged to the floor, clawing long blood lines as she went down.

Dropping my pistol, I let the two snarling hogs grab me and have some fun beating on me for a while with their crackling shock-rods.

After all, they'd earned it.

-11-

When Drusus' face loomed over me, filling my limited field of vision, I blinked at him and made groaning noises.

I was flat on my back. Each hog had a boot on one of my arms. They also had their shock-rods upraised, ready to land more blows on my criminal person.

"McGill?" Drusus asked. "What was the point of that? Sheer emotionalism? An outburst of anger directed at—?"

"Check her..." I grunted out. "Check her belt."

Not liking the fact I'd gotten out a few intelligible syllables, the two hogs rained down kicks and sizzling shocks until Drusus waved them back again.

"What are you talking about? You're not making any sense, McGill."

I spat up some blood. "Maybe a few more kicks will fix me," I suggested.

Frowning, Galina and Graves moved away. They walked to Deech's corpse. Galina knelt and fished around.

"Tribune?" Drusus asked. "What are you...?"

Galina stood up with an illusion box in her hands. "Deech was not Deech," she said. "She was Claver. Look."

Drusus didn't look. He showed his teeth instead. "Arrest Tribune Turov," he ordered the hogs.

I tried to get up as they moved away from me, but I wasn't in good shape. My limbs were numbed by repeated applications of the shock-rods.

That's when another shot rang out. Drusus spun around and dropped.

Stunned, everyone looked at Graves. He had his gun out, and he had just killed the highest ranked military officer on the continent.

The hogs dropped their shock-rods and drew their pistols. Graves surrendered immediately. The hogs were white-faced with confusion and near-panic.

"Hold it," Turov said. She straightened up and stood again, this time over Drusus' corpse. She held another illusion box. Holding one of the devices up in each hand, she demanded that the hogs identify the dead people.

"They're... they're clones," the lead hog said. "How is that possible? Isn't this a Galactic violation...?"

"Yes," Turov said. "This man's name is Claver. He's been playing both parts—Deech and Drusus. Unfortunately he's human, so his cloning violations must be kept secret, or all of Earth could be blamed."

"I'm pissed at myself," Graves said. "I should have spotted one of them."

"Not your fault," I croaked from the floor. "He was in charge."

"Where do you think the real praetor is?" Turov asked.

"The same place as the real Tribune Deech," Graves said. "They're both dead. The enemy has taken out our top officers. And there might be more of these clone agents around."

Turov looked alarmed. She began making calls on her tapper.

Graves turned to the hogs. "Get everyone up here. An investigatory team, bio people, the works. We have to find out how this happened and where our leadership has gone."

"Wait..." I said from the floor. "How do we know you two are legit?"

They looked at one another. "Good point," Graves said. "Get techs up here with EMP wands. We'll short out everything on our bodies. It's worth frying some electronics to be certain we've flushed all the moles. McGill? Can you stand?"

"I'm actually feeling pretty good lying down right here, sir."

He frowned at me, and for a second, I thought he might shoot me in the head. But he didn't—not yet.

"You know I don't like slackers, McGill. Pull it together, or I'll print out a new officer."

"Right Primus. You're all heart, sir."

Straining and grunting, I fought my way up to one elbow, then eventually to all fours. I puked at that point, then struggled onto my knees and finally my feet. By the time the office had filled with emergency personnel and MPs, I was able to stand straight as long as I leaned on Drusus' blood-streaked desk.

The bio people fussed over me for ten long minutes. I thought for sure they were going to run me through the revival machine to "freshen me up" but they didn't. They gave me some injections and about a liter of nu-skin spray instead. Soon, I was slightly high but able to walk unaided.

We were all subjected to EMP wands, frying out everything except our tappers, which they thoughtfully shielded first. The three of us all proved to be legit, and we relaxed a little.

As I could talk more clearly now, I reported my run-in with two Clavers just the day before out in the city streets. I'd written it into a report, but I hadn't emphasized the implications.

"This is a full-scale invasion of Claver Clones," Graves said.

"He's no longer trying to hide his intentions," Galina said. "He's a threat to all of Earth. How many clones do you think he might have? How many are operating as agents on Earth right now?"

"Thousands, maybe," Graves said thoughtfully.

"Say," I said, speaking up and addressing the two of them. "I'm kind of hungry. I haven't had a bite since my last revive. Anyone want to accompany me down to the mess hall?"

"How can you think of food at a time like this, McGill?" Turov asked me.

"Easy," I said. "I'm hungry."

"You're always hungry. Go get something and report back when your brain is working right again."

I left Drusus' office, staggering a bit in the passageways. After I ate my fill in the officers' club, and drank a few rounds of beer, I felt pretty good. Sure, my ribs ached every time I breathed, and my head felt like it was floating above the rest of me, but overall I was in a passable state.

My tapper lit up then, and Graves came into view. I winced, not wanting to talk to him right now.

"Can this wait until morning, Primus?" I asked. "I could really use a good night's sleep."

Graves seemed to find this amusing. "Did you forget something, McGill?"

"Uh... probably."

"Get your ass back up here. You'll get your beauty rest soon enough."

Closing the connection, I wandered back up to Drusus' office. Along the way, I figured out what he meant: I was still supposed to be delivered to Squanto as a peace offering.

This had to be one of the luckiest days of my long life.

-12-

When I got back to Drusus' office, there had to be a dozen hogs wandering around investigating and scowling. They didn't seem to like me at all. Maybe they blamed me somehow for what had happened, but if that was the case, well, they could screw themselves.

"You know," I said loudly, "it's too damned bad security here at Central is so frigging lax. I mean, how the hell could these clones wander in here and take over like this? Are you guys all Clavers too?"

The sour glances and scowls turned into glares of outright hate. None of them argued with me, but they weren't happy at all.

I didn't care if they felt bad, so I kept right on shooting off my big mouth until Graves came up and shut me down.

"McGill, stop antagonizing the investigators."

"It's a keystone cops show here, Primus. These boys couldn't find their own asses with two hands and a flashlight. Why don't you call in some of the tech nerds, or maybe Natasha? Someone with some brains."

He appeared to give it some thought. "We've got bigger problems right now. We can't find Deech or Drusus. They're nowhere in Central. They've been replaced and vanished without a trace."

61

"Huh…" I said, chewing that over. "Maybe that's what they had planned for me. Just yesterday… I think it was yesterday… a couple of Clavers tried to put me down out in Central City."

"Yeah, yeah, you told us about that."

"But wait: why would they do that? Maybe they did the same thing to Drusus and Deech. Maybe they planned to replace me as well."

Graves squinted up at me. "Then why didn't they do it when they had you down and out?"

"Um…" I thought about the state I'd been left in, and the state I'd left them in. "It didn't go cleanly. Maybe they wanted to get me to a certain destination to do the switch, and my reaction made them change their minds."

Graves chuckled. "Your reaction, huh? I can just imagine. But all right, I'll widen the search. Where did you say the assault happened?"

I gave him the cross streets, and he ordered a stack of additional hogs to comb the area.

"You sure are putting a lot of effort into finding these bodies, sir," I told him.

Graves slid his eyes to me and crooked his finger. I leaned closer.

If there was a man on Earth who didn't really know how to whisper, it was Graves, but he gave it a try. "Think, McGill. If we can't find Drusus or Deech, we can't revive them. Do you know who might be next in line to take over in that case?"

I blinked at him. "Not Turov?"

"No, no. It would be Wurtenberger. He's a good man, but he knows nothing of real command. He's been flying a desk for fifty years."

"Huh… yeah, I get it. You want to revive Drusus quickly, so Wurtenberger won't try to take over?"

"I see you understand our peril. Now, shut up about it." He walked away, and I wished him success.

I spent the next hour walking around the crime scene, ignoring all the stink-eyed hate I got from the various hogs. They cleaned up the bodies, the bloody desk, and everything else. Drusus would have a spotless office when he returned—if he hadn't been permed that is.

The thought of Drusus being permed did concern me. I wanted to get to the bottom of this and figure out what Claver was really up to.

Before I'd had time to learn jack-squat, the desk lit up again. It was a call, and it was coming in over the deep-link.

"Uh…" I said, "Graves?"

He turned and rushed to the desk. "Jesus…" he muttered, and he ordered all the workers to get lost. "We have to take this, it's from Rigel."

Nodding, I stepped up to the conference table. "I'm right here with you, sir."

"Are you insane, McGill? You're not talking to Squanto."

"Of course not, sir," I said, snagging a pair of auto-cuffs off the belt of a hog who was backing out of the camera pickup range. I slipped the cuffs onto my wrists and let them squeeze-up until they were quite snug. "I'm your prisoner, remember? I'm to be seen and not heard."

Graves looked a little desperate. "All right. Just keep quiet."

He stabbed the accept-call button with his finger and made a gesture over the desk, causing it to open the channel. The desk immediately bubbled up an image that looked like colorful liquid between us. It projected a hologram of the ugliest damned bear-dude I'd seen in ages—and that was saying something, because all of them were nasty-looking to me.

"I am High Lord Squanto," the bear said. "To whom am I speaking?"

"I'm Primus Graves."

"Primus? Do I hear correctly? I know your ranking system, human. I'm being insulted from the outset, forced to speak with a servant. Where is your commander?"

Graves squirmed a little. I almost opened my mouth, but I managed to contain myself and maintain an idiot's grin on my face.

"Ah… Praetor Drusus isn't available right now. Maybe I can get another officer."

I knew Graves was in a tough spot. This negotiation and the entire spying project were both highly classified. Most of the brass we had crawling around the upper stories of Central didn't even know about it.

Paging through his tapper, Graves sighed. He pushed the emergency tab and sent a message.

"Praetor Wurtenburger has agreed to come to this meeting. He'll be here shortly," Graves assured Squanto. "In the meantime, please tell me why you're calling us today."

"We've lost contact with some of the people we were negotiating with," Squanto said. "We suspect you're backing out of your part of the bargain. In such a situation, this war will not only continue, it will escalate."

Graves pointed at me. "Here's proof we're in earnest."

Still smiling big, I lifted my wrists and shook the cuffs vigorously.

"You might remember this legionnaire," Graves said. "He tends to make quite an impression."

Squanto focused on me, and his eyes narrowed to slits. He looked like a wet bobcat. "James McGill…" he said slowly, as if tasting each syllable. "I've waited for so long for this. Do you recall, McGill, that the last time we met you abused my person?"

"Uh…" I said, eyeing Graves sidelong.

He shook his head at me, clearly indicating he wanted me to stay silent.

"I remember!" I said, unable to help myself. "Are you talking about the time I rode on your back like a kid on a pony? That was on Storm World in front of the scupper queen."

Squanto's eyes had been slits before, but they narrowed farther down to lines. His teeth showed as his lips curled up. "That was not the occasion I was thinking of. Do you recall the day you confronted Sateekas with me?"

"Oh yeah! That was a day to remember. I traded you straight-up for Floramel. You can't still be sore about that. We made a deal, Squanto. I was just making sure we both kept our bargains."

A commotion off to my left caught my eye. It was Graves, and he was frantically making throat-cutting motions with his finger. I figured he wanted me to shut up.

"You are indeed the McGill," Squanto said, leaning closer to the camera pickup and staring. It almost seemed like he was turned-on or something. "I have waited so long for this day."

"That's right," I said. "You're one lucky bear cub. Is there anything special you want me to wear? Like a skirt, or something?"

"Your utterances lack meaning. Your torment will be exquisite, McGill. I'm glad your flesh is high in volume, it will take much longer to abuse every living cell."

I opened my mouth again to make another snappy retort, but before I could get it out, the door opened.

Praetor Wurtenberger strode into the office, backed by a pair of hog guards. Wurtenberger was a fat guy with a Euro accent and four stars on his shoulders. I'd met him before, and he seemed like a pleasant enough guy, if a little pretentious.

"Ah, Primus Graves," he said. "And who is this alien on the deep-link?"

"That's High Lord Squanto," Graves said.

Wurtenberger blinked. "Isn't this matter something Drusus should attend to? He's handling these negotiations..."

"That's right sir, but we believe Drusus is dead, and we can't revive him until we find his body."

Wurtenberger frowned. "He's dead, but you don't have a body? These two statements are incongruous."

"Right sir. He's in limbo right now, so he can't perform negotiations at this time."

"How inconvenient... Very well, I can see why you summoned me with urgency."

Wurtenberger confronted Squanto then, who had been growing more and more impatient.

"High Lord Squanto," he said. "What can we do for you?"

"Are all humans imbeciles? I'm demanding payment. Deliver McGill, and this war is at an end."

Wurtenberger glanced at me and shrugged. "It would seem to be an equitable bargain for peace. But what will you give us in return?"

"What's this? Promises followed by deceit?"

"Not at all, High Lord," Wurtenberger said. "An exchange has been arranged and agreed to. We're giving you one of our officers, as I understand it. What will you return to us in the spirit of giving?"

"Such foolishness," Squanto complained. "I can see now why our species are always in conflict... but very well. I will deliver one of my officers of similar status."

"That sounds reasonable. Who will this officer be?"

Right then, the Devil gripped my soul. I opened my mouth, and I blurted out a name.

"Give us Claver!" I shouted at the hologram. "He's your renegade, and we hate him as much as you hate me."

Graves and Wurtenberger looked startled. But Squanto... he looked thoughtful.

"It's actually a workable concept..." he said. "Claver and his legions are troublesome. Worse, they are demanding. Our contract is soon up for renewal, and all the Claver speaks of is an increase in his rates."

I laughed. "Same old Claver."

"Excuse me," Wurtenberger said. He frowned and approached the screen. "Am I to understand you have a human in your employ? In a military capacity? A turncoat, in other words?"

"Damn straight they do," I said, but Graves made shushing motions. I closed my mouth and stood there waiting for my fate to be decided.

"Your species is despicable," Squanto said. "Selling your military to the highest bidders, even when the job is to slaughter your own people."

"We do have mercenary legions," Wurtenberger said. "But they're strictly forbidden to fight against Earth."

Squanto gave one of his gargling laughs. "Ignorance? That is your claim? I'm almost willing to believe it. We employ Claver and his countless clones. They do a poor job, and they are over-priced, but at least the chosen people don't have to die in battle."

"The chosen people?" Wurtenberger asked in confusion.

Graves leaned closer to him. "That's what the Rigellians call themselves."

"I see… Very well then, High Lord. I agree to your terms. We will send McGill to you, and you will give us Claver in return. Where will this exchange take place?"

"At Claver's home planet, of course," Squanto said. "If you take any sample of him somewhere else, you're sure to be dealing with a counterfeit."

Turning toward Graves with a fresh shocked look on his face, Wurtenberger sputtered. "This individual has a planet? A heavenly body he owns and calls his home?"

"He sure does," I said. "I've been there several times. But I can't say I know the coordinates."

With eyes as big around as saucers, Wurtenberger stared at me and blinked a few times. He nodded at last. "We'll take care of several outstanding errors at once, then. Tell us where Claver's world of clones is hidden, Squanto. I'm very curious about it."

Squanto gave us the coordinates. Unsurprisingly, it was in the middle of the frontier buffer zone between Earth and Rigel.

"Ah yes…" Wurtenberger said as he worked the computerized desk. "I've plotted it. Eridani 77, I see it now. We have no survey information on that star system as yet. But notice: it's within thirty lightyears of both Blood World and Dark World."

That made perfect sense to me. Back when I'd visited Blood World, Claver had shown up to fight in the contest. He'd wanted a planet of his own at that time. Later on, during the Dark World campaign, we'd met up with a Lady Claver. Had he gone and colonized Eridani 77 with his twins in-between those campaigns? It stood to reason, because soon after that he'd revived me on his Clone planet to talk more than once.

Squanto and Wurtenberger agreed to the details and set a date six months in the future. Squanto then faded out, and Wurtenberger turned to face Graves and I. The praetor seemed decisive.

"This whole situation is intolerable. We'll be glad to put it behind us."

"Why such a long lead time?" Graves asked. "We could deliver McGill to that planet in two months' time, easily."

Wurtenberger blinked at him, then shook his head. "That is not our mission," he said firmly. "It would be too great of a lost opportunity."

"What do you mean, sir?"

"We're going out there to Clone World, yes, but we're doing it to wipe out Claver and his illicit hive of duplicates. After that, if the council is interested and Squanto is still agreeable, we'll make the trade."

"That's going to be hard to do!" I said, walking up to the two of them and towering over both.

"Why's that, McGill?" Wurtenberger demanded.

"Because all those frigging Clavers are going to be stone dead by then! How will they keep their part of the bargain at that point?"

Wurtenberger laughed. "I like your madman, Graves—but you should keep a tight leash on him."

"I try to, sir. I try."

-13-

Less than a month later, Legion Varus loaded up aboard *Legate*. The huge ship was the legion's most comfortable troop transport we'd flown in to date, and we loved her.

One of the best things about her was the fact she had a special berth for Blood Worlders. Now, I wouldn't want people to think that we didn't like our near-human friends—but they could be hard to live with. Even worse was the pack of arrogant Cephalopod officers and noncoms that gave them their orders

This time out, our Blood Worlder formation—or "zoo legion" as the rest of Varus referred to them—was more autonomous than usual. They bedded down in their over-sized berths, free to stink up the place all they wanted to. Their life-support system and ours were completely separated, so we couldn't even smell them through the vents if we'd wanted to—which we didn't.

"Hey, Primus Graves," I said about a week after launch. "Who is the new tribune for the zoo this year? I'm pretty sure old Armel quit the job."

"He did indeed, and we'll soon retire him permanently as a just reward," Graves said, smiling. He was the only man I knew who smiled big when he talked about perming people for reals.

"Uh…" I said. "But who…?"

69

"Come on, McGill," he said. "I know you're just making a joke. It's not funny, and I'm tired of hearing my officers laugh about it."

Confused, I gave my skull a scratch. "Uh... I think I missed something."

He ran his eyes over my slack-jawed, confused-looking face for a few moments before sighing. "All right. I'm going to take the chance that you really don't know who is leading our brother legion, and that you're going to behave with decorum when I tell you."

"You know I will, sir," I said, becoming more curious by the minute. After all, who might have taken over the job of zoo-keeper and made Graves so reluctant to tell me? Deech was still playing dead, as we'd never recovered her corpse. Drusus was in the same state. I was baffled.

"It's Primus Winslade," Graves said at last. "He's been given the job of sub-tribune on a trial basis, so he's the acting officer in charge of our sister legion."

Twice, my eyes opened double-wide. I was processing this shocking information for a few blissful seconds. Then at last, a huge grin began to form on my face. It quickly grew to improbable size.

"This is what I was afraid of..." Graves complained.

"HA!" I roared. I almost choked, I started laughing so hard. "Winslade is a zoo-keeper! HA-HA-HA!"

Graves sighed and shook his head. "He outranks you now by two steps, technically."

"No he doesn't. He's a *sub*-tribune. That means he's lower than any human officer in a *real* legion. He's—"

"Shut up, or I'll give you clean-up duty on the lower decks."

I swallowed my laughter, but it was a hard thing to do. Winslade thought quite a lot of himself, and this fate was a perfect conclusion to his hard-scrabble career in the legions.

"You're right, Primus," I told Graves when I'd regained my composure. I wiped the wet corners of my mouth and eyes. "When you're right, you're right. Old Winslade deserves this honor. He's worked for years to get to the top of the heap, and I shouldn't make fun of a man's achievements. So what if he has to carry a shovel to dig his way into his own office every morning? Shoveling manure is a manly thing, isn't it? There's no shame to it, no shame—"

"Shut up, McGill. I'm not warning you again."

I smirked. "I hear you loud and clear, sir. I wouldn't want to get handed over as a prisoner to be tortured and permed or anything."

Graves dismissed me from his office, and I walked out. I fell against the walls laughing the moment I was out of earshot.

Winslade had found something lower in the universe than being a hog. I didn't think he could do it, but he'd found a way.

Rushing back to our unit's module, I passed on the news with glee. Carlos and Sargon loved it the most.

"You're *shitting* me!" Carlos said. "He took a job cleaning up after a herd of near-humans?"

"He sure did!" I said. "By all reports, he loves it, too. Maybe he'll marry one of those beasts—and I'm not talking about a pretty Rogue World lady, neither."

"Yeah..." Carlos said. His eyes were alight with the possibilities. "I hear the women who gestate those twelve-foot tall trackers are real lookers."

"This has got to be some kind of a scam," Sargon said doubtfully.

"What do you mean?" I asked him.

"Just think about it: Winslade's an evil weasel—but he's not dumb. Why would he take this kind of assignment?"

"Because it's the only way he could get ranked as a tribune," Carlos said. "He's greedy for rank. Everyone knows that."

"I don't know..." Sargon turned and walked away. He was a suspicious man, and he was usually right to be so.

"Hey," Carlos said, slapping me in the gut with the back of his knuckles. "You should go visit Winslade down there in the animal pens. Just make up some kind of excuse."

"What for?"

"I don't know, invent a story. You're the professional liar in this family."

I frowned down at him. "That's not what I meant. Why should I go down there at all?"

71

"To find out what Winslade is hiding. If he's poop-scooping for a legion of retarded apes, there's a reason. A very good, very evil reason. You need to know what it is."

I wasn't quite following his logic. "I don't need to know crap."

Carlos smiled. It was a knowing smile. We'd been friends for so long, we were like old marrieds. It was disturbing to have someone know you that well. Especially when it was a hairy, annoying pug like Carlos.

"Just do it," he said. "You know you want to. You know he's hiding something."

"*You* do it," I said.

"Nah, come on, man. I'm a noncom, and I'm not even good at lying. Hell, I get caught for things I *didn't* do."

He was right of course. If anyone was going to succeed in this kind of spying mission, it was would have to be me.

"All right," I said. "I'll think about it."

Carlos gave me a knowing laugh and clapped me on the shoulder. "You do that, big guy. We both know you're going, but I appreciate the attempt to obscure the truth. I guess it's pretty much reflexive for you now."

He walked off, and I stared after him with an unpleasant expression on my face. I didn't always enjoy his personality. Most people didn't.

I held out for nearly an hour after that. I made a point of displaying myself all over the module, walking this way and that and checking equipment and duty rosters. Every time I glanced at Carlos, he grinned back and gave me a "bon voyage" kind of wave.

At last, I couldn't take it anymore. I exited the module and headed toward the elevators.

It was time to learn the truth.

-14-

Winslade was a thin, wiry man with evil eyes like a possum. Finding him wasn't hard, he had the nicest office on the nicest deck in the zoo-zone.

As I walked among lumbering oafs and startled-looking squids, I acted like I belonged there. As I was a centurion—a *real*, human centurion, nobody asked me what the hell I was doing. Sometimes, there were side-benefits to working with alien troops. They were much better conditioned and genetically predisposed to accepting authority, unlike human troops who questioned everything.

The place did reek, however. That was the worst thing about being around near-humans, every deck smelled like a neglected monkey cage in July. They were big people with no concept of deodorant and very little knowledge of soap—it wasn't pretty.

Finding Winslade turned out to be easy. He was on the highest deck in the zone, partitioned from the rest by a big set of steel doors with a heavy-trooper guard standing on each side. These guys had nothing to do all day other than open those big doors, but their lumpy, slack faces didn't look bored. They were perfectly suited for guard duty.

Giving them a salute and a smile, I made a hurry-up motion suggesting they should open the doors.

The two hulking men, each around three meters tall, just blinked at me. One of them shuffled around a little, something I knew they did before speaking up. They didn't talk much, normally. It didn't seem to come naturally to them.

"Centurion?" said the meatball on the left. He was the one doing all the shuffling, so I figured he must be the smart one.

"That's right, trooper. I'm Centurion James McGill. Now, please open up these doors, pronto."

He did the shuffle-thing again. Right foot up, down, then left foot up... and down again.

"Not on list, sir," he said.

"Yeah... that's right. I'm not on the list."

I noticed now that he had a very simple device in his hand. It was about the size of a pistol, but it looked small in his big hand. At one end was a handle which he had in his massive fist. At the other was a sensor of some kind. On the top of it was a light. A single, bright LED. The light was shining red, and he was aiming the device at me.

Near-humans didn't have tappers. That was a problem all by itself, but they also weren't usually smart enough to use something as complex as a personal computer anyway. I could tell right off that someone had gone and designed a piece of tech that operated at a level they could understand. All they had to do was aim it at a person and activate it like a handgun. If it shined red, that person wasn't allowed to pass. If it shined green, I assumed, it meant the man in question was permitted inside.

I was impressed and annoyed with this bit of tech all at the same time. It was way too effective.

Still smiling, I put my hand out. "Can I see that for a second? I'm good with technology. Maybe I can fix it."

The two glanced at one another. "It isn't broken," the smart-guy pointed out. I was beginning to think of him as a "smartass" but I kept my smile planted and even curled up the corners a bit more.

"Well, my man, I must argue with you on that point. This thing is clearly broken because it's shining red at me when it should be shining green."

Stumped by my logic, the guy nodded after a few seconds of further contemplation and handed it over. I took it and quickly stepped between them.

"Ah!" I said immediately. "I see the problem. See? It's green now!"

I had it in my hands and aimed in my general direction, but not precisely. It was missing my body and hitting the other guard. He, of course, had permission to enter.

Happily, the smartass shuffled his feet and nodded. "It works again," he said. "That's a good thing."

"It sure is," I said. "Now, could you fellows open the door? I'm going to be late getting to Tribune Winslade's office if I don't hurry. You boys wouldn't want to be blamed for that, would you?"

They shook their heads with vigor and flung the doors wide. I handed the detection device back and slipped away quickly before he could think hard enough to aim it at me again for a second check.

I needn't have worried. He put away the ID gun, and the doors swung immediately shut behind me.

Whistling an old tune, I walked through the command deck. It was like *Legate's* Gold Deck on the main module above, but this level didn't control the ship in any way. It was also chock-full of squids.

Among non-humans, the smartest members of our many allies were the Cephalopods. They were used to command near-human legions as sub-officers. In any zoo legion, there were about ten to twenty humans with the rank of primus. They served a human tribune as combat officers leading each cohort, while the rest of them were staffers.

That was it. Except for a fistful of humans, the other ninety-nine percent of the legion wasn't from Earth. It was kind of weird, when you thought about it. I had to wonder how long we'd keep our top-dog spot with so few of our own kind in charge.

As usual, the squids gawked at me, the near-humans looked at me stupidly, and the few primus types gave me a frown.

75

They figured if I'd made it past their bouncers at the door, I must belong. They didn't ask any questions, and that was a good thing, because I was short on answers.

Such was the key to success in missions like this one. A security system helped a man like myself as much as it hurt me, because if I could fool it, everyone would accept my legitimacy.

Winslade's door was obvious. It wasn't tall, but it was ornate. A silver-coated relief of Earth dominated the center. I hammered on the shiny bumps depicting South America like I wanted candy.

At last, the door opened. It wasn't Winslade, but a rather surprised-looking adjunct. She was easy on the eyes, and right off, I knew why Winslade had picked her to be his aide.

"Hi there," I said. "You must be new around here."

"Hello Centurion. Yes, I am. How can I help you? Do you have a message from Graves?"

My face almost faltered, but I managed to catch it. "That's right," I said. "Personal courier from the big Gold Deck upstairs."

She smiled politely and stuck out her hand. I had nothing to offer her, so I shook my head. "Directly in the tribune's hands. Those are my orders, sorry."

"No problem. Please, come in."

I followed her into a sumptuously carpeted office foyer. Another door, again decorated with a metallic relief of Earth, stood at the far side of the foyer. This time, however, the surface had been done in gleaming gold, rather than silver.

Without hesitation, I marched over to Winslade's door and repeated the pounding I'd given the first one. I felt one of the ridges on the Andes crinkle and indent a little, but it couldn't be helped. I had to see Winslade right away. If I didn't, someone was bound to figure out I had no business being down here.

"Centurion?" the adjunct said in alarm. "Could I trouble you to sit down?"

"No trouble at all," I said, and I kept on hammering until Peru was as flat as Florida.

The door popped open, and a confused Winslade appeared. "What in the nine hells—oh no. You have got to be kidding me. McGill…"

He said this last word like it was some kind of curse. I'd heard it pronounced that way many times before, so I took no offense.

"Tribune!" I said, all smiles again. "So good to see you, sir. I'd like to congratulate you on your promotion to zookeeper on the behalf of all Varus—"

"Stop prattling, McGill, and tell me what you're doing here."

"Doing? Why sir, I thought you knew. I was sent here with a special message."

Winslade blinked once, then twice. His face underwent a transformation. "Really?" he asked. "I didn't know… but I should have expected this. You're just the sort for it. Come in, come in."

I had no blessed idea what he was on about, but I was more than happy to waltz into his inner sanctum. I took the opportunity to crane my neck around and smile at the pretty adjunct, who looked kind of worried about the whole situation.

"You see?" I told her. "No trouble at all! I'll tell you what, when I get out of here, I'll take you up on that offer for lunch."

"What? I didn't…?"

"And don't worry, I'm paying. It's the least I could do."

"Do shut up and get in here, McGill," Winslade insisted.

I went inside, and Winslade slammed the door shut behind me.

He licked his lips and eyed me critically. He didn't even say anything for a few seconds.

"Uh…" I said, not knowing what was going on inside that pointy head of his.

"Claver is amazing," he said, lowering his voice to a conspiratorial whisper. "In what capacity will you be serving? And don't you dare tell me that you've been promised a legion of your own. It's entirely inappropriate if you have."

"Uh…" I said, blinking stupidly. My mind had begun to spin, but it wasn't going in positive directions.

What had started off more or less as a joke was rapidly turning into something serious.

-15-

Winslade twisted his lips up and put his hands on his hips. "You're acting like a moron, McGill—even more than usual. What *are* your instructions?"

"Graves sent me down to tell you about the exercise tomorrow."

Winslade frowned. There was an exercise, but everyone already knew about it. There was absolutely no need for anyone to tell anyone about it in person. It was the only vague excuse that I could come up with.

"That's it?" he demanded. "Everyone knows about that!"

"I'm sorry sir. I guess Graves just wanted to be sure. You can check with him if you like."

Just as I expected, Winslade shied away from my upraised tapper. If he was involved in something illicit, the last man aboard *Legate* he'd want to talk to was a straight-arrow like Graves.

"Graves sent you?" he demanded even as he waved my offered forearm away. "Not… someone else?"

"You did say something about Claver, sir. But I haven't met up with that particular criminal for years."

Winslade suddenly looked nervous. His tongue darted out, swept over his lips, and then darted back into his mouth again. Watching that was enough to make me squint in disgust.

"Just so…" he said, talking fast. "I spoke out of turn, that's all. Never mind. There's a highly classified matter going on, you see. I'd assumed—well, never mind. I was in error. We're no longer as close in rank as we once were, and I'd thought you were aware… but no, never mind."

"Uh…" I said, trying to puzzle things out. "Did you just say 'never mind' three times in a row, sir?"

"If I did, perhaps it would be best if you took my advice. Hmm?"

"Sure thing, Tribune. Always listen to the brass, that's my motto. I guess I'll be on my way."

Winslade's eyes narrowed further, although I wouldn't have thought it possible. "Just a minute. This isn't what it seems, is it?"

"What do you mean, sir?"

"Coming down here talking about a message every janitor aboard has already heard. A pathetic ruse. But *why* would you come down here with no good reason…? And how did you get past my new security measures?"

I shook my head in bewilderment and gave him a dumb-ass grin. "I have no idea what you're going on about, sir. I just wanted to see how you were getting along with your new zoo. How's the old sniffer doing? Do you have to wear a facemask during roll-call?"

He was barely listening to my best jibes. I was sorely disappointed to see not a single one of these insults had landed. He was still too freaked out about why I'd come down here at all.

I considered telling him the real reason—that I wanted to laugh at his new job—but I didn't bother. He wouldn't believe it, I could tell. His mind was on much darker paths, and it was best to get out of his presence as soon as possible.

"Well sir," I said loudly. "I'll be taking my leave now, if you don't mind. I'll see you tomorrow in the exercise room."

"Yes…" Winslade said in a voice that was a little bit hissy. "I'm sure that you will."

Walking out, I took my time lingering over the adjunct's desk. She blushed, and I could tell that she was enjoying my attentions. Unfortunately, I could also tell I wasn't getting anywhere fast. Deciding to make the best of it, I gave her a few more heartfelt compliments and walked out without pressing for a date I wasn't going to get.

That was part of the beauty of growing up and learning new things: a man came to understand it was best to fight the battles he could win, saving the rest for another day.

On my way past more baffled squids and watchful near-humans, I made it all the way to the zero-G drop-shaft that connected *Legate's* various modules before anyone made a move to stop me. I sensed eyes on me, but no one said a word as I almost trotted toward the exit.

When they finally did make their move, it was a serious attempt. Three slavers were waiting for me. They were near-humans, as tall and gangly as heavy troopers were broad and bent.

In retrospect I figured it only made sense: back on their homeworld, these slavers were specialists in scouting, kidnapping and the like. They were smarter and quicker than any heavy trooper. If a giant had been sent, well, they probably would have killed me rather than attempted to capture me. Their minds were limited, and any captives would probably just get squished in the process.

As it was, the trio of slavers was obvious about their intentions. They stood in a group, holding nets of silvery mesh in their hands. I knew those nets would give a nasty shock, paralyzing their victims as well as tangling you up in unbreakable cabling.

Approaching the three, I gave no hint that I was on guard. I whistled louder, in fact. Swinging my fists high with each stride, I moved with what could only be called utter confidence.

Giving them the briefest of salutes, I walked as if to pass them right by.

Their over-sized ears flapped. Their muzzles dribbled spit in anticipation. They watched with unblinking eyes.

As I knew they would, they took no action. They would wait until the moment I passed them by, then attack from behind. It was in their DNA to do so.

Predictability is a weakness in almost any adversarial situation, doubly so in combat. Therefore, I always made it my goal to surprise the enemy.

In this case, just as I drew even with them, while not even looking up at their crackling nets and low-hanging genitals—I struck.

My blade was out and the first man was down a half-second later. I'd hamstrung him, stepping between those legs that were like the trunks of two bent palm trees and slashed him down.

Now, as I did this, I really did hope Winslade had set this group on my trail. I felt sure that he had, but I would've felt downright guilty if they'd all backed away in horror.

But they didn't. They sprang into action—at least the two did who weren't on their backs, howling and grabbing at their heels in agony.

The key with slavers was to get in close. They've got super-long arms that are even stronger than they look—but if a man can step in close enough, they lack the leverage to push you away.

That's what I did now. Pressing my attack, I rushed the second one, with my head coming up to about the level of his balls. Seeing all the blood and pain I'd delivered upon his friend, he let go of his net and reached out with those big hands, reaching for my face and arms.

Another mistake. My blade was wet, but it wasn't done yet. When those hands came for my face, looking like a couple of giant five-legged crabs, I slashed twice. Fingers as thick around as Winslade's wrists fell thumping to the deck.

He did manage to land one of those palms on my skull, however. The giant hand was short a few fingers and the blow was more of an open slap—but it was enough.

He was just too big, too strong, too heavy. A splash of white light exploded in my brain. At the same time, I went flying, doing a cartwheel before landing in a mess on the deck.

My lungs gulped air. I was stunned—but concussion or no, I knew I had to get back into the game.

Anticipating the next move again, I set my long knife up vertically. The blade was tip-up, and the metal hilt was firmly planted on the deck.

The third man had again followed his instincts. He'd tossed his net, snapping and sizzling with an electrical charge. This came down over me, and I don't mind telling you it didn't feel good.

The only thing that saved me from outright paralysis was my knife, which served to short out the net, connecting it prematurely with the metal deck under my sore back.

I was hurting. My skull felt like it was dislocated, if such a thing is possible, and my jaw wasn't lined up with my face.

Even so, I didn't scream. I didn't move at all. I barely twitched. Instead, I waited.

The third slaver came to crouch over me warily. There was an evil intelligence in those big, jack-o-lantern eyes of his.

As further evidence of his wisdom, he didn't try to pick me up. He kicked me in the ribs instead.

Now, maybe to this half-ton four meter tall scarecrow, it was only a nudging of the big toe. But to me, it was a full-on field goal planted in my side. My ribs crackled like sticks. My body burned, and I couldn't fake it any longer. I rolled half up on one elbow, groaning.

That's when he came in, knees bent low, those long, long arms flung wide. His eyes were those of a predator making a kill. I doubted he would show me mercy now. He wasn't looking like a man determined to bag me gently—his face was all harsh lines and full of murder.

Taking the one shot I had, I threw my knife. End over end, it thunked into one of those outsized eye-sockets. Squealing and lacing long fingers over his injured face, he turned and rushed away.

The fight was over.

Coughing and standing up slowly, I took a look around. The other two slavers had found better places to be. I'd taken a big chance not pulling out my pistol, but I hadn't wanted to kill them. The legion's bio people could almost always repair any damage a knife dealt to a man.

Hobbling the rest of the way to the drop-shaft, then floating in zero G all the way back to my part of *Legate*, I felt glad none of them had been killed. It wouldn't have been right if I had finished them. The legions didn't usually revive nonhumans.

More importantly, I didn't hold any real malice toward them. I was pretty sure they were just following Winslade's orders.

-16-

By the time I made it back to my own turf, I was in bad shape. One of those ribs the slavers had kicked in had punctured my lung.

You can always tell when you've got a punctured lung. Not only does it hurt, but you start coughing up pink stuff. Then, it gets harder and harder to breathe because air leaks out of the lung and accumulates inside your chest. As it fills up the space, you can't get a breath anymore. It feels like you've got a weight on your chest that's suffocating you.

I was in that kind of state when I reached Blue Deck. Every transport like *Legate* had one or more medical decks that were collectively called Blue Deck by everyone.

The bio people knew the second they spotted me that I was in trouble.

"Centurion? Are you all right?"

"Just out for a stroll," I said, then I coughed up some of that pink stuff and spat on the deck.

"What happened?" asked the bio. Looking concerned, he offered me a shoulder to lean on. Although he was a man of slight build, he looked strong enough to hold me up, so I took him up on that.

"Just a training accident. I could use some bone-splints and nu-skin, if you don't mind."

"Right through here."

I was taken into a ward and gratefully sat on a table covered by crinkly paper. Waiting there, I checked my tapper.

I was surprised to find a lot of red messages blinking on my arm. Red messages generally meant they'd been sent by a superior officer.

They were all from Graves and Winslade. I only read the subject lines—until I got bored, that is—but even those lines contained a lot of curse words.

I reflected on how people lost self-control when they got angry. It was a bad habit to get into.

Letting my arm sag down, I tried not to cough again. I had to put up a good front when the doc came in. If I looked too rough, they might get funny ideas about recycling me.

When a bio finally did show up, she was looking down at her medical tablet, frowning. At least she was an adjunct. That was customary, to have an officer work on an officer. It helped with discipline issues. You didn't want to outrank your doctor by too much, as it became harder for them to get a patient to do as they were told.

"Centurion McGill…" she said, then she looked up, and I recognized her.

"Evelyn?" I asked, surprised. "I thought you left Varus!"

She looked down again and shrugged. She was trying not to look flustered, but it wasn't working out for her.

Evelyn Thompson and I had a weird thing going some years back. At first, it had been unpleasant: we'd tried to kill each other. In fact, we'd both managed it several times. As nobody got permed, we eventually got over it.

What we couldn't get past came later on, when Evelyn worked as a spy for Galina Turov. She'd been assigned to figure out what I was up to, and one thing had led to another. Eventually, she confessed about the working side of her interest in me, and we'd parted ways.

I'd been hurt about it, but not too badly or for too long. After all, I'm not the kind of man who pines away over a single woman forever. It just isn't in me.

"This is awkward," she said, "but let's just make the best of it, shall we?"

"Uh…" I said, "awkward how?"

She flashed me a tight-lipped expression of disapproval. As women went, she was smaller than most, and a bit on the thin side, but she had a nice look to her all the same. I stared at her and smiled, liking what I saw.

She flushed and looked down again. "To business, then. You've got eight broken ribs, numerous contusions, a dislocated jaw—"

"No, no," I said, rubbing at it. "I got that back into place, see?"

"There is damage at the joint, McGill. The autodoc doesn't miss a thing like that."

"Yeah..." I admitted. My mouth did hurt every time I spoke, but it wasn't something a man like me couldn't ignore. "Are you going to get cracking with the nu-skin or what?"

She looked up again and sighed. "The computer is recommending something more drastic."

"What? A recycle? Hell no, I'll be fine by morning if you start working some of your gear. Did we leave all your instruments back on Earth?"

"It's about the recovery time, James," she said. "The computer has you down for six days of bed rest for a full recovery. Even if you go half that—it's not fast enough."

"Uh... why not?"

She blinked at me. "Because, you're leading the training tomorrow. Have you forgotten?"

Confused, I lifted my tapper. I wanted to cough again, but I held it back. "There were some messages about that. They just came in, and I didn't get a chance to read them."

"No... of course not. Listen, James, as I understand it you have a critical role to play in the morning. You have to be in peak condition. If we recycle you now, you'll be fine in an hour. Otherwise... there's no way you can lead the event. Your superiors have already communicated this to me."

"Uh... you mean Graves?"

She shook her head. "No, it was Tribune Winslade who called."

"That cock-smoker!" I burst out. "Dammit, I guess he's not done yet!"

"What are you talking about, McGill?"

My hand reached out and grabbed her wrist. She looked alarmed, but not really fearful. After all, we had a past.

"Listen, Evelyn, you've got to help me out."

"What is it?"

"Make a copy of me. A scan. A physical back-up on one of those disk things."

Frowning, she gently pried my fingers off her arm and tilted her face up to look at me. "You're serious, aren't you? What have you gotten yourself into, James?"

"Something bad, I figure. Winslade, maybe some others, they want me dead. Really badly. I have a feeling that once I do die, I'm not going to come back so fast. They might have a software glitch. Maybe my body will come back, but I'll lose a month of mental updates, something like that."

Evelyn narrowed her eyes. "You're always getting into trouble. If I help you now, they'll find out, and I'll be in your spot."

"It's not my fault, girl. I just overheard something—something about treachery. Sellouts. Turncoats."

Evelyn winced at these unwelcome words. She looked more nervous than ever.

"You owe me, girl. Make a copy. You might never have to use it."

"That sort of thing goes on record. You don't just download a body scan and a matching set of engrams without it being logged by the data core."

"I know. Just do it anyway."

She heaved a sigh and turned to walk out.

I didn't grab her again. My very existence—or at least my memories—were in her hands now. Further arguing wasn't going to do it. I had to hope for pity.

When the door opened again, I expected to see Evelyn with a body scanner and one of those little silver disks they used to store them physically.

But I was disappointed. Instead of Evelyn, it was Graves.

He had a pistol in his hand and a look on his face to match.

"Hold on, sir!" I said, and a coughing fit ensued.

Graves shook his head and checked his pistol's charge. He leveled it at me coldly.

"You should be grown up about this by now," he said. "You've been AWOL and gotten yourself hurt. That's a crime, McGill. You've damaged Varus property without permission. What's more, you did it while wandering around down in the zoo zone—and no, I don't care to hear why you were down there."

"All right, sir," I said, lifting my hands up in a gesture of surrender. "You can do what you have to do. Claver couldn't have engineered this better. My hat's off to him."

Graves sighted along his pistol barrel. The red laser-dot gleamed on my cheek.

He hesitated. "What's this horse-hockey about Claver?"

"Nothing that won't wait, sir. Assuming I do manage to catch a revive after this, we can talk all about it."

Graves' eyes were slits. "Why wouldn't you get a revive?"

"Because people that know too much about a mutiny sometimes get removed from the picture. If I wake up and don't recall anything since leaving Earth—or if there's some funny error and I don't wake up at all—well, it'll all be your problem."

Cursing, Graves lowered his weapon. "Two minutes. That's what you get. Talk now, or forever hold your peace."

I did the best I could between coughing fits to tell Graves what I'd heard. He frowned, then he looked thoughtful.

"Hmm... there has been a sudden change of plan. You've been slated to lead tomorrows blue team. You know about that, right?"

"I get it. That's why I have to die right now. Very convenient."

Graves tapped the barrel of his gun against his chin.

About then, Evelyn showed up. She had a body-scanning gun in her hand.

Graves smirked at her. "I see you've been given this line of crap from McGill as well."

"Primus?" she asked primly. "Can you excuse me? I'm doing a back-up of this soldier before the... procedure."

Graves gave a rumbling laugh. "Before I scatter his brains, you mean? All right, proceed."

"Not a word to anyone, sir," I said as Evelyn scanned my mind, body and soul. "If they don't know we have a backup, they can't come to erase it."

"You mean Winslade and his apes?"

"I think there are more than just them involved, sir."

Graves didn't like that. He waited impatiently. When Evelyn had finished her work, she gave him the thumbs-up.

Graves aimed his gun at me, smiled, and pulled the trigger.

-17-

When I returned to life, I felt myself wondering how many times I'd been killed by that man, Primus Graves. I figured he was probably my greatest nemesis if you counted every occasion, all the way back to my first training. Could you really call a man like that a friend? I don't think that anyone could.

"What's his score?" Evelyn asked.

"He's an eight. Make that eight-point-five."

"I'll take it. Sit him up."

Bleary-eyed and aching a bit, I sat up and groaned. Sitting up caused a bolt of pain to shoot through my chest. That was a shocker.

"What the hell?" I asked, then I coughed. I coughed hard and deep. It really hurt.

"He's bleeding again."

"Nano-inject the site. Get the stints in. We have to cover this up."

Right about then, I became alarmed. If I wasn't mistaken, I still had a full rack of broken ribs to contend with.

The whole damned point of being recycled was to get rid of injuries like the ones I was feeling right now. Reaching up to touch my mouth gingerly, I felt a loose tooth and a loose jaw to match.

"Who screwed this up?" I rasped.

"We didn't do it," Evelyn said. "Your data was lost, just like you said it would be. We had to revive you from that disk backup. Your injuries were recorded, and we didn't have the time or the authorization to try to edit them out."

"Shit…" I complained.

"Listen James," Evelyn told me, getting into my face. "You were as good as permed, at least until we got back to Earth."

The implications were grim. There had to be someone working here inside Blue Deck with Winslade. Or, it could have been some kind of tech wizard hacker. He couldn't have erased my files on his own.

"What am I supposed to do?" I asked.

"You have to fake it," Evelyn said in my ear. "Don't act hurt. We've patched you up, but you're going be really sore for a few days."

"How long have I got until the training exercise begins?"

She glanced at her tapper. "Three… maybe four hours."

"It's morning?"

"It's four a. m. We didn't want to do this while people were watching. We're in the middle of the graveyard shift on Blue Deck."

Blinking and rubbing at my eyes, I found that every movement was painful. All my injuries were working overtime. They'd been patched over, but they were still there. Modern medicine could do amazing things, but there were limits. I felt like the layered-on nu-skin might rip when I took a deep breath, for instance.

"Shoot me up with something," I said. "I have to walk and talk like I'm feeling fine."

She didn't want to do it, but in the end, she did. A few minutes later, I was feeling kind of floaty…

On the way out, I made a grab for Evelyn. Surprised, she let me scoop her up and plant a big kiss on her. I set her back on her feet, and she stared, open-mouthed.

"Just a country boy thank-you," I said. "I owe you one, Adjunct Thompson."

She shooed me out the door, and I ambled up toward my module again. I did my best to project an aura of comfort and well-being. The drugs helped a lot with that.

Double-locking my door, I eased myself into my bunk and slept for three hours. That was more than I should have, but I needed the rest.

When the inevitable tapping on my door came, it was diffident.

"Yeah?" I called out. I had to fight down an urge to cough.

"Sir? Are you alone, sir?"

It was Harris. Obviously, the other adjuncts had volunteered him for the duty of waking me up today.

"I'm alone, and I'll be out in second."

Hissing with pain, I got into a sitting position and began dressing. It was harder than usual with all the sore spots.

The bones had set. That was due mostly to nano-netting enclosing the ribs and cinching tight. With a lot of growth stimulants, I was more like five days into the healing process, rather than five hours. They still hurt plenty bad. Anyone who's had a brace of broken ribs can tell you that the fifth day isn't a good one.

Ninety seconds after that first tapping came, I opened the door and strode outside. I moved like I felt fine, but internally I was sweating a little due to the pain. My whole side had stiffened up. Maybe the nap idea had been a bad one.

Just get through one exercise, McGill, I told myself. *Just one, and you can crash.*

Slamming my hands together, I walked out in front of my assembled unit. They were all lined up for roll-call. Some of them, my officers in particular, looked curious. But I gave them nothing. No explanations, no apologies, just a stern gaze.

"This is going to be a bad one," I said loudly, despite the fact I had yet to read the briefing. "We're going to win it, but it won't be easy. Let's move out to the mess hall."

"Uh…" Harris said behind me. "That's already happened, sir."

I tossed a glance over my shoulder at him, then Leeson, who stood on my other flank.

"That's right," he said. "We fed these dogs at six."

"Right," I said. "Good move. Let's get to the floor, then."

Internally, I was groaning all over again. No food, banged up, and fresh from the revival machine. I hadn't even had a shower. This was going to be a fun day.

While we marched toward Green Deck, I checked over my tapper. The information there was confusing.

"It says we're to head on down to Violet," I said. "The hold?"

"That's right, sir," Adjunct Barton said. She had moved up to my side. She looked concerned, but the other two looked disgusted. "Are you okay, Centurion?"

"Right as rain," I said, faking a confident smile. I must have done it right, because she smiled back.

Barton was a square-shouldered woman who'd come from Victrix originally. She was the most by-the-book officer I knew in Varus—except maybe for Graves.

"It's to be a hard vacuum op, sir," she said quietly. "Shielded suits, needlers and nothing else. They turned off the gravity, too. It's supposed to simulate a fight in null-G."

"Ah… that sounds sweet!" I said, hiding my horror with an even bigger smile. "Nothing like twisting, turning and fighting like rats in a sewer. Uh… any news concerning our opponents?"

She wet her lips. "They're squids, sir. About a hundred of them. All the sub-officers and noncoms from Winslade's legion."

If it was possible, which I doubted, I felt a little bit sicker than I did just thirty seconds ago.

"Squids, huh? You don't say…?"

"Yes. They can be revived. They still don't have good equipment for printing out the near-humans. The heavy troopers and slavers still don't fit into the output tray of most revival machines."

Cephalopods were about three meters tall if you stretched them out flat. They weighed in at around five hundred pounds. Still, that was only half the displacement of a full grown heavy trooper.

"Well, don't worry about this one," I said. "It's all just for show."

But for me, I knew it wasn't. I was hurt, and I couldn't risk dying again. Who knew when I'd catch my next revive?

We were met at the door by a delegation of brass. Graves was there, as were both Tribune Turov and Sub-Tribune Winslade. I'd daresay I didn't see a single face in the crowd that looked happy to see me. Maybe they'd all worked together to lose my data file.

"Attention!" Harris bellowed.

We stopped our advance and stood tall. The three high level officers approached. Galina's face softened as she looked me over. Apparently, whatever Winslade had been telling her wasn't impressing her now.

"I see nothing wrong with this soldier," she said, looking me over then glancing toward Winslade.

He shrugged, and his mouth twitched with tightly pursed lips. He looked like he smelled garbage.

"It's a fine day to die!" I boomed, grinning. My confidence seemed absolute and foolproof. "Wish us luck, sirs!"

They nodded and saluted us—all except for Winslade, that was. He looked disgusted. I figured he was probably pissed off to see me here at all, especially as I appeared to be hale and healthy.

Without further discussion, the cargo airlock that led into Violet Deck rumbled open. It was a deep-freeze, an extra cold zone low down in the *Legate's* belly. The nice thing about spaceships was the ease with which things could be frozen. All you had to do was open a window and zap! Everything was a block of ice.

Graves' voice came into my helmet, overriding tactical chat. Every man in my unit could hear him. "Welcome to our first zero-G exercise, soldiers. Today, we've got a new kind of challenge for you. With light weapons and light protection, you're to use the cargo hold on Violet Deck as a sparring arena. We've turned off the gravity, the air, the heat—everything."

He sounded pretty happy about his list of absent amenities. I wondered how long he'd sat up over previous nights to dream up this hellish experience for his troops. I figured he'd had a grin on his face the whole time.

"The mission is to defeat your opponents. We're not going to make this a to-the-last contest. If either side capitulates, the match is over."

At that point I got a private message on my tapper. It was from Carlos, so I ignored it.

"That's the good news," Graves said. "The bad news is you're all going to be nearly unarmed. Nothing but needlers, which we've toned down a bit. They'll work best at short range. You'll find they'll take about a one-second burn-time to get through a standard spacer suit."

Needlers? That was a stunner. Normally, a needler could slice up a man in a thin spacesuit rather easily, but was useless against armor. Apparently, they'd seriously nerfed the weapons. That got my mind to churning on alternatives.

"For the Varus side, the human side of this contest, we've got the 3rd Unit of the 3rd Cohort. Centurion McGill will be leading his infamous dirty-fighters in hopes of victory. On the other side we've got a team of Cephalopods from Varus sub-legion Alpha. The Alpha team will be commanded by Sub-Centurion Bubble."

For the first time all day, a real, honest-to-goodness smile erupted on my face. I couldn't help it.

"Bubbles!" I said, laughing. "We're up against Bubbles!"

"That's great, McGill," Harris said. "He hates you, doesn't he?"

"He sure does. That's probably why they chose him."

"Maybe he volunteered for the job," Leeson suggested. "Just to get back at you."

"Could be," I admitted.

In the meantime, Graves was wrapping up the pregame talk. "…may the best team win. Either way, I'm sure you'll make Varus proud. Decompression begins… now!"

The air began to hiss out of the airlock. It wasn't any ordinary airlock, but rather a huge affair big enough to hold a town meeting in. That was because it had to be big enough to move anything the ship's crew might want inside the ship through it. If it didn't fit through the cargo hold airlock, it wasn't going to fit aboard *Legate*.

They turned off the gravity next. We floated off our feet and began pushing off. Some of the men cuffed each other, sending both into a laughing spin.

"Grab a handhold around the edges. Hang on!" I shouted at them.

They quickly stopped screwing around and found a loop to hang from. The airlock was circular in shape, about twenty meters across. There were loops all around the outer edge to grab onto in case of emergencies. To me, the entire situation qualified as one giant emergency.

Moller was my best veteran. She was still cuffing a few recruits into grabbing handholds when the situation drastically changed.

The airlock's interior door that led into the cargo hold shot open with shocking speed. This change came early and without warning. It caused serious problems, as they hadn't yet pumped all the air out of the airlock.

I suspected Winslade had arranged this trick, but I couldn't prove it, and it didn't matter right now anyway.

We all had our helmets on and sealed, thank God. But not every soldier had a handhold yet. Those that didn't were surprised by the gust of depressurization. They were whisked away into the vast empty region known as Violet Deck.

Moller was one of these people. She'd been helping recruits find loops to hang onto. I reached out a huge boot, kicking her in the gut. She took no offense, she just grunted and latched onto my boot. She knew instantly it was meant to save her. She even had the quickness of mind to reach out and snatch another recruit who went twirling by and hang onto him as well.

All and all, only about fifteen of my men were left floating off into the hold, shouting and struggling in the darkness of the vast hold.

"Tell them to use blasts of compressed air to return to the group," I ordered.

"We don't have more than an hour's breathing time," Leeson said.

"That's their problem."

"McGill is right," Harris said on command chat. "If they're so dumb they're out of control in the first five minutes, they

97

aren't going to last an hour against an army of squids, anyway."

"What a way to kick-off a battle…" Leeson complained, relaying my command.

Soon, we got all our people into one place in some semblance of order. Looking like a school of fish floating over a seabed at night, we advanced into the hold as a group.

There was no sign of the enemy yet, but it was only a matter of time.

-18-

Violet Deck was cold, huge, and dark. There was frozen gear everywhere. Anything that could freeze, had long since frozen and then some.

There are even qualities to gear left in the hard vacuum of space that are difficult to explain to someone who hasn't seen them. Not just water freezes, for instance. Gases freeze as well.

The typical temperature in interstellar space, where we were flying at the moment, was almost negative three hundred degrees C, or negative five hundred in Fahrenheit. That's pretty damned cold. Even liquid nitrogen is only negative two hundred degrees C.

Due to this extreme temperature, the environment was brittle. Cargo nets wrapping around cartons of stored goods might snap at the touch. There were icicle-like crystalline structures hanging from those nets, too, which were even more brittle.

The icicles were formed not just of frozen water, but frozen carbon dioxide, better known as dry ice. There were lumps of frozen methane as well, strange ice-balls that would burn if you took them into the ship and lit them on fire. Burnable ice, we called it.

The main overhead lights had been switched off as well. I knew right off why that had been done: Cephalopods had pretty good dark vision. They had better night sight than humans, being deep undersea predators.

Winslade hadn't missed a trick when he'd put his thumb on the scales for his squids. I wasn't sure if he was hell bent on winning, or just hating on me. I guess it didn't matter which it was. In the end, the two goals meant one and the same thing to my men: we were screwed.

"Lights out," I said, "run night optics in your helmets."

"That's not as good for targeting," Harris said. "These cold-blooded aliens already got a heat signature that's dark as hell."

He was the type to argue, but today I wasn't interested in his opinions. "Adjunct, kill those lights!"

"Yes, sir."

The lights snapped off all along the advancing, floating line of troops. We were using one hand to pull ourselves along, from one roped carton to another, over the bottom of the cargo hold. The other hand of every trooper clutched a needler. They were about as useful as cigarette lighters, but they were all we had.

"Any sign of the squids?" I asked Harris.

"Nothing yet, Centurion."

My tapper beeped again. I was in command chat, meaning I could only hear my officers, but I relented and answered this time, opening a private channel. "What is it, Carlos?"

"This is a set-up, McGill!" he said.

"Tell me something I don't know."

"This is total bullshit! No lights, no gravity, no air—nothing. Everyone knows squids swim in space. It feels natural to them."

He was right about that, but I didn't feel it was worthy of note. "Is that all you've got? You're just calling to complain?"

"I haven't even started yet. Graves is a monster. A bastard of the highest order. He put us in here, and he's leaning on us to help the squids. He probably wants to save wear-and-tear on the few precious revival machines that are big enough to handle birthing a squid."

"You're wrong," I said. "It's Winslade who's screwing us."

"Really? Why?"

"He just became their new CO, didn't he? He wants them to look good their first time up at bat."

"Winslade, huh?" Carlos asked. "That evil cock-smoker. He'd sell out his own species for a promotion, wouldn't he?"

"I'm pretty sure that he would. Now, shut the hell up and kill a squid for me. McGill out."

Switching channels, I spoke to command chat again. "Barton, field your lights. Scout thirty meters ahead. The rest of you, stop here, and hold the line. I like the looks of that depression in the cartons below us. Everyone circle up in there for now."

"Not much cover," Harris complained. "If I was commanding the squids, I'd have them swim hard around behind us and flank."

"That's why I said circle-up. Move it!"

The team glided apart, forming a rough circle. We soon had eyes looking in every direction. Every few seconds, I glanced up at the ceiling. It was shadowy up there, but I was pretty certain I'd see the squids if they tried to make a move to flank us that way.

The cargo hold was running on emergency lights only. Combined with our night-vision enhancements in our helmets, we could see pretty well in a green-and-black universe.

Still, somehow, the squids managed to surprise us. They were sneaky bastards by any measure.

"Behind us, Centurion!" shouted Cooper. "They've circled around to our rear!"

It was only then that I realized I should have used my two Ghost Specialists, Cooper and Della, to do my scouting for me. I'd been concentrating on advancing my whole force as a single group, rather than using the scouts I had. Maybe the pain meds were affecting my judgment.

Spinning around, I didn't see a single squid, but I ordered Barton's light troopers to fall back, tightening up our defensive position in the mounds of cartons.

The squids must have interpreted this move as prey that was trying to escape them. They launched their attack the moment we tried to ball-up.

101

Huge shapes came at us out of the dark. They'd been gliding low, drifting over the lumpy surface of crates and equipment. To them, it probably seemed like a very familiar environment. After all, they were pack hunters, apex predators from the depths of their own ocean-covered world.

Shouting erupted on tactical chat. "Squids, sir! Dozens of them!"

"Fire at will!" I ordered my whole unit, and we engaged.

We didn't have any choice. They were coming in close, and I knew why. Each squid weighed four times as much as a big man. They were large, physically powerful and ruthless.

All along our lines, beams flashed. When they struck the cargo, they melted the ice on them and sent up plumes of vaporized gas. The enemy did the same, returning fire and scoring our suits with black burn-marks.

"The needlers aren't doing shit, sir!" Harris called out.

Proving his point, I shot a squid as it dove down from above us. It didn't stop him—hell, it didn't even puncture his suit.

Speaking on the unit-wide tactical chat channel, I made a fateful announcement: "Forget the needlers. Drop them, they're underpowered. Use your belt-knives—or your teeth, if you have to."

"Why not just tell us to use our dicks?" one of my troops dared to retort. I thought it was Carlos, but I couldn't swear to it.

All around the hold, the battle was going badly. The squids fired their needlers at us, but they didn't do much. They seemed to expect that, and they plunged closer and closer.

"They're going into hand-to-hand. Draw your belt-knives, everyone. Remember, you don't have to kill a squid, just cut his suit open. Nature will do the rest."

They reached our lines at all points almost simultaneously. The whole thing smacked of a setup. It was as if they'd known where we'd enter, and they'd been allowed to encircle the spot and lay in ambush.

Cooper bought the farm first. His position in the far rear had made him an outlier, and they found him somehow despite

102

his stealth suit. Probably it didn't work well in hard vacuum. For all I knew, squid eyes could see right through the effect.

Whatever the case, he was yanked out of a gap between cargo cartons and two squids fought over him. They plucked off both arms first, then a leg. After that, they tossed him in a spin that went straight up toward the ceiling. A ruby spray of frozen blood droplets flew with him like a swarm of bees.

Then their main force hit our lines, and we crumpled. Their weight and mass was such that we might as well have been charged by a ring of hungry great-white sharks.

"Knives, people!" Harris shouted. "Stick-em!"

Varus legionaries are a resourceful lot. We were actively trained with every imaginable weapon, both advanced and mundane. Having been killed and reborn somewhere between ten and hundred times each, we didn't face deadly situations with the kind of panic most men did. We fought with commitment, like starving wolves.

Thrusting out with our blades to meet the enemy charge, many men penetrated the squid suits. They were thin, after all. The fabric was too tough to tear through normal means, but it wasn't capable of withstanding an edge that was a single molecule wide.

Our knives weren't standard issue stainless steel. Far from it. They were tempered for strength, and their edges were artificially aligned at the molecular level. They had to be sharpened by computerized nanotech. If you touched one to a regular whetstone, you'd ruin it forever.

Fortunately, I'd had my troops run every blade we had through the sharpening machine when I'd first heard of this "exercise" and it was really paying off today. The blades slid right through the enemy spacesuits, and right through the rubbery flesh underneath. Tentacles, curling and writhing for a full second after being severed, floated away from the scene in a dozen fights.

One squid came at me, and I lunged, thrusting my knife deep. Most men slashed, but I wanted to be sure I punched through to the organs. I managed that and more. The stricken squid convulsed in agony. My blade had gone between his reaching tentacles and cut deeply into his main bulbous body. A few eyes popped, leaking gore.

He slapped at me, giving me a massive ache as my cracked ribs sang a song of woe. But I hung onto consciousness, stabbing him more deeply.

All of a sudden, he lurched and withdrew. He'd had enough. Unfortunately, he took my knife with him, wedged in what served a Cephalopod for guts.

Similar fights went on all around me, in a ring of struggling forms. People shouted, screamed and begged—but they fought on.

Despite the initial bite we put on them, we couldn't withstand their strength and weight. They were big, vital, and far stronger than any man. They got in close, wrapping each stabbing legionnaire in crushing tentacles. I'd expected them to wield spears or knives of their own—but they didn't. They didn't seem to have anything other than weakened needlers. Dropping these useless guns, they wrapped us with their numerous powerful limbs and squeezed until our bodies were broken.

My men died, but after a full minute of chaos, the injured squids began to die as well. Most of them had lost their suit integrity. The incredibly cold nothingness that we all swam within began to work its evil magic.

They stiffened, spasmed, and did odd, wriggling dances. Often they died while holding crippled and broken men in a death grip. For the most part, our own suits were intact, and our survivors watched the squids die all around us.

Bubbles called for a retreat. Moving as one, the surviving Cephalopods launched themselves straight up, avoiding us with a single mighty thrust of their numerous limbs. They glided away with the same grace and unity they'd used when they attacked.

Like snarling apes, we stabbed and cut at the retreating forms. We then formed a knot of survivors, hooking our feet in the frosty cargo webbing. We waved our blades overhead, shouting until we were hoarse and jeering.

"Count off," I gasped, breathing hard. My lung was punctured by a loose rib again, I could feel it. I wasn't going to last an hour—but with luck, I didn't have to. "Moller? You there?"

"Here sir," she slurred back. "I'm a little banged-up, but I'm good."

"Roger that. Leeson? Harris?"

No answer came back to me. "Adjunct Barton here," Barton said. "I hope you're not disappointed, sir."

I was, but it was better to have one surviving officer than zero. "All right, let's group up. Help the wounded, finish any squids that look lively."

We checked, but there were precious few survivors on either side. You were either able-bodied and escaped death, or you'd been ripped apart. The squids hadn't fared much better. One good cut through their suits led to death within a minute or two. It was simple physics. Even squids needed air and some level of warmth to survive.

On our side, I had less than thirty men left out of about a hundred-twenty. The squids had really caused a lot of damage.

"Grim losses, Centurion," Barton said matter-of-factly. "Um… who do you think has won this?"

I looked at her in surprise. Violet Deck wasn't completely dark. There were dim emergency lights far above us. Now that our eyes had adjusted, I could see the outline of her face inside her helmet.

"Who won?" I asked. "This isn't over with yet. Squids don't give up easily—and neither do we."

She didn't say anything, so I marshaled the troops we had left.

-19-

Sometimes, especially in the legions, dying in the first engagement of a long battle was a good thing. The survivors who had to struggle on, injured and exhausted, often came to envy the dead. This was just one more thing that revival machines had changed about the way we viewed war in modern times.

"Bubbles?" I called out, trying to contact my enemy commander. "I know you're still alive. A few of your squids got away, and I know you're the biggest chicken of them all, so you must be out there somewhere."

I'd often found the best way to get a creature talking was to sting its pride. If there was one deadly sin that every alien seemed to indulge in, it was that one. They all had an undue belief in their own self-worth.

"The McGill…" Bubbles called back, and I thought I detected a weariness in his voice. Could he be injured? "You are in error. We withdrew to allow you to die quietly from your injuries, like the prey-animals you are."

"Ah, is that it?" I asked loudly, broadcasting my words to make sure everyone in the exercise and all those watching could listen in. "I thought you were plain cowards. All the same, now that the fight is over, I'd like to offer you my congratulations. You fought well here today. Defeat isn't the worst thing—not if you face it with honor."

"You're utterances are empty," Bubbles told me. "It is you who have been clearly defeated. You hide like shellfish among rocks, fearing to face us in the open."

"Fear? That's a funny thing that you should bring that topic up, because I wasn't going to be the one to do it. I've got to tell you, we've got a lot of frozen ink back here all over our camp. Your boys not only ran for their lives in terror, they inked themselves when they did it."

"Sir?" Barton said, drifting close to my side. "Why are you goading him? Is that wise?"

Keying off my headset, I turned to her. "Just keep your troops alert and watching for squids, will you?"

She drifted away, and I went back to talking big to old Bubbles. I watched her go, and I couldn't help but admire her athletic form. It was funny how you could always tell a woman's shape from a man's, even in a bulky spacesuit. Well... I could tell with Barton's shape, anyway.

"Bubbles?" I asked. "Are you still there? You haven't called Graves and quit yet, have you?"

"I have no intention of—"

"Good, good," I said. "Some of my boys here laid money down that you'd had enough, but I bet on you to keep going. Don't go and piss yourself and quit on me, you hear? I'm betting on your reliably stupid behavior."

"I fail to comprehend how you've come to misunderstand this situation so drastically, McGill. Even now, we're advancing to finish your microscopic command. You've lost eighty percent of your force. We will end this within minutes."

That was good intel from my standpoint. I stuck out my lower lip and nodded appreciatively. It didn't sound like I was going to get him to make another disorganized rush, but at least I knew he was on his way back.

"I'm glad to hear it," I told him honestly. "Hell, we thought we were going to have to dig you out of whatever hole you've gone off to hide in."

"There is no such—"

"Hey, it's been good talking to you, Bubbles, but I've got to go. I'll buy you a beer when this is over."

"My name is singular, and alcohol is inert to my species."

"That's a damned shame," I said with honest feeling. "McGill out."

"Have we got any techs left?" I asked Barton.

"No. Only one of the bio-people is left. They seemed to sense our weakest fighters, and targeted them first."

"Who's the bio—oh."

Carlos came gliding up to me. Just like Barton, I recognized his shape. He was kind of walrus-looking.

"Okay," he said. "I'm here and ready for abuse. What heinous death do you have planned for me this time, Centurion?"

"With luck, it will be the squids that die badly today. We need new weaponry—and we've got about ten minutes to come up with it."

Going through the roster, I found Sargon was still among the living. I summoned him and gave him some special orders.

"You see those cartons below us? In that frozen webbing? Dig in there. I want you to find something we can mount these knives on. Let's turn them into spears. We've got three knives per man now—see what you can do."

"On it, Centurion," he said, and he began ripping into the cartons and modularly stacked gear. There was no hesitation in his movements. He obviously didn't care what kind of damage he did.

"Centurion?" Barton said moments later. "Is that man damaging—?"

"He sure is. Get some of your boys to help him. We don't have long."

Soon, Sargon dug out rods. These were about eight feet long and served as pins in the cartons had that hinges. The rods weren't much to look at, but they would have to do. We used the needlers to weld the knife handles onto these titanium poles and formed crude spears.

"Anything to give us some reach," I told the rest. "Get cracking, people. You've got five minutes left to live. Don't be shy."

Soon, my entire command was digging and gouging at the cartons. We found all sorts of junk. Medical supplies, food, even a few rifles. Reluctantly, we dropped those. We'd been explicitly told we couldn't use our standard gear.

But no one had said anything about cannibalizing or modifying what we'd been issued. Normally, in Legion Varus, innovation was encouraged.

It was Carlos who came up with a real gem—an oxygen bottle. It wasn't plumbed right for us to use, however. It was teamed with an acetylene tank, a cutting torch system essentially. We didn't have the time or inclination to do much with that, but Carlos kept toying with the fittings.

"I've got an idea," he kept saying.

"That's great," I told him. "Whatever it is, make it snappy."

A few more minutes went by, but the squids didn't attack. After about twenty had passed and we'd made as many spears as we could, I began to get bored. I was about ready to call up Bubbles and call him a liar.

But then they made their move. All around us, a dozen of the enemy had squirmed in between the cartons, sneaking up on us without coming out in the open.

"Spear 'em!" I shouted. "Gig them like frogs!"

Sargon was a known expert with spears. We only had about a dozen, but he threw three before they reached us. He managed to skewer one squid, opening his suit and dooming him to depressurization.

Still, I was worried. We were badly outweighed by the enemy. The simple fact was they'd killed eighty percent of my troops last time while we'd only managed to kill maybe half of them. This time, we might be better prepared, but they were going to overwhelm us.

Baring my teeth, I prepared to fight to the bitter end.

"Squids!" Carlos shouted. "More of them—up on the roof!"

My eyes rolled up, and I almost couldn't see the ceiling— but then I spotted a rippling tentacle. They were up there, another dozen of them. They coiled up those flappy tentacles of theirs preparing to spring down into our midst.

"This is it!" Carlos called out. "I'm doing it—everybody duck!"

We winced and glanced in his direction. In the middle of fighting squids with spears, we'd kind of forgotten about him.

Sensing our distraction, the squids who were trying to infiltrate our defensive setup lunged. Tentacles slid up between us and grabbed men—pulling them down into the cracks where they howled until they died.

What I saw next, however, I'd never have credited if I hadn't witnessed it with my own bare eyes. Carlos had that oxygen bottle he'd been messing with for nearly half an hour now. He fully opened up the valve, and it sprayed out a white gust of vapor—pure oxygen freezing into particles in the absolute cold of Violet Deck.

The real shocker was Carlos himself. He'd built a rocket of sorts, but instead of letting it fly like any normal teenager on Unity Day, he rode with it. In his hand, he had a red, gleaming light.

What the hell was he up to? I had the focus of mind to think that single thought—and an instant later, I knew.

"Take cover!" I roared, throwing myself flat.

A blast wave rolled over me. A gush of orange flame blossomed, and I swear I felt the heat of it right through my suit.

The squids on the roof, however, were much closer to the blast. Carlos' makeshift missile went off in the middle of them, even as they tried to pluck him off his gas tank. He was blown to bits along with half of Bubble's troops. Apparently, he'd managed to light it off with his needler. I suspected he'd just held the trigger down and cooked a hole clean through the tank.

"Huh," I said. "Someone got some use out of those worthless needlers after all."

The rest of the squids struggled among the cartons, but the fight seemed to go out of them. We speared a few more in between the cartons while they wriggled away in full retreat.

Right off, I suspected I knew what had happened. "Hey, Bubbles," I called out on an open channel. "This is McGill. Talk to me, Sub-Centurion."

There was no response for about thirty seconds. Finally, however, another voice answered. "McGill? This is Sub-Veteran Ripple."

"Really? All right, Ripple. Where's Bubbles?"

"Sub-Centurion Bubble was killed in the last engagement."

"Is that right? Well then, who's in charge of your team?"

"As best I can determine... I am, sir."

"Okay, now we're getting someplace. Come on out of hiding and fight like a squid, will you? We're getting tired of watching you ink yourselves and run off. It's embarrassing."

"Sub-Centurion Bubble is dead, sir. Therefore, you have won this conflict."

"You quit?"

"That is not an appropriate description of the situation. When one side's commander has perished, whatever conflict he initiated—"

"You're quitting, aren't you! Hot damn! You hear that, Graves? Winslade? This is over. The squids have surrendered!"

Ripple kept on complaining about my misuse of various terms, but it didn't matter a hill of beans to me or my cheering men.

"Yes, McGill," Graves said. "We're listening. This contest is officially over."

"There will be an inquiry!" Winslade said in a whiny tone. "Illegal activity permeates your unit, Graves. I'd forgotten how dishonorable and even criminal your outfit can be. I should never have agreed to—"

"No you shouldn't have, Winslade!" I shouted. "Your squids got their tentacles blown off."

There was more like that, but Turov's voice overrode all of ours and shut us down. "The contest is over. I hope you enjoyed yourselves. Now, get your asses out of my hold before you do any more damage. Graves, this is the last time we're using Violet Deck for an exercise. McGill has trashed valuable equipment."

I didn't care to listen to anymore nonsense. Me and my men were just too damned happy. We howled and helped each other toward the exits of the frozen hold with grins on our faces. Those of us who had survived couldn't stop smiling.

Later on, the bio people on Blue Deck put me to death, but I barely cared. I'd beaten Bubbles fair-and-square, and I'd always wanted to do that.

-20-

When I came out of the revival machine with a smile on my face, the bio people did a little mind-check before they let me go. I guess they figured that a grinning rebirth was unusual enough to suspect brain damage.

I let them do it, as I was in a great mood. At last, shaking their heads, they let me go. My brain wasn't perfect, but it functioned well enough to keep me walking and breathing right. What more could the legion ask for?

Marching toward Gold Deck, I didn't even bother to check in with my module. My troops were grown-ups. They could take care of themselves. After all, we'd won, and that should relieve any trauma they might be feeling after a tough fight.

"McGill?" my tapper spoke up.

I lifted it up into my field of view, surprised. It was Tribune Galina Turov. She had an odd, suspicious look on her face.

Now, that expression wasn't an unusual one for her, but what really surprised me was that she was talking out of my tapper without me having touched the "accept call" button.

"Uh…" I said. "Hello sir. How did you…? I mean, I hadn't even had chance to answer yet."

"I know," she said. "I called you three times already. The moment you got out of Blue Deck, I began calling you."

Naturally, I knew all that. That's why I was walking up to Gold Deck, but I hadn't bothered to answer her repeated calls.

112

I was a man who preferred to speak face-to-face with people. Text messages, phone calls and the like—they tended to get nastier. There were more misunderstandings, and I also suspected the anger expressed in such communications was inherent to the nature of man.

If you're in the physical presence of another person, you're less likely to yell at them. That is a plain and simple fact of existence. Why? Because you instinctively know you're more likely to get your ass-kicked if you mouth off face-to-face, that's why. That's my own opinion, but I bet any psych worth his salt would agree.

"Uh..." I said. "But how did you make my tapper answer your call, sir?"

"That's an update. How do you like it?"

"Hmm... I can't say that I do. Also, I have automatic updates turned off on my tapper."

She smiled wickedly. When she was in a mood, her smile could be downright evil at times. "You died, didn't you? That resets your settings."

She was right, of course. Grumbling, I went into my settings screens to turn off the auto-updates. After doing it, and moving to tap the exit button, I saw a strange thing. The damned sliding button for updates had glitched back again, going to full-auto.

"Damn..." I said, tapping away.

While I did this, I got an earful from Galina. I didn't listen to most of it, but what I heard made some kind of sense.

Apparently, Winslade was butt-hurt over the fact I'd beaten down his squids with such impunity. He was claiming all kinds of fouls, cheats, and general dirty-dealing had occurred.

None of this surprised or impressed me. Winslade had never taken personal defeats well. I figured he'd get over it eventually.

"The inquiry will be held in my office. Get up here as soon as you... oh."

Tapping politely on her door, I was let in by her boy-toy assistant Gary. He twitched his lips at me and nodded toward the interior door.

113

Brushing past, I marched to the bigger door and lifted my hand, but my knuckles never landed. Galina snatched the door open and looked both ways.

She still had that pissed-cat expression going on. Narrowed eyes, tight mouth, head swiveling around like something bad might be hiding in every corner.

"Get in here," she said.

Happy as could be, I walked past her, lounged on her couch and heaved a sigh.

She stood over me with her fists on her hips.

Damn. Those were some nice hips. I'd kind of forgotten. Galina and I hadn't been together since the Armor World campaign.

"Looking good, Tribune," I said.

"McGill, you are insufferable. Look at you, you're so pleased with yourself. Do you know how many quartermasters want your blood today?"

That one kind of threw me. I blinked stupidly and frowned. "Quartermasters?"

"Yes. You wrecked twenty million credits worth of gear. It's hard to believe, but you managed it all in a single hour's time."

"Oh… that. I get it. Well, what moron had the bright idea of setting up a death match in the dark on Violet Deck in the first place? Maybe they ought to take it up with him."

Galina licked her lips, studying me. "You don't seem to be any different. I'm not sure where you stand…"

"Uh… could you throw some light on that cryptic statement, sir? Where I stand in what context?"

She cocked her head and narrowed her eyes a little more. It was calculating look. I knew it well. She was thinking dark thoughts.

"You know about Claver, right? About his offers? Don't even try to play the idiot this time."

I blinked once, that's it. Then I got my surprise under control and did a little shrug and a tiny smile.

That was it. She figured I knew everything. Sometimes, the best lies were told with body language. People always believed your body couldn't lie. Usually, they were right. But I pride myself on having become a man who possessed rare talents over the years. I was what I liked to call an *advanced* liar. A man who had truly studied the art form. I'd taken my natural proclivities and turned them into mastery.

"Of course..." she said in a hissy tone. "You've been approached. Of course you have. Absurdity, the mere idea you should be allowed to operate a legion—but then, Claver has always been fascinated by you."

"Well..." I said, talking slowly in hopes she would jump in with more details. "What did he offer you, exactly? I figure it must be at least the rank of imperator. After all—"

"Shut up," she snapped. "You know full well he's offered me nothing. It's an insult."

"Ah..." I said, nodding. "He is a petty man. Willing to give up on the best of the best out of sheer spite."

It was her turn to blink in surprise. "You really think I'm the best?"

"You've got the rank, don't you? Do you really think he'd offer me a legion, but not give you the time of day? You must have thirty years of experience wearing the brass ahead of me."

"Right..." she said, softening her tone. I could tell my implicit compliments were having their desired effects. "But maybe it's more than spite. Maybe he doesn't trust me. Maybe he thinks I might be an effective rival in this revolution of his."

I frowned, just for a second. *A revolution?* What the hell was everyone else aboard this ship involved in?

To cover for the frown of concern, I looked at the deck and nodded seriously, as if I was truly interested in the in-fighting among our local traitors for the top spot in Claver's scheme.

"What are we going to do when we get out there?" I asked her.

She stopped staring into space and looked me in the eyes. "That's the real reason you're here today. I wanted to know if you stand with Claver—or with me."

"Uh..." I said. "You're not on his side, then?"

"I just told you he didn't even invite me! That prick thinks he can do this alone. He thinks all he needs is a few sycophants like Winslade at his side—but he is sorely mistaken, let me assure you."

A smile glimmered on my face. "So, it's a fight, then? Not some kind of wild chicanery coronating Claver?"

"Not if I have anything to say about it."

"Hot damn! Count me in!"

She proceeded to complain about Claver and Winslade some more, but I got bored and stopped listening. Eventually, a tapping came at the door.

Galina's face went feral for a second, then she regained her composure. She was still angry, but she wanted to hide it.

She stepped to the door and opened it. Winslade and Graves stood there, and she invited them inside.

Winslade sauntered in, but he did a double-take when he spotted me lounging on the couch. "What is this man doing here?"

"He's here at my order," Galina said stiffly.

Winslade recovered quickly and shrugged. "Fine. As long as we arrest him at the end of this farce, I'll be satisfied."

"Just so. Sit down, please, Sub-Tribune."

Winslade sat opposite Galina's big desk. Graves took another chair off to the side of the room. He didn't say anything, and his face resembled a stone mask. That didn't mean squat, however. He pretty much always wore that expression.

"For the last time, Turov," Winslade said, daring to drop Galina's rank. He figured now that he was in charge of a zoo legion he was on an even keel with Galina. She figured differently, I could tell just by looking at her. "Are you going to arrest this man, or not?"

"On what charge," she asked smoothly.

Winslade began ticking things off on his skinny fingers. "Insubordination. Destruction of legion property—wanton destruction, I might add. Additionally, three murders—all perma-deaths—were suffered by my slavers only yesterday."

"Now, hold on just a damned minute!" I interjected, coming halfway off the couch. "I didn't murder those men. They were alive! They were a little damaged, maybe, but they were breathing just fine when I left them."

116

Winslade rotated his head on that skinny neck and gave me a knowing smirk. "Do you know what use this legion has for crippled near-humans?"

"Uh…" I said, thinking that over. "Not much, I suspect, but you could always just airmail them back to Blood World and get new ones. They could get the care they need back home and—"

Winslade cut the air with a nasty laugh. "How little you understand our savage brethren, McGill. What? Do you think they have *hospitals*? Or convalescent homes, perhaps, for the aged and the weak? Such absurdities. If we did bother to send them back, they'd have been executed within minutes."

"So… what did you do with them?" I asked.

"We saved ourselves the power surge of using the gateway equipment. We put them to death. But really, *you* are their executioner, aren't you McGill? All in order to resist a valid arrest."

"Arrest?"

Winslade produced a rattling length of computer paper. He handed it to Turov, who took it with little interest.

The words displayed on the electronic document no doubt accused me of countless crimes. He'd probably made it up right before the meeting and back-dated it.

"Here are the orders they carried," he said. "They're valid, and I demand they be carried out immediately now."

Turov sniffed, glanced at the document, then let it slide out of her fingers onto her desktop. Her thin arms crossed over her breasts, and she eyed Winslade.

"This is my ship, Winslade," she said. "I'm a full-fledged Tribune, and I'm commanding both Legion Varus and your sub-legion. This mission is my operation, and I'll give the orders here."

Winslade sputtered. He looked pissed. Maybe this kind of power struggle was exactly why he'd opted to go for whatever it was Claver was offering him. He didn't like still being under Galina's thumb. Hell, no one ever had.

"Fine," he said suddenly, standing up. "I'll be going then. If you and your boyfriend want to circumvent the law, then I'll bring it up with Central when we return to Earth."

There it was. Winslade had gone and done it. He'd shoved his dick in the proverbial light socket and flipped on the switch.

Galina was many things, but above all she was prideful. She didn't like people talking about her, um… relationships. I was pretty sure she wasn't proud of any of them, but if there was one boyfriend on her list she didn't want the public to know about, it had to be me. We'd had an odd on-again, off-again love affair for over a decade now, but she still didn't want to admit it.

"Not so fast," she said. She glanced in my direction, and her eyes were full of hate. "McGill, arrest this man."

I sprang off the couch like a terrier who'd heard the mailman coming. One of my big hands landed on Winslade's shoulder a moment later.

Galina smiled at Winslade's fuming and fussing.

"Graves," she said. "We've discussed this man's treachery at length. What has your investigation turned up?"

"You were right, Tribune. Although I'm not sure how you knew about it… he's been in contact with Earth's enemies. He seems to be taking direction from them."

For the first time, Winslade looked seriously alarmed. He glanced to his left at Graves. I stood even closer on his right side, with one big hand on his shoulder.

Then, realizing the game was up, he turned back to face Galina. He raised his chin, and a sour smile crossed those thin lips.

"Do your worst. It will mean nothing in the end."

Galina's eyes faltered, just for a second, then she steeled herself. She produced a computer paper of her own. She read it, and at the end, declared Winslade a traitor.

"I sentence you to be executed immediately."

She nodded to Graves, and he put his pistol up to Winslade's head.

"Don't think you've won anything," Winslade told all of us spitefully. "I'll meet you all again, soon enough."

Then Graves shot him dead. With his skull popped like a melon and some of it splashed on Galina, Winslade slumped onto the deck.

118

"Gah!" she said, wrinkling her pretty nose. "Get that mess out of here. He's bleeding all over my carpet."

We hustled the corpse out and gave the body to Gary, who looked like he might be sick.

I tried to slip back into Galina's office, but she slammed the door shut on me. Waiting just a second, I called her and hit the "force answer" button. That was new.

Galina was in the bathroom when her tapper woke up on her arm and I started talking and looking at her.

"Tribune? I'm sorry, but I—oh..."

She'd stripped down to her waist. I guess she'd gotten some blood on her uniform and was changing into a fresh one. Unable to help myself, I ogled her breasts as they bumped right into my face—after all, a person's inner forearm was typically aimed that way while they did things.

Finally, a very annoyed face came into view. "McGill? You're spying on me now?"

"No, no, sir," I said. "I just called you and—"

"That frigging update! I'm rolling that back. What a piece of shit—"

"Uh... sir? I have a few things to discuss... could you open your door?"

She paused, looking at me. I tried hard, real, real hard, not to dip my eyes down and look at her bare skin. Like a laser sight, I kept my eyes in contact with hers.

Galina sighed at last. "All right."

The screen went blank, and the lock on her office door clicked. I let myself in.

She was still in the bathroom scrubbing and cursing. I made a drink and waited patiently. She came out looking fresh again. Not a drop of Winslade's blood was in sight. She must have poured nanite powder on the carpet to eat up the stain.

"What do you want here now?" she asked, putting her fists on her swelling hips.

"Uh..." I said, "I just arrested and executed a man for you, sir."

"That's half-right. Graves shot him... but your point is well-taken. It was an act of loyalty. I do feel gratitude, as you chose to follow me rather than Claver."

119

"Damn-straight," I said, offering her a drink I'd poured.

She sighed, and she sat on the couch beside me. Soon, we were smiling and kissing. One thing led to another, and I soon managed to peel that fresh uniform off of her once again.

The truth was she seemed kind of turn-on by the whole violent event in her office. It was like she'd struck a blow for justice or something. She was really pissed to be passed-over by Claver for an offer to join his rebellion.

Hours later, she kicked me out.

"Just so you know, James," she said. "This is not going to develop into an affair. I consider it a relapse—and it's over with. Understand?"

"Uh…" I said, my mind working on some weaselry. But I stopped myself. I forced a smile and nodded. When a woman dumps you, your best chance to reverse it is to take it in stride. Caring too much was almost always a mistake.

"Okay," I said, and I kissed the top of her head. She let me, then I walked back through the long passageways to my module.

Thinking over the events of the day as I stretched out on my bunk, I soon fell asleep. My drifting mind thought that maybe Galina had made a valid point. Claver really *ought* to have invited her, if only because he was going to regret not doing so now.

Hell hath no fury like a woman scorned, and Galina Turov was living proof of the concept.

-21-

The next day, they announced a new officer had taken over Winslade's job. They were to display the swearing-in live on every open wall aboard *Legate*.

We were all curious as to whom it might be—but none of us suspected the truth until we saw the new man take the job.

"Primus Fike?" Leeson asked in shock. "Wasn't he with the Iron Eagles?"

"Not last I saw," Harris said. "He was playing sidekick for old Armel when he was in charge of that garrison legion on Storm World."

"That's right," I said, chewing over the new information. "That's where I saw him last, too."

Primus Fike was an arrogant, by-the-book sort of officer. When you were around him, he never let you imagine he wasn't better than you. Not for a moment.

For all of that, I kind of liked his spirit. His swaggering and boasting wasn't entirely unwarranted. He'd fought well every time I'd seen him in the field. Overall I'd have to admit he was an effective leader—even if he was an asshole.

"Fike's a good choice," I said. "He's been playing second banana with a zoo legion on Storm World for years. I'm sure he'll know how to handle his own command."

"But why would he want to work with Varus?" Harris insisted.

I shrugged. "Maybe that part wasn't his idea."

Harris laughed and shook his head. "No, I bet it wasn't."

Fike was given a handshake by Turov, and she welcomed him aboard. He'd stepped through the ship's gateway from Earth only minutes earlier.

"Sub-Tribune Fike," she said. "Let me be the first to use your new title publicly. I want you to know that aboard this ship, our near-human legion is considered to be Varus' largest and most important cohort."

Fike blinked at that. I could tell he wasn't quite sure if he'd been insulted or given a compliment. I could have told him it was a little of both. It was the sort of thing Galina was famous for—faint praise.

"Now then, if you'd like to address everyone aboard, feel free." So saying, Turov stepped aside, letting Fike take center stage.

He kind of reminded me of a larger, younger, more flashy version of Graves. His voice wasn't a rumble, however. It was resonant and clear. The perfect officer's voice.

"Legionnaires," Fike said. "I hope we're all going to become tight allies. The fight ahead, by all reports, will not be easy."

Here, he turned to Turov. "Have you briefed them yet on what we're facing?"

She made an easy gesture with one hand toward a camera pickup. "They know the basics. Go ahead and tell them of our latest intel from Earth, if you would."

Nodding, he turned back to us. His blocky face was like a mask of professionalism. He gave no hint of emotion, other than stern resoluteness.

"Legionnaires, Earth is facing a new danger. A renegade, originally from legion Germanica, has performed countless Galactic Crimes."

This caused a lot of whispering to arise around me. His words didn't shock me much, of course, as I'd performed countless Galactic Crimes myself. The trick to it was in not getting caught.

But for the average troop in the rank and file, any Galactic-level crime was an unthinkable risk. The Galactics weren't

122

generous rulers. They often took a very broad view of guilt when handing out punishments. Families, towns, even planets and entire species had been found guilty by association in the past.

Even less appetizing was the only known punishment meted out for infractions at such a level: mass death.

"That's right," he said. "This individual, known to us as Adjunct Claver from Germanica, left Earth's employ decades ago. Since then he's been considered an unpredictable, self-serving danger to us all. Operating as an interstellar trader, he's been found useful to deal with at times—but no longer."

He paused to sweep a set of steely eyes over us all. "This time, Claver has gone too far. He's raised an army and declared a planet he's squatting on to be a sovereign state."

There was an increased volume to the chatter in every module aboard *Legate*. This irked Harris. "Quiet!" he bellowed.

At last they settled down, and Fike went on. He was quite the showman. It was as if he could hear us and knew how we were reacting in our individual chambers.

"That's right," Fike said. "The man is clearly insane. And who, you might well ask, is manning these legions of his?"

For the first time I frowned in concern. I'd heard several references to what Claver had specifically built out on this planet known as Eridani 77. People had talked about an army thousands strong—but entire legions? That was a shocker.

"We don't know how many men he has," Fike explained. "But we do know that he's been cloning himself. His army is made of men who are all degenerate, illegal copies of Claver himself."

He paused again, letting that one sink in. It wasn't well-received. "Insanity!" I heard from the front ranks.

The recruit who'd said it was right. Cloning yourself just once was far too bold of a move. But to do it over and over, making an army? I could hardly imagine something that would piss off the Galactics more than that.

"We've got to take him out," I said quietly. "Fike's right."

My adjuncts looked at me. "We're going to, Centurion," Leeson assured me. "Don't fret about that."

"The enemy is essentially an army of clones," Fike continued. "But they aren't just copies of Claver. They're specialized. Several types exist, some more intelligent or physically capable than the others. We don't know everything about them yet, but we know we can't allow them to be discovered by the Galactics. They must be removed from the galaxy, once and for all. We're going to burn them out, and we ask that Legion Varus accompany my new legion, supporting us in this heroic endeavor!"

People were standing and cheering at the screen. I began slamming my hands together, and others joined in support. I had to hand it to Fike, he knew how to gin-up a crowd.

"Thank you, Sub-Tribune," Galina said suddenly, stepping forward.

Fike glanced at her in surprise. I suspected he was just warming up—but she was shutting him down.

"That was a rousing call to action," she said, and she smiled like she meant it.

But I saw signs that suggested the opposite. The tightness of her pretty little mouth, for instance. Those lips were bloodless, rather than red and full. You don't sleep with a woman—even off and on—for a full decade without learning to read her mood. She was pissed but trying to hide it.

Graciously, Fike got over his surprise and nodded to her. He pasted on a smile just like she did, and he stepped aside.

Galina took center stage. She gestured toward the wall behind her, and a star map was unveiled.

"This is our target," she said, putting her hands around a small star and making a spreading motion with her arms. The scene zoomed in, and we soon saw a hot, white, F-class star fill the screen.

"Eridani 77 has only six planets that we know of. One of them is habitable, the one farthest out from the central sun. F-class stars burn hotter than our own sun, so this world is quite warm, probably tropical, even though it is pretty far out. The rest are lifeless irradiated ovens."

"It is tropical," I said aloud with certainty. The truth was I'd visited the place at least twice—that was all I could remember, it could have been more times than that.

Adjunct Barton and the other officers around me gave me a strange look. Leeson shook his head. They knew I'd seen and done things none of them had dreamt of—but they were smart enough not to ask for details.

Details could get a man permed sometimes.

Turov proceeded to talk more about the planet, but she really didn't know much. I could have done a better job of describing it than either of the officers. In fact, I probably knew the place better than anyone else aboard *Legate*.

At least, I hoped I did. There might still be more traitors wandering the passages of this big ship.

Turov went on, talking way too long as usual. I soon got bored and stopped listening. Instead, I admired her form and thought about the night before. Maybe I should visit her again later on—but what would be my excuse this time?

Maybe, I thought to myself… yes, my mind had just hatched an idea. A good one.

I smiled, even as the others surrounding me looked upset and uncomfortable. They all found the briefing disturbing. They hadn't known Claver was a madman who freely liked to make copies of himself.

To me, that information was old-hat. I just smiled up at Galina, thinking over my new plan.

-22-

The very next day, I wandered up to Gold Deck again. We had at least twenty days of travel to go before we made planetfall over Eridani 77, so I didn't feel any urgency to prepare for the invasion.

Instead, I'd worked up a different kind of plan. I wangled my way past the guards onto Gold Deck, and after suffering through a half-hour of bullshit from Gary, I finally got in to see the Tribune.

Galina didn't look as happy to see me as she had the night before. I shrugged that off and offered to pour her a drink.

"You got any straight bourbon?" I asked, looking over her miniature bar with distaste. It was full of all kinds of fruity stuff that I hated. What was the point of making Vodka, for example, with vanilla in it? Some ideas were abominations in disguise.

"Get away from my alcohol and get to the point, Centurion," she said in a stern tone. "I let you in here because you said you had critical information. Now, what is it?"

"Just a way to get inside Claver's organization, that's all. Is this all the ice you've got?"

I'd found a pair of matching tumblers with shiny gilt rims. I poured the least sugary beverage I could find, which turned out to be from a small bottle of blue gin. It smelled only slightly sweet, and it was pretty strong. Mixing in some fizzy stuff and lime, it tasted okay.

Galina stalked up to where I could see her. I'd kept my back to her as I made the two drinks.

"You never listen, James. I'm not drinking with you. I'm not doing anything with you, other than kicking you out."

"Is that so?" I said, turning and handing her a beverage. "That's a crying shame. I guess I'll just have to reach my goals alone. It will be harder—but I'll get it done."

She glared up at me. I could tell she was indecisive. Sure, I might be full of shit, but then again, sometimes I had ideas that worked. She knew that, and it was driving her nuts.

Finally, she reached for one of the drinks and took it from my hands. She gulped half of it.

"Tell me your plan—and it had better be damned good."

"Sure thing," I said, stretching out on her couch again. "It goes like this: we're heading to Clone World, right? We'll be there in less than three weeks. When we arrive, we'll check out the lay of the land. It should be easy to see that we're outgunned and outnumbered, both in space and on the ground. After that—"

"Hold on. What are you talking about? How do you know what we'll be facing?"

I made an easy gesture with my free hand and sipped my gin with the other. "I don't know what we'll find—not exactly. But it stands to reason it will be superior to our force. That much is obvious."

The word "obvious" was a trigger word. I used it when I wanted to piss people off. Just try it yourself sometimes, it always works. The word implies that if another person doesn't agree with you, they must be some kind of an idiot.

People usually got mad when I pulled that trigger, and Galina was no exception. She put her left hand on her hip and pointed with her right toward the door. "Get out of here. You don't know anything. You're fishing, and I won't fall for it—not this time."

Sighing, I made a production of getting up off her couch. "If you say so, sir. I'm sure you won't regret a thing when we make planetfall. What do I know about Claver and his clone armies? Surely you've been out there to his planet a dozen times—more times than I have."

I took two steps toward the door. Then she kicked me in the butt.

I turned around, surprised. The kick hadn't hurt, but she'd meant it to. She was fuming.

"You haven't been dismissed yet," she snapped.

"Uh…" I said, thinking over the last thirty seconds. "Actually, I think you ordered me to leave."

"Shut up and let me think."

Galina started strutting around angrily, talking to herself. I watched and sipped my gin. It tasted better with each sip.

Finally, she stopped pacing and stared up at me. "Well?" she demanded.

I was caught flat-footed. She'd been talking a lot while she did her little march-around thing, but I'd been staring at her curves. I hadn't heard a word.

"Sounds good," I said loudly.

"No, no it doesn't. You fool—are you even listening?"

"Uh…"

"Pour me another drink and tell me whatever insane scheme is in your brain today."

Happily, I complied with her demands. Soon I was back on her couch and talking freely.

"You see, it just came to me yesterday. When I realized that Winslade and Armel had both been recruited by Claver and that you knew about it, the whole thing became obvious."

"Stop using that word. What's obvious?"

"First off, Claver doesn't do things haphazardly. Even more telling, Winslade barely cared when we executed him. Don't you think that's strange?"

"No, not at all. The man is vile. He's a traitor to Earth."

"Yeah, yeah, sure. I get that. But why would he be on this ship then? Why didn't Claver just kill him back at Central and print out a new Winslade on his home planet?"

She blinked at me twice, absorbing this.

"You have a point. Claver doesn't care about Galactic law. He doesn't care about making copies. He makes thousands of them."

"Exactly. He already had Winslade in the bag, but yet he was having him fly aboard *Legate*, bringing him out here from Earth at the head of a zoo legion. Why do that? Why not just transfer Winslade directly?"

She looked thoughtful. "Perhaps there are others aboard who are working for him?"

I snapped my fingers and pointed at her. "Now you're getting into the mindset I'm living in. You see, *Legate* is playing the part of a delivery boat."

"You're saying he *wants* us to bring Varus to his homeworld? That's madness."

"Maybe… or maybe it's just like Claver. He's a tricky bastard, the very worst. He wouldn't reveal himself to me, to you, to Winslade and God knows how many other officers without a good reason. Not without feeling very confident he could handle all the firepower we represent."

Galina began to look concerned. "You think he's prepared for us?"

"Does he know we're coming?"

"I guess we have to assume he does. Winslade was in his employ, at the very least."

"Exactly. So he knows we're coming. In fact, he's got spies everywhere. He knows *exactly* what he's up against."

"And yet… he invites *Legate*. Two legions… He's fearless—or at least prepared."

"Bingo! That's where my head is right now. Can't you see it? Claver doesn't make rookie mistakes. Old Silver, that's what they used to call him. He's an evil genius. Remember fighting him down on Blood World? He ran a legion very smoothly back then."

"He did…" she said, and she handed me her glass.

I looked at it questioningly.

"Fill it," she said.

I obeyed, and Galina stared at the star maps that covered her back wall behind her desk.

"What's he got out there?" she asked the wall. "What's he got that has filled him with such confidence?"

"We're playing delivery van," I said. "That's what I think. Winslade, others—they're aboard, waiting to defect the

129

moment we get to our destination. Winslade might have planned to take his whole legion with him."

She turned to me in alarm. "All his officers? Defecting? But why would they do it?"

I shrugged. "You were the one that was upset that he didn't offer you the job. What were you expecting?"

She glanced down with maybe a rare hint of shame. "I don't know… wealth. A slice of his planet. Maybe he'd make me a duchess or something."

"Would you have taken that deal?"

"No!" she insisted. "Of course not! He and his band of rebels will all be hunted down like dogs in the end. Slaughtered in the dirt. I just…I guess I was insulted that he didn't even offer."

"Ah!" I said, grinning again. "Now I know *why* he didn't make the offer!"

Her face puckered up. "Why?"

"You just said it! You wouldn't have taken the job. Claver knew that. He only makes sure-fire deals. He doesn't offer people things they'll refuse—not unless he's desperate."

"Hmm…" she said, and I could tell she liked that idea.

She'd been thinking Claver considered her to be incompetent. My fanciful version of Claver's thought process was far more appealing.

In truth, I knew Claver thought Turov was a disaster. She was good at gathering power and getting promoted, but she wasn't any kind of tactician. It wasn't that she lacked the brains for the job, but rather that she couldn't stop thinking of herself. She cared more about personal gains than she did her own legion. That tended to lead to defeat.

"What you're saying makes a lot of sense, McGill," she told me.

"Damned-straight it does. Claver would never pass up the top officer of Legion Varus for a flunky like Winslade. You and I both know that in our heart of hearts."

I grinned at her, and finally, at long last, a tiny smile flickered on her face. She hadn't smiled at me like that since I'd arrived at her door today.

We had our third drink, and we talked about what we could do if we were heading into a trap. We came up with wild ideas that became increasingly unworkable with each shot of gin we consumed.

At last, without any conscious signal, I knew the time was right. I kissed her, and she kissed me back with passion.

"I missed you..." she said, straddling my wide body. "I'm glad you came back and weaseled your way into my office again."

"Me too..." I heard myself saying. Strangely, those words might be the only shreds of truth I'd spoken since I'd wandered into her presence today. The rest of it had all been conjecture.

Galina and I made love like two teenagers. It was funny, how she and I could be spitting venom one minute and climbing all over each other the next. I had yet to figure out how our relationship worked, but then, I'd never devoted much time to thinking about such things. Most of the time I just go with the flow.

By the time we were finished and suiting up again, our tappers had lit up with a dozen important messages and calls.

"I sure as shit hope everyone can't break in and force my tapper to open a channel," I remarked.

She laughed. "No, I rolled back that shitty update."

"It was bad. What if you'd called me last night, and I didn't answer? You might have seen something you didn't like."

She glanced at me reproachfully. "Like the sight of you with some fresh recruit in your bunk?"

"I don't date recruits."

She snorted. "What about that girl, Sarah?"

I blinked twice in surprise. I hadn't thought she knew about that. Damn. The girl was sneaky.

"Well... that was years ago, and it was after we'd mustered out."

She twisted her lips into a pout.

I'd blown the mood, and in order to fix it, I touched her shoulders lightly. I tugged her tight uniform into place, and she let me do it.

"There have to be more traitors aboard," I said. "How are we going to smoke them out?"

She looked me up and down. "Can I trust you?"

"Cross my heart and hope to die."

She nodded slowly. "Good… You'll probably get your wish."

Then, she told me her plan. The one she'd been hatching while we were entangled. It was bold, and I was pretty impressed that she could think clearly like that during such intimate moments.

Me, I couldn't have done it. Complex thoughts never occur to a man while he's with a lady he really likes. We're just not wired that way. We think like apes when we're with a woman, we really do.

-23-

For the next several weeks, much to the chagrin of staffers like Gary, I became a regular item in Turov's office. We took turns hatching half-assed tactical plans and making love on a daily basis. It had to be the best time of my life in the legions, at least with respect to my experiences on Gold Deck.

Each night at around eight pm I was promptly booted out of her bed and sent to stay with my troops in the modules. That was okay with me, but I did have to endure the scorn of a half-dozen pissed-looking hens who were stationed down there. Della, Kivi, Natasha and even Adjunct Barton—they were all twisting-up their lips and glancing sidelong in disgust. Somehow, they'd gotten wind of my extended visits abroad, and they'd soured toward me, one and all.

I didn't care. After all, a man could only be bothered with the weighty task of keeping one woman happy at a time under the best of circumstances. Even that much was often beyond the scope of my admittedly weak romantic skills. I figured as long as Galina was happy, I should be happy too.

When the big day came at last, I found myself standing on Gold Deck, watching it all happen. Our plans went into action the minute we arrived at Eridani 77. The trick was we didn't come out of warp and immediately approach the sixth planet, the farthest from the central sun. Instead, we stayed in warp and circled around to the far side of that bright-white F-class star.

Captain Merton, commander of *Legate,* wasn't happy with these last-minute changes. Turov had to pull out her operational command orders on him. As the senior officer, a real tribune leading a human legion, she'd demanded the change to the flight plan. What was really bothering the crew was she hadn't let anyone know about the navigational juggling until after we entered the star system. Only a few navigators and glum-looking helmsmen even knew what was happening.

As Turov's chief accomplice, I got to stand on the bridge with her and the crew. That was kind of cool. Usually, when I was summoned to this holiest of holies—the nexus of *Legate* and the inner sanctum of brass aboard any transport—it was a bad thing. The old McGill tended to get himself into trouble as a regular part of life. Being hauled up to Gold Deck generally meant punishment of some kind was in the works—but not today.

"How long until we get to Claver-land?" I asked the helmsman excitedly.

The helmsman wasn't a half-bad looking woman, but she was Fleet, and that meant she was too good for a grunt like me. Still, such barriers had never kept a man like myself from smiling and admiring.

"Same as the last time you asked, Centurion," she said. "We'll come out of warp soon, but we'll still be an hour out from planetfall."

"Hot damn! I'm sick of being cooped up on this ship."

Turov glanced at me, and I met her glance with a grin. This was all part of the act, of course. Just in case part of the bridge crew was dirty, and in the employ of our friend Claver, I was given the job of blathering about things that we didn't actually plan to do.

Standing just a bit too close, I looked over the helmsman's instruments. It was relatively easy to understand the big ship's controls. The icons were all Imperial standard, and I'd even flown a vessel like this one briefly in the past.

"Do you mind, Centurion?" she asked.

I hadn't even brushed up against her, but apparently, I was invading her personal space.

I took a half-step to the right, giving her some room to breathe. "Sorry, Commander. I'm just looking forward to the next step."

She frowned at me. "Anything I should know about?"

"Don't tell Turov about my big mouth," I said, leaning in close again, "but I'm leading a commando raid, a teleport-suit blitz on Claver's headquarters the minute we get into range."

She blinked once, then twice as she absorbed this false information. "Really?"

"That's right. I'm watching your console for the perfect moment to suit-up."

She bit her lower lip. "I see."

After that, she seemed distracted, but I didn't care. I watched her fine hands on every control. With deft motions, she brought the big ship out of warp something like twenty minutes later.

We glided into the Eridani 77 system from an unexpected direction, moving in from deep space like a prowling shark.

"What's that?" I demanded suddenly, pointing a big finger at her console.

The helmsman had just reached out nonchalantly and opened another screen. A series of glowing sensor options greeted her.

"We have to ping our surroundings," she said evenly. "There could be asteroids, or—"

"Are you shitting me? Tribune!"

Galina stepped around to the helm, frowning at both of us sternly. "What is it?"

"Are we supposed to contact Claver's spaceport and ask about the weather?" I asked.

"Certainly not. Maintain radio silence, Commander. Do not release a single pulse."

"But what if—" the helmsman began.

"What if we run into a chunk of ice, or a rock? Then, Commander, we all die. Is that clear?"

"Yes sir."

Both the helmsman and I stared at her big board, but Galina didn't leave. She watched us instead, and I got the feeling she didn't approve of the way I was hovering over the commander.

At last, she wandered off to scold the crewmen who were operating *Legate's* sensor arrays. She demanded everything that wasn't purely passive be switched off.

"You're starting to get on my nerves, Centurion," the helmsman told me.

"You wouldn't be the first, sir."

She gave me another odd glance, but she didn't say anything else. I saw the lines of her cheek muscles bulging. She was annoyed.

Despite this, I clung to her station, watching her every move. Galina and I didn't trust anyone farther than we could spit—not half that far, in my case. After all, I was a gifted spitter.

We glided close, but before we'd cut the distance in half, an alarm sounded.

"Hull breach," the computer said. "Hull breach. Hull breach. Hull—"

It just kept on going like that, and I found the sound of that robotic voice set my teeth on edge.

"What sector?" Turov demanded.

"Aft, sir. Something hit us in the fantail."

Galina and I exchanged concerned glances.

"If it was a rock," I said, "it would have hit us in the nose."

"Right," she said. "McGill, take a unit to the aft decks. Locate the breach and report back on the situation."

The helmsman frowned at me as I left her side. "Aren't you going to teleport—?"

"All in good time, my lady."

I left her puzzling over that one while I rushed toward my module. My troops met me halfway and soon we were tramping through the passages toward the back of the big ship. By the time we got there, Graves was leading another unit of legionnaires at a jog.

"I thought you were some kind of a golden-haired pet today, McGill," Graves said.

"That's right, sir. I'm a dog, and I'm in this hunt."

136

Graves gave me a sidelong glance. He didn't know what my angle was, and he hated that situation. He and his team broke off, taking another passage toward the rear of the ship.

My unit trotted another two hundred paces, if that much, before *Legate* suddenly did a somersault. At least, that's what it felt like.

Without warning, we were thrown off our feet. We were tossed into the air and cracked a mixture of skulls and helmets on the ceiling.

"Helmets buttoned down!" I roared. "Visors locked, advance, double-time!"

My people picked themselves up and flew after me. A few weren't moving, but I didn't have time to check on their status.

We'd lost gravity, but that didn't stop an experienced legionnaire. We propelled ourselves with gloved, clawing hands and scrabbling feet.

We'd been slowed down, but not stopped. Graves contacted me a minute later.

"McGill, there's no pressure in the next section. It's sealed and they're calling for an evacuation. You'll have to take up a defensive posture—"

"No-go, Primus. I've got my orders. I'm going straight to the breach."

He didn't answer right away, but when he did it was without anger. "Turov knew this was coming, didn't she?"

"No sir, but we've made plans for a contingency like this."

"How the hell could Claver be hitting us so soon? We came in from an unexpected angle of attack. We're too far out to get a fix on, and we're gliding in silence. How could—?"

"With all due respect, Primus, you're not asking the right questions. We lost power, and we've suffered a breach—but I don't think Claver did it. At least, not directly."

Graves was quiet for a second, then the light went on in his straight-arrow brain.

"Sabotage? Another traitor is in our midst?"

"You didn't think Claver would lure us all the way out here just to deliver up Winslade, did you, sir?"

137

He hesitated. "No," he said at last. "No, I don't suppose he would. Carry on, I'll marshal the ship-defenders and back you up as soon as I can. Go play first-responder."

"Roger that."

I was glad Graves was onboard with my actions. In truth, it wouldn't have mattered if he hadn't liked what I was doing. He would've been forced to shoot me to get me to stop—but it was still a nice feeling to have him on my side all the same.

We passed through an airlock into a powerless, airless dead-zone. I never stopped advancing to the point where the breach had been reported.

Behind me, my unit traveled in a swarm. We looked like a bouncing herd of jackrabbits, but we were still making pretty good time. Every handhold, every caged light fixture with a dark tube inside, they all served as a pushing off point for us as we advanced, surging ahead.

All of a sudden, in the gathering darkness that filled the passageway, we ran into another formation of troops going the other way.

They were flying in the airless, Null-G environment as well. The big difference is they weren't humans—they were Blood Worlders. Slavers and squids, all of them. They were wearing emergency suits and helmets, just as we were.

"Sub-unit!" I called out, addressing the group. "Who's your sub-centurion?"

"I am the sub-centurion in command, McGill."

Now, you would never have thought that I could recognize a squid's voice. After all, they're all translated by artificial devices. It wasn't like I could really hear the clicking of that hidden beak with my own ears. It was buried in the squid's suit, for one thing.

But in spite of all that, I *did* recognize the voice. There was something special to the cadence, to the disgust that was evident in those mechanically translated words.

"Bubbles?" I asked. "Is that really you?"

"Yes."

"I knew it! Sub-Centurion Bubbles, you are one arrogant squid. I'd know your voice anywhere. Caught a revive since the last time we met, huh?"

He didn't answer me.

I got moving again, and my unit pressed through the formation of squids. We continued to advance into the darkness. Oddly, they milled for a bit, then began to follow us. They were better than humans in this kind of environment, less clumsy, so they kept up easily.

"This is our defensive zone, McGill," Bubbles told me. "I'll have to ask you to withdraw."

"And I'm answering not just no, but *hell no*, squid!" I told him. "You can follow my unit if you like, but stay out of the way of the rest of the coming cohort. They're right on my heels."

Bubbles hesitated. His troops had stopped their languid movement forward and roosted in a loose mass on the roof. It was like having two dozen bats the size of elephants squatting above you, staring down.

"That's right," I said, confirming my lie with absolute conviction. "My unit is just the spearhead of an army. Graves has sent nine more units in my wake. We'll soon be massing up right here."

"What is the purpose of this 'massing up' Centurion?"

"To find out what happened..." it was right about then that I realized something. My tapper, which had been leading the way to the breach location, had stopped pointing arrows ahead. It no longer directed me to push onward.

Location reached, it said in green. I lowered my tapper and stopped advancing. My troops gathered around, breathing hard in their suits.

My eyes lifted up to stare at Bubbles, who still crouched on the ceiling. He stared right back at me.

It was right about then that I realized there was a patch of stars next to him. His group of squids entirely encircled it. The ceiling had a hole in it, and that hole appeared to go right through a number of layers until it reached open space.

Now, I'm not the most intuitive man in the universe. I'll be the first to admit that I don't always notice things everyone else in the room seems to understand.

But today, there was one thing I knew for certain: Bubbles had caused the hull breach. Somehow, some way, he'd blown a hole in *Legate's* thick skin.

That asshole, I thought to myself. I hoped it wasn't something I'd said that had driven him to it.

"Unit!" I roared. "Take down those squids!"

They didn't need a moment's further encouragement. None of my people liked squids, and we didn't trust them either. We'd held our rifles aimed at the deck out of respect, but every man in my unit was feeling twitchy.

Less than a second passed before the passage lit up like it was Hegemony day in the sticks. Lances of fire crisscrossed in blazing streaks across the passageway, dazzling our startled eyes. Purplish afterglows were burned into our retinas.

The squids didn't jump down to attack us, however. Instead, firing to cover their maneuver, they all bolted up through that hole. I think they'd been more ready for my attack than I'd been ready to attack them. If they'd outnumbered us, we'd have been toast—but they didn't. I had a full unit, about a hundred and twenty soldiers, and they had less than thirty saboteurs. Wisely, they ran.

We only shot down two of slavers, nailing them in the butt as they scrambled for the exit. As they were nowhere near as graceful in null-G as the squids, they didn't have a chance. The air bled from their suits and they convulsed until they froze solid.

"McGill!" Graves said in my ear. "I'm monitoring your position. I'm picking up a firefight—are we being boarded?"

"Uh... sort of, sir. Except, not like you think. The enemy was already here. We brought them out here with us from Earth."

"Explain yourself."

Staring after the squids that had bolted out into the dark, I made my report. "I've driven a commando team of squids onto the outer hull. I believe they created the breach. Should I pursue?"

"Negative, McGill. Hold the breach. Help is incoming."

As I waited for reinforcements from Graves, it became more and more clear in my mind that the real danger we faced came from the near-humans aboard *Legate*. Sure, a few of humanity's worst could be bought. Fellows like Armel and Winslade, for example. They'd joined Claver when they thought the price was right.

But the squids had infinitely better reasons to switch sides. They were effectively Earth's conquered subjects. They had zero love for humanity, and plenty of reasons to hate us.

Fike showed up a few minutes later. Behind him was a veritable wall of heavy troopers. That didn't make me happy at all.

"Whoa!" Carlos said, sidling close to me. "Keep an eye on those freaks, McGill. They're probably all traitors."

I couldn't directly refute his statement, so I pushed him aside and moved to greet Fike. He studied the gaping hole in the roof and listened to my report.

"Traitors…" he said, as if greatly concerned. "You did well to chase them off the ship, Centurion. They must be hiding out on the hull somewhere. Stand your ground here, I'll mop them up."

"Uh…" I said, watching him as he leapt to the roof and pulled himself, hand-over-hand, out into open space.

At his back, dozens of heavy troopers followed. My own men shuffled, gripping their weapons tightly and glowering. We didn't know who to trust.

It wasn't long before a terrific firefight broke outside on the hull. At first, we couldn't see it, but we could hear the radio traffic. Fike seemed to be having quite a time of it.

"We're pinned down," Fike said on command chat. "Fire is incoming from all sides. Requesting back up."

"Graves?" I called. "McGill here. My boys are itching—"

"Negatory, McGill. Hold your position. You're my plug holding them back in case Fike is overwhelmed. Help is less than ten minutes out."

Harris stepped closer to me. He stared upward at that patch of stars, hunkered over his rifle. His eyes were big, and you could see the whites all around.

"McGill…" he said. "There's no way that only thirty squids and slavers are putting out that much firepower."

"That's true…" I said. "Sounds like there's no way Fike is going to hold out for ten minutes."

Harris looked at me. "You going out there?"

I took a deep breath. It was hard to watch your own troops get chewed up—or rather to hear it. "Cooper!" I shouted. "Get over here!"

"Right here, sir."

I didn't see him, but I knew he was standing nearby. As usual he'd donned his stealth suit the moment we'd gotten into a combat situation.

"Scout for me, Cooper. Kivi, send up buzzers."

I waited for another thirty seconds. I thought I saw a shimmer between me and the stars outside, but I wasn't sure if it was the buzzers or Cooper. It could have been either, as the buzzers used compressed air to maneuver in null G.

"I've got eyes on the fight," Cooper reported in thirty seconds later. "You're not going to believe this."

He piped the vid down to my tapper. I watched in amazement.

There had to be a thousand enemy combatants surrounding Fike's heavy troopers. Human, or at least humanoid, the enemy approached from every angle. They were all about the same size and height. They moved methodically, firing as they approached Fike's encircled unit, which was hunkering down in the crater formed by the hull breach.

I knew right off who the approaching enemy was. They weren't men—not exactly. They were Clavers. Class-threes.

A whole army of them.

-24-

A man named William Claver was among the most interesting of people I'd ever met in my life. As long and storied as my existence has been, it's nothing when stacked up against his.

Now, I don't want to come off as some kind of a Claver-expert, because I'm not. No one was, as far as I knew. Plenty had studied him over the decades, but there was too much of his background and exploits that were unknown.

In brief, he was one of the first legionnaires ever to join Earth's forces and fight among the stars. There had been plenty of other good men in those days, naturally—but they hadn't all stuck with it the way he did.

Most men figured out that fighting and dying over and over wasn't a great way to live your life. That was especially true in the old days, when the revival machines were more experimental. They hadn't been fully attuned to our DNA strands, as I understand it, and there were... mistakes.

Even today, there are what we call "bad grows" now and then. Sometimes, when you die and come back, something goes wrong. A mutation. A deformity. A twist of the body—or worse, the mind.

That's what most people think happened to Claver. He'd always been a smart man, a strategist and a masterful officer. But one time or another during a chain of deaths and revivals, he went from an exemplary officer to a scoundrel. Perhaps it was due to a slowly introduced error that grew over time, or maybe the mutation had hit all at once. No one knew the truth, but Claver was definitely a bad grow of the worst kind.

I believe that in the twenty-odd years since I'd met him, he's become even stranger still. He's now not just an interstellar con-man. He's become an evil genius with grand plans even I don't comprehend.

One thing he'd done recently was make clones of himself—a whole planet-full of them. I don't know how many Clavers exist now. I don't even know how many *types* there are.

Those I have had personal contact with came in five flavors. There were Claver-primes, leaders who were the most similar to the original, if a little twisted. There were also less adept Clavers, Class-Twos. These are used as run-of-the-mill specialists. If a Claver revived you, he was a Claver-bio and therefore a Class-Two.

From there, things got a little strange. There had been at some point, and possibly still were, Lady-Clavers…

Now, that point took some getting my head wrapped around, but apparently females and breeding were off-limits in Claver society. All the Clavers had agreed that they'd stick to cloning themselves to reproduce. That made sense, to a point. But maybe some of them had gotten tired of not having any companionship that was more stimulating. Anyway, an unknown number of Lady-Clavers had been produced. I'd never met a live one, and it kind of gave me a shiver just to think about it.

Next up was the strangest Claver of all. Claver-X, I called him. He was a renegade Claver. A man who passed for a Prime, but who dodged the rest and did as he pleased. A con-man among a race of con-men. I kind of liked him, but I didn't see him often.

Lastly, there was the combat-model: Claver Class-Threes. As best I could tell, they were by far the most common. They were muscle-bound dumb-asses. Brutes built to fight and take orders. They were as loyal and mean as attack-dogs—and just about as smart. The pitbulls of the Claver Clan.

That's the type I saw on *Legate*'s hull today. About a thousand Claver-Threes, all armed and fighting determinedly. They weren't elite soldiers, but they were as determined as all get-out.

Fike's near-human troops didn't stand a chance. They were surrounded and outnumbered. Still, for all of that, they put up a good show.

Like the near-human heavy troopers, the Claver-Threes weren't geniuses. When Fike ordered his men to hunker down, they were no longer easy targets for the Class-Threes. Taking this in the most simple-minded way, the Clavers advanced to close with them.

It was dog-logic. If you couldn't reach the bad man and bite him in the ass, well, you advanced to where you could reach him. Problem solved.

An avalanche of Claver-Threes advanced en masse, and they quickly got close enough to fire on the heavies. Fike had ordered those poor bastards to hunker down on the uneven exterior of the ship, on their bellies. There was something of a crater in the exterior skin of the ship, due to the outward blast Bubbles had set off to make the hole in the first place. It wasn't much, but Fike and his men were making the most of this cover.

When the Claver army marched close enough, Fike ordered his heavies to rise up and go into close-combat with the enemy. Some of them were shot down immediately. A storm of fire took down several. But the rest reached the Claver ranks. They tore into the smaller men, who weren't used to fighting hand-to-hand.

A terrific melee began. Again due to Fike's orders, I saw the heavy troopers engaging in a smart tactic. Fike's men were using their great strength to pluck the smaller men from the *Legate*'s hull and pitch them, tumbling ass-over-tea-kettle, out into open space. This was easy to do as everyone was only holding onto *Legate*'s hull with magnetic boots.

Flying off into the void, many of these Class-Threes fired back down at the mass of struggling forms below. But as they were spinning and there were more Clavers than near-humans, they hit their own troops more often than not. Another win for Fike's strategy.

"Dammit, dammit, dammit..." I cursed and bared my teeth. "They're fighting hard out there. Fike is giving them hell."

"Don't do it, McGill."

I turned brooding eyes on Harris. He knew me well. In moments like this, he could tell what I was thinking—possibly even before I did. That was an occupational hazard of spending decades fighting with another man in countless campaigns.

Looking at Harris, but not really seeing him, I recalled a different day. A time back on Dark World, when I'd let Fike charge in and die to the last man in a similar, hopeless battle.

Sure, Fike had been a grade-A asshole then, and he still was today, but that didn't mean he wasn't a man who deserved respect. He fought well, and he fought with everything he had, and here I was hiding like a spider in a hole watching the action on my frigging tapper.

"Unit!" I roared. "Up and out! Pop-up attack! Get high, and hose them down with fire from above! Then turn on your magnetics and helmet-thrusters. Get back down to the hull within ninety seconds."

"Shit, McGill! Shit!"

It was Leeson. He showed me every tooth he had—but he wasn't smiling. Fortunately, I didn't have to look at his ugly face for long. I shot myself up and out, straight through the hole above.

The pop-up attack was a specialized offensive tactic we'd practiced in our null-G training, but it was rarely employed. The idea was to launch yourself up high over the heads of your enemies, who were focused on the battle at hand. With high ground and no obstacles, you could theoretically hose them down with rapid-fire plasma bolts before they knew where the attack was coming from.

All that was theory, of course. As a kicker, you got to put your dick in the breeze, with no cover if the enemy got their act together and returned fire.

But I didn't care. Fike's people weren't going to last long out there on that barren stretch of metal. His troops were bigger, stronger, better led and just plain meaner than any

146

Claver that had ever been spawned—but they were badly outnumbered.

As I'd given the order, and I was directly below the opening when I'd given it, I barreled out into space before anyone else even got into position to follow.

Above me were only stars. Off to the left and low was a glaring white sun. It was distant, but you could just tell it was kicking out a lot of radiation.

Stretched out below me was the curve of the *Legate*'s hull. It was pitted and burned in places, where the Clavers had been trying to break through. They must have been teleported out here to invade our ship, but hadn't managed to make it through the transport's shielding and hull.

The whole scene was breathtaking, but I didn't even bother to breathe. I made an animal sound and held down the firing stud on my morph-rifle. It was in assault-mode, and it stitched the darkness with flashes of radiation brighter than the sun itself.

Operating the undercarriage, I released a series of grav-grenades, lobbing them toward the Clavers in the rear ranks. These guys were shoving and reaching for the fight, but unable to reach it due to their own vast numbers. I knew from experience they were grunting and snorting in an animal fashion as they fought, full of a primitive excitement that wasn't entirely human.

The second I'd released my fourth and final grenade, I pulled the ripcord, sending my feet back down toward the hull. Legion Varus troopers were equipped with emergency gear that let us propel ourselves back down if we got too high in a low-grav situation. Apparently, Claver-Threes didn't warrant the expense. The men Fike's heavy troopers had hurled into space were still spinning and struggling helplessly.

More of my unit's members were on hand now, firing up out of that hole in *Legate*'s skin like popcorn. Like me, they each blazed down death briefly then retreated to the center of Fike's circle, joining the fray.

Unfortunately, there seemed to be at least two brain cells to rub between all those Class-Threes collectively. They'd finally noticed they were getting pasted from above and began to return the favor. They shot up several of my men, and I ordered the rest to stop with the pop-up attacks and just crawl out of the hole like the rodents we usually resembled.

But the damage had been done. The grav-grenades had been our most devastating attack. They'd not only torn up handfuls of the enemy with every silent, blue-white flash of released energy, they'd also caused many more to lose their grip on *Legate*. If I had to guess, we'd killed two hundred men and sent another several hundred spinning into space.

The Clavers were tethering up now, running lines to one another for safety, but it was too late. Sure, they were harder to throw off the hull now, but they were also getting tangled up and restricted.

Even Class-Threes could apparently feel fear. We'd killed half—more than that, I reckoned. As manipulated as their minds and bodies were, they were still men. They still retained their basic instincts of self-preservation at the deepest levels.

They pressed us hard, but with Fike's men and mine fighting side-by-side with practiced expertise, they couldn't overcome us.

All of a sudden, they just stopped trying. It was kind of weird to watch. They had a group-mind, in a way, since they were all copies of the same man. So, logically, when one of them decided to run for it, they all did.

Their ranks melted away before us, and we shot them down as they ran. There wasn't really anywhere for them to go, so Fike called back his littermates before they thumped after the retreating enemy.

The heavy troopers were as hard to control in battle as Claver Class-Threes in their own way. They tended to go mad when one of their brothers died—and pretty much every group of nine had been broken in this hard fight. But Fike managed to hold his men back, and my respect for him went up again.

Stumping close to me, he peered up into my helmet. It was dark, but his face lit up in recognition.

"McGill?" Fike said, recognizing me in the starlight.

"Yes sir."

Fike nodded, and stuck out a gauntleted hand. I took it, and we shook.

148

"They say you love a good fight, and today you proved it. We probably could have taken them—but the outcome was in doubt."

That was Fike in a nutshell. He was twice as arrogant as Winslade on a good day. He'd had no chance of survival until I came to help, and we both knew it. But he would never admit it—we both knew that, too.

"I couldn't sit down there and watch you have all the fun, sir," I told him.

Fike grinned. His face ran with sweat inside his helmet, which was fogging up in places.

"Outstanding," he said, and he let go of my hand.

That was it, the equivalent of a hearty thank-you from Sub-Tribune Fike. It hadn't been much, but it was probably more than he was accustomed to giving.

Harris came up to me and spoke privately a moment later. "Leeson's dead," he said matter-of-factly.

"Doesn't matter. We won."

"That's right," Harris said with sudden emotion. He stabbed a thumb into his chest plate. "*We* won. *We* did this. Fike's fancy-pants, Iron-Eagle-ass was *toast* out here until we—"

I lifted a hand to stop him. "Doesn't matter," I repeated. "We owed him this one."

Harris glared at me. He knew what I was talking about. He'd been there when we'd let Fike and his men die in a vicious fight with Vulbites years back.

He nodded finally and dropped it. He looked around at the dead, which were everywhere. Clavers, humans, near-humans—hundreds of them surrounded us. When he spoke again, the anger had drained from his voice.

"Must be five hundred dead out here," he said. "They look like seaweed at the bottom of the ocean."

"Yep. Limp plants on a windless day."

When you died in null-G, the results were kind of morbid. There was no gravity to make a man fall flat. You usually were still clamped to the ship by your magnetic boots, so you sort of stood there, swaying a bit. With your arms floating around, you looked like a plant, anchored down but lifeless.

"What do you think Graves is going to say?" Harris asked me.

I shrugged. It was a hard thing to do in armor, but I managed it.

Glancing at my tapper, I saw it was full of red messages, blue alerts and lavender notifications. The lavender stuff was new—that had probably come with another recent unwelcome update.

I kind of figured most of these frantic attempts at communication had come from Graves. I'd silenced my tapper when I'd launched myself up to attack—it would only have been a distraction.

"I bet Graves is real happy about all this," I said.

Harris rumbled with laughter and slammed a fist into my back. Fortunately, I barely felt it through my armor.

-25-

When I reached Gold Deck, I expected a lynch-party would be waiting for me. But that didn't happen.

Instead, the place was alive with frantic officers and crew. Everyone was rushing around in a big hurry. Even the near-human guards looked antsy. They kept stepping from one big foot to the other, doing an uneasy dance in slow motion.

I grabbed a tech by the arm and swung her around. "What's up?" I asked.

She blinked at me twice, then caught her breath. "Centurion? Don't you know? Ships are coming at us. Fighters."

I let her go, and she scurried off. My heart quickened in my chest, and I headed for the bridge.

If there was one thing a ground-pounder didn't want to hear it was that a space battle was coming. We were as useless as tits on a boar in that kind of fight.

Fighters?

As far as I knew, I'd never even laid eyes on a fighter in space. I heard of such things, of planning and contingencies, but Earth had never built a fighter for use in space.

"Fighters?" I asked the bridge crew when I reached that most important chamber. "Why fighters?"

151

The helmsman I'd pestered the day before glanced at me, running her eyes up and down my long body. "McGill? Are you on the roster today? We're under attack, you know."

"That's right. Under attack by fighters. How is that possible? Earth doesn't even build fighters."

The helmsman shrugged. "They're not practical for Earth. Fighters have short ranges. They're too small to travel between the stars alone. We build big ships like *Legate* and pack them with gear and weapons. Fighters can only defend a single star system."

"Huh…" I said, chewing that over in my mind. "I guess that makes sense. We have to have mobile forces that can move to defend any of our planets that needed defending. But couldn't we build a carrier?"

"A what?"

"A big ship, like in the old days. They used to build carriers to carry lots of fighters."

She shook her head. "Maybe we could build something like that. I don't know. I steer ships, I don't design them. Are you even supposed to be here, McGill?"

"Of course I am," I lied with utter conviction. "Take a look at my tapper, see all these messages? That's Turov and Graves looking for me. They want my advice."

She blew out a puff of air. Her bangs flew up a bit. "Sure. Looks more like they want to hang you."

"That too, probably…" I admitted. "Say, when you get off duty—"

"I'm surprised it took you this long," she said.

"To what?"

"To hit on me."

We looked at one another frankly for a moment. This girl was pretty direct. I didn't mind that. She had the kind of blonde hair that had red and brown streaks in it. I didn't mind that, either.

"Well?" I asked.

She sighed and covered her nametag with her hand. "What's my name?"

I'd seen this dodge before. "What? You think I'd ask you out without knowing your name? What kind of a scoundrel would attempt such a thing?"

"You would, according to every girl on the ship. What's my name?"

Fortunately, I'd taken the time to give her nametag a glance. "You're Lieutenant Commander Janet Easterbrook. That's a mouthful, but I never forget a name or a face—at least not a pretty face."

Janet eyed me for a moment, letting her hand drop from her nametag and back to her boards. The fleet people didn't use Roman ranks, they used the old traditional naval ranks of centuries past instead. I think the new service had done that just to set themselves apart from the rest of us grunts.

"All right," she said. "That stunt you pulled down there at the breach—everyone is talking about it. We might owe the ship to you. If we survive the coming attack, I'll go out with you."

I grinned. "I stopped them from boarding, but you're about to stop these fighters from catching us. We're two heroes, and that's worth a drink anytime!"

Janet gave me a small smile, and I wandered off. It was best to move off early when you got a date set up. I never gave a girl time enough to get tired of old James McGill. There would be plenty of opportunities for that later on.

Two steps. That's all I made it before I ran right into Turov.

"Here you are, you crazy bastard. What are you doing on my bridge?"

"Uh…" I said, showing her my tapper. "I've been summoned to—"

"No you haven't. I know full well that most of those messages are from Graves, demanding that you hold your position. He's pissed at you, and he's placed you on report for disobeying his orders."

"That seems extreme."

"Not at all… but now it's my problem."

She put her hands on her hips and looked me over with a critical eye. While she did this, she noted the helmsman standing just behind me.

153

I think it was Janet who gave us away. She was acting nervous. She fidgeted, glanced at me nervously. Then she slid her eyes around to check out Turov, then back at her instruments. She did this twice, and I suppose Turov caught on.

"I see..." Galina said quietly. "Two weeks of fun, and you're bored already. Fine."

"What?" I asked.

I was playing dumb, and I was working it. All the while Galina had been inspecting me and deciding my fate, I'd done my damnedest to look like an innocent ape. Janet had blown it, however.

Galina crossed her arms and narrowed her eyes. "Graves is right," she said firmly. "I can't let this kind of insubordination go unpunished. Even if you did succeed in stopping a boarding attempt, you disobeyed orders today."

"Aw now, hold on, sir," I said. "We'd be up to our armpits in Clavers if I hadn't of—"

"Immaterial. Report to Gray Deck. You've volunteered for a special mission."

"Dammit... all right."

I slunk away. As I was leaving, however, the screens around the bridge all flared into life at once. They brightened, zoomed, and displayed what looked like a star cluster.

Pausing on my way out, I stopped and stared. I realized I wasn't looking at a star cluster. The pinpricks of light were too numerous, too bright—and they seemed to be in a triangular formation.

The fighters were coming. How many? There had to be at least fifty of them.

My mouth ran dry. *Legate* could fight, but she was designed to stop a few missiles, or to blow a large capital ship like herself out of the sky. She wasn't really built to handle a full wing of fighters.

The crew shouted and the ship came about, directing her broadsides toward the approaching threat. Like all our ships, *Legate* was equipped with a battery of sixteen heavy, fusion-warhead-throwing guns.

But against agile little craft like these, it would be like shooting at sparrows with a row of cannons.

154

-26-

Although I'd been ordered to move to Gray Deck, I didn't leave the bridge right off. Things had just gotten interesting.

"New course set," Lt. Cmdr. Easterbrook announced loudly. "Locked in."

The big ship wheeled to bring her broadsides to bear.

"Captain Merton," Turov said. "I leave it to you to stop those fighters from destroying us."

The captain gave her a wary glance. I could tell he didn't like the idea that she thought she should even say that—but he probably appreciated the implicit trust. Turov was indicating she was going to be a bystander on the bridge during the ship-to-ship action.

"Load dispersal-shot!" Captain Merton ordered, turning to his crew. "Fire when ready!"

The big guns moved with the audible rumble of vast gears under our feet. The broadsides and the fire control room were all below the bridge.

After perhaps ninety seconds, which seemed far too long for my taste, the big guns finally roared.

As a veteran of such events, I kept my feet under me when the deck bucked up under them. Turov did the same, but she did throw both hands wide, gripping the sides of a console.

It was Lt. Cmdr. Easterbrook who seemed to be the most surprised. She stumbled, but she didn't do a facer. That would have been an embarrassment for the entire bridge crew.

Looking startled, Janet threw a wild look over her shoulder at the weapons crew. Apparently, they'd fired the instant they'd been primed to do so without making any announcements about it. I couldn't blame any of them. They were acting in the moment, and they weren't accustomed to all-out space battles.

"What's dispersal-shot?" I asked Galina. "That sounds new."

"It's sort of a shotgun approach. Instead of one big warhead, each cannon throws out a capsule filled with hundreds of smaller smart-bombs. That way, the likelihood is much greater we'll hit these fucking fighters before they get close."

I glanced at her. She looked stressed and angry.

"You think they'll take us down if they get past our barrage?"

She shrugged her shoulders. "Probably. That's why I'm angry. Claver foresaw this situation. He built these fighters to screw me and my ship."

"You really think so? You think he's planning on taking down transports that come to invade?"

She looked at me. "Isn't it obvious? We've been planning for weeks, and he has as well. He had to have known that we would come for him. We couldn't just allow him to sit out here in space and build up his forces forever.

Today was the showdown. With luck, we'd win, and that would be the end of it. But I was feeling less lucky by the minute, and Galina didn't look like she felt too good, either.

The first barrage sped toward the approaching enemy. Sixteen streaks of light, sixteen warheads that soon split apart, forming thousands. It was like a fountain of fire, of sparks, like a gush of flame that became a glowing cloud of destruction.

The fighters ran into this expanding cloud, despite taking emergency evasive action. They rolled and twisted, firing afterburners and spreading out in every direction at once.

156

The central mass of them, however, couldn't escape. The warheads had multiplied, and there wasn't much time as our courses converged.

"Six hits… nine… fifteen!" the weapons op kept reeling off the numbers with growing excitement.

Galina's face was glowing again. "We're crushing them."

I touched her hand, and she gave me a squeeze. Then, all of a sudden, her face shifted.

"McGill?" she demanded. "What are you still doing here? Go to Gray Deck!"

"Yes sir! On the double, sir!"

I ran off the bridge like my tail-section was on fire. I figured there wasn't much I could do from here anyway, even if it was interesting.

As I ran, I heard commands reverberating throughout the ship, each word being echoed via my tapper. The captain's voice ordered the big guns to fire again.

Taking momentary refuge, I grabbed onto a loop of protective webbing and held on. The guns were very close—I was just outside the control room.

But after gritting my teeth for maybe ten seconds, I frowned.

"Fire control!" Captain Merton shouted. "Release the second volley *now*! The enemy are spreading out, moving out of optimal position. Fire!"

The big guns remained silent. Growing curious, I changed direction and rushed to the control room doors.

They didn't open at my touch. Now, there's nothing usual about that. Not really. During a battle, the control room was locked down and heavily shielded. The operators must be allowed to work their cannons without interference.

All the same, my fist came up, and I hammered on the door. It didn't budge, and no one answered me.

"Fire control! Fire barrage two—immediately!" The captain was roaring through the loudspeakers all over the ship, sounding like voice of the Almighty himself—but no one was obeying him.

Right about then, a security squad showed up. They were carrying drawn pistols.

157

"Centurion!" their leader barked at me. "What are you doing here?"

"Trying to get into this control room. You got the code? Open it!"

The squad leader looked at me warily for a moment before ordering a sidekick to approach. The man was a security specialist, and he worked the door lock for several seconds. He shook his head.

"Jammed."

The security chief approached and wasted several more precious seconds. I watched this with growing impatience.

"It's locked from the inside," he said, baffled. "Could there be traitors in there?"

"Either that, or the enemy," I said, getting sick of his half-assed handling of the situation.

I stepped up, deciding it was my turn. A big hand and arm hauled the squad leader off his feet and tossed him on the floor. The security boys huffed and spat—but they shut up right-quick when they realized I was spilling all four of the grav-grenades in my rifle onto the deck.

"Back up, ladies!" I called out.

They scrambled, and I followed them. When the blast went off, it was a pretty impressive one. The lower half of the doors was a gaping hole, and the left door hung funny.

A few of the security punks hadn't moved fast enough, they were left squalling on the deck—but I didn't care about them. If I was right, we were in a bad way, and one more puke with a pistol wasn't going to fix anything.

The haze of smoke cleared quickly, and I threw myself prone. A storm of fire came out of the hole I'd made. Plasma bolts streaked overhead, scarring up the passageway and burning troops. Most of the bolts were aimed low, and they struck men in the legs and guts. Steaming corpses shivered on the deck all around me.

Claver-Twos. I'd recognize them anywhere. They looked pretty much like Primes, but they weren't talkative or super-smart. They were the working-joes of Claver-land. The specialists who made up his army's medics, technicians—and fighter pilots.

"Tribune!" I shouted into my tapper. "We've got an infiltration! There must be a dozen Clavers in the fire-control room!"

"McGill?" Galina hissed back at me. "What are you doing down there? Don't wreck my CC, you dumbass! Don't you *dare*!"

"Orders received and understood, sir!"

Another storm of fire went off, with shots traded through the smoking doorway in both directions.

The security chief bellied up next to me. At least he'd survived. "Was that the Tribune?"

"Sure as hell was."

"What's she want us to do?"

"We have to take back the CC, no matter what. Nothing lives."

His face hardened. "Got it."

He stood up, and I have to give the man credit. He wore a grim mask. It was the face of a man who knows he's facing certain death and yet charges anyway. I'd been convinced he was a born hog in his heart-of-hearts up until that moment, but now I stood corrected. Crewman or not, he had balls as big as anyone in my beloved Legion Varus.

"Rush them!" he called out, not even bothering to look back to see if his own men were following, or if they could do so if they'd wanted to.

Ducking in and firing repeatedly, he was cut down within five seconds. But during those seconds, he lived well.

His squad followed him, all those who could. I locked a fresh battery into my morph-rifle's breach and set it for high-output assault. Bringing up the rear of the team, I waited until the security men were cut down, giving me a free field of fire.

What can I say? I hosed the place down. There were probably no more than five of the enemy pilots left alive by that time, and some of them were wounded. But they were hiding behind consoles for cover, and widely dispersed around the room.

Still, one man in armor can take a terrible toll on a team of men in spacer suits who are armed with pistols. Beams flashed

159

and metal sizzled and melted. The Clavers were taken out with one methodical burst at a time.

After the room quieted, and I walked among them, I took note of their gear. Each man carried an oxygen bottle, a spacer's suit, a single pistol and a teleport-rig.

Immediately, it was clear what had happened. These pilots had been flying the attacking fighters, and they'd been shot down by our surprise barrage of spreading warheads. In the last instant before death, they must have pulled their eject cords, teleporting them onto *Legate*. Once aboard, they began working to stop the very guns that had been killing them.

"It almost worked, too..." I said aloud to no one, then I triggered the big cannons to fire again. There were two triggers separated by several meters, so I had to use the hand of a dying security man by dragging him to it and ordering him to squeeze for all he was worth. To his credit, he did this with a stoic mask of pain on his face.

After the ship bucked and the scattershot was away, I checked the bodies. Everyone was dead. I made sure, gunning a few extra bolts into any crawling Claver-pilot who looked like he had some juice left in him.

This part of the battle was over.

-27-

When I told my tale about ten minutes later, Galina went from snarling with rage, to thoughtful, then to worried.

"They have a way to teleport through our shields, then?" she asked with real concern.

"Actually," a nerdy weapons tech spoke up. He'd come up from engineering to man the broadsides since the mainline gunners were all dead. "Our forward shields were down at the time of the boarding attack. The fighters had managed to knock down the shields, although their armament did little more than scar our hull once they penetrated our defenses."

Turov turned on him. "What if they'd gotten through with a full-force attack? What if that trick with the warheads hadn't worked to wipe them out?"

The weapons tech shrugged. "The fighters only touched us using their best weapons at very long range. Their strikes didn't have any punch in them. *Legate* probably wouldn't have survived if they'd hit us full-force at close range."

Galina looked around with growing disquiet at the pile of bodies in the command center.

"James, this is unacceptable," she said, turning back to me. "They keep surprising us. They keep hitting us. One of these times, Claver is going to get through and kill us all."

I shrugged. "Maybe. Or maybe we'll keep swatting Clavers down like flies."

161

She eyed me again. "I want you to go to Gray Deck now—no more detours, please. I admit this side-trip was warranted, and it was quick-thinking. In fact, I'm willing to admit that what you did to defend the ship at the breach was a good move as well. But we don't know what's coming next. We have to take the initiative."

"Uh... what's waiting for me down on Gray Deck?"

Galina smiled, but it wasn't a pleasant smile. "The techs have a surprise for you. They will provide an opportunity for some payback."

"Great..."

Without thinking about it, we both took a step closer to each other. We couldn't kiss or anything, since the CC was crawling with techs and bio people, but I felt that she wanted to.

Giving her a crisp salute I marched down to Gray Deck. There, a team of tech specialists handed me a teleport harness and began pulling it over my limbs when I hesitated.

"Hey... is this what I think it is?"

"It's not a tuxedo, Centurion."

"Shit..."

I let them fart around suiting me up. They quickly discovered wounds in the process from the gun-battle with the Clavers. Tsking, they summoned bio people. Pretty soon, I looked like some kind of a movie star who was late for a scene. They swarmed over me, grabbing, tugging, tucking and spraying nu-skin without so much as an "excuse me" from the pack.

"There you are, McGill," Graves said. He walked up and looked me over. "The tribune told me you did well with your detours today."

"I sure as hell did, sir."

"Well, I don't like it. I suggested we use another man, but she wouldn't hear of it. Are you affecting her judgment in some way, Centurion?"

He gave me a hard look, so I played dumb. "Uh... like how, sir?"

Graves shook his head. "I don't want to speculate."

162

I brightened suddenly, deciding to take his comment the wrong way. "I get it. You're right, Primus. I'm influencing everyone in high command today. Just like you always say, outstanding performance in battle tends to inspire even the brass. Isn't that what you always taught us back in the old days, sir?"

"I literally never said that. No one should do anything with the intent of impressing superior officers. You do it because it's the right thing to do."

"Oh right... sorry sir. I must have been thinking of Winslade."

His mouth twisted up, but my distraction seemed to work. He stopped complaining and speculating about me and Turov. "All right, whatever. You're going on this mission. When you're suited up, you'll port out to join the rest of them."

"Hmm..." I said, wondering if I should ask for details. Finally, after a few seconds, my curiosity got the better of me. "Where, exactly, did the rest of *who* go, sir?"

He looked disgusted. "Is your head in this game, McGill? I must have sent you a dozen battle plans over the last two hours."

"Ah! That would explain it! You see, with all the fighting, my tapper has taken some hard knocks."

He frowned, grabbing and examining my uninjured arm. "Looks okay to me."

"Well it does *now*, sir. It's been repaired."

The techs surrounding me gave us a few quizzical glances, but they didn't argue with my lies.

"Well, it doesn't matter. All you have to know is the commando unit has already left. You'll join them as a backup auxiliary. Follow their lead and help out where you can."

"Um... but exactly where are we going, sir?"

"Claver-land, of course. Where do you think? Your target LZ is the very headquarters building that you reported about years ago. In fact, you're the only man on this mission roster who's been to the target planet. That's the only reason I didn't erase your name from the list."

"That's mighty considerate of you, Primus."

"Just shut up and port out."

163

Someone handed me a fresh morph-rifle. The techs slapped my helmet to let me know I was good to go. They stepped back, and I reached up to my chest-plate.

I was tired and sore all over, but I was still game. I grabbed hold of the knob I found there and twisted it. I twisted it hard over to the left, as far as it would go.

The universe began to waver and turn blue. The blue light deepened, going into a cool, gloomy undersea shade. It was like seeing the world from the bottom of the ocean.

Gray Deck and *Legate* faded from existence. A few seconds passed, during which I couldn't breathe. That was always one of the most upsetting parts of teleportation travel. You felt like you were suffocating—or maybe like you were already dead.

In any case, it was several long seconds before the world began to come back into focus. When it finally did, I was in a very different place.

-28-

Flickering lightning lit up the sky overhead—at least, that was my first impression. But it didn't take long for even my fuzzy brain to realize that there was a battle going on and what I'd assumed was lightning was instead live gunfire.

The air hummed with bullets, beams and mini-missiles. These last were possibly the most dangerous, as they were intelligent. They shot up then sang down at sharp angles, spinning and trailing vapor. Traveling at half the speed of a bullet, they were far worse than a hunk of lead. Bullets didn't steer into you, nor did they explode when they struck home.

Like any trooper who pops into an unknown battle zone, I threw myself on my belly. My chest-plate scraped over rocks as I used my HUD to determine where friendly contacts were located. Heading in a direction my helmet had chosen to call "south" I wormed toward a set of green dots that were about ten meters off.

Before I made it to them and slithered into a half-assed trench, something had spanged off my armor twice. I didn't bother to check out what was hitting me, I just crawled faster.

"Centurion?" an adjunct asked when I arrived and shoved my bulk into what amounted to a double-wide foxhole with him.

"Hi there, uh… Adjunct Garlock," I said, reading his nameplate. "Glad to make your acquaintance."

165

"You are McGill, right?"

"In the flesh. Can you fill me in?"

Before Garlock could speak further, a raking spray of fire stitched our vicinity. We both had to sink down on our butts. The foxhole was so shallow our knees poked up when we got our heads down into the hole completely.

"Sir, this is what they call a charley-foxtrot of the first order," Garlock told me.

I could tell right off that he'd made an accurate assessment of the situation, and that I was going to like this man. "Where's your commander?"

"The centurion is dead, sir. There's just me and two other adjuncts. I'm not senior, so…"

"Point the way."

After a moment's hesitation, Garlock aimed a gauntleted finger across an open swath of greenery. "In those trees, sir. Last I saw of her."

I frowned. There was no cover higher than a foxtail all the way over to the trees he'd indicated. Crossing that no-man's land would be certain death.

"Okay, so we're pinned and taking fire from that tower over there?"

"Right. We landed as close as we could to the main building—the place you spotted Clavers living years ago, I hear."

He looked at me for confirmation of this rumor, but I wasn't in a chatty mood. I gestured for him to hurry up.

"Right… well, they were right here waiting for us. The building is shielded, but certain areas around it aren't. I think it was a trap from the start. A setup to lure a teleport team into landing here where we could be torn up."

Surveying the land, I thought he might be right. It would be just like Claver to bait a trap and make it look good—then snap the jaws shut when someone fell for it.

"Yep," I said. "This looks like the shit-show to end all shit-shows. You say your centurion is dead?"

"Yes sir."

166

"Good enough for me. We're pulling out. Signal your team on command chat. We'll all jump together, as closely as we can in time, to return to *Legate*."

"Um… that's not what our orders—"

I grabbed him by the collar and hauled him into view. He was a small man, and it would have been easy to toss him out of the foxhole.

"I like you, Garlock," I told him, "but you're getting on my nerves real fast. Now, if you don't want to be the last man on this rock, relay my instructions."

Garlock was all out of arguments. He signaled the rest of his unit.

"Some of them don't have the power to jump, sir," he told me.

I frowned at him. "Cannibalize it off the dead. Don't they teach you anything in boot camp anymore?"

He flushed and then relayed the command.

Still, as fast as my command went out and was obeyed, things got worse. I saw humping shapes coming from the towering building a few hundred meters off. They were probably more Claver-Threes.

"Tell everyone with a good power charge to fire at the approaching troops. The rest can try to find power wherever they can."

As my suit was fresh and had a brimming charge, I laid into the approaching enemy. They were cagey for Threes, but not geniuses by any means. As often as not they looked up over the edge of a trench to have a look around.

Bam! That was when I hit them with a full burst. I'd popped four by the time Garlock told me ninety percent of the survivors were good to go.

"Jump!" I ordered, bypassing him and roaring the command over general chat. All around me, the wavering blue glows began to thrum up and up, rising in intensity.

Apparently the enemy heard me or saw the glow. The Claver Threes scrambled up and charged us, looking for easy kills while we were porting out.

As I had yet to activate my suit, I took the opportunity to paste the advancing line. I chugged out all four of my grenades, then went full-auto and hosed them down with power-bolts.

Laughing, I sank back down on my butt and activated my suit. The blue light wavered, shrouding me—but it wasn't fast enough.

My display of bravado had singled me out. A swarm of those mini missiles were released. They arced up then down again. Before I could dematerialize, my foxhole, my armor and my body were blasted to smoking ruin.

* * *

I came out of the revival machine laughing. I seemed to do that more often these days. A good joke was almost worth a death to me now, as long as it was quick.

The guy who was there to preside over my birth, however, wasn't in such a jovial mood. He was a cold-handed, speechless man who checked me out like a prize-winning pig at the fair.

"His status is acceptable."

"Good, good," said another man. "You can leave us now."

That second voice seemed familiar somehow, but my fuzzy new mind couldn't place it immediately. I blinked my eyes experimentally. It was painfully bright. The first hint I got that something was wrong came from the ceiling.

"Alabaster?" I croaked out.

"What's that, McGill?"

That voice... again, it was familiar, but it didn't seem...

The figure near the gurney I laid upon had a slight Texas twang. When he spoke, there was an edge to every word, like he was laughing at you no matter what you said.

"Claver?" I rasped.

"That's right, dummy! Who else would salvage a wreck of a hero like you?"

Blinking, I fought to clear my vision, but it wasn't working. Bright lights, fresh-grown eyes—they were always a bad combination.

168

"Why revive me? How...?"

"How did I do it? Is that a serious question? I didn't figure you were still that big of a moron. Let's do the math, shall we? You died on my doorstep, son. Worse, you were permed, unless someone from *Legate* decides to come back down here to identify your scattered remains. What would you bet on the odds of that happening? Huh?"

Permed? The thought hadn't occurred to me until now, but Claver was right: it was a possibility. After all, I'd stayed behind to fight when the rest of the unit had jumped out. On their tappers, I'd be recorded as living at the last point of contact. If I'd managed to jump after them a few seconds later, all would have been well.

But I hadn't. Instead, I'd died alone on an off-grid world... that was the stuff of nightmares for any legionnaire. One of the main ways you could get your ass permed in Earth's service was to pull a stunt like that.

My heart pounded, and I tried to think. It was hard, but I worked on it.

"Why revive me even if I was permed?" I said, trying to sit up.

That's when I noticed there were straps over my chest. Big bands of cold steel, by the feel of them. I wasn't sitting up on my own anytime soon.

Claver gave a dirty laugh. "Because I like you, McGill."

"Really?"

"No. I don't like you at all... but I *am* fascinated, and I do have a grudging respect for your animal prowess. You're a wrecking ball. A dumbass wild bull, hell-bent on destruction. The shit you pulled out at Rigel last month, for example—that was sheer magic."

"So, you liked that, did you?"

"I sure did. I got several fresh contracts from those bear cubs in the aftermath. They're convinced Earth is a clear and present danger to all their planets. That translates into orders for a whole lot more Claver-legions needed for extra protection."

"Claver-legions, huh?" I asked, craning my head as far as I could. I couldn't see much. "If you don't mind my speaking out of turn... they seem to kind of suck."

For the first time, I got a solid stare from him over that comment. He was a Prime, I could tell that much. I'd been delivered by a Class-Two, or a Beta Claver... whatever. But this guy, he was a Prime. The real deal.

"You're rude, but you're accurate. Most of my legions lack good leadership."

At this point, Claver signaled for a couple of beefy Class-Threes. Without a comment or a grunt of acknowledgement, they stepped forward and began wheeling me out of the revival chamber.

The Prime walked with us as we traveled through the building. It was kind of weird, having two versions of a man pushing you along while a smaller, third version paced alongside.

We soon reached another chamber. This one was full of high-tech gadgetry. I ignored the gear and focused on the man. The longer you could keep a guy talking, the harder it would be for him to cut your balls off, I always say.

"So," I said conversationally from my gurney. "You've been recruiting leaders from Earth. Like old Armel, I guess. By the way, you should have seen the look on his face when I screwed up his command back on that space station orbiting Rigel."

I laughed, but Claver didn't laugh with me.

"You're a cold one, McGill. That wasn't just any space station. You brought down a space *city*. A resort for the young and wealthy. Thousands of families are still mourning their losses."

"Uh... no revives, huh?"

"Just like Earthlings, they don't track every mind and scan every physical body. They only revive members of their ruling elite. Politicians, military officers, people like that."

"I see... bastards like Squanto, then. That explains why I keep running into that dick."

"Exactly. Speaking of which, you'll be delivered into his tender care soon."

170

Up until this point, I'd been fairly relaxed about Claver's intentions. To be honest, I'd kind of figured he'd offer me a job. After all, that's what he'd been doing with the others aboard *Legate* who were of officer rank.

But handing me over to Squanto? That wouldn't go well. Squanto had already made a play to get his claws on me back on Earth. Now he was at it again.

Squanto was some sort of middle-grade overlord in the Rigel government. He'd met up with me several times, but we'd never gotten along.

The more I thought about it, the more I began to frown. My new face almost pulled a muscle the longer I pondered meeting with Squanto again, but this time as a prisoner.

There'd been that time I'd given him a juice box—convincing him it was a bomb—then made fun of him for believing in my trick later on... Then, another time, I'd ridden him like a dog and transmitted the video live for laughs. The cherry on top had to be the recent mass civilian casualties... Taken as a whole, I had to figure old Squanto was pretty annoyed with the antics of James McGill by now.

"Uh..." I said. "Don't you need a new commander? For one of these Claver-legions?"

"What? Are you out of your dim-witted mind, boy? If I wanted to destroy another of my precious legions today, I'd just as soon march them into a meat-grinder as put you in charge!"

He laughed and shook his head. We stopped in a small chamber which had a lot of complex-looking equipment in it. He began making careful adjustments to a gadget he was messing with. It looked like a communications box.

After watching him for a while, I decided it was a deep-link rig, an Imperial standard-issue unit he'd stolen or borrowed at some point.

Deep-links were devices capable of transmitting sound and video over interstellar distances without worrying about the irritatingly slow speed of light. They used some kind of trick of aligned-photons. It was quantum stuff I didn't really understand.

"Dammit," Claver complained after a few minutes. "This thing is misaligned again. Toro! Get your butt in here, girl!"

Toro? I hadn't heard that name in a decade...

Sure enough, the woman I'd long known as Adjunct Toro walked into the revival chamber. Her eyes only glanced in my direction, and I might have been mistaken, but they seemed a tiny bit apologetic.

-29-

My mouth gaped, but Toro avoided my gaze as she stepped to Claver's side.

"What is it, Commander?" she asked.

"This damned thing… it's not aimed at Rigel anymore. Who's using this when I'm not around?"

"I'm not sure, sir. If you'd like me to pull the security videos and run a check—"

"Forget it. That will take hours. McGill needs to be wrapped up and delivered by then. He's long overdue at Rigel."

I snapped my fingers and tried to lift my arm, but of course, it was shackled to the gurney.

"Hey!" I said, rattling my chains. "That's what you were up to back at Central, huh Claver? That copy of you I met with the Claver-Three in the bombed out zone of Central City. You were trying to capture me and take me back to Rigel, right?"

Claver made a sour face. "Yes. You were as uncooperative then as ever. Today will be different."

My eyes swung to Toro. "Good to see you again, Adjunct!"

She glanced at me. "I can't say the same, McGill."

"Aw, come on. You can't still be burned about being kicked out of Varus at the start of the Dark World campaign, can you?"

"An injustice of such magnitude isn't easily forgiven."

"But I didn't do it."

"Maybe not, but you're still a representative of that ghastly organization."

That was Toro in a nutshell. She'd always been touchy and kind of prissy. It really wasn't a good match for the rough-and-tumble life style of Legion Varus.

It occurred to me that mentioning such a fact wouldn't help my case any, so I moved on to something else. While they were fooling with the deep-link, I snapped my fingers again.

"Hey!" I said. "You must be one of the most senior officers here on Clone World by now, right? What are you, an imperator?"

She tossed me a frown.

"Uh... a tribune, then? Surely, you *must* be a tribune. Hell, those boys I fought back aboard *Legate* had the kind of leadership even a Claver-Two could beat. They sucked *balls*."

Claver was ignoring me. He was too busy realigning his equipment. But Toro, she could never let a barb go by. Like I said, she was really too sensitive for Legion Varus. Besides, I'd known her for years, and I knew how to press her buttons.

"I'm a primus," she said. "Special operations. For your information, I commanded that brave attack you've been denigrating, McGill. We were defeated, but it was a close thing. Bragging about it is unbecoming of your position."

"Whoa!" I said, all the while thinking *bingo* inside my head. Toro had always been a half-assed adjunct. When raised to the level of a primus, well, things were bound to go badly in a tough fight. "I'm sorry about that. I had no idea there was a human commander involved. I hope it didn't hurt too much."

She frowned at me. "What didn't hurt too much?"

"When you died out there, I mean... Hold on, you didn't run out on your cohort and survive, did you?"

Her frown deepened. "Of course not. I was never there—physically. I directed the force from my command station here in our headquarters building."

"Uh-huh..." I said, thinking that over. Right off, I suspected that her chicken-shit command style had probably contributed to the failure of her attack. But seeing as telling her this wasn't going to make her any happier with me, I decided to leave such thoughts unspoken.

I turned my eyes and my mouth toward Claver again. "Hey Claver. Why don't you just print out some extra Primes and make them tribunes. I mean, it can't be hard to do, and you've always been a solid officer."

Claver paused and looked at me seriously. "I can't do it," he said. "It would break our pact."

"The pact between you and the other Claver-Primes?"

"Yes. You see, if one of us gets a loyal legion to command, the others wouldn't be happy. Most of my kind are operating as free-agents. We would naturally be at a disadvantage—politically speaking, of course."

"Ah... I get it. You don't trust yourself."

"On the contrary. I trust human nature. I trust *my* nature. Which is to say, it would be best not to put a man like myself in charge of a large independent military unit."

"Yeah..." I said, thinking it over. "None of you want the other guy to declare himself to be Caesar."

"Exactly."

"So... that leaves you hard-up for good human officers to lead your own clones around. Damn, that's a weird situation. You sure you don't want me to do the job? Maybe even as a primus? I mean, I just beat this candy-ass ex-adjunct Toro with one hand tied behind my back. You know full well I could do that every day of the week, if I had to."

For the first time, Claver seemed to consider my words. He paused, turning slowly to face me. Then he looked up at Toro and smiled.

Toro didn't like my words. She was pissed, and she had her hands on her hips, glaring down at him.

"I'm afraid I'm going to have to decline your offer, McGill," Claver said. "I've got a better deal all set up."

That's when I knew the truth. Toro and Claver were screwing on the side. The situation was delicate, and I was going to have to maneuver with great care.

When they finally got their deep-link rig operating, they transmitted a canned message and switched it off again.

"That's it. He's on his way."

I nodded. "Good deal. It'll feel good to screw over that bear cub one more time."

Claver chuckled. "You're still full of piss-and-vinegar, aren't you boy? I have to admit, there are times when I could use someone like you around here. Maybe after I ship you off, I'll print out a new McGill and take his offer. He'd never know about you, of course."

Claver grinned, and my face fell—but Toro... she looked deeply annoyed. Claver seemed to miss this, and to me it was no wonder he'd always had trouble picking up the ladies. A man had to at least know when he was pissing off his woman.

Laughing about it, Claver-Prime left the room. He gave the Claver-Threes orders to take me down to the docking station, whatever that was.

"Hey!" I called out to Toro as she turned to walk away. "Want me to tell you a secret?"

Toro stopped, but she didn't turn around right away. She was thinking about it.

I said nothing. When you were fishing, you didn't scream and carry on. You didn't *beg* the fish. You just baited the hook, and you sat back and waited. The fish had to make that fatal decision all by itself.

Finally, she turned back around and walked alongside the gurney.

"What's your secret, McGill?" she asked.

She had her arms crossed over her breasts, and her eyebrows were cinched together tightly. She wasn't liking me much right now—she never had.

"You're the one who's been messing with alignment on deep-link, aren't you?"

She looked startled. Her eyes flicked to glance at the two Claver-Threes who were slowly wheeling my naked ass down the passageway.

"Don't worry about these dummies. They're not interested."

Her eyes came down to meet mine.

"How'd you know about the deep-link?"

"How do you think we traced our way back to Clone World?" I asked. "Don't you think it's odd that we found you, way way out here?"

Her eyes were furtive. "You're full of shit. No one can trace a deep-link call."

I opened my mouth wide and laughed. "That's right, no one can trace anything. It's frigging impossible. You and I are astrophysicists, after all, and we know all about that kind of stuff."

"What you're saying is ludicrous," she said. "But, let's say for a moment that I believe you. That Earth did trace us using emissions. What has that got to do with me?"

"It's been a decade, hasn't it?" I asked. "Since you got kicked out of Varus and—"

"And then I was executed. Permed."

That part slowed me down. I'd heard some people were going to get permed if they released secrets. Maybe Toro had done so. Rather obviously, she'd had some kind of relationship going with Claver. When Central had found out she was a spy, well… they'd taken steps. Harsh steps.

"You were Claver's squeeze way back then too, huh?" I asked.

She blinked twice. "You have a way of putting things that—"

"I've got a real talent for a sharp turn of phrase, I know. Lots of ladies have told me that. But listen, let's forget about who is porking who, and who's a traitor, and all that malarkey. I know your secret. You got bored and lonely out here after Claver revived you. Sure, he was nice enough to unperm you, and you felt grateful—but the sex thing… that's probably something you'd best—"

"*Shut up!*" she hissed.

"Okay, okay. I'll drop that. You got bored and called your mom, or your old boyfriend—whatever. Central traced the call to here, since it was a beam coming into Earth from an unknown source. It's all very understandable. I'm sure Claver would totally forgive you for this tiny error—"

She was showing her teeth by this time. "McGill. If you don't shut up, you might not make it to the docking station alive."

"Right. Got it…" I said, and I did shut up. After all, I was still lying on my back with my balls in the breeze. Her hand had moved to the butt of her pistol, and I was reminded she had been Varus material at one time—a killer, through and through.

Toro stared at me thoughtfully for a few seconds. I knew she was thinking it over. Maybe she was working out scenarios in her mind as to how she could off me and be rid of my annoying ass.

"Look," I said. "I can help you out—or I can hurt you real bad. That's how it stands."

That was it. She drew her weapon and aimed it into my face.

The Class-Threes stopped pushing the floating gurney along and stood still. Oddly, they didn't look at either of us. They just waited, and I got the feeling they weren't going to intervene if Toro got a bug up her butt and shot me dead.

-30-

I'm a bluffer, almost to a fault. So I went with my instincts on this one.

I grinned at Toro. "Hey," I said, gesturing with my chin at her gun. "Go ahead. Fire away. Claver will revive me again, no matter what kind of lame excuse you give him. Then my story will have much more weight to it. After all, why would you kill me if I was lying?"

"You're playing with fire, McGill," she said, pressing the gun barrel into my cheek.

I kept on grinning. "Come on," I said. "You really think I'm going to shiver and piss myself? I'm a Varus man. I'm not sure what you're used to out here on this rock, but I'm not some candy-ass push-over."

She swallowed. That was a tell. She was feeling the stress. She didn't know what to do.

"Let's cut a deal," I said cheerfully. "We've both got cards, here. Let's put them on the table."

Toro's mouth opened, but not with a smile. It was more of a grimace. Her tongue rubbed at her teeth.

I sure hoped she couldn't come up with a good plan, because I knew she'd burn my ass down in a second if she did.

At last, she made a sound of frustration and disgust. She stared ahead again and put her pistol back into its holster. She

179

signaled the Class-Threes, and they began walking again, as solemn as pall-bearers.

"All right," she said quietly. "What do you want for keeping quiet?"

"How am I being sent to Squanto?"

"Through a pair of gateway posts. We have a direct connection from here to Rigel."

I nodded thoughtfully. That made sense—and it was also alarming. Effectively, Claver's home planet was serving as an advanced base for Rigel.

What I didn't like was the implication: Our enemies were organized and using the same tech as Earth to move forces around quickly.

"The main thing I want," I said, "is to avoid going through that gate into Squanto's loving arms."

"That makes sense," she said, and she gave me a secret smile. I think the idea of Squanto torturing me to death was appealing to her. "But I don't know how I can stop it."

"Think of something. Fast."

We'd reached the docking station Claver had mentioned. Apparently, that's what they called their connection nexus.

The big doors swung open, and a room such as I'd never seen was revealed. There wasn't just one pair of gateway posts, oh no. There were a dozen. Each stood in an alcove. In the center of the large space was an operator, a Claver-Two no doubt, working the equipment.

I whistled, long and low. "It's like frigging Grand Central Station in here!"

The Class-Threes that were pushing me along headed toward the central booth with its lone operator.

"This is the package bound for Rigel?" the operator asked.

"Yes," one of the Class-Threes said. I wasn't sure which one it was.

Craning my neck painfully, I looked around. I didn't see Toro at first—then I spotted her hindquarters. Her hips were in full sway as she walked rapidly away from me. I'd been ditched.

"Hey!" I shouted after her. "I'll tell Squanto. Don't you think he's going to be interested? He'll give the info back to Claver, you know he will!"

Toro stopped. The two Class-Threes had selected a set of gateway posts. They were methodically marching me toward them. The posts ran with an evil, sickly-green light. They were warming up for the transmission of my sorry ass to Rigel.

Toro's left arm did a little hopping jig of frustration. Finally, she spun around on her heel and walked after me.

"Hold it," she said.

The Class-Threes stood motionless. The Class-Two watched with mild interest, but he didn't say anything. He was genetically predisposed not to ask questions.

Toro's glowering face came into view. "Squanto is going to execute you. He won't believe a damned thing you say."

"Probably not," I agreed in a mild tone. "But you know he won't miss a chance to interrogate me. He's no fool, after all. He'll ask all kinds of questions, and I'll sob, beg, and crap like that. Then... somehow... the truth about you will just come out. How you're a mole, and all. How you're a deep-plant, the center of all human resistance to—"

Her gun was out and shoved into my mouth. My teeth clacked on the barrel, and all speech was cut off.

The two Class-Threes shuffled a little at this, but they still held their peace. They rolled their eyes at us, reminding me of draft horses that were becoming concerned about the antics of their angry-monkey masters.

"You're not going to threaten me. You're not going to sour the deal I have here. I've put up with years of bullshit, and I'm not going to let you screw that up. I'll blow your dick off, first."

I watched her as she worked the problem in her mind. It was all up to fate, now. A woman like Toro was a feisty, emotion-driven creature. Most people were at times like this. I'd stated my case clearly, and she had to make her decision.

Finally, the gun came back out of my mouth. The metal left a bad aftertaste.

"There's been a mistake," she said loudly. "We have to return him for processing first."

The clones all looked confused. "Come on!" she shouted. "I'm a primus, I order you to walk this prisoner back to the storage facility."

Surprised but obedient to a fault, they turned around and started walking toward the exit. I don't mind telling you that my heart did a happy slow-down, and I took a few gulps of fresh air.

The Class-Two operator stood up in his booth. "Primus," he said.

"Yes, Specialist?"

"I must log a reason for this change of plan."

"I already told you the reason. There's been a mistake."

"I must log a reason."

He was short on imagination, but I could tell he was a stickler for the rules. I looked up at Toro curiously, wondering how she was going to get out of this one.

"Fine," she said. "We'll do it right here."

Her face raging, she shot the Class-Two dead. He took the shot in the chest, staggering back. She fired twice more, throwing the shots wide. She seemed to be doing this with deliberate care.

The Class-Two died with a shocked look on his face. The Class-Threes took notice, but they still didn't argue. She was a primus. She could shoot people if she wanted to.

"He was a traitor," she said calmly.

Walking between the two Clavers, she unbuckled my straps and handed me her gun.

"Uh…" I said. "You sure about this?"

"It's all I've got," she said.

I nodded. "I'll remember this. Make sure you erase my files when you get a chance, so Claver can't bring me back to life just to check. But even if he does—I won't tell him."

She nodded. The two Class-Threes were rolling their eyes and shuffling nervously again.

I shot them all. The two Class-Threes, then Toro herself. She just stood here, teeth gritted, waiting for it.

"That was a proper death," I told her as she gasped on the deck. "You really did belong in Varus."

She might have smiled, but then again, she might have been expiring. It was hard to tell.

Quick as a rabbit, I ran toward the nearest set of gateway posts and vanished in-between them.

Where was I going? I had no idea, but I figured it had to be better than here.

-31-

When I stepped out of the gateway, I felt woozy. It had been a long hop, and I had no idea where I was.

After a few seconds, however, that sensation passed. The air wasn't fresh, but it was familiar—homey, even. The gravity, the blue skies... Yes—I was back home on Earth.

I could hear the distant sounds of ground traffic, the peeping of birds... No question about it, this was Earth.

My immediate surroundings, however, belied that conclusion. I wasn't outside—not exactly. I was in some kind of pit—a tunnel mouth, to be more exact.

Dirt, chunks of puff-crete, concrete and twisted rusty steel were all around me. Looking back, I saw the gateway posts glimmering. They were set back in the tunnel behind me, and the rest of the place looked like a bomb-shelter that had recently taken a direct hit.

Walking up out of the pit, I realized I was buck-naked. Shrugging, I pressed onward. There was nothing I could do about it, and hanging around the gateway wouldn't improve my odds of escape.

I tried my tapper, but there was interference. That made some kind of sense. Whoever had setup this hideout with the gateway hadn't wanted anyone to report on it. They'd probably put up some kind of a transmissions jammer in the area. They'd probably come to check on whoever had just used the gateway any minute now, too.

Gazing with longing back into the dark tunnel, I consider running down there and hiding. If nothing else, I'd skip out on the opportunity to show the public my wand as I ambled out onto the streets I could hear nearby.

I resisted the urge to hide. Bold action often brought unexpected rewards, so I decided to continue to press my luck.

Scrambling up a mound of broken masonry, I heard a voice behind me. It was familiar, monotone, and deep.

"Where's the Prime?" it asked.

Slowly, so as not to startle the idiot, I turned around. My best smile spread onto my face. "He's right down there in the tunnel," I said. "He brought me back to Earth with him."

He was dumb, but he moved fast. He knocked the pistol I'd taken from Toro right out of my hand.

"I don't see the Prime," the Claver-Three complained, peering into the dark tunnel mouth.

"He's in a shy mood today. If you would just—"

The brute eyed me with purpose. I steeled myself, but he had a rifle and I had skin and fists. I didn't think much of my chances.

Looming over me, he waved his rifle, indicating I should proceed him into the tunnel.

"You will not escape," he said.

"No, I sure won't. Not with you on the job!"

I walked toward the gateway, but stepped on a rock and bent forward. I didn't have to fake the pain in my bare foot, even though I'd stepped on it purposefully.

"Damn!" I called out. "You got any extra shoes?"

In way of an answer, the Three clubbed me in the back with his rifle butt. I staggered ahead, but I didn't fall. I stopped again, messing with my foot.

He walked up confidently, lifting his rifle for another blow—but it never landed.

I kicked at his knees, and I heard one crack. The side of the knee is a weak spot in humans, even in specially-bred clones. He staggered, and I sprang on him.

185

It was a struggle. I'll give him that. He was strong—maybe stronger than I was. His breath came out in puffs, and he grunted like a rutting boar, but in the end, I twisted his neck until it crackled. After that, he just sort of lay in the dirt, snuffling and drooling.

A shot rang out, and a power-bolt struck the rubble. I had the guard's weapon in my hands by that time, and I spun around.

We both aimed, the second Class-Three and me, at the same time. We fired and we both struck the other. He took it in the chest, I took it in the guts.

For about fifteen seconds, I lay bleeding and making mud in the dust. I said some bad words, and I made some animal sounds.

When I could look up again, I saw both the Class-Threes were dead. Unfortunately, I wasn't in good shape, either. Having been shot any number of times, I've come to be a pretty good judge of such things. I wasn't going to live long.

Struggling to get to my knees, I used the rifle to lever myself up. I had two options—no three, if you counted just dying on my back right here in the dirt.

The other two were rough, but more to my liking. I could crawl to the gateway, head back to Claver-land and hope things went better in round two. Or, I could try to climb four meters of filthy rubble and get up to street level.

I took the last option on the list. I'm not a quitter, and I didn't think anyone back on Clone World was going to help me. Not today.

Accordingly, using the rifle as a cane, I worked my way with great pain and numerous injuries up the shifting mound of loose gravel, dust, and sharp rusty metal. A stripe of blood, dark as spilled varnish, painted my path behind me. I was bleeding out, and already my eyes were rolling up into my head now and then.

Sweating, grunting and working hard, I made it to the top of the heap without passing out. Having a look around, I saw a few scrubby trees, ruined foundations to destroyed buildings—and the looming dark hulk of Central behind it all.

"Central City..." I rasped.

I had truly made it home. This had to be the way Clavers were infiltrating the city. Even half-dead as I was, I marveled at Claver's ability to worm his way into events and places where he didn't belong.

The street. It was only another three dozen steps away. If I could keep on my feet, I might just make it.

There was a fence surrounding the property, and I headed toward it. As I did so, I sensed a tingling on my body. It felt like I was passing through a soap-bubble. That had to be Claver's defensive field. It only made sense that he'd deployed something which created interference to hide the gateway. It probably even muffled the sounds of gunfire.

Crashing through the weed-overgrown barrier, I fell onto the sidewalk, facedown. I'd lost the rifle somewhere, I didn't even recall where.

When I hit the pavement with my face, it felt kind of good. Cool... soothing...

"Hey mister? You okay?"

A kid. I reached out my hand, as I couldn't speak, and I clamped onto the kid's ankle. I tried to look up at him, but he wasn't in my field of vision. I tried to speak, to ask for help, but it came out as croaking sounds.

"Filthy bum!" a man roared suddenly.

An explosion hit my face. He'd kicked me in the teeth. He drew back and did it again. The force of these kicks rolled me over onto my back. My hand relaxed, and the kid ran off crying.

"Oh shit..." the dad said suddenly. He must have seen my wrecked, bloody guts. "I'm sorry, man. I thought you were some kind of pervert."

I lifted a wavering arm. I was beyond speech, but I reached up, and he grabbed my hand in his. Anyone looking at me had to know I was dying.

My eyes, blurry and half-closed, looked at my tapper on my arm. There it was, and as I watched the signal lights spun, turned green, and...

I smiled with the half of my face that still worked. I'd gotten a clear, strong signal.

My tapper was synching up and uploading.

187

Looking at the confused, flustered dad, I kept smiling. He was talking, but I couldn't hear him, and I didn't really care to hear his apologies, anyway.

This James McGill's existence had come to an end.

-32-

"What have we got?" asked a female voice.

"He's an eight."

"Good enough. Call the praetor's office. Tell him he's awake."

The praetor? That was probably Drusus they were talking about. No other high-level brass had ever taken an interest in the life and times of James McGill.

My eyes snapped open, but the world was still a blur of lights and shadows. I tried to get up. Small, weak hands pushed me back down. I had the strength of a newborn—but it was coming back fast.

"Just lay back, Centurion. You've got an important visitor coming. Save your energy for him."

Taking in deep breaths, I soon regained the power of speech.

"This *is* Central, right?" I asked.

"Last I looked," she said.

"Have the patrols rooted out that nest of the enemy?"

"Um… what's that, McGill?" the bio asked.

"The Clavers—in Central City. There were two of them—probably more."

"McGill… are you confused? Orderly, run a brain-scan."

189

She moved around, so I could see her face and she peered into my eyes again. I felt like slapping her hands away, but I didn't. Bio people hated that.

"McGill, you were found dead across the street from one of those new city parks. Witnesses said you crawled out of an empty lot full of rubble and began harassing passersby."

"That's a damned lie," I mumbled.

Another presence entered the room then. I could feel him, rather than see him. It was in the way the others hushed and backed away.

It had to be Drusus.

"Praetor?" I asked, squinting in the right direction.

"McGill..." he said, his voice both wondering and tired. "What brings you home early from deployment this time?"

"Uh... it was sort of an accident, sir."

"Right... countless accidents. This occasion has to be a mark of distinction even for you, however."

"How's that, Praetor sir?" I croaked out. The bio people had come near again, and they shined lights in my earholes and whatever else they felt like.

"According to Graves—who is still out in deep space aboard *Legate* where he's supposed to be, I might point out—you ported down to an LZ. Immediately after your arrival, the mission failed, and then you disappeared... All within eighteen minutes?"

"I'll admit, that does sound like a record."

"After most of your troops withdrew," Drusus continued, "there was a search. They couldn't verify that you'd died, so you were marked down as MIA—the epitaph of many men who've been permed."

"I'm well aware."

"Indeed... Let's bring this story full-circle. Approximately twenty hours after your disappearance, you turned up here on Earth—in Central City no less. You were found naked, accused of accosting children, and you managed to inexplicably die again on a peaceful public street. Did I leave anything out?"

"I'd have to argue with that part about me causing the mission to fail back on Clone World, sir," I said. "We didn't stand a chance. The Almighty himself would have been pinned down and crushed by that crossfire. They were lying in wait for us at the LZ."

"Be that as it may, how did you find your way back to Earth... again?"

"Well sir, it was a bit of luck and quick-thinking."

I told him a greatly edited version of the events that had transpired on Clone World. In my version, I escaped the Claver-Threes and rushed through the first gateway I saw. I didn't even mention Toro's name—after all, a deal was a deal, even with a cast-iron bitch like her.

Drusus squinted at me while he listened. I could tell he believed some things and doubted others, but he couldn't tell which was which. At last, he sighed and shook his head.

"All right. We'll check out the location where you were discovered, we'll give it a full scan. As to your story: you were captured, and you escaped. That's really all I need to know, right? Is there anything else you'd like to tell me, McGill?"

"Uh..." I said, thinking hard. My eyes could see clearly now, and I'd noticed there were some hogs lurking out in the hallway. They could have been here to guard Drusus or even to protect yours truly—but I doubted it. They were most likely on hand to perform any arrests that needed to be made.

"I've got some tapper feed of what happened."

"We've already pulled all that. It's mostly blank."

I frowned. I'd worked to record key events. Maybe Claver's system had overridden that.

"We did get tapper recordings from some of the last men to teleport out of that firefight back at the LZ. They back up your version of events to a point."

"Excellent, Praetor sir!"

I was all grins, but he was giving me nothing but suspicious stares. He sniffed when I didn't offer anything new.

"McGill..." he said. "Are you aware that certain offers have been made to otherwise loyal Varus officers? That—reportedly—some people have been tempted and accepted these bribes?"

There it was. Drusus was worried I'd been bought off and switched sides. That kind of pissed me off, to be honest.

191

"Now look here, sir. I'm many things, but I'm no traitor. To be clear: I've heard these vile rumors, but Claver didn't offer me squat. He had a far worse fate in mind for me."

"Really? Such as?"

I told him about Claver's plan to sell my sorry bare ass to Rigel. Drusus knew all about Squanto, and all the reasons that diminutive alien had to hate me, so he laughed out loud.

"All right," he said. "I believe *that* story. Squanto hates you more than any living being ever has. It's good to hear you're still on Earth's side, McGill. In fact, it leaves me in the awkward position of having to offer you a special mission."

"Another mission, sir?"

"That's right. I want you to ferret out traitors—before they make their move to join Claver. Identify them and give the information to Graves. He'll take care of the arrests, and he'll do it quietly so as not to scare the rest of the fish away. Not until we have them all."

"Uh... that's great, sir. How do I do it?"

"You've been cleared, but your part of this campaign isn't finished yet. Your new orders are to return to your unit via a gateway connecting Central to *Legate*. All transports have them now."

"Of course, sir. But what I meant was how do I find the traitors?"

"You've already identified several. Use your judgment. I can't afford to lose any more officers."

"Anything else?" I asked with only the slightest hint of sarcasm.

"I think that's sufficient. You're dismissed, Centurion. Head down to Gray Deck for processing."

And that was it. Without so much as a handshake, he kicked me out of the revival room, out of Central—and off Earth itself.

-33-

When I got back to *Legate*, Graves was waiting for me. He didn't look even half as happy to see me as Drusus had been.

"Great to be back with Varus where I belong, sir!" I told him, giving him my heartiest grin.

Graves shook his head. He was watching something on his tapper—it looked like the destruction of the team he'd sent down with me to Clone World. He glared at the flashes of fierce combat.

"All right," he said at last. "Drusus claims you're not a traitor. I'll take his word for that. But if you're not a traitor, you're an idiot."

"Uh..." I said.

"Follow me, Centurion."

I walked after him unhappily. I'd kind of hoped to sneak away and get some much-needed bunk time. "No time for a shower, huh?"

"No, dammit. Come on!"

I walked after him, with my new body feeling all sticky inside my uniform.

"Uh... what's the hurry, Primus?"

"The hurry is that we're not getting anywhere. This mission has stalled. We're in enemy territory and every move we make fails."

I thought about that. Turov and I had come up with a list of plans of action over the preceding weeks. So far, she'd only tried the tame moves. I knew that it would soon be time to try something more drastic.

"How many revival machines do you think Claver has in this system, McGill?" Graves asked me suddenly as we reached the lift and stepped into it.

"Well sir, I only saw the one—the one I came out of."

He nodded. "That makes sense, but it's too bad you didn't see more details while in his fortress. You've been here several times, as I understand it, and you've never done a good job scouting the place."

I recalled those prior visits vividly. Every time, the security had been tight. Claver-Threes had literally glommed onto my arms. I hadn't been able to take a step on my own to investigate the place.

Graves looked up as we reached Gold deck. He gave me a hard stare. "What has Turov got planned?" he asked me.

Shrugging, I blanked my face. "How would I know anything about that, sir?"

Graves snorted. "Come on, give me a break. What's next on the menu?"

"Well sir…" I began reluctantly. I was thinking of some of the crazy things we'd come up with. "I think that's better heard coming from Turov herself. After all, she's the mission commander."

Graves looked pissed. "McGill, has it occurred to you that I'm second in command of this legion, and yet you seem to know more about our commander's plans than I do? Doesn't that seem odd to you?"

"Well sir… we've had loyalty problems. Not with you, of course, but the more people who know what's coming…"

I trailed off, and he gave me a hard look. At last, he nodded. "All right. I get it. She trusts you to keep quiet—which seems odd on the face of it, until I consider all the times you've kept a secret by lying and playing the fool… All right."

That was the end of it. Graves finally stopped grilling my ass, and that was an honest-to-God relief for me. I didn't like lying to Graves. It was like lying to my parents. Sure, I still *did* lie to them—all the time, actually. But I'd never enjoyed the process. It just felt wrong, somehow.

When we reached Gold Deck and the bridge, Turov was there, strutting around like a prized hen at the fair. She didn't care if she was breaking traditions, stepping all over the toes of *Legate's* captain—she was running this show directly.

"Perhaps, Tribune," began Captain Merton, "if you could allow me and my crew—"

"Forget it, Merton. I can't let amateurs run this show. Not today. We've lost too much already. Here's the plan: you will bombard the planet with the broadsides."

"That has been considered, sir," Merton said carefully. "But it's quite impossible. We can't get close enough—not by several million kilometers. If we try, the enemy's defensive batteries will destroy my ship long before we're within range."

"You're under my mission command, Merton," Turov said dangerously. "And you will follow my orders accordingly."

Merton straightened, and he seemed to grow a spine. "You are the mission commander, but I'm specifically allowed to override your orders if I see them as unacceptably dangerous to this ship and crew."

The two squared-off. I was smiling, ready to applaud. Old Merton had been a whipping-boy the whole trip out. It was good to see him finally grow a pair.

"Captain, I—"

"I do not have to endanger this ship," Merton interrupted. "I see your orders as suicidal, therefore I won't follow them."

"And if I have you arrested?"

Merton paused for a moment. "Then you can explain that action to Central, should any of us be lucky enough to make it home alive."

Turov nodded. "All right. You win. We won't approach and fire. Instead, we'll warp from here to orbit, then fire and land. Does that make you happy?"

Merton blinked repeatedly. "That's against regulations. The radiation released by a warping ship near an inhabited world is strictly—"

"We're not coming here to colonize!" Turov reminded him. "We're coming to *bomb* them!"

I understood Merton's difficulties. Normally, Earth legions didn't go in for total war options. We fought limited engagements. Our broadsides were rarely used, and usually only on fortifications if we're talking about firing on a planet. Once a missile battery or other installation was destroyed, we usually invaded and conquered.

This was different. This was a rogue planet. The people down there were human, technically, but they were all illegal clones.

Still, hearing Turov's plan, I was left frowning. We'd discussed this one, but it was indeed extreme. She'd gone right

195

from regular operations to opting for total destruction. She was gambling with the ship, with her legion—with the entire mission. Maybe that was due to Merton's resistance, I wasn't sure.

"Uh…" I began, thinking to make a calming suggestion.

Graves hushed me by snapping his fingers in my face and shaking his head.

I shut up and watched.

"Well…" Merton said, "that's dangerous for the ship, highly irregular and—"

"But will it work? Can you steer this whale well enough to pull it off?"

Merton nodded. "We can do it. We'll have a window— perhaps three to five minutes—before we'll have to warp away again to stop the enemy defenses from taking out the ship."

Turov smiled and began to strut again.

"That's right," she said. "We'll do it. This is a stalemate, and I'm going to put an end to it. Graves, put everyone you can on a lifter. *Legate* will warp into position, fire a barrage to take out the defensive batteries, then your job will be to drop from orbit and mop up the resistance."

"Will you be dropping with us, Tribune?" Graves asked.

Turov gave him a glittering stare. She didn't like to get down in the dirt. She liked that fact being pointed out in public even less.

"Yes," she hissed after a moment's hesitation. "I *will* be dropping with the legion."

She looked back at Merton. "Will that be alright with everyone? Or should we put this to a vote?"

Captain Merton was blinking in surprise. Slowly, the realization that he was getting rid of Turov—possibly on a permanent basis—was dawning on him. He began to smile.

"No need sir!" he said. "I'm in complete agreement. Don't worry, *Legate* will stay out of harm's way."

"That much I'm sure of," Turov said sarcastically.

After that, things got crazy. The big ship swung around and accelerated. Her warp engines shimmered into life.

All over the ship, Legion Varus was called to action. We were ordered to Red Deck.

We were landing within the hour.

-34-

After scrambling to Red Deck, we found the lifter pilots were prepping to launch as well. I tried to contact Graves, but he was too busy to brief the curious.

"I've seen this before," Leeson said. "Back about a decade before you joined up, McGill, we had a short drop-window like we do now. To speed things up, not everyone will be deployed with drop-pods. To get all the manpower and equipment off the transport as fast as possible, they'll dump three or four cohorts with drop-pods. The rest of the troops and all the heavy equipment will come down on lifters."

"That's dangerous," Harris said. "Lifters are too big, too easy to hit with defensive fire."

"Then let's pray the broadsides do their job and destroy those defensive gun batteries," I said.

They looked glum enough to pray, but no one did it out loud among the officer's ranks.

3rd Cohort was lucky enough to get drop-pod duty. I call it lucky because we couldn't get wiped out with one well-aimed shot.

We got into position, geared-up and sweating in our suits. After forty-one minutes of that crap, the ship jumped. I'd been waiting for the moment, and we finally slipped into a warp bubble and sped toward our destination.

Turov had pulled it off beautifully, in a way. We suspected we had spies aboard *Legate*, which was why Claver had always been one jump ahead of us on this campaign. But since we were far out in the system, even if someone wanted to warn Claver about our surprise, there wasn't time.

This was due to the limitations of radio transmissions. Radio traveled at the speed of light, and we were more than a light hour out from Clone World. Even if someone had reported the moment Turov announced our intentions, a radio signal didn't have time to get from *Legate* to the target planet.

It was possible, I supposed, that a secret enemy deep-link unit was aboard *Legate*—but I highly doubted it. They were too expensive, too large. It wasn't something you hid aboard a ship without people noticing.

As *Legate* formed its warp-bubble, scooting through space much faster than light could travel, we reached our destination before any traitorous signals could arrive to warn the enemy.

Materializing in low orbit, our big guns swung and locked on target. They fired in unison, and the men who were already being chugged out in drop-pods were jostled and nearly lost their footing.

It was Leeson's turn, in fact, when the big guns spoke. They knocked him half off his stride, and he went into the tube kind of off-balance.

My mouth split open in a sympathetic grimace, and I made a hissing sound. Poor Leeson. This wasn't his lucky day.

The two halves of the capsule slammed into his body as he dropped out into open space under the ship. I saw it on my tapper, and it wasn't pretty.

The trouble was Leeson hadn't come down the chute nice and straight. He'd fallen down at an angle. He'd tried to right himself, throwing out an arm to brush the side of the chute and steer himself back to center—it was a desperate, but logical gamble. Sure, he was bound to lose an arm doing that, but he'd at least avoid the worst.

Unfortunately, the worst happened anyway. He was sideways when the two halves of the capsule smashed into this body. His head and one arm were crushed on one side, while both feet were chopped off at the other end.

Harris glanced at me grimly. "At least it was quick."

"You're up. Go!"

Harris stepped out and vanished. There was a pro for you. The last man was hamburger, but Harris took his turn without hesitation. It made me proud to see it.

Behind me, I heard Veteran Moller shouting and slamming her gauntlets into various troops' skulls. She had to keep them moving. There couldn't be any backing up, no recoiling in horror, no panic in the tubes. You just had to take your turn, and you had to do it on time. The machinery was relentless.

It was my turn next. I stepped into space without a moment's hesitation. I hoped my example would calm the troops and keep them coming.

A moment later I was cocooned in titanium. My body was spun around, my legs bent at the knees, and the inevitable hammer-blow to my boots came a half-second later. I'd been launched out of *Legate's* belly.

All around me, I knew, men were falling like swarms of tiny bomblets, and lifters were screaming toward the planet. The broadsides were firing over and over as fast as they could to destroy the enemy fortifications. With any luck, their shields would be overwhelmed and their defensive installations reduced to rubble.

The plan had called for *Legate* to stay over the target for no longer than four minutes—but Captain Merton hung there for six. I could only surmise that Claver's defensive people were as surprised as we'd hoped they would be, and they had to retarget our ship in a panic.

"Two minutes," I said to myself as I screamed down in my pod, the capsule growing hot from the steep angle of reentry. "It must have taken them two minutes to aim and fire…"

We'd calculated that Claver's missiles could reach the *Legate* in four minutes. But they must not have launched the moment we appeared over their base. There must have been a much-needed delay.

Still, this was war at a lightning pace by any definition. The sky cracked open before I reached the LZ, and *Legate* winked out as suddenly as she'd appeared.

We were on our own. I shrunk down all my thoughts of the battle to my own situation. Theory, strategy, planning—they were all useless if you were dead in your boots.

The pods rained down in a swarm and landed not far from our last LZ. The difference was the area had been struck by heavy bombardment before we got there.

When my pod slammed into the dirt, I winced, but I didn't pop the hatch—not yet. I took a radiation reading first.

"Four hundred rads…"

Not good. Three hundred was a deadly dose. We'd have to keep our helmets on and breathe canned air, at least until the wind changed.

"Team," I broadcast to my unit, "keep your kits buttoned up. We've got some hot rads to worry about."

Popping open the hatch on my pod, I climbed out and surveyed the area. A strong, blistering wind was blowing. Trees were down, and everything organic about this place looked dead. The air swimmers had been incinerated. The leafy fronds of the jungle had been transformed into black finger-bones. They rattled and clawed at the radioactive winds.

We'd really done a number on this place.

-35-

Harris landed a big gauntlet on my shoulder. I spun around, frowning.

"Look..." he said, breathing hard. "The enemy's innermost dome—it's still up."

I looked, and I marveled. I saw a glimmering dome of force. It didn't have that glossy solid glass-bowl look anymore. Instead, it was shimmering, crawling, *running* with a weird effect that reminded me of heatwaves coming off a highway in summer... but it was still there.

"Shit," I said.

"Agreed."

"Get the men together," I told Harris. "Put Sargon in charge of Leeson's platoon."

Harris rushed to obey. I took stock of our status on my tapper. It wasn't horrible, but it wasn't great. We'd lost thirteen souls in the drop. We were down to about a hundred and ten effectives.

But any Varus unit could take a hard knock and keep marching. We gathered up what we could and advanced toward the dome. The forest we'd used for cover the first time we'd come here was gone—at least it was absent outside the central dome.

All around me, in a circular region some ten kilometers across, troops were hustling to encircle Claver's fortress.

Behind us, the lifters roared down and landed. There were dozens of them, and I was glad to see them all make it safely to the ground.

"Hey," I said to Adjunct Barton, after checking all the reports, "we didn't get through all their shields, but we did manage to destroy their anti-space batteries. They didn't shoot down a single lifter!"

She gave me an honest grin. We both passed the info on to everyone in the unit. They could use some good news about now.

Harris caught up with me a few minutes later. "What's the op plan now that we're on foot, Centurion?"

"We're going to advance and mop up. Anything that's still alive gets shot."

"That's it?" Harris asked in dismay. "No organizing, no forming proper lines—"

"Harris, we just gave them a surprise punch in the mouth. We're the shock-troops, the first ones to rush in to prevent them from recovering. When you've got an enemy down, you keep on kicking until he gives up."

He knew I was right and that Gold Deck had made the right choice this time, but he didn't like being part of any mad rush. Participating in such actions frequently resulted in death. Grumbling, he marshaled his platoon and trotted ahead.

We marched forward in a ragged line. As we got closer to the dome, the destruction got worse. The hot bed of radiation got hotter and the dust got so thick you could hardly see your gun in front of your visor.

We didn't find anything alive. Even the trees were dead. The ground itself was uneven, broken up and blasted with craters as big as football stadiums. The ground inside these craters crunched under our boots, the earth having been flash-melted into dirty glass.

At last, we reached the dome and halted, hunkering down under what cover we could find. A hundred meters away a glassy wall of force rose up out of nothing.

"What do you see?" I asked Harris, who was leading the lighter troops right to the edge of the dome itself.

"I don't see shit. Outside the dome, it's a dust storm. Inside, it's a jungle."

"A jungle? Untouched?"

"That's what I said. Everything near the borderline is all burnt up and dead, but there are plenty of trees, and even some balloon-looking things floating around deep inside their safe zone."

The fusion warheads from a broadside barrage not only struck with fantastic force, radiation and heat, they also released a brilliant light. Anything with eyes was often blinded for miles around. I was surprised the scene inside looked tranquil.

"Light platoon," I ordered, "advance and enter the dome. See if we can penetrate it."

"What? Now?" Harris called back.

"You heard me. Move!"

They hustled forward, and I brought up the heavy troops with Barton behind Harris. Since the last campaign, I'd given Harris the lights again. I felt it was only right, as Barton had been stuck with them for years.

I watched as Harris' lights reached out with the muzzles of their snap-rifles and touched the glossy surface. It buzzed and flashed, but it let them through if they moved slowly enough.

"Aw, this is nasty!" Harris complained as he put a foot into the wall. "It's like walking into a wall of Jell-O."

"Jell-O that tingles your balls with static electricity," I added. I came up behind him, giving it a try.

Only a dozen paces behind Harris, the heavy platoon entered next. There were complaints about the sensation up and down the line.

I didn't care. We'd advanced a long way with no resistance to speak of. They should be happy we were still breathing.

The dome was about a hundred steps thick. As we pushed our way inside, the weird feel of it was intense. Every cell on the surface of my skin felt like it was being tickled. Every hair on my body was individually tugged.

After walking for perhaps three minutes, we were through.

"The dome can't stop troops," I said, gasping for breath. It had felt natural to hold my breath when I was in the force field's grip. "The dome only stops bullets and bombs."

"Great," Harris said, standing next to me. "Orders, sir?"

"Keep advancing until we make contact. That's what we're supposed to do."

He rolled his eyes and shook his head, but he kept moving forward. He in turn ordered his ghosts to sprint ahead of the lights, and they vanished.

Off to my right and left, I saw similar contingents of troops advancing on both flanks. Could it be Claver's forces had been caught outside this dome and been destroyed by the bombardment? I dared to hope it was true. His legions might have been placed in defensive positions, outside the central fortress. If so, this might be a cakewalk.

No sooner had that happy thought crossed my mind than the first ripple of gunfire raked our lines. It was a light turret, manned and firing plasma bolts. At least five hundred bolts per second buzzed out, hosing down Harris and his advancing lights.

They threw themselves to the ground, but many of them wouldn't be getting up again.

"Take cover!" I shouted, echoing the calls of every officer and noncom in the unit. "Sargon, take out that turret!"

The enemy up there had little more than a machinegun, but they did have a clamshell lid on top of their gun. It was rotating evenly, humming with electric motors. I recognized the type of emplacement. There would be a crew of three working it, and unless we took it down fast it would destroy my infantry.

There was plenty of return fire from our side. Grav-grenades, bolts from morph-rifles—but that stuff couldn't penetrate. Most of our fire spanged and sparked, flashing off that sealed shell.

Methodically, it roved over the scene, chewing up my crawling men. They were desperate to take cover, but the enemy gun knocked down trees and lanced beams right through mounds of dirt a meter thick. The gunners knew their business, they were shooting men right through the cover they'd taken.

Then, three beams lanced out from our side. The beams struck the clamshell from three angles, hitting all at once.

The turret swung toward the first of these focused beams, stitching the ground with dark, smoking holes. If they could get lined up—

The turret exploded. The belchers had penetrated the armor and ignited the troops and the ammo inside. A very satisfactory plume of fire shot up ten meters, and smoke licked the roof of the dome itself.

We'd survived our first encounter with the enemy—or at least, most of us had. Scrambling back to our feet, we marched forward again, but with greater caution this time.

Not a single man in the unit walked with a straight back after the ambush. All of our dreams of a peaceful invasion had evaporated.

-36-

Resistance stiffened as we penetrated further into the domed region. For a time, I couldn't get in touch with Graves, and that freaked me out a little. Naturally, I didn't let on. I told my troops that our forces were pressing the attack on every front.

Finally however, I called a halt less than a kilometer into the domed area. We had found an area with good cover, and I wasn't willing to press ahead without knowing what we were up against, or who was supporting our flanks. It was one thing to push an enemy hard, and another to commit tactical suicide.

Radioing a good friend of mine, Centurion Manfred answered my call. It was a relief to hear his friendly, British-accented voice.

"Hey Manfred," I said. "I'm out of contact with Graves. How about you?"

"Same here," he said. "He's not inside this dome yet, as I understand it. Communications can't penetrate it. Are you still pressing deeper?"

I looked around at my tense, crouching troops. We'd lost a nearly a platoon's worth of men by now, including those who died during the drop, and no one was joking around any longer.

"Nope," I admitted. "We're holing up in this jungle, waiting for fresh orders."

"Yeah… probably the right move. I'm going to call a halt after we take this outbuilding."

"What outbuilding?" I began to ask, but I heard fire opening up.

Turning my head, I realized Manfred had to be pretty close. No more than a few hundred meters off. I could hear the gunfire off to our right.

"How's it going?" I asked Manfred, frowning at my tapper.

"We've got a nest of Clavers here, McGill. Signing off."

He disconnected, and I heard the gunfire continue. In fact, it grew in intensity.

"Unit!" I called out. "Gather your gear. We're moving toward that skirmish. With luck, we'll hit a battle group of Clavers in the ass."

They hustled and soon we were marching through the jungle again. Ahead, the forest was lit up by flashes and a lot of noise. It didn't seem to be letting up.

"Kivi, get your buzzers into position, I want a live stream. Harris, get your light troops out there on both our flanks. Barton, heavies in the center—pick up the pace!"

We moved at a jog through the trees until we reached the conflict. The ground here was open and low, a depression that might have served as a mining zone or something like that…

The buzzer feed finally came in, almost too late to be useful. I saw the scene now, from an aerial point of view. The depression was some kind of a dried up artificial pond. It appeared to have been full of water at some recent date— probably before we'd blown up all the surrounding land and destroyed whatever river fed this spot.

Pouring into the muddy middle were hundreds of Claver-Threes. They seemed to know that they had an enemy camp to face here. They were coming in force.

Behind the wave of Clavers, a row of vehicles hummed. They were open-backed transports. Little more than floaters with rails and big motors. Fast, easy transport for a lot of troops. The Clavers must have sighted Manfred here at the pond and swooped in with mobile infantry to trap them.

"Orders, sir?" Harris asked.

"When you see a target, halt and engage. Heavies, continue to press in closer."

On both our flanks, my advancing line stopped and began peppering the enemy troops with fire. Manfred's unit was hugging the shoreline opposite us, and they were stubbornly holding their own against a force that outnumbered them by at least four to one.

But then we hit the Clavers in the ass. They were slow to recognize the new threat—but then after a moment of milling around, they did behave intelligently. They dismounted from their vehicles and advanced on foot. Half of them turned to attack us, while the rest drove onward toward Manfred.

That made me frown. They were operating like they had a brain. Someone was directing them with smart tactics.

Zooming in with my helmet's optics, I scanned the center of their formation. There! I saw someone differently dressed, differently shaped.

It was a woman, and it wasn't Toro. Who could it be? Who was commanding these men?

Before I could hope to identify her, I was deep in the shit. About two hundred Clavers had turned and formed a line to advance toward us.

My unit had the higher ground, and we had some cover from the trees. The enemy, in comparison, were slogging through mud and made easy targets even when they threw themselves flat and crawled in our direction.

Still, it wasn't easy. They had a lot of firepower, and it wasn't easy to break their morale. They didn't surrender, or run, they shot at us and kept coming.

"Stay in the trees! Fire from cover! Choose your targets, and put each man down!"

It was a grim battle. Usually, modern fights with humanoids were fought at a distance of one to three kilometers. You shot at puffs of smoke, and they fired back at you.

Not this time. These men were taken by surprise, and we were all within a hundred meters or so of each other. We hosed one another down with guns set to full-auto, blazing away like there was no tomorrow—because there wasn't.

But soon, our superior training, organization and position began to tell. My men were better shots, and we had more heavy weapons. Grav-grenades rained down on the men in the mud, and the few that came back at us failed to strike more than a handful of my troops.

Belchers fired in wide arcs, blinding and burning the approaching knots of troops. They died hard, fighting until the last, but in the end, we overwhelmed them.

When the smoke cleared, I stood up and approached the shoreline. It was a massacre. Dead Clavers were everywhere, in every imaginable state of repose.

"Hey, sir!" Barton came near and touched my elbow.

I looked at her in surprise. She was pointing down, down into the muddy core of the pond full of dead men.

Right off, I saw what she was talking about. A single white cloth was waving down there. A strip of someone's shirt, by the look of it. They didn't even seem to have a stick to put it on.

"Huh…" I said. "Looks like we've got ourselves a prisoner."

"But Clavers don't surrender, Centurion," Barton said suspiciously. "We should gun them down, whoever they are."

I pushed her snap-rifle down, laughing. "Damn, girl! Varus has gotten into your blood, hasn't it? Let's see what this turncoat officer has to say."

"Turncoat?"

"That's right."

Advancing toward the waving white strip of cloth, I slogged through bloody mud and stood over a drainage pipe of some kind. It was in the middle of the pond, and must have been used to draw water from it before disaster had struck this world.

"All right," I said loudly, lifting my rifle and training it on that fluttering flag. "Come on out and leave your weapons behind."

When she stood up, I was dumbstruck.

It wasn't Winslade, or Armel, or even Toro. It was Centurion Leeza, formerly of Legion Germanica.

-37-

You have to understand, Centurion Leeza and I went *way* back. We'd had run-ins over many years, some good and some bad. One time she'd discovered me sleeping on a pool table naked, for instance. On another occasion, she'd overseen a duel to the death between myself and Tribune Armel.

She wasn't a bad-looking woman, as they go. She was tall, lean, and kind of mean-looking in the face. She wasn't the nicest person I'd ever met—but then, neither was I. She'd long served under Armel as a personal assistant in Legion Germanica. I'd never examined that relationship too closely—I hadn't wanted to.

"Centurion Leeza?" I shouted, tilting my morph-rifle up at the sky. "Fancy finding you out here in this pathetic mud-puddle. Tell me, did all these bad Claver-men kidnap you? Are you a woman in distress?"

Leeza climbed out of her hole in the ground and looked around with narrowed eyes. As far as she could see, there was nothing but dead bodies, blood and mud. From either direction, a ragged unit of Varus troops approached. She had to have around a hundred guns aimed at her skinny ass. In fact, I was probably the only human present who wasn't aiming a gun at her and scowling.

I grinned instead, like I'd found a long-lost cousin hiding under my porch.

"James McGill…" she said, spitting out the words. She had a faintly European accent. "My good fortune is overwhelming."

"That's right. You're one lucky lady today. How about you come all the way out of your bolt-hole and put your hands on your head?"

She did so, and my men captured her properly. She was manacled, but not roughed up. I gave the Varus boys a stern look to make sure.

Another individual approached the scene across the mud flats. He was as broad-chested as I was tall.

He was Centurion Manfred, the one and only. We clasped hands, and he grinned.

"Good to see you, mate," he said. "Although I have to protest on this glory-hounding behavior."

"How's that, Manfred?"

"Here I am, having the time of my life slaughtering a thousand-odd Clavers single-handedly, when your lot shows up to steal a share of the credit."

I snorted. "That's right," I said. "I've always been like that. It's a character flaw."

We laughed and turned back to Leeza. Manfred pointed at her. "I see you've caught yourself a new girlfriend, eh?"

"Hardly that. She's a traitor, and an enemy of all Earth."

He nodded in agreement. "Shall we execute her now, or interrogate her first?"

"Hell no, we shouldn't shoot her! Not yet. Barton! Disable her tapper!"

Leeza's hands were manacled behind her back. Barton took two strides forward, and she stabbed her combat knife into Leeza's right foreman. She did it quick-like, as if she'd been itching to do it since we found her.

Leeza's tapper went dark. It would no longer transmit anything about her status—or about us—to Claver-central. She hissed in pain, and Barton sprayed her arm with a pink foam of fresh skin-cells.

"If we kill her now," Barton said conversationally. "She might be permed. She's not on the grid any longer—theirs or ours."

"Good point," I said. "Unit, move out! Let's get out of this mud-pit before more Claver's show up."

While we marched back into the jungle, I took the time to question Leeza. "You remember that time you caught me on the pool table?" I asked her.

"How could I forget?"

"You remember what you said back then?"

She frowned. "Something about never wanting to catch you raiding the officers' bar again."

"That, and you said you were in my debt. You let me go because you owed me one."

At that, Leeza glanced up at me, sidelong. "Are you suggesting a deal, McGill?"

"Of course. Start talking. If you give us information that makes this action go smoothly, you probably won't get permed at the trial at the end."

She huffed. "That's not much of a deal. I'll tell you what: transmit my engrams to Claver's fortress. In the clear, right now. If you do that, I'll be revived there. I'll claim legitimacy, kill my clone, and I'll owe you a favor once again."

"Uh…" I said, chewing over her words. "What are you talking about, kill your clone?"

"If you haven't noticed, Claver doesn't play by Imperial rules. As soon as one of us has lost contact, they're marked for dead and a new officer is born. I'm probably half-way through the gestation process already."

I thought that over. It did make sense. Whenever Claver was executed, he never showed much concern. He knew he'd pop out of the oven again somewhere.

Apparently, that was now true for all his compatriots as well. I recalled that Winslade had been self-assured at his execution that he wasn't in any real danger either.

"Huh…" I said. "Is that the appeal, then? Eternal life? You can't get permed if you join up with Claver?"

"Not just that," she said. "He's got bigger, more powerful allies than Earth does."

"You mean Rigel? Those bears are tough, but we can beat them. We've done it several times."

"Maybe so… but can you beat the Skay, McGill?"

213

I halted, and we locked eyes. Centurion Leeza wasn't the kind of woman who joked around. She played things straight—she always had. I could tell she was telling the truth now.

My face didn't show it, but I felt a chill. The Skay were Galactics—nasty ones. They were like the Mogwa, but worse. They were machine intelligences. Each member of their race was the size of a planet and moved as they pleased around the cosmos. Just one of those ships could destroy a hundred worlds out here on the frontier, where our tech was comparatively weak.

"That's not good..." I admitted. "So that's the situation? Claver threw his lot in with Rigel, that much I knew. But the Skay..." I shook my head. "They're worse than the Mogwa. Who wants to be enslaved by alien AI?"

Leeza cast her eyes downward. "I didn't choose this—not really. Armel did. He was angry because he lost Germanica and was given a legion of stinking animals to preside over. At least Clavers are fully human."

I could have argued with her on that point, but I didn't say a word. She was talking freely, and I wanted to hear it all.

"How were you recruited... exactly?"

She shrugged. "Armel and I have long been... close. After we met the Skay, and he disappeared from *Legate*, we all returned to Earth. Armel followed me there, somehow. He tracked me down to my home, and he confided in me. I told him he was a madman. He smiled, shook his head, and informed me that he wasn't *asking*, he was *telling* me about my future. Then... he murdered me."

I thought back to the last time I'd seen Armel during the Armor World campaign. It had been aboard *Legate*, and he'd killed a lot of Mogwa with a wrench, as I recalled. "He came back to Earth... probably through one of Claver's secret gateways. He murdered you? As in permed you?"

"That's right. When I was revived, I was on this strange planet. Armel was conciliatory, and in time, I was given the rank of primus. It beat being dead."

She was claiming to have been shanghaied. Pressed into service against her will. It was possible—but I didn't buy it. She was probably giving me this line to gain sympathy and set up a possible defense in case I managed to drag her to Earth to stand trial.

"Okay," I said. "Let's say I believe all that malarkey. I'll even testify that I do, if it comes down to it."

She glanced sidelong at me again. I think I'd surprised her.

"How many troops has Claver got inside this dome?"

She shrugged. "A legion's worth, I'd say. You destroyed two more legions with the broadsides. But James—none of that really matters."

"Uh… why not?"

"Because the Skay are coming. Claver is fighting defensively, buying time with his troops, slowing you down—he only needs to keep it up for another day or so. Then, he'll have his reinforcements and the game will be over."

I felt a sick hole forming in my stomach. If she was telling the truth… We were well and truly screwed.

"I've got to get ahold of Graves!" I begged Natasha a few minutes later. I'd put out an urgent summons for her, and she'd come running.

Natasha had been reassigned to my unit when Graves and Winslade got promoted. They'd no longer needed a sidekick tech specialist—and everyone knew she was the best in the cohort. I'd pulled strings with Graves to get her back.

She looked worried when she reached my camp. "Kivi's dead," she said.

"Yeah? Well then… you're it. Build me a way to communicate. I don't care if you have to run a cord through the dome itself."

She looked down, thinking hard for a second. "Can I use your ghosts?"

"Cooper is dying to die for this."

"I'll need both of them…"

"Della too…? All right. Go."

Natasha got up and raced away. I had total faith in her. If it could be done, she'd do it. If she failed, that meant it was impossible in the first place, so it didn't matter.

I turned my mind to other things and found myself conflicted. I passed on what I knew to Manfred and the other nearby centurions via buzzers—but I didn't want to broadcast it.

After all, we knew we had moles in our officer core. I could understand why at this point. Claver was offering the assurance you could never be permed. Our troops were mercenaries to begin with, and I knew a lot of them only fought for Earth to gain a painful sort of immortality. If Claver could offer them one better than that: no chance of perming due to capture or missing-in-action problems... Well, some of these Varus boys were bound to be tempted.

Worse still was the news about the Skay. We'd been worried about Rigel, but we'd always figured we were pretty far apart, about 800 lightyears, and we could stop them before they reached Earth.

But not the Skay. We had cut a shifty deal with them the last time they'd come out here, but we couldn't fight them. Hell, the Mogwa seemed to be having a great deal of trouble doing it. They had thousands of advanced ships. If they couldn't stop the Skay, what chance did measly humans have?

Leeza watched me as I went through these stages of worry. She knew exactly what was going on inside my head—the turmoil her words had started. She didn't look guilty, not exactly, but she didn't look happy about it, either.

"You're going to fight to the very last, aren't you, McGill?"

"Damn straight I am."

"I almost admire that about you. It's like watching a pilot battle the controls of his craft, even as it plunges hopelessly toward the sea. You're doing everything you can—but you won't win. Not this time."

Pacing around her, I ignored her words. At another time, I might have been tempted to give her a good shaking and demand to know why she felt so smug about turning traitor on humanity. But not today. At this moment, all I could think of was getting the word out about what we were facing.

Carlos showed up, and he was all grins. He hadn't heard about Leeza's confessions. From his point of view, we'd just won a big victory over the Clavers.

"Hey, big guy. Are you chubbed over that win, or what? That was nothing short of military genius."

216

I glanced at him. So did Leeza. Neither of us smiled.

"What?" he asked. "Not even half-chubbed? I'm disappointed. Is your new girlfriend here giving you a hard time?"

"In a manner of speaking, yes," I said.

Carlos looked bewildered. "Well, hey, the troops are asking if they can break out a ration of—"

"No," I said.

"But they just—"

"No. We haven't won anything. Not yet. Tell them to stay alert and man their posts. Rotate the watch. One third of you must be eyes-peeled in every direction every hour."

Carlos sighed. "So it's like that? More Clavers marching our way? Great."

"Be ready to move out with five minutes' notice," I continued. "Tell everyone. Move!"

He turned around and trotted out.

"What possible positive quality could you see in that pig of a man?" Leeza asked me.

"Loyalty," I told her firmly. "That's his secret ingredient. Loyalty to Earth, to me—to his friends."

She shut the hell up after that.

-38-

Through non-standard wizardry, Natasha managed to get me a line to Graves, who relayed me up to Turov.

Despite what she'd said about landing with the legions, she'd stayed way behind the lines. She was on Clone World somewhere—but I doubted it was anywhere near the front. I could tell this by the background displayed around her pretty, scowling face. There was warm sunshine, a lovely lush forest and plenty of those air-swimming things floating around like jellyfish.

"McGill? This had better be good."

"It's not, sir. It's bad. Real bad."

I repeated what I'd heard from Leeza. Turov's eyes softened, then widened in alarm. "So... a Skay is coming? *Here?*"

"If Leeza is telling the truth, then yes."

"Well, Claver clearly wants to keep us from taking his fortress. His fall is inevitable, but he's causing it to take more time by making counterattacks. Are you sure she's not just helping him stall?"

I didn't think Claver's defeat was inevitable, but I decided to keep that thought to myself. I just shrugged.

"It all seems genuine to me."

She looked away, checking reports. "I guess this makes some sort of sense. Claver would only be fighting a delaying tactic for a sure reason.

"What are your orders, sir?" I asked.

"The same as before. Penetrate the enemy defenses. Keep advancing. We've got a full near-human legion, plus Varus. According to reports, Claver's men don't fight very well. You just wiped out hundreds of them."

"Uh... but we haven't gotten to the fortress itself yet. How are we supposed to—"

"McGill! Don't turn chicken on me now. If the Skay arrive before this is over, we'll have to run. That will mean leaving behind anyone who's stuck under that dome. Do you understand?"

Unfortunately, I did understand. I knew right off she was sitting at a safe distance with the lifters. She'd bug out and leave aboard *Legate*, and with the poor communications, some of us were bound to be left behind. In that situation, we were as good as permed.

It was a grim set of circumstances, but I could see her side of it. Legion Varus had to act now. We had to do or die.

Her face softened for a moment. "Into the valley of death rode the six hundred, McGill," she said.

"What?"

"It's from a poem... *the Charge of the Light Brigade*... It's about a battle that went badly. Anyway, my thoughts and prayers are with you. I can't give you much more than that, the dome is preventing my staff from running this operation properly."

"Charge..." I said. "We've got to charge, you're right. I'll talk to Graves."

She signed off, and I thought she might have felt bad about seeing me like this. Maybe she did care, a little bit, when perma-death was a real possibility.

Graves came back on, and he was easy to hear and understand. There was no fuzz or lag to the signal now.

"Are you inside the dome now, sir?" I asked.

"We've moved through the dome, yes. It was disgusting," he said. "I hated that sensation—pressing through that dome was unnatural."

"Damn straight. What're your orders, sir?"

I felt a surge of relief. Graves was the best of the Varus officers. He was our Blood-Primus, our second in command. It wasn't only that he was very experienced, having served on some of the first missions in Earth's mercenary history, but he was good at his job, too.

"McGill, you and Manfred team up. Pick up stragglers from the seventh and tenth units. They've both been broken and are down to a handful of men."

I blinked at this unwelcome news. Apparently, the Clavers hadn't done so badly on other fronts. The small engagements we were fighting all over under the dome hadn't all gone our way.

"Will do, sir."

"Both of those units are closer to the fortress than you are. You're dragging your ass, McGill. Get off your can and advance to contact. Graves out."

Before I could do so much as say 'yes sir' again, he was gone. I got to my feet in a rush.

"Unit!" I roared.

Every conversation stopped. Everyone who was loading or cleaning a gun froze. Scores of faces turned to look at me.

"Move out!"

Without pausing to answer any of a storm of questions, I grabbed my gear and started marching toward Claver's fortress. I could see the structure now, in glimpses between the treetops. It was less than five kilometers off. Not that long of a walk on a warm night.

All around me, people scrambled to break camp and follow. They hustled and complained, and some of them shook their dicks, cutting off a good piss mid-stream.

I didn't care. It was time to march. Graves, Turov—they were right. We had to attack, and we had to do it now. Waiting around just meant we might lose this whole thing.

Claver had gotten us to feel paranoid. He'd fed us troops in foolish counterattacks. But for all the crazy nature of these moves, whether they'd been orchestrated by Armel or Claver himself, they'd served to make us cautious. Like blazing a wild spray of gunfire over the heads of an enemy, they'd kept us ducking.

No more. We had to bring this fight to a conclusion, win or lose.

"Sir! Centurion, sir!" I turned to see Sargon. He had someone with him. Someone who was staggering and being half-dragged along.

He had Leeza by the arm, our treacherous prisoner. "Look, sir," Sargon said. "If we're going on the offensive, I can't be dragging her and my belcher at the same time. Barton handed her off to Harris, who handed her off to me. I—"

I halted and put up a gauntleted hand. "Don't worry about it, Sargon. You can leave her with me."

Around us troops streamed by heading toward the fortress. Every eye was aimed forward, scanning in every direction where the enemy might lie in wait.

Sargon blinked twice, but he nodded. Still, he hesitated, not wanting to walk away.

"Uh... sir? Are you—?"

"McGill," Leeza said, her thin face sharp in the dark. Her eyes were two glints that shone wetly. She stared at me. She never blinked, not once. "McGill... I want out of Claver's army. I want to get away from Armel, too."

"I can't do much about that."

"I know—but remember me. That's all I ask. When you find out that I spoke the truth today—you remember that. I gave you a break a long time ago, and I gave you another one today. You owe me."

Thinking that over, I nodded. "I'll remember."

Then, while Sargon watched open-mouthed, I shot her. She fell, and he looked at me in surprise.

"We can't take a prisoner with us while we assault Claver's castle," I told him. "She knew that, and you should have, too."

Sargon didn't say anything. He just nodded and walked back to his platoon. He was a veteran, not an officer. He would probably never advance to the officer ranks. He was where he belonged in this legion, and that wasn't a bad thing. The way I

221

figured it, the universe would be a better place if more people knew where they belonged in life.

Shouldering my rifle, I marched into the darkness. All around us, thousands more troops were advancing on every front. We had encircled Claver's fort, and we were going to make our assault before dawn.

-39-

It's one thing to assault a fortified position with artillery behind you, pounding the defenses—but we didn't have any of that. We didn't have air cover, space-borne bombardment, or even a few star-falls to soften them up.

We had men, we had rifles, a few belchers and plenty of armored suits. It was crap, really. We didn't even know how many of the enemy we were facing. For all I knew, Leeza had lied her ass off, and we were outnumbered two to one.

It didn't matter. We crept closer every hour. We were determined, we were willing to die, and we were professional troops. In the morning we would win, or we would lose. It was as simple as that.

The Blood Worlders hit the enemy lines first. I could tell, as a firefight erupted a long distance away, on the other side of the fortress. The fighting rapidly spread. According to reports, the battle had begun the moment the near-humans had dared to step out of the gloom of the forest.

"Look alive!" I shouted over tactical chat. "They're going to engage us before we get to their walls. Claver must have significant numbers to—"

That was as far as I got with my little speech. Plasma fire erupted from in front of us, tearing up trees and the muggy night air. Long before dawn pinked the hazy skies, we reached our first serious obstacle.

There were three turrets this time instead of just one. Manfred's unit and mine, along with other troops we'd gathered on the march, all threw ourselves onto our bellies.

We'd come to the forest's edge. My first troops had just set foot in the open, walking out into a shallow depression that looked like a wide, dry canal.

It was a killing zone if I'd ever seen one. The three turrets tore into our lines all at once. The trees lit up overhead. They caught fire, and burning branches fell. Here and there, a man went down, rolling, cooking and screaming.

Scrambling for their lives, the troops in the lead withdrew and took cover. For a few minutes, they were nothing more than targets, crawling in the dirt, ducking fire.

"Natasha! What's on your buzzers?"

"I've got nothing, sir. I sent out five, but they've all been brought down. I think they're using EMP pulses, or radio interference."

"Roger that. Ghosts!" I called out. "Advance and recon!"

The bushes rustled nearby. Cooper and Della, already stealthing in their suits, raced across the broad ditch toward the turrets. In the meantime, Sargon and his weaponeers were firing mini-missiles and belchers at the turrets, trying to take them out. So far, they'd yet to score a hit.

"Sir," Sargon called to me. "We can't get focused fire on those turrets. Against three of them, we can't coordinate safely. I've already lost one weaponeer."

"All right Sargon, stand down. I'll see if I can improve your odds. Harris, pepper the turrets with snap-rifle fire. Let them hear metal rain on their clam-shells. Keep them nervous."

"On it, Centurion."

There had been sporadic fire from our side up until now, but for the most part, my troops had been trying to keep low and stay alive. Now, a rattling storm of small-arms spanged and sparked on the clamshells. It wasn't going to do much, but it might give my ghosts a chance to—"

"McGill?" a breathless voice came into my ear.

"Della?" I demanded, recognizing her voice.

"I've made it across. I'm at the center turret."

"What have you got on the ground? Any supporting enemy troops?"

"Negative. I'm alone down here. I don't see Cooper, but he might have made it across, too. James, I'm going to climb this ladder and squeeze a grav-grenade into their front grill."

My teeth showed themselves. I grimaced for a moment, like a dog who was thinking about snarling. I'd never liked ordering Della to do anything insane. She was, after all, the mother of my only child.

"Do it," I said. "I'll adjust our covering fire."

I ordered Harris to get his lights to lay off the center turret. That took about half a minute, then I watched and waited for perhaps twenty seconds more…

Whump!

The center turret flashed and crumbled. It had been knocked out.

As if stung, the two outer turrets both swung toward their dead brother. They hosed the jungle with fire. Violet flashes tore up the brush, the ground, the smoking turret itself. They rained death on the area with abandon.

"Della!" I shouted, but then I noted her name had gone red in my HUD.

"She's gone, sir," Cooper reported. "I'm at the left turret. I can take it out the same way."

"Hold on… Sargon? Try to knock them out while they're distracted."

Sargon's weaponeers stood bravely and melted down the last turrets with focused fire. The Claver-Twos operating the guns were so busy tearing up the jungle to make sure they got Della, they'd given us a window.

A minute later, all three of the turrets were smoking wrecks. The jungle fell quiet again.

We hustled over the patch of open ground and advanced into the trees on the far side. We were getting close now. Soon, we'd face the fortress itself.

Taking a breather to patch ourselves up, we huddled in an outbuilding. The roof had been torn off and a few dead Clavers decorated the floor.

Centurion Manfred swaggered into the building and approached me. "Nice place you've got here, McGill."

"I call it home."

"Sorry to hear about your lady-friend, but she did a number on that turret."

"She sure did," I agreed. "How many men did you lose in that action?"

"Six. You?"

"Seven, I think."

Manfred laughed. "You always have to one up me, don't you?"

"It's in my blood. Listen, has your tech specialist managed to keep a buzzer in the air?"

"No, no one has. Claver has some kind of trick that keeps knocking them down. We're marching into his lair blind—only you've been inside before."

"I didn't see that much of it," I admitted. "I know there are at least ten floors, and a room down low has several gateways in it, including ones that go back to Earth."

"Seriously? That cheater. That's how he gets around so easily. He clones himself and slips from world to world like a ghost."

"That might be all over with if we take his fortress down in the morning." I thought that over, and Manfred kept on talking—but I didn't listen to any more of it. I soon nodded off.

I felt a boot kick my boot. I woke up with a start.

"Is it time?"

"Yeah," Manfred said. "Half an hour until dawn."

I snorted and stretched out again. "Wake me up with fifteen minutes to go."

He left, and the next thing I knew Kivi was shaking me. "McGill! Time to move out!"

"All right," I said, and I climbed to my feet and stretched. I rammed pocket-warmed rations into my mouth, chewed, swallowed and guzzled some water. Five minutes later, I was moving, and my unit gathered up with me. We marched toward the fortress and reached the limits of the forest.

"There she is," I said.

The fort was encircled by a bald area of land. It sat on a low hill surrounded by knee-high grasses. A circular wall surrounded the building itself, which was blocky and ugly-looking.

"Pure puff-crete," Manfred said from my side. "It's not such a much, now is it?"

"I guess not." For a few seconds, I watched the air-swimmers drifting near the high windows. I wondered what attracted them up there to flutter around. Did Claver feed them? Somehow, I doubted he'd bother.

We waited for the attack signal, and we didn't have to wait long. Graves came onto command chat and gave us a few choice words.

"Legion Varus and support Legion Twelve, you're about to get your chance for revenge upon one of the greatest criminals in human history. Adjunct Claver, who's gone by countless names in his countless existences, is about to meet justice. I hereby order you to kill every person in that structure. Have no mercy. Have no regrets. They won't have any for you if we lose today."

It was quite a crappy pep-speech, even for Graves. No one cheered much. A few grumbled, others angrily spat and stared at Claver's walls.

Sensing a mood-lifter was in order, I lifted a fist and pumped it in the air. My visor flipped open, I roared "Varus!" over and over.

Others picked up the cry. All up and down the front line, a hundred throats shouted together—then a thousand.

"That's what I like to see," Graves said. "Now, get in there, and take them down. Don't be afraid to die. Let the bio specialists sort out the dead. Advance!"

Despite Graves' words, not all of us were cleared to charge immediately. Instead, about half the men ran off toward the walls, which were perhaps four hundred meters distant.

Predictably, dozens of turrets folded out of the outer wall and opened up on us with chattering fire. Men and near-men were cut down by the hundreds.

The light troops in the front absorbed most of these lethal bolts. In response, every weaponeer we had focused return fire from the rear ranks. A gush of belcher plasma, mini-missiles and other weapons roared and lashed the turrets. Some were knocked out, others continued their withering fire.

When the front rank was about two hundred meters from the base of the wall, Graves ordered the second rank to advance. Manfred and I moved forward at a brisk trot. Those walls looked taller with each step we took.

"We'll never scale them," Manfred said. "Not even with grav-boots."

"Nope," I agreed. "We'll have to bore through, or use charges to blow a hole in the base."

Manfred gave me a worried look which I didn't return. Sure, I knew that chewing through puff-crete with small-ball weapons was easier said than done. But there was no use arguing about it. This was our time to do or die.

"Look out! Up top!" roared someone off to my left.

I looked up, and instinctively lifted an arm to shield my visor. Dozens of enemy troops—no hundreds—were now standing on the top of the wall. They had assault rifles, and they were blazing away into our charge.

"This is insane!" Manfred called out next to me. "Graves must have sold out!"

A bolt spun him around then, and he fell. I ran to him and picked him up by his ruck. "You okay?"

"Just got the wind knocked out of me," he rasped.

He was on his feet, so I let go of him. He staggered in my wake.

It didn't matter if he was dead on his feet or not. We had to reach that wall.

-40-

My legion's first wave was pretty much destroyed. A few turned to run, and we tripped them and jeered. Sure, we were about to get ours. Maybe we'd be broken and routed by ninety-percent casualties, too. But for now, we had to keep our morale up, even if it was at the expense of our own panicked comrades.

Throughout history, even the best armies of Earth tended to break somewhere around the point of a fifty percent loss. The animal in every man's mind can't take much more than that. Almost anyone can panic and run even when you know you'll be shot in the back. Honestly, you aren't even thinking at that point.

Professional legionnaires, however, were a different breed. We were more akin to the crazies of history: the Viking berserkers, the Spartans, or the Samurai. We knew we could die and return to life. Even more importantly, we were intimately familiar with death in all its grisly forms. This combination of experience and know-how left us uniquely able to keep our cool under fire.

And so we charged those tall, slick walls. They loomed up, thirty meters or more, impenetrable to any light weapons. It usually took star-falls or something stronger to blow a breach in a wall like this one.

Fortunately, we hadn't been sent into this battle without equipment. We had tube-punches with us, one per unit. These were simple devices intended to punch a hole in just about anything. They were tubes with an explosive at one closed end. The explosive had a shaped armor-piercing shell sitting on top of it. This specially designed weapon only worked once, but it could penetrate several meters of granite, or a few centimeters of collapsed armor.

Puff-crete was tough, tougher than tempered steel, but it wasn't stardust. When we got to the base of the wall, most of our troops fired up at the enemy on the battlements. They were firing down at us, and we were dying three to one in the exchange.

But this distraction allowed a few weaponeers to get their tube-guns into position. Like the sappers of old, they blew head-sized holes in the puff-crete. That wasn't enough to take it down, of course. It didn't even penetrate to the other side—but that wasn't the purpose.

"Fire in the hole!" shouted a man nearby.

I dropped my rifle and threw myself on top of it. A shockwave rolled over my back. Chunks of puff-crete struck my armored back-plate here and there, feeling like a shower of bullets.

Scrambling up, I got my rifle to my shoulder just in time. The smoking breach was there, no more than two meters wide—but it was wide enough.

We rushed inside. More Clavers met us, again as if they'd expected this.

A grim fire-fight began. I soon realized that the enemy strength *was* low. They'd been fighting hard, and they seemed to be numerous, but if Leeza had been right, we'd outnumbered them two to one from the start. We'd destroyed thousands outside this wall. Now the castle garrison was facing us, and as best I could tell, it was all they had left.

Even though they had the drop on us, we killed them all. We did it by simple numbers. We had a hundred men coming through that breach, and they had maybe twenty defenders. When these had been cut down, we rushed to the central building itself.

Inside the walls, it didn't look quite like a fortress. It looked more like a tall, blocky building. I'd been inside it, and on each occasion, it had seemed very utilitarian. I don't think the Clavers had really envisioned fighting over this ground. Maybe the walls and the dome itself were afterthoughts. He'd depended on the secrecy of his location to protect him.

Cheering hoarsely, we marched toward the doors. They were steel, nothing more. We blew them down and walked inside. Clavers ran from us, and we gunned them down. Most of these were Class-twos, not really fighters. They barely resisted our advance.

"Where is the enemy?" Harris demanded.

We looked at each other in the smoky corridor, breathing hard and coughing.

"They've either been wiped out, or... come on!"

The elevators had been disabled. I rushed toward the stairs leading down, having a sudden thought.

A few more Claver-Threes met us on the stairs and battled grimly, but we overwhelmed them. I had a score of men at my back, and we weren't in a charitable mood.

"Where are we going, McGill?" Harris demanded. "Isn't the king at the top of this castle?"

"No. Not this time. He's down low, on their version of Gray Deck."

He looked at me, and his eyes bulged. "A teleport room? You think they're bugging out?"

"Of course."

Howling as if personally affronted, Harris rushed with me down the steps. Confused troops raced in our wake.

I knew what was motivating Harris. After a tough fight, he liked to execute his enemies. He wanted to see them dead for all the trouble they'd brought to him.

We reached the portal room, and it took a few minutes to break through. Finally, we managed it, and we charged inside.

A familiar figure sat in the control booth in the center. The gateway posts were all demolished, smoldering piles of delicate electronics—except for one of them.

Instead of a Claver-Two operator, the man in the booth was a Claver-Prime. I could tell the difference instantly. Instead of

231

having a blank, slightly concerned expression, his face was full of calculation and amusement.

"Well done, McGill!" he said, and he lifted his resting boots off the control panel. He pointed toward the last operating set of gateway posts. "I'd hoped the cavalry would arrive in time, and it has, but I hadn't dare dream it would be you."

"Shut your filthy hole!" Harris roared—advancing on him with his rifle trained on his chest. "Surrender, Claver!"

"Oh, I surrender. But McGill… time is wasting. The officers, the traitors you seek—they went that way."

My eyes went to the gateway posts. I wasn't sure where they led to. There was no indication—no signs, no colors, no pictures—nothing. But I was sure this wasn't the same set of posts I'd gone through the last time I'd teleported to Earth.

"Uh…" I said, as men filled the room behind me.

Other officers and troops were arriving every second. Most of the invading force had gone upstairs rather than down, but even so, I knew it was only a matter of time before some uppity officer like Fike would show up and take over the situation. If I was going to do anything unexpected, this was the window I had to work with.

"Claver-X?" I asked.

He pointed his finger at me, and he grinned. "That's right, McGill. Every time we meet, my estimation of your brain's quality rises. Most of my brothers consider you to be a lucky ape, did you know that?"

"I'd gathered as much."

"Well, they're wrong. No one gets lucky as often as you do. I'd stake my reputation on it."

"Centurion?" Harris demanded. "Can I at least arrest this man?"

I thought that over for a few seconds. "No. Stand down, Harris. Claver, talk to me. What's this about? What's on the far side of that gateway?"

Claver-X stood up.

Harris tightened his grip on his rifle. His finger massaged the trigger lovingly.

232

Taking no notice, Claver-X smiled and sauntered down to meet me like we were best friends at a picnic. He was watching me, only me.

This version of Claver was an enigma. He was a twisted member of his shared genome—you might even call him a mutant. Bad grows were bound to happen now and then. The phenomenon was more common among those who are revived over and over. Biotic copies are messy, and they didn't always come out perfect. Sometimes, there was a twist of the body. I'd been born missing my toes once. Another time, I'd become a murderous scoundrel.

But Claver-X was a different kind of clone. He was nicer and more compassionate than his countless brothers. He'd been born smart and mean like the rest—but with different goals. Seeking something more than trade and trickery, he'd tried to create a female Claver. That had been a cardinal sin according to his clones, and they'd banished him. Like all Clavers, he'd proven to be harder to get rid of than one would think.

I stepped forward, allowing my rifle's muzzle to dip toward the floor. Just like him, I offered up a big smile and a welcoming handshake.

We clasped hands like buddies and shook. Everyone behind me was gaping at the display. Here I was, almost making out with this villain, and the crowd of troops surrounding us couldn't believe it.

"Claver," I said quietly when we were up close and clasping hands. "I can only keep this situation from going bad for about another minute. Primus Graves is on his way down here—and he doesn't like you. He'll take charge, and he'll probably execute your ass in five minutes flat... if you're lucky."

"Graves is here?" Claver-X asked, and a flicker of concern ran over his features.

"Damn straight he is," I lied. "Now, why don't you tell me the nature of your offer before this gets ugly? Where does that gateway go to?"

He shook his head, and a sly expression grew on his face. "You know I can't do that, McGill. I have to have an edge."

"What do you propose, then? We've got like ninety seconds left."

Claver's eyes slid toward the exit. More men were wandering in now, looking bewildered. Only Harris looked angry. He still had his gun aimed at Claver's head, but that seemed to have no effect at all on the wily bastard.

"All right," Claver said. "You drive a hard bargain, but I'll walk through with you. We'll step out, and we'll see the answer to your questions."

I snorted. "Why the hell should I do that? Why should I let you go anywhere?"

He shook his head. "You're not thinking, McGill. I waited here for you. I could have left—everyone else did. Winslade, Toro, Armel—everybody. Why did I wait here to make this offer?"

I thought that over, and I didn't have an easy answer. "I don't know. Why?"

"Because I'm trying to help! Let me help. Let me show you something interesting."

Damnation. Claver was so good at this kind of bamboozling. Did he really just want to capture me? Just to say he'd done it?

But if that were true, he wouldn't be Claver-X. He would be Claver Prime, trying to screw me. I decided to test him.

"What was the lady-Claver's name?" I asked him.

"What?"

He was blinking now. His face sagged a little. He hadn't been expecting this line of questioning.

"You heard me. You made her. You brought her into the world, and then you let her get killed. What was her name?"

"How could you—never mind. A test... I get it... Her name was Abigail. Happy now, McGill?"

I nodded. I was happy. He seemed saddened, but not pissed off. Normally, regular Clavers lost their minds when I brought up the Lady Claver. They denied her existence and became violently angry over the topic. This truly might be Claver-X.

"All right," I said. "Let's take a walk."

Moving with Claver-X, I walked toward the single set of operating gateway posts. Harris objected immediately.

"Sir! Centurion McGill! Don't take this the wrong way, sir, but have you lost your frigging mind?"

At the gateway, I turned back to face him. "If I don't come back, I got screwed. Give a full report to Graves. I absolve you of any guilt in regard to this decision."

"That's very nice of you, sir," he said. "But this has to be the most bat-shit—"

I didn't hear the rest of it. I'd stepped out with Claver-X. We went together, vanishing into the unknown.

-41-

Trust is a funny thing. When you come right down to it, there are two flavors that I know of.

One is the trust you have in your tightest allies. The men you've fought with for years. The wife you've been happily married to for a decade. That sort of thing.

The other kind of trust is based on logic. If I give a man half the money for something I'm buying up front, and I know he wants the rest real bad, I have a reasonable level of trust that he'll deliver on his promise to get the rest of it.

That was the kind of trust I had with Claver-X. I knew he wasn't always on the same side I was, but I also knew he wasn't my sworn enemy. He'd helped me out several times, in fact, and I'd let him slide now and again as well. We had the kind of trust a cop has with a gangster informant. There was no bond of friendship, no history of great times—just a reasoned expectation that the other guy would probably hold up his part of any given deal.

Another reason I stepped out was related to the general personality of all Clavers. They were traders—the best Humanity had ever produced. They often made deals with aliens who would have killed anyone else on sight.

How could he have managed to build up such a series of deals and repeat customers if he screwed everyone along the way? The answer was that he couldn't have. When a Claver made a bargain, he kept it, even if he regretted it later on.

And so it was that when I stepped into nothingness and exited the other side, I had no expectation of arrest or death. I didn't know what I was getting into, but I knew that this man wouldn't go to all this trouble just to screw me over. He wanted to show me something, and he wanted to show it to me desperately.

When I first stepped out onto an overgrown hilltop, I knew right off I was on a different planet. The trees ran with sap and were shaped like pineapples. The sky overhead—it was dark. At first, I thought it was night, but then I saw that strange, smoldering sun.

"Dark World?" I asked in surprise. "You took me back to Dark World?"

"Yes."

"But why?"

"Come this way."

I followed him, and he showed me another pineapple plant with thick, bulging roots. These were swarmed with large dark shapes.

Unslinging my rifle, I almost shoved Claver away when he put a hand on the muzzle, pushing it down.

"They're harmless," he said. "They're feeding, that's all."

"They're Vulbites!"

"Shhh… Of course they're Vulbites. This is their home planet, remember?"

"Yeah…"

I looked around, disquieted. When any man saw a two hundred kilo insect, he felt an immediate urge to kill it. I was battling with this instinct right now.

"Look up," Claver-X told me. "You might see something else that's familiar."

Following his pointing hand, I squinted into the dark skies. What was weird about Dark World was its sky. The sun was a brown dwarf—a sun so dim and small that it was like the dying embers of a campfire that's long since run out of wood to burn. You could see the stars at the horizons, far from the glimmering sun itself.

"Uh…" I said. "I don't… wait a second. Is that part of a space station?"

"Yes. They're rebuilding it. The orbital shipyard. These bugs—the Vulbite race—they do more than fight for Rigel. They're relentless factory workers."

"And this star is halfway between Earth and Rigel," I said. "We can't let them rebuild this base. They'll churn out ships and attack."

Claver-X watched me closely, listening. He didn't cackle or say snide things—at least not as often as the regular Clavers did.

"I took down the first space factory," I told him.

"I know."

"That's why you brought me here, isn't it? Well, I hate to disappoint, but I don't think I could pull it off again."

Claver snorted. "I know that. Damn, no wonder the others are always calling you a dumbass. You've got to go back to Earth, McGill. You've got to show them this, use your suit cams."

I touched them, having forgotten—fortunately, they were recording. They had been since the battle back on Clone World.

"All right," I said. "I can do that."

I turned to go, but he called me back.

"Wait. Have you heard anything else about Abigail?" he asked.

That question floored me. He honestly seemed to want to know.

"Uh…" I said, considering a half-dozen cruel lies. "No, I'm sorry. Not really. I know that just mentioning her to other Clavers drives them crazy. That's about it."

He nodded. "A pity. If you ever do learn something… keep me in mind. I'd owe a favor to anyone who could give me concrete information."

"You mean she might be alive? Or you want to know who killed her?"

"Either," he said. "All Clavers are hard to stamp out, you might have noticed. I… I still have hope."

"Okay, then. It's a deal. Are you staying here? On Dark World?"

"Yes. I must. I must rejoin the others."

I blinked, and I understood. "So the rest of them are here too? Building a fleet? Building ships to carry legions of Class-Threes?"

"Yes."

Right then, I gripped my rifle, and I thought about putting him down. One less crazy Claver running around...

But I didn't. I *couldn't*. This guy had helped me out with vital intel. He wouldn't have done that if he hadn't wanted to help Earth. At least, that's how I figured it.

"You want us to stop your brothers, don't you?" I asked. "From taking over humanity? From ruling Earth with Rigel's help?"

"Yes, I do. It's not natural. We're not conquerors. We're a race of traders. We should stay in our lane. Sometimes, I think my other selves are madmen."

"Okay," I said. "I can believe that. The only thing I know about Abigail is what we found here at Dark World. I know our techs ran a DNA sample and found out she was female—and your relative."

Claver-X nodded thoughtfully. "Who did the DNA sample?"

"Natasha, I think."

He nodded again. "Okay, thanks for the lead. I'll check into it."

I frowned a little, wondering if I'd made a mistake. Using DNA to reconstruct a person from scratch was possible if you'd lost a body-scan, but you also needed the engrams. What use would a body be without a mind and memories to help it function?

"That's all I've got for you," I said, wondering if I'd already said too much.

"Farewell," Claver-X said, and he offered his hand.

After a moment's hesitation, I shook his hand. Then I stepped back through the gateway posts.

On the far side, a snarling team of techs and officers grabbed me when I appeared. They scolded me, arrested me, questioned me, and even kicked me in the balls a few times.

"You went AWOL," Graves said firmly. "That's what I know."

"Sir, I was investigating an interesting lead. I was talking to Claver-X."

"Stop calling him that. You were tricked, McGill. All the Claver-Primes are evil. There isn't a Santa Claus hiding in the pack. Not one."

They replayed the vids my body-cams had recorded, and they tried not to look impressed. A few minutes later, I saw a fire-team rush through the gateway posts I'd just come from. They had their weapons ready, and their power-armor humming.

"Uh…" I said. "That's a bad idea."

"What?" Graves asked. "Are you the only one that's allowed to wander off and do as he pleases? Those men are going to arrest your Claver and bring him back for questioning."

"Ha!" I said, grinning. "Now I know you're having me on. Claver-X—no Claver ever born—would have left those coordinates alone. He'd rewire those posts. Your men are either in limbo, or in some flaming pit of hell-fire."

Graves looked toward the posts in concern. He blinked twice, and then he turned to one of the techs. "Has the failsafe member of the team come back yet?"

"No sir. Not yet."

Graves glanced back in my direction, and his face soured. "You're telling me those men are permed?"

"Look," I said. "I half-invented the failsafe 'one-man-returns' tactic. Either they've been wiped out, or they're solidly screwed. Even if your tech is still getting a connected-circuit signal back from those posts—they aren't coming back."

We waited for about ten minutes. Graves finally growled in frustration.

"Should we send another team, sir?" the tech asked.

"Do you want to go?"

The tech's face turned gray. "Uh… no sir."

"That's what I thought. Mark them down MIA. Damn that Claver..."

Now, at this point, one would think that Graves would be in a more conciliatory mood. That maybe, just maybe, he'd be contrite and thankful for my warning. After all, only four good men had been permed. If he'd sent another team, that would have made it eight.

But no. That's not how people work most of the time. They usually vent their rage on the messenger of bad tidings.

"All right, McGill," he said with clenched teeth. "If you're done having a chuckle at my men's expense, let's talk seriously. We know they're rebuilding a fleet at Dark World. That makes it a direct threat to Blood World—but not to Earth."

"Things are worse than that, sir. If they can reproduce the space factory, it will churn out warships—"

"Yes, right. But stop and think, McGill. Don't you understand that we're doing the same thing even now? We've got advanced bases of our own in the frontier zone."

Blinking, I considered his words. They did make some sense. I didn't know everything about Earth's military efforts. Many secrets were floating around these days. Earth was stronger than ever, and we were still building up our military all the time.

"I guess that makes sense," I said. "Still, it can't be good news that they're building so near one of our planets."

"Of course not. But let's get back to your unsanctioned actions: By stepping through and reporting back, you've just confirmed to Claver Command that we know about their base. They'll *expect* an attack."

"You mean... you already knew they had that base?"

"I can neither confirm nor deny that."

"Huh... so you're assuming that Claver-X was bullshitting me? Maybe showing me things to lure us in?"

"That's my assumption. Now we can't assume we'll have the advantage of surprise. Here are your new orders, Centurion: get out of my sight. Stop screwing around with things you don't understand."

241

I slunk out of his office, considering his words. He could be right. Like Claver-X had said, it was best to stay in your lane.

-42-

We'd mopped up the Clavers on Clone World, but I strongly suspected that more of them would pop up here and elsewhere. That's how Claver liked to play the game, he always planned for the worst. He assumed he would be killed at some point, and so he built a web-work of lies, deals, hideouts and secret stashes to make sure he'd breathe again.

So, even though we'd destroyed this nest and burned it clean, there were bound to be more of his kind springing up like cockroaches in the future. Hell, I'd already been treated to the sight of one of them by Claver-X.

On the third day after the fortress fell, I was summoned from a search-and-destroy patrol back to *Legate*. A meeting of the brass was in progress there. Apparently my name had come up in strong terms.

Ambling to a lifter, I was transported back to *Legate* in comfort. Nineteen minutes flat after I'd received the summons, I was helping myself to some alcohol from a blue bottle in the Gold Deck conference room.

"What's this all about, sirs?" I asked.

A line-up of officers watched me pour and mix their booze in stony silence. Graves was there, as were a dozen other Primus-level subordinates. Surprisingly, Sub-Tribune Fike and Tribune Turov were both in attendance. They had their hands on the big conference table, fingers laced.

"You look like you're about to start praying," I said, but a laugh died in my throat.

"Centurion McGill," Turov began, "do you recall when the Skay first visited Earth?"

"Uh…" I said. "How could I forget? Is that big basketball orbiting our homeworld again? Is that what this is about?"

If it was, then I could understand all the long faces. The Skay were a recently discovered race of superior beings. They were Galactics, just like our own overlords the Mogwa—but the Skay were even scarier.

"No, not yet," Turov said. "But they are coming here… aren't they?"

"Um… maybe. I don't know, really. Claver-X said something about it, as I recall."

Fike rattled a computer paper, and he leaned forward. Galina nodded to him, indicating he should take over. "Right, Centurion. We know about that. Since we've gotten that bit of intel, we've been scanning long-range for any kind of unusual fleet movements from the Galactic Core. Do you know what we discovered?"

My eyes slid from one of them to the other. They had a certain look going on now, and I recognized it. I'd seen this sort of yellow-eyed suspicion and cageyness on the faces of authority figures countless times in the past. The day I'd collapsed the roof of my high school drama department, for instance—it had been a freak accident, of course—but they'd had that same damned *look*. Every teacher and administrator had stared at me back then, the same as these officers were doing now.

I took a big gulp of my beverage. "So… something's coming?"

"Yes," Fike said. "Not just one something, but *two* somethings. Two very large contacts are approaching this star system. They are converging on our position and will arrive within the next few days."

"Well sirs…" I said, taking my beverage to one of the two open chairs at the table and making myself at home. I noticed the spot I'd chosen was at one end of the long table, while the other seat opposite was vacant as well. I wondered vaguely who it had been reserved for. "Sirs, I have to take this moment to point out how quickly my scouting efforts have paid off in this instance."

Fike blinked at me. "How's that?"

I gave him a warm Georgia smile, but it didn't seem to have any effect. "I can't recall a day when my efforts at gathering military intel have paid off so handsomely. I told you just yesterday the Skay were coming to dinner, and here we go and detect them today. I can only conclude that this gathering is meant to honor my contributions to the valiant history of Legion Varus."

A scoff erupted. I didn't see who'd made the sound, but I scanned for the culprit. It was rude, after all, to rain on my parade that way. I couldn't figure out from their sour expressions who it might be. It could have been any of them.

Fike leaned back and crossed his arms. He had a look of disgust on his face. Turov sucked in a breath and leaned forward, taking over this inquisition again. I took the momentary pause during their switchover to gulp my beverage. It was mostly gin, but the expensive, fruity kind. It wasn't too bad.

"McGill," she began. "This isn't funny. We know you shared your body-cam data. Your tapper's astronomical detection software also confirmed you actually did visit Dark World on the seventh of—"

"Hey!" I interrupted, leaning forward with a sudden thought. "Did that fire team that stepped out to Dark World ever come home?"

"No," Graves said in a stony voice. "They did not. They've been effectively permed."

"Four more good men lost due to your unapproved actions, McGill," Fike chimed in.

I shrugged. "I didn't order them to do it."

The officers exchanged glares. I might have poked a sore spot, but if you don't do that now and again you'll always get blamed for everything. After all, the truth was on my side in this case.

"McGill," Turov asked, "let's get to the point. These two distinct contacts can only be sizeable groups of ships, or one

245

very large vessel, in each case. Who do you think is coming to Clone World?"

I blinked at them in confusion. "Can there be any doubt?"

"Just tell us what you know, dammit McGill," Fike said.

"I don't know anything. But I can perform basic logical operations. One of those contacts is an individual Skay. The other one is probably a large fleet, something about the size of old Battle Fleet 921. In other words: the Mogwa."

You could have heard a pin drop after that. They all stared for maybe five long seconds. That can be a very long time when you're getting stared at by two dozen hostile eyeballs.

Honestly, I think they already knew the truth of my words. Hell, if I could figure it out, they should be able to as well.

Leaning back and sighing, Turov looked like she wanted to put her face in her hands. But she didn't. You couldn't just go and do that sort of thing in front of a load of brass.

"How much longer until he arrives?" she asked.

Fike glanced at his tapper. "He's overdue. But he's not onboard yet, I have alerts watching."

"Me too," she said.

"Uh…" I said. "Who else is coming to dinner?"

My long arm with a long finger at the end of it pointed toward the opposite end of the table, where the sole empty chair was waiting.

"Praetor Drusus, of course," Galina said. "He's stepping out from Earth at any moment now."

My jaw sagged a little, and my mouth hung opened. I closed it with a snap.

-43-

Drusus arrived a few minutes later. I'd always liked Drusus. When I'd first met him, he'd been in Turov's seat. He'd been the best tribune of Earth's worst legion, and he'd led my beloved Varus like no other.

Now, many years later, he was leading Home Planet defense. It only made sense that he was involved in this one. He'd been placed in charge of coordinating Earth's defense on two distinct occasions in the past, so I wasn't surprised he'd taken an interest today with this new looming threat.

"Ladies, gentlemen… and McGill?" Drusus said this last when his eyes finally came to rest on me.

I stood and saluted like the rest—and I grinned hugely. No one else was smiling, so I figured the top dog could use a friendly little boost.

"I'm not even going to ask why a centurion is here in a senior officers' meeting," Drusus said, taking the last seat at the head of the table. "Who here can tell me if anything new has been learned about this approaching threat?"

My hand shot up. Drusus pretended not to notice. He turned to Turov instead. "Tribune, you're in charge of this expedition. Has anything happened here that might engender the interest of not one, but two forces from the Galactic Core?"

"We were discussing this as you arrived, sir. It's this committee's belief that one of the forces was sent by the

Mogwa, the other by the Skay. We don't know that they're hostile, or the nature of their compositions. However, as the Mogwa and the Skay have been at war recently, we might find ourselves caught in the middle."

My hand slowly lowered itself. Galina had just taken my idea, spruced it up and served it to the top brass like it was her own. I thought about complaining, but I decided not to. After all, the important thing was that Drusus knew about the theory.

"I see…" he said, looking down again. "Now the question is: why are these two combatants coming here? What possible use is Clone World when the majority of the inhabitants have already fled?"

My hand bounced up again. Sometimes, I think it has an evil will of its own.

Sighing, Drusus finally met my gaze. "Yes, Centurion? Do you have something material to add to this discussion?"

"I sure do, Praetor, sir. I think they're coming here to fight it out."

Drusus blinked once. "And why's that, McGill?"

"Well sir, the Skay are working with Rigel, and Rigel is working with the Clavers. The Skay must have gotten a distress call from Clone World. Why else would they come all the way out here to the boonies? The second group, however, that's harder to figure out. What I would assume is that they're the Mogwa. After seeing the Skay launch a fleet toward Province 921, they've decided to intercept it."

"And what special knowledge might you have of the situation that would lead you to these conclusions?"

"Uh… just plain common sense, sir, that's all. The Mogwa don't give a rip about this province. The only thing that would bring them out so far from the Core is an opportunity to block their worst enemy."

"Hmm…" Drusus said, nodding slowly. "Your scenario does make sense…"

"Excuse me, Praetor," Turov interrupted in a mild tone. "I don't recommend that anyone take McGill's advice on anything at face value."

Drusus faced her. "What's your theory, then? And this time, please follow-up your theory with a recommended action."

That stopped Turov cold. She was always long on talk and short on plans of action.

"I see," Drusus said after a painful moment during which Turov remained silent. He slewed his gaze back to me. "McGill, I understand that you recently traveled to Dark World."

"That's right, sir."

"You saw evidence of enemy forces building up there. Did you see anything that would indicate they had a fleet big enough to pose a threat directly to Earth?"

"Uh…" I said, chewing that one over. "I did not. But I was only there for a few minutes. I couldn't scan what was in orbit with nothing but a tapper."

"I understand. Turov?"

"Praetor?"

"What do you think we should do now?"

Galina looked flustered. "I think we should pull out. Pull everything back to Earth. Defend the homeworld."

Drusus nodded thoughtfully. "Tribune Fike? What do you think?"

"It's probably inappropriate for me to provide input, sir. But I would withdraw, too. The risk of getting involved in a serious battle between two Galactics is too great.

Drusus gazed at him for a moment. At last, he nodded his head.

Then he looked at me. "McGill. What would you do?"

I was stunned, and from the looks of it, so was everyone else. He hadn't asked for input from any of the others present, who were all primus-level officers. He eyeballed me instead.

Staring back at him, I thought it over for a moment. "I'd bring every battlewagon we have right here, sir. Make a stand—or at least pretend to."

"Bold," Drusus said.

"Insane!" Turov squawked.

"Why would you do that, McGill?" Drusus asked me.

249

"Well, here's the way I see it: everyone will assume we're running for Earth. Therefore, right here is the one place they won't expect to find us. The Rigel boys might send a fleet out here, but they probably won't. If the Skay and the Mogwa have come to fight, we should at least watch it. We can join either side we want to, or just sit neutral and look tough. Either way, they can't help but be impressed by the size of our new fleet."

Praetor Drusus slid his eyes toward Turov next. "Is McGill wrong?"

She threw up her hands. "Probably not. But we're playing with fire, Praetor. If any of our enemies surprise us at Earth, the homeworld will be defenseless."

"What good is a fleet that sits forever in your home port, sir?" I asked. "If this battle is tight, we can choose an ally and help them win."

"Praetor," Fike said, leaning forward and indicating me with a thrust of his chin. "Why are we even discussing this with McGill? He's not known for his strategic ingenuity."

"No. Only his gut-instincts. You people invited him, so I'm including him. Does anyone else here have a good idea they'd like to share? A third option?"

No one moved a muscle, not even Graves. They were typical mid-level brass: scared of their own shadows.

"Precisely," Drusus continued. "I'll have to think this over... how long do we have?"

"Ninety hours before the first fleet arrives," Fike said. "Four hours later, the second fleet will reach this system."

"Which one will make it here first?"

"The one that looks like it's coming from the Skay provinces, sir."

Drusus winced. "That does change things... with that new detail, I believe we have to stay here."

"Why's that?" I asked out of turn.

He looked at me seriously. "Because if the Skay reach Clone World, and they find we've destroyed it—where do you think they'll go next?"

"Oh... Earth, right?" I asked.

250

"It's a strong possibility, and it's a risk we can't take. We've left a trail from Clone World to Earth. We can't allow the Skay to make the connection and chase us."

"This is turning into a holding action then," Fike said grimly. "We've got to keep the Skay occupied for four hours—long enough for the Mogwa to arrive."

"Wait!" Galina said in a near panic. "Ninety hours isn't long enough to get our fleet out here!"

Drusus checked his tapper. "Normally, you'd be right. But Earth has already sent them. Every ship we have is on the way here, right now."

The officers looked stunned. "When did you make this choice?"

"About an hour ago the joint council in Geneva gave the order. They're watching us all—right now, in fact. This conference is being transmitted home live via deep-link."

A few stunned eyeballs rolled toward the corners of the room, including mine. They looked around at the camera pickups. They were pinpricks of light—glowing blue dots. But they always looked like that. We had no idea we were being broadcast.

"But..." Galina said, "ninety hours?"

"Yes. We can do that with our core fleet. Our new ships are faster. Older models and transports like *Legate* are much slower, of course. Speed has been a design goal of our new fleet for years. If you have a growing volume of space to protect, you increase the value of your forces by making them faster."

"Of course," Fike said. "Speed is a force multiplier. If you can't get your ships to the battle in time, they're useless."

"But..." Galina repeated. "Such a dramatic increase... I didn't realize we'd made such advances in propulsion. Three days instead of three weeks? That's very impressive."

She was looking kind of stunned, like her mind was recalculating certain realities she'd been counting on. That made me wonder if they'd kept these advances a secret up until now because of her, and other officers with questionable loyalty.

"I came out here," Drusus continued, "to see if there was better intel on the battlefront. Sometimes people can see a tactical situation more clearly from ground zero. But this visit has only confirmed our plans. We're going to meet the Galactics in this star system."

Turov still looked sick. Fike was pale, too.

But me...? I was grinning. I'd guessed the right move, and Drusus and all the council members watching us back home knew it. That was kind of cool.

-44-

Praetor Drusus wasn't one of these fancy new admirals in their slick new starships. No sir, he was an old-fashioned ground-pounder. He'd risen through the ranks in the early days when Earth's battles were fought solely on foreign worlds from one continent to the next.

As a result, he was respected by just about everyone. We readied our ship, running drills and positioning *Legate* far outside the star system, so we couldn't be surprised by the arrival of the Skay right on top of us.

At first, I didn't see much point to doing infantry drills in what was bound to be a nasty space-battle—but I was wrong. The drills mostly had to do with jump-suits.

If we could penetrate the enemy defenses, we were going to get a chance to fight. Wearing new rigs and teleporting into the enemy ships, we could do some serious damage.

"Uh…" I said, inspecting the equipment on Gray Deck. "I've run some tests on this gear, sirs, and I've found a fatal flaw in the design."

Graves and a few unsmiling techs looked up at me, halting their huddled conversation.

"I assure you, Centurion," said a prissy, hog-like tech girl. "That's not possible. This equipment has been tested and it works perfectly."

I snorted and lifted the battery pack into view. "You see this sorry excuse for a battery? You can't even charge up enough to port a lightyear with this garbage."

"That's right McGill," Graves said. "We've lightened the load for each soldier, and simultaneously reduced the cost for each rig so much we've been able to manufacture thousands of them."

"That's all well and good, I'm sure, Primus. But how are we going to even launch?"

The prissy tech girl took over, stepping up to place a teleportation rig on a weird-looking prong. I saw it was a charging hook of sorts. "Each combatant will wear the rig and plug into this launcher—really, it's just a charging port. A high-voltage burst will power the device, and the subject will be launched almost instantly."

"Okay…" I said. "I get that, but how the hell do we get back?"

They looked at me like I was some kind of moron. I get that a lot.

"McGill, McGill…" Graves said. "Do the math. I'm sure you're up to it."

Shaking his head, he turned and walked away. The prissy tech and a few others walked with him. They were all kind of snickering about it.

I stood there with my brows furrowed in a deep frown, and my eyes were all squinched up. I couldn't—

Then, suddenly, a realization hit me square in the ass. "We're not supposed to come back at all…" I said aloud. "Shit… Harris is going to love the hell out of this deal."

Right about then, Harris showed up. He must have heard me use his name. It was like he had radar or something when you spoke his name.

"What's this skinny fanny-pack full of wires going to do for us?" he demanded.

I pointed to the charging hook. "First, we stick that prong up our butts. Then it launches us on a one-way trip to wherever they want to send us."

Harris looked this over with growing alarm. As always with him, surprise quickly turned into rage.

"This is bullshit! This is abuse, plain and simple! We'll all be permed! You've got to do something, McGill!"

Throwing up my hands, I pointed after Graves, who was now inspecting more sinister-looking gear. A huge rack of warheads was being filled up as we spoke. Each warhead had a timer, a detonator... but I didn't see any delivery systems. No missiles, no nothing... just bombs.

"Hey! Primus Graves, sir?" Harris called out. He marched toward the primus, and I ambled in his wake. I was mildly surprised. Harris usually chickened when it came to confronting brass—but not always. Today was one of those exceptions.

"Sir?" Harris asked, holding up the flimsy rig. "Are we really being used as cannon-fodder?"

Graves shrugged. "What else good are ground troops in a space battle, Harris? You're going on a one-way trip to do some damage to the enemy fleet—if we get close enough we'll knock down their defensive systems."

"But... we'll all be permed, sir!"

"No, no. We're making sure there's no way anyone who ports out can survive long. See this rod here, in the back of the rig? It's really a charge with a timer. It will pop open any trooper wearing it after about an hour. That way, we know you're dead. No one will be permed."

It was Harris' turn to gape at this like a dummy.

"A suicide vest—in more ways than one..." he marveled.

"That's right. There's nothing to worry about," Graves said. "Now, get your men prepped, I'm busy."

Harris grumbled continuously as we walked back toward our module. "This is the worst," he complained. "Abusive, that's what it is!"

"How come you didn't tell Graves that?"

"Because he wouldn't have listened."

"That's right, and I don't want to hear it, either. Oh, and one more thing, Harris: keep your mouth shut about these rigs. The troops don't need to start off demoralized before the battle begins. Remember, Earth is depending on us."

Harris grumbled bitterly, but we walked to our module and made the best of it. The troops and other adjuncts had a million questions. I smiled, and I lied, and I told them whatever they wanted to hear.

"Uh-huh, that's right. This will be a cakewalk. Cross-my-heart-and-hope-to-die!"

Harris stayed quiet, his face stormy, his arms crossed. He looked about as unhappy as I could remember him looking. That wasn't that surprising, as Harris hated dying way more than I did.

I didn't care. It was time for him to step-up, to do his part to save Mother Earth.

* * *

When the hour came and the Skay finally arrived, I was suited up and standing on Gray Deck, ready to lead my suicide unit against them. It was beyond hopeless—we'd probably be dead before we got a shot off if we teleported out to the surface of those planet-sized aliens. But we were ready and willing to do it anyway, one and all.

The techs walked among us, tugging on straps and checking gauges. Sixteen at a time, we were pronged onto those coat-hook looking chargers. The charging meters showed green, and we were ready to pop out any time.

"How do you even make these things go?" Cooper asked, puzzling over the new rig. As a ghost, he'd been chosen to go out with the first batch—even though I doubted stealth was going to do him any good on this mission.

"You don't," a nasty-voiced tech explained bluntly. "*We* decide when you go, and where you're going. Just be ready to deliver your payload as quickly as possible when you arrive at your destination."

Cooper frowned dubiously at the basketball-sized warhead in his hands. "But how do you—"

I stepped in and put a heavy hand on his shoulder. He craned his neck angrily, but his face softened when he saw who it was.

"Centurion, sir," he said. "Glad you could make it to this party."

"Wouldn't have missed it for the world."

"Can you tell this hog-in-training there are obvious design flaws in this new cut-rate teleportation equipment?"

I smiled. I couldn't help it. Cooper was a lot like me, but less refined. He had a sharp wit, an acid tongue and a set of brass balls that were too big for his pants.

"Look, Cooper, this is the shitty deal. We've got these rigs, and they're cheap and disposable, yes. That's why we can afford to send out waves of men with them. They're mass-produced."

"Uh-huh," he said. "This is some kind of bullshit suicide mission, isn't it McGill?"

"Everyone has to die sometime, Cooper. Unless you want to go on that final journey at this very moment, I suggest you shut your overworked mouth."

"Got it, Centurion. Loud and clear."

I removed my heavy gauntlet from his shoulder and walked to the next scowling complainer. What was with the younger Varus soldiers these days? Did they seriously think they were going to live forever?

Right about then, my tapper started squawking—in fact, everyone's tapper did. So did the ship's PA. Every bulkhead, from starboard to port, rattled out the same message.

"McGill to Gold Deck, immediately. Centurion James McGill, you are to proceed to Gold Deck this instant."

The voice was Galina's.

"Oh shit…" I said, and I began tugging at the monkey-suit harness they'd strapped onto me.

Natasha stepped up to me and put a hand on my tapper. "I've got a hack. Can I use it?"

"What the hell are you talking about girl?"

"I can port you up to the bridge—right now."

I looked at her, and she looked back at me. Her eyes were lit up like a kid opening Christmas presents. There always had been some glee in her whenever she broke a security system and got to show it off. That was the only reason Varus had managed to recruit someone so gifted—she was a criminal at heart.

257

"Uh…" I said, thinking it over. I might end up dead, partially fused with a bulkhead. Or I might kill somebody when I arrived, with my skull intertwined with some hapless victim's hindquarters.

But then I grinned. "Do it—she did say immediately!"

Natasha connected her data-port to the teleport rig I was still wearing.

"Hey!" shouted the annoying tech-girl. "What are you doing?"

"Hook yourself to that charging prong," Natasha said.

I did so without hesitation. A moment later, the world rolled with blue, wavering light. Then, I vanished.

-45-

Needless to say, my arrival on the bridge created quite a stir. I didn't merge up with anyone fortunately, Natasha had seen to that. But that didn't mean it was a safe reentry.

I appeared about two meters above the navigator's station. The ceiling was a high one, so I didn't collide with any of the cables and equipment that was suspended up there—but I did fall.

"Whoa!" I whooped, and I landed on a navigator—at least, I thought he was a navigator. He was kind of flat-looking after I got to my feet again.

"McGill?" Galina snarled, stepping close to me and looking like she was ready to slap me. She might have done it, too, if people hadn't been watching. "Get up and stop fooling around. We have a message incoming from the Skay. They are the first to arrive and join this shit-storm." She turned toward a startled communications operator. "Play it!"

An odd voice filled the room. I'd know it anywhere: It was the God-like voice of the Skay.

"Creatures. We have arrived to punish you. Present your leader, the individual known as McGill. Compliance must be immediate, or your punishment-level will be enhanced."

"Huh…" I said. "He thinks I'm the leader of humanity? That's pretty cool."

"No, McGill, it isn't cool," Galina complained. "But I know why he might think that. All that negotiating you did with the Skay last time we encountered them—that was unauthorized, I might add."

"The word you're looking for is diplomacy, sir. And by the end, Drusus approved all of it."

"Only because he had no choice," she said bitterly, beginning to get angry all over again.

"Tribune," Fike said loudly. "We have to present McGill to the aliens."

"But we don't even have a plan yet!"

"I'm ready!" I said.

They looked at me. "What are you going to say?" Galina asked.

"Uh…"

"That's what I thought. You're going to wing it, aren't you?"

But then, in that moment, I realized I *did* have a plan. It was a good one, too.

My best schemes came unbidden into my thick head in the spur of the moment. I just wasn't the kind of guy who held lots of meetings, who took committee votes, and who wrote everything down first. I was more the kind of guy who operated on flashes of insight—hunches, you might call them.

"I'm going to tell him we serve the Skay," I said. "That we are faithful subjects of the empire, keeping down all barbarians that invade this Imperial province."

"Really?" Fike asked. "And when the Mogwa arrive? We'll attack them together with the Skay?"

"Uh…" I said, having not really taken the idea that far in my mind yet.

"We have a visual," the comms officer said. "Displaying it now."

The big holotank in the center of the bridge lit up. I fully expected to see one large, Moon-sized sphere on the long range scopes—but I didn't. Instead, there were three.

They were of varying sizes. Two were big-boys, almost the same size. They were grayish in color. The third was smaller, about half the mass of its brothers. It was bone-white.

"Three of them…" Galina breathed. I could tell she was scared enough to piss herself. "Put McGill online with them."

"But Tribune—" Fike protested.

"Now," she said, and the comms officer obeyed her.

"Channel opened. Transmitting…" The comms officer looked at me expectantly.

Stepping up to the hologram, I addressed the three killer spheres.

The Skay were a strange race. They were probably the weirdest aliens we'd ever met. They were AI-based, with electronic brains. But they did use organics as well. Their minions, which operated kind of like blood cells in the human body, came in many forms. They liked to disassemble any organic life they encountered and build new cyborg constructs to serve them. Sometimes they resembled soldiers. Sometimes they were more like tanks filled with meat. But always, these minions had computers for brains.

Inside each of those colossal spheres was an entire ecosystem of creatures, and all of them served the Skay in some way. When we fought with them, we were treated like an invading disease—or morsels of food to be broken down and digested.

"Uh… hello Mr. Skay," I said. "This is James McGill, ruler and spokesperson for Earth and all Humanity."

Fike grunted in disbelief at my invented title. Galina gritted her teeth and squinched up her eyes, but she knew me well, and she didn't really seem surprised. If you handed the keys over to old James McGill, well sir, you had to take the good with the bad.

"This is the same speaking ape we dealt with previously?" the Skay asked.

"One and the same, sir!"

"Excellent. You will explain your actions ·in this star system immediately."

"Uh… of course, sir—or is it sirs? Are you individuals?"

"We are. I'm the largest of the three you see before you. I am the same individual that you infected previously. These others serve me, as I am greater than they are."

I got the feeling the Skay society was all about dick-size. That made perfect sense, given their poor personalities. I wasn't sure exactly how they "grew" as their hulls were constructed with stardust, but I didn't much care to ask right now.

"What is your individual name, or title, Mr. Skay?" I asked.

"It is appropriate to refer to me as 'Master'."

"Uh, okay... Master Skay, what actions can I explain to you?"

"Why is there an Earth ship in this system? Why have you attacked the base here and destroyed it?"

"That is our sworn duty, Master Skay. Remember, Earth's job is to keep this province pacified and under the control of the Galactics—among whom you are our current overlords."

The last time I'd met up with these strange, monstrous aliens I'd cut a deal to serve them rather than the Mogwa. I'd argued that Humanity was just like a rental security man—we served whoever paid us and rightfully owned our home province. This bit of fact-shuffling had allowed around ten billion humans to continue breathing.

"You have made an error. The base here was constructed by humans—humans in our employ. You have damaged our efforts to annex Province 921."

"Uh... sorry about that. I would suggest that next time you inform us first, because we're really good at our job. Just look at this situation. The home world of these Clavers was taken out by a single ship—and we have thousands of ships. Might I further suggest you employ better agents next time? Clavers can't really fight worth a damn."

The Skay was silent after that for several long seconds. I knew from experience they were doing some deep thinking.

"Your statements match the observable data. The Clavers were poor servants if they couldn't resist a single ship from Earth."

"That's right. We could have sent more legions—but we didn't even bother. These guys are serious losers."

"We will now move on to the next infraction. We have detected a large group of ships coming from Earth to this star system. If you only needed one ship to conquer the Claver

262

homeworld, why are there so many coming now that the battle is over?"

"Well, Master Skay, sir," I said, "that should be obvious. Are you capable of detecting the other fleet—the one coming from the Core Worlds behind you?"

"Of course, human. Your question is impudent."

"Sorry Master, sorry. Well then, simple deductive logic should be applied. We're here to fight the invading force if necessary. This is Province 921, and we have been charged by the Empire to defend these local stars. Accordingly, we're positioning ourselves to do so."

"Interesting..." the Skay said. "Alarming as well. By implication, you believe you could defeat a Core World fleet?"

"It doesn't matter," I said. "It is our job to do our best. If we all die, so be it. We are willing to give our lives—all of them—to serve the Empire."

"That is an excellent attitude, slave. I'm impressed by your supplication."

"Why, thank you Master Skay. We take pride in our service."

The Skay stopped talking then. The silence went on for several minutes.

"What are they doing?" Galina hissed. "Did you blow it somehow, McGill?"

"Don't see how..."

"They're still closing, moving in on Clone World," Fike said. "They're going to scan it, then decide to trash us. All this bullshit McGill is throwing around isn't working."

I gestured for him to shut up, and he glared back—but he did stop talking.

Several more long, tense minutes passed. A couple of times, we tried to transmit a fresh greeting, but the Skay either weren't listening or weren't interested.

Finally, when the officers around me were losing it, they called back. "Here are my decisions, humans," the Skay said, "you will bring your fleet to this star system. You will stand at our side, and you will fight the invading ships that have followed us from the Core Worlds. For this service, you will be allowed to continue your existence for the foreseeable future."

-46-

The deal offered by the Skay might not seem all that generous to the uninformed. But to an experienced starman like myself, it seemed more than equitable.

"All we have to do is stand with your fleet? We're more than willing to do that, Master. We'll do it with bells on."

"No audio devices will be required. This conversation is terminated."

Just like that, they hung up the phone. I turned to the other officers on the bridge with a big Georgia grin on my face. "Did you hear that? They bought it all, and they even gave us a guarantee to continue breathing! Sometimes, my negotiating powers impress even me."

"McGill," Graves said, speaking up at last, "has it occurred to you that we're about to engage in direct battle with the Mogwa? That if the Skay lose, the Mogwa will be within their rights—no, it will be their *duty* to exterminate our species?"

"That's not McGill's fault," Galina said, pacing the deck. She didn't look at Graves, so I decided to ignore his pessimism as well. "It has always been coming down to this. This moment in time has been coming for a long time. Once the Skay arrived and challenged the Mogwa for this province, we were involved. We're finally being forced to make a decision. Shall we declare our loyalty to the Skay? Or should we stick with the Mogwa? Or… should we try to be tricky?"

The rest of them looked sick, but I was pretty happy. After all, if it hadn't been for me, we wouldn't be making any choices—we'd already be well on the way to extermination. Even if we flipped a coin now, we had at least a fifty-fifty chance of survival. That was a pretty big improvement in the odds, from my point of view.

I took a moment to turn to one of the marines hanging around the entrance. I took off my teleport rig and handed it to him.

"What's this, Centurion?" he asked. He held the load of straps and wires like a dead opossum.

"You should run that down to Gray Deck and give it to the techs. It's programmed to explode after you teleport someplace. It should be going off pretty soon, by my reckoning."

He blinked at me like I was crazy.

"Well? Go on, get going!" I urged. "I'm busy, and time is wasting."

With growing alarm, he trotted off the bridge.

"We can't make this choice on our own, sir," Fike was saying. "We must consult Drusus."

She made a dismissive wave of her hand. "He's gone back to Earth through the gateway posts."

"Of course, but we can still contact him on the deep-link and ask his advice."

Galina stopped wandering around, strutting her butt in front of us all. She turned on one sharp heel and marched right up to Fike. "You will do no such thing. *We* will make this choice—it's our prerogative. I'm in command of this task force, and I have operational authority."

"Exactly," Fike said evenly. He wasn't cowed, I gave him that much. "Operational, but not *diplomatic* authority. This goes beyond the scope of our operation. We're talking about starting a war, here. We must contact—"

"Arrest the Tribune!" Galina shouted, pointing at Fike.

The poor man blinked and stared. His jaw dropped open a bit, too. I could have told him not to go up against a tiger like Turov without having a firm hold on her tail. You just didn't mess with her unless you had an edge of some kind.

After a moment's hesitation, the marines on the bridge looked at *Legate's* captain. He gave them a small nod, and they moved on Fike.

Primus Fike wasn't a weak man, nor was he a chicken. His hand strayed to his pistol—but he didn't draw it.

That was a sheer mistake, I could have told him. The marine guards were spooked already. You didn't go for a gun in these situations then chicken out. When the marines got to him, they whipped his ass good with their powered truncheons. Crackling clubs rose and fell, sizzling through the air with electric pain.

When he was no more than a sagging rag between two burly veterans, they hauled his butt off the bridge.

"Take him to the brig," Turov ordered. "No torment, no abuse—just lock him up. He's had an emotional breakdown due to the stress of this moment. It is forgivable—but not admirable."

No one else spoke up after that. Turov had cleaned house. She was a ruthless little witch when she wanted to be. Fike hadn't understood what he was dealing with. He was more of the gentlemanly type, an old-fashioned soldier that lined-up real neatly and shined his kit until it was like chrome.

That wasn't the Varus way. When we left Earth, we were officially off the chain. We lived by our own code of conduct—and died by it.

"McGill," Turov said. "You set this up so we could choose which Galactic to fight with—correct?"

"That's right, sir," I said proudly. "We've got three choices now."

She nodded. "Fight with the Skay—or turn against them when the Mogwa arrive and stab them in the back—or... what's your third option?"

"We refuse to fight at all. We stand down, and we watch the Galactics duke it out."

Galina frowned. "I don't know if that option is available to us at this point. The Skay have given us orders. If we disobey, they'll count us as an enemy. Therefore, we might as well attack."

266

"You just leave that up to me when the time comes, Tribune."

Her eyes darkened. "No. I will do no such thing."

"Uh... well, you've got another problem to worry about. When our home fleet arrives, the commander of that larger force is going to take over."

Galina's face was full of thoughtful evil today, and she smiled at my words as if she enjoyed hearing them.

"I've already thought of that," she said, "don't worry. If we decide which way to go now, our actions will make the future irreversible."

"Huh..." I said. "What, exactly, does your plan involve? If you don't mind my asking, sir?"

"I do mind. For right now, keep your brain focused. Which side do we choose?"

"The Mogwa," Graves said, stepping forward. "They're our original masters. If we stick with them, no one other than the Skay is going to be upset. If we rebel against them openly now, every Galactic species in the Empire will know we're traitors."

"I understand the sentiment, Graves," Galina said. "And I really do appreciate your point of view. Yours is always a traditional, loyalist stance. What could be more admirable than that?"

"My position isn't some kind of romantic nonsense," Graves said. "It's based on observable data. The Skay are machines. They're difficult to convince of anything. Better to work with a biotic species we can better comprehend."

Galina frowned at him. "Are you going to tell me I'm out of line?"

"No sir. You're in command."

Graves shut up after that threatening exchange. As far as I was concerned, that demonstrated a wisdom that Fike hadn't possessed. Graves was rarely arrested. In fact, he was so smart in that area that he usually *did* the arresting.

"Good..." Galina said. She stepped up beside the helmsman, the one I'd flirted with some time back. "Steer this ship toward the Skay," she ordered.

Nervously, the helmsman did as she had been ordered. Now and then, she glanced at Galina, her captain, and the

267

stains that Fike had left on the deck. She didn't look happy. No one did—except for me.

I didn't much care where we stood. When the time came, I had one more trick to play. I hoped it would impress.

The three Skay ships moved into far orbit over Clone World. *Legate* sidled up to them. The size difference made us seem completely insignificant. Our ship looked like a pet cricket following three grown men around an open meadow.

The Skay didn't contact us about our maneuvers. After all, they'd ordered our fleet to join theirs. To them, it must have looked like we were following those orders eagerly.

-47-

About two hours after Fike had been arrested and dragged from the bridge, something changed. Something bad.

It started with the comms officer and the sensor ops guy. They stepped together and had a little conference. They didn't look happy—not at all.

"What's going on?" I asked the helmsman.

She was worried, too. I could tell by the way she kept flicking her eyes over to the others, watching out of the corner of her eye.

"Something's wrong. There's another contact—it's coming in fast."

"Yeah...? From where?"

"They're arguing about that. See that? On my screen?"

I looked over her fine shoulder. I got a little close to do this, but before I could even enjoy the scent of her hair, I saw something that made me frown as well.

"That's a whole lot of ships. They're not coming from the Galactic Core, either. They're coming from the opposite direction."

"That's right," she said.

As we watched, the contacts went from white to yellow. The battle computer was trying to classify them, and it was failing. They weren't friendly, but they weren't definitively hostile, either. Not yet.

Three long strides took me from the helm to where Galina and Graves were having a powwow of their own. They weren't looking at sensors, they were going over reports of our own fleet's composition.

"Hey," I said. "Sirs? There's a problem."

"What is it, McGill?" Graves asked me. "Did you get shot down by our pilot over there?"

Galina looked instantly pissed. She didn't mind when I chased another woman now and again—but not when I did it in plain sight of her, and other people noticed.

"Nothing like that, sirs. There's a new fleet arriving any minute now. A fourth fleet."

They blinked at me in shock. Galina marched to the sensor ops station, and she starting kicking tail. Captain Merton was called in, and he got a scolding, too. He was lucky he wasn't arrested and dragged from the bridge like Fike. I knew Turov, when she got on a roll, it was best to stay clear. If she hadn't needed *Legate's* bridge crew badly right now, there might have even been some executions.

"I'm not going to tolerate *anyone* who undermines my authority."

"This is a Fleet matter, Tribune. We're underway, and—"

She shut the captain up with a reach for her pistol. "You've got a few goons on this deck, Captain Merton. But I've got twenty thousand more aboard *Legate* than you do."

Turov said this with an evil voice. She meant business, there was no doubting that much. To prove her point, I stood behind her, as did Graves. The marine guards who had arrested Fike earlier were standing at the main entrance, looking fidgety. I supposed they weren't sure what to do—but they would probably obey the captain if he decided to stage a showdown.

Fortunately for him, Captain Merton realized he was outgunned in the larger sense. His handful of marines couldn't stand up to a legion.

"When we return to Earth," he said stiffly, "a court of inquiry will be called."

"That's fine," Turov spat out. "*If* we return, and *if* there is an Earth left to return to, you can have your investigation then.

But for right now, we're going to discuss this development you've been hiding. What do you know about this new fleet that's approaching us?"

"Look sir, I'm not hiding anything. This formation of ships only just appeared on our scopes. It could be a ghost contact, or maybe the Earth fleet is arriving earlier than expected."

"Is that even remotely possible?"

He examined the data closely, and he shook his head. "I don't see how. This situation is becoming increasingly dangerous. Earth's fleet, two Core World fleets—and now this? I don't know what to make of it."

Galina didn't eye the data, she eyed him. She read his face, and at last, she nodded. "All right. I believe you. We've been screwed somehow. That can't be a friendly fleet—every fleet we know of in this region of space, every alien who has a powerful force of ships is already here! Who are these aliens? What do they want?"

Suddenly, like an ice-cold bolt of lightning, the answer hit me right between the eyes. I knew without a doubt who we were about to be dealing with.

"Uh..." I said. "There's only one answer that makes sense, sir."

They all looked at me with a mixture of disgust and agitation. I was the proverbial turd in their punchbowl.

Finally, Galina made a rapid circular motion with her hand. "Well? Out with it, McGill!"

"It's got to be Rigel," I said. "They're the only interested party that isn't already here. They probably got the same distress call the Skay got, and they're coming to help the Clavers. No one else on the frontier has a fleet that size, and they're even coming from the right direction, see?"

I used a long finger to draw a line on the interactive mapping screen. The line arced right back toward the frontier—toward Rigel.

They all stared, and no one spoke for a moment.

"They're making the same gamble Drusus decided to make," Graves said thoughtfully. "They're leaving their homeworld open, and they're coming out here for a showdown."

"Whose side will they be on?" Galina demanded, sounding stressed.

"Not ours, that's for damned sure," I said.

"The Skay side," Graves said. "They're coming out to fight for the Skay."

Galina was staring at the screen where my big-ass, finger-drawn line led back toward Rigel. The whole scenario was clear to anyone who had half a brain.

Her eyes were darting all over the place. "Damn it!" she shouted at last. "Damn it, damn it—damn it all to Hell!"

She was breathing hard, staring, and we were all looking at each other, shrugging our shoulders.

Apparently, some plan of hers had just been blown wide open—but I had no frigging idea what that might be.

After Galina's outburst, no one wanted to talk too loudly. She wasn't in her best mood, and she'd already trashed Fike. We stood around quietly, hoping she'd give us a hint as to what she wanted done next.

"All right," she said, taking in a deep breath—then three more. "All right. We can deal with this. We have no choice now. Those fucking little bears…" She closed her eyes, sucked in another breath and let it out. "All right… back to your posts. Get Drusus on the deep-link, and connect it to the conference room."

She stalked off the bridge, and I followed her—no one else dared.

"Uh…" I said to her hunched back. "Galina? Are you okay?"

She winced at my words. "McGill? What are you doing?"

"Checking on you," I said. "Something's wrong—I don't know what it is, but I know it's real."

She stared at me for a few seconds, then she relaxed a bit. "Follow me—I could use a loyal man right now. That frigging captain might try to pull a move on me. Keep your eyes open and one hand on your pistol."

That was the kind of order I was born to follow. I hulked after her, looking like her watch-gorilla. She was half my size at best, and people tended to skitter out of the way when they saw the two of us barreling along through the passages.

When we got to her office, she shut the door. Then she locked it, and she kissed me.

That was a surprise. In fact, I flinched when she grabbed my head and stood on her tippy-toes, not knowing what the hell to expect.

But her soft kiss was pleasant, and I smiled.

"You're loyal," she said. "Like a good dog. I really appreciate that."

"Uh... okay."

She let go of my face and turned back to her office. "We've got a problem, James."

"You don't say?"

Rummaging in her liquor cabinet, I found the item with the least amount sugar in it and poured us both a shot. It was bourbon, decently aged and orangey-brown in the bottle.

"James," she said. "I thought I had this worked out—but I don't. I wanted the Skay and the Mogwa to fight it out. We could claim neutrality as they are both Galactics. Whichever won, we would swear allegiance to them."

Frowning, I thought that over. I did see a certain logic to it. "But now there are four fleets rather than two," I said. "Things are getting complicated."

"That's right. Drusus couldn't hold his water, and neither could Squanto. They're both upping the ante. This is going to be a massive cluster-fuck."

"Huh..." I said, unable to argue with her point.

"My plan had been to wait until Drusus arrived with Earth's fleet. I thought I could persuade him to stand back, to wait until these titans battle it out. But now... I don't think it will work. Even if Drusus does nothing, Squanto will attack us. We'll be dragged into this battle, and we might well lose."

I shrugged, pouring us both a second one. "That's the nature of war. You can't always predict every outcome."

"But that was the beauty of my plan!" she said, looking up at me. "It didn't matter who won, who lost—we'd pick the winner and go with them. Now, we might be on the wrong side. All of Earth, all of humanity might be lost by morning."

"Yeah... we'll just have to go with the flow, I guess."

273

"You're not bothered? You're not filled with uncertainty and worry?"

"Uh… no. Not really. Every legionnaire dies on a regular basis, and we never really know if we're waking up or not after. I guess I'm used to it."

She shook her head, then shook her body. It looked good.

"James… if we do live through this, I want you to spend the night with me. Not one of your sluts you pick up all the time. All right?"

"Hell yeah!" I said, loving the invite.

We kissed again, but I had to answer a call. My tapper had started going crazy, as my unit on Gray Deck was ready to port out. This battle was kicking into high gear.

Heading to Gray Deck, I stood next to that prong-thing that would charge and launch me. I was handed a fresh rig, as I'd ditched mine.

Natasha had hacked the external vid feeds, and I listened to command chat. Together, these two elements gave me a clear picture as to what was going on outside *Legate's* hull.

First off, the Mogwa fleet arrived on the scene. They didn't make their presence known instantly, but came in stealthed. Only by using our gravimetrics could we detect them at all.

The Skay, however, weren't fooled. They left orbit over Clone World and wheeled toward the out-system zone. They stalked forward confidently, releasing various forms of radiation, which we figured were some kind of active sensor sweeps.

Realizing they weren't fooling anyone, the Mogwa appeared in space. There were a surprising number of ships—at least a thousand of them. Most were cruisers, but there were smaller ships around the outer edge and a few honking big battlewagons in the center of the formation.

"Damnation…" I breathed. "That's bigger than Battle Fleet 921."

"Newer, too," Natasha breathed in my ear. She was watching the feed, the same as I was. I had to accept that, as every hacker always helped themselves to the choicest bits of intel when they found them.

Command chat was buzzing, but they weren't coherent. I got the feeling they were as rattled as everyone else. Finally, I caught a sensible order from Turov.

"Fall back slowly. Let the Skay get ahead of *Legate*—way ahead. If they ask about it, we'll pretend our engines aren't up to the task."

I smiled. She was still trying to play this on the sly. You had to give the girl credit, she was a natural schemer.

Minutes passed, but the Skay didn't demand that we keep up. Probably, they'd calculated that one Earth ship wasn't going to do diddly-squat in this battle of titans.

Both fleets glided to a stop about ninety-million kilometers apart. That was pretty long range, even for high-tech ships.

"What the hell are they doing now?" I asked.

"Talking, I bet," she said. "I'm catching all kinds of RF. I suspect they're trading coded signals, demands, threats... who knows?"

The two alien fleets stood off, not firing a shot. Three gray-white spheres the size of moons faced a thousand sleek warships. It was kind of cool, if terrifying, to watch.

This went on for some time, and I got bored.

"All this for nothing?" I asked. "They've gone chicken, that's what it is."

"If you're right, that's great news, James," Natasha scolded me lightly.

She was right of course, but I didn't like a specialist telling me so in quite that tone. If we hadn't had such a long history together, I might have complained—but I didn't.

After ten more minutes, I got audio. I was surprised. Natasha had hacked into their channel—or at least to the feed that they were listening to through their translators up on the bridge.

"The Grand Admiralty of the Mogwa again repeats our demand. You are Skay. You do not belong in Province 921. You will withdraw—"

"The Skay do not recognize your authority," interrupted the strange voice of the AI beings.

"According to the treaty of—"

"The Skay do not recognize the treaty referenced."

275

It kind of went on like that, and it was even more boring than I thought.

"What the hell are they both waiting for?" I asked. "Why don't they duke it out?"

Natasha's tongue wet her upper lip nervously. Even though we were both wearing spacesuits, I could see her face. She didn't look happy.

"They are waiting for something…" she said. "It must be the other fleets. The ships coming from Earth and Rigel."

I snapped my fingers. "That's it. They're screwing around talking big, hoping for an edge. They must feel they're evenly matched, or they'd move on each other right now. Which fleet is due to arrive next?"

"Our fleet," Natasha said, and she looked at me. There was fear in her eyes. "What will Drusus do when he gets here, McGill?"

"Uh… he'll probably stand with the Mogwa. He's almost as big of a boy scout as Graves."

She nodded, and I put a hand on her shoulder. "We're going to do fine," I said. "And if we don't—well, we'll die in a blaze of glory!"

Natasha gave me a flickering smile. She didn't look comforted.

I knew what the trouble was. She was thinking about Earth. She didn't care all that much if we blew up, or got fried in space. But all those citizens back home, she couldn't get them out of her mind.

"Hey," I said. "Don't worry so much. I've got this wired."

"What? How?"

I grinned. "It's going to go our way. I guarantee it."

She eyed me, judging my face. I gave her my best liar's grin, trying to appear like I had a secret ace in the hole.

Finally, she nodded her head and smiled. "That's a relief. Thanks for telling me, James."

"Any time."

A few minutes later, the space around good old Clone World got a little more crowded. Earth's fleet had arrived at last.

When Drusus came out of warp with hundreds of cruisers at his back, we all cheered. The brass had seen fit to display this sight on the bulkheads all over *Legate*, touting the event like it was the Second Coming.

Drusus appeared a moment later on the bridge of his flagship, the United Earth Ship *Berlin*. "To all Earth forces in this system. We've made a choice—one that we had to make. We're fighting with the Mogwa today. We can't stay neutral, or choose sides later. We must commit and pray for victory. I know you'll all do your best and make Earth proud of this day."

The image fuzzed out, and people slammed gloved fists into one another's backs all around me. We marveled at the look and feel of our graceful new fleet. Sure, we didn't have a thousand ships—it was more like three hundred. Neither did we have ships that were quite as high-tech and massive as the others, but they were wicked-looking all the same.

"Those wrinkly old spiders need us. Our ships aren't only better than Mogwa ships," I boasted loudly without a shred of knowledge on the subject, "they're manned by humans, not chicken-shit Mogwa. As to the Skay—don't even let me get started!"

Men within earshot cheered.

"Um... McGill?" Natasha asked.

I looked down. She looked nervous again. "One of the Skay is backing up. It's moving toward the planet."

"Really! That's fantastic! Those big chickens! I always knew—"

"James," she hissed. "*Legate* is still hanging around Clone World. They're moving toward us."

"Oh..." I said, getting the picture at last.

What had happened? Had they decided that if Earth's ships were on the Mogwa side, they might as well get rid of that one lone transport on their flank?

It wasn't a bad idea, from their point of view. After all, *Legate* had fallen back out of formation with the big Skay ships. When Drusus had appeared and ordered the Earth fleet to join the Mogwa, the Skay had figured out at long last that humans just weren't their friends.

277

"Fine," I said. "Maybe the brass will deploy us at last. I'm getting itchy in this harness."

Natasha's eyes were wide and her face was pale. She didn't seem to be as enthusiastic as I was.

The scene on the walls changed about a minute later. Galina's face, as big as you'd like—and maybe bigger than that—appeared all over the ship.

"Crew, legionnaires, soldiers of Earth. We've been contacted by Drusus. We're to join his fleet. Prepare to warp out."

More whooping and cheers broke out. Possibly, they were even louder than before. A great feeling swept us all, we'd been saved from an ignoble death in the harsh radioactive hell that was open space.

"Before we jump, however," Turov continued, "I'm ordering a cohort to board the smallest of the three Skay. It's approaching us with its mouth open, and it's therefore vulnerable to a sneak-attack."

The crowd on Gray Deck quieted. The mood went from a rock concert to a funeral within the span of seconds as we absorbed this unwelcome information.

A big countdown timer appeared next, flipping red numbers. Shouted orders came into our helmets.

"Close visors, hook up those teleport-rigs! We jump in eight... seven... six..."

"Tell me this isn't happening," Carlos complained off to my left.

"Ready-up!" I shouted, and I saw them button up all down the line. "It's time to grip your rifles and piss in your suits, kids. Charge-up and fly!"

All around me, troops connected their rigs to the dangling plugs. Sparks flew in some cases, but no one was electrocuted outright.

A few seconds later, the throbbing blue waves of light from a hundred spots became blinding. We were jumping out—my whole unit at once.

-48-

The situation wasn't ideal. We were jumping—to where again? I had time to think that over as I was blinking out—oh yeah, we were heading into the mouth of the smallest of the three Skay.

If the attack was successful, that wouldn't necessarily save *Legate*, but I tried to put that out of my head. It didn't matter for now. What mattered was our mission—our one tiny part in this monstrous battle.

Even the smallest of the Skay was a massive being. When we coalesced into a swarm of troops again, we were pretty high up off the inner hull. Small jets flared into life, and we fell toward the concave deck below which was the inner surface of the stardust shell.

Visible off to one side was the mouth of the Skay. I wondered at first exactly why the enemy had seen fit to open its maw right now—but the answer was plain to see.

A flood of sleek, black ships flowed out into open space. They were reminiscent of the landing craft we'd seen the larger Skay loose when it had first invaded Earth.

These ships were probably fighters, however, rather than some kind of landing craft. Maybe the Skay used one ship design for both functions.

Fifty, a hundred—two hundred. The dark ships flowed by, but the moment the last of them sailed out into space, the great mouth closed.

"Holy shit," Leeson said in my ear. He was using my command chat, which was limited to unit officers right now. "That wasn't enough time. We can't have more than five hundred of us in here. Half a cohort in strength, at the most."

I had to agree. Gray Deck was a better launching facility than it had been before. With all the streamlining they'd done over the years, a transport like *Legate* could fire a lot more teleporters a lot faster than ever before.

That said, there were limits. We'd only had a minute or two as a window of time.

"Centurion?" Barton called to me. "My tapper says a second wave was launching just as we arrived—when that door closed."

"What happened to the rest of the cohort?" Harris demanded. "Are they out there on the outer hull, crawling around like ants locked out of a lunchbox?"

"Probably so," I said encouragingly.

"Nah," Leeson argued. "They're spam by now. Their teleport suits are dumb. They'll be embedded in the outer hull like bugs hitting a windshield."

I glanced at him disapprovingly. He wasn't helping morale any, even if the officers were the only ones listening in.

"Gather up your platoons!" I shouted. "Head-counts! I want head-counts!"

That got them busy. We'd only lost two due to accidents. My unit was full strength and ready to fight.

We looked around, seeking a target. As before, when I'd invaded my first Skay, I didn't see much around the landing zone. The life that crawled and consumed anything it could find inside the guts of every Skay, a living ecosystem of an alien nature, wasn't common near the great mouth. The various forms of the "children" of the Skay, as it called its idiot abominations, couldn't survive in hard vacuum.

"Unit march, this way!" I said, and I picked a direction almost at random. Ahead, I'd spotted a cluster of hills with odd hairy growths on them. It would do.

A voice rumbled into my helmet then, and I was very pleased to hear it.

"McGill?" Graves called. "Where are you going?"

The primus had jumped with us. That made me feel good. All too often, when I got caught up in one of these cluster-fuck operations, I'd been the top officer on the scene. Now that the operation was much larger, Turov had seen fit to send her second-in-command into harm's way.

"Primus?" I called back, striding steadily with clear purpose. "I'm taking cover before we're attacked. The Skay always have living sub-creatures inside them—those constructions of meat and machine operate like anti-bodies, attacking any invaders they detect."

"Right... carry on."

Glancing side-to-side, I saw the other units pick up their gear and hustle after us. We spread out into a ragged line. Soon, we were at the foot of the low hills we'd been heading for.

In the low gravity, we were able to cover ground quickly with an odd gait. It was kind of like skipping the way a kid might, but in this case, each skipping step carried a man a meter or so up and a dozen meters over the curved hull.

This Skay was a lot smaller than the one we'd first invaded over a year ago. Instead of being moon-sized, something like three thousand kilometers across, it was more like a third of that. Still, it was pretty damned big. I couldn't see all the way to the hanging gloom of the far walls. I could see the gentle curvature of the inner hull, however. That was much more pronounced than it had been the last time I'd been trapped inside the belly of a beast like this one.

We heard something as we mounted the hills. The air inside this strange world was thin, but it existed. A flapping sound, that's what it was.

"Rifles and peckers up!" I shouted. "Look sharp, they'll hit us from the air!"

Sure enough, a swarm of big bat-looking things came flapping at us. They swooped and dived, flying low over the hills. They used the initial tactic of slamming into a target to knock it flat.

Gunfire erupted along with a storm of curses as my men were suddenly up to their asses in flying assailants. They had bodies like metallic manta rays, and this version seemed to be larger than the ones we'd fought long ago. Was that due to the lower gravity? Could a larger creature travel through the air here inside this smaller Skay? I didn't know, but it stood to reason.

I didn't have much time for contemplation when one of them roared down at me, making me hunker my shoulders. I was in mid-flight myself, having just taken one of those skittering hops. My gun and my trigger-finger, however, were up to the task. I fired a long burst, and the creature came apart into a puff of blood, metal scaling and—I swear—what looked like springs. This mess hit me with a meaty slap, almost knocking me on my can, but I kept my feet and landed about halfway up the hill.

Looking around, breathing hard, I was surprised to see a lot more of these flapping things. They were all coming off the hills we'd run toward, launching themselves at the cohort of troops.

My unit was in the lead, but we were by no means alone. All along our drawn-out front line, fighting was going on in earnest.

"Put them down!" Graves ordered over tactical chat, hitting every receiver on the battlefield. "Help your buddy, keep your gear, advance to cover. Take these hills before something worse hits us."

The troops, who had all been stopped to battle these startling creatures, got moving again. We hadn't lost many soldiers, as the bird-things hadn't been well-armed. I figured they'd hit us first because they were the fastest moving elements the Skay could deploy. But for all of their savagery, they hadn't done much more than delay us.

Soon, we were swarming on the hills and seeking firing positions. The troops were spooked, aiming every which-way. I couldn't blame them.

"Leeson!" I shouted. "Set up your weaponeers at the high points. Barton, move your lights to the outer perimeter. Scan, snipe and report any sightings. Ghosts, come to me!"

My two Ghosts, Cooper and Della, were naturally invisible. They came trotting to me in their stealth gear and stood near, nervously awaiting their assignments.

"I need intel," I told them. "Della, you hit that copse of dirty-looking broccoli-growths over there. I don't want an ambush coming that way. Cooper, you're going farther out. I want a report on the next set of hills."

Cooper rustled in his suit. "All the way the hell out there, sir?" he asked plaintively. "That must a kilometer or more."

"Almost two," Della said, "I'll do it."

"No, no..." Cooper said, sighing. "I'm on it. Wish me luck."

"Luck..." Della said, and he was gone.

"James," Della said. "You aren't protecting me, are you? That's not fair to Cooper—or me, really. I can do this job."

"I know you can, girl, and I'm doing no such thing. Move out!"

She trotted off. "Luck, Della," I muttered.

I'd lied of course. I always protected Della whenever I could. Sometimes, she told my daughter Etta about what she'd encountered out here among the stars. Etta in turn would tell my mother. That was all I needed when I was resting up dirt-side, a good scolding from the women in my family about my battlefield decisions. No sir, Della lived a charmed life in my unit.

When we'd shot down the last of the flapping things, we hugged our limited cover and dug in. Graves walked over to my team to talk about our next tactical move. That made me puff with pride, as I could tell right off he was seeking my advice on the matter.

Throughout my tenure with Legion Varus, from the first day to the last, I'd mostly been scolded, admonished, reprimanded and flogged on a regular basis. I could have counted on one hand the number of times my immediate superior had asked me for help on any decision, no matter how small. This time, we were in a bad fix. Maybe that's what brought Graves to me—he had no better options.

"McGill, what the hell do we do now?" he asked. "We've got what... thirty-two minutes left before the bombs strapped to our backs pop—and that's it. If *Legate* is still around, they'll start pumping out new versions of all of us."

"Yeah…" I said, knowing he was right. "We can't sit here, we have to find the enemy and hurt him bad. Otherwise, this attack was a waste."

Graves ran his eyes over the landscape. "This mission is hopeless," he said. "I can't believe I signed up for it."

"It's the only play we had, sir. The only chance a ground-pounder has to affect the outcome of a battle like this."

"Right. Any useful suggestions?"

"Uh…" I said, mulling it over. "I might have one, but you probably won't like it."

"That's what I thought," he said, sighing.

"How about we get an expert to help?" I asked. "Let's talk to Natasha."

He looked at me sharply. "You're not planning to hack something, are you?"

"Why, sir! I'd never sanction such a thing. That kind of conduct is beneath the consideration of any Varus officer, no matter how low."

"Right… get her over here, I'll listen to anything at this point."

I called her eagerly, because I actually *did* have an idea—and I sincerely hoped it would turn out to be a good one.

-49-

I described my thoughts to both Natasha and Graves at the same time to save a few precious seconds.

Graves didn't like it. I'd known he wouldn't, but putting it out there in front of Natasha, who lit up at every word as I spoke, changed the feel of it.

"This isn't what we were ordered to do," Graves complained. "McGill, your scheming is going to get us into a big violation with the Galactics, and they're in this frigging star system with us right now!"

"That's right, sir," I argued, "but in case you hadn't noticed, we're struggling for our very existence today. We're literally taking up arms against the Skay, who are by all reports at least as powerful as the Mogwa. Neutrality and rule-following? All of that happy horseshit has gone out the window—if you don't mind my saying so, sir."

Graves did mind. His face was stormy, and he gritted his teeth. Gripping and re-gripping his rifle, he did a little march-around circle. He stared at the odd, gloom-filled horizons that surrounded us.

During this performance, Natasha gave me a significant look. I nodded quietly, and she moved off to start working. After all, she needed every second we had left. We couldn't wait around all day for Graves to make the decision he was being forced to make.

"All right, dammit!" Graves said at last, wheeling around and heaving a sigh. "Just do it. I don't want to hear any details, just—where's Natasha?"

"Uh…" I said, looking around in a startled fashion. "Damnation! That girl should have been trained as a ghost! I'm sorry, Primus. She must have had to pee or something. I'll have her up on report for this. It's downright unprofessional."

Graves sighed. He was no fool—not most of the time. He knew I'd ordered her to proceed with the project the moment I'd thought of it. That was the trouble with knowing another man for decades, you got to where you just couldn't fool one another.

Shaking his head, he walked away from me to see to our defenses. "Let me know how it goes, McGill."

"Will do, Primus."

Natasha did work fast. It helped that she'd already hacked these rigs previously in order to air-mail me to Gold Deck just hours earlier.

"We can do it," she said, "but we need power. We don't have enough."

I chewed that over and worried for a spell. "Well…" I said. "If we don't have the power source at hand, we need more time. Can you fix that?"

She looked startled. "You mean… turn off the self-destruct timers on the rigs?"

"That's it."

She made a face that reminded me of Graves. She showed lots of teeth and hissed. Then she shook her head. "I don't know, James. I mean… I was a duplicate once before, remember? When the timer goes off, they're going to assume we're all dead. They'll start the revivals immediately—making twins out of all of us. Are you sure you want to deal with that?"

"No," I admitted. "But right now, we can't complete our mission in the time allotted to us. The mission comes first. Besides, you should look on the positive side—we can always blow ourselves up somehow later on—it can't be that hard to do."

Uncertainly, Natasha hacked my rig first, and she turned off the self-destruct. Using a relayed update feature, she broadcast the fix over our unit LAN. Within a minute, it had spread to a hundred others.

Graves walked up to us about ten seconds later. He had a frown on his face. "What's this priority update my tapper is flashing at me over and over? I keep cancelling it, and it won't stop popping up again."

"Uh…" I said, looking toward Natasha.

"There are power problems," she began. "We don't have enough of it. So—"

I could tell right off she was going to blow it by being honest, so I jumped in.

"So," I said loudly, "we need all the troops to accept this update. That will give us what we need to get started."

Graves narrowed his eyes and stared at me for a few long seconds. "This update is necessary?"

"Damn-straight it is."

"Then why didn't you send it to the entire cohort?"

My lower lip puffed up, my eye-brows rose high and I nodded, considering the prospect.

"You know what?" I asked Natasha. "The primus here has got a point. Relay that update to the entire cohort."

"But sir… are you sure about that?"

"Just do it, Specialist," Graves complained. "We're running out of time."

Sighing, she managed to keep a straight face while she transmitted the stealthy virus-type update to everyone inside the enemy Skay's hull. Graves followed that up with an order to allow the update to install.

A big old-fashioned download party started, and after around three minutes, everyone had gotten the update and installed it. The next thing that happened surprised us all.

The latches on our rigs clicked and the straps fell away, dangling. They had been locked onto our bodies—but no more.

"Hey," Carlos said "I like this. Can we take these things off and toss them?"

"No," I ordered. "Strap it back on."

"Just the way you like it, big guy," he said, and he walked away.

"Come back here, Specialist."

Reluctantly, Carlos returned.

"You're not doing anything useful right now," I told him. "I need you to go around and collect the power packs on every support person's harness, plus all the power modules we have from our dead. You got that?"

"Um… if you don't mind my saying, that sounds like grunt work, sir. I'm more of an idea-man."

My face darkened. "Get your ass moving Specialist, or I'll give you a snap-rifle and add you to Barton's light platoon."

That got him going. He trotted away without another smart-ass remark.

I sent off a dozen others with the same mission. Graves was pacing while Natasha worked hard on the teleport rigs. He looked worried, so I moved to join him on the nearest hilltop.

"What's on your mind, Primus?" I asked. "Any sightings?"

"No, and that worries me. The second we got here, we got hit with the fastest force the enemy had available. Since then, nothing. That's not good."

"Uh… why not, exactly?"

"Because it means they're gathering up all their strength. They're doing it at a distance, out of sight. When they come at us again, they'll be using their big machines. Abominations like those tanks we fought back on Armor World."

"Huh," I said, not arguing the point. It stood to reason that he was right. They knew exactly where we were. They knew from experience what we were capable of. Logically, the quietness of our LZ could only mean one thing.

They weren't communicating or making probe-attacks. They were building up an overwhelming force. It was only a matter of time until we were surrounded and destroyed.

Natasha and several other techs worked furiously, assembling a charging system using power-plants from dead troops, batteries wired together, and anything else they could think of. Soon, we had a dozen harnesses with enough of a charge to jump again.

Using her hack, she mapped out destinations all over the inside of the spherical Skay. That part confused me.

"Huh… why are we spreading out so much?"

"Think, James," she lectured me over her shoulder. "We don't know where the nexus is—where this thing keeps its brain. We have to send scouts out to every anomalous region we've spotted with lidar so far—"

"You've spotted some?"

"Yes. We've identified about twenty-one hundred likely spots to investigate. We'll investigate them, holding back an assault team to launch a final strike if anyone reports back a promising find."

"Huh…" I said, immediately identifying a few problems with her plan.

Natasha sighed. "Yes, you're right. We don't even have that many troops, assuming we could launch one at every target. Fortunately, many of them are close together. Others can be ruled out for various reasons."

"Like what?"

She shrugged. "A few hundred of them match the profile of known enemy structures. Like that hive of a nest we investigated the last time we were inside a Skay."

Thinking hard, I turned and peered into the gloomy distance. "Say, Natasha? Do you recall that big tower-like structure? The thing that was the size of a mountain?"

"It looked more like a termite mound," she said. "I remember it, yes."

"Have you found something like that? My team died trying to reach a structure like that last time."

"Yes… we have. But James, that's no reason to think it's something special just because it's big. It could be an atmospheric processor, for example. Or the engine that drives this huge ship. Who knows?"

I nodded. "I understand. But that's where I want to go. Send me there."

She blinked at me twice. "Send you? I thought we'd send light troopers on these missions. The most expendable—"

Reaching out, I put a gauntlet on her shoulder. I was gentle, and I didn't squeeze or anything. After all, she wasn't wearing armor like I was.

"We're not going to have long," I said gently. "We might get wiped out at any moment. If everything starts to go to shit—send me there."

Her smile drooped. "All right. This whole thing is a desperate play anyway, isn't it? We might as well go out the way we want to."

I grinned. "That's the spirit!"

As it turned out we had less time than we'd imagined. After charging maybe fifty suits and sending out various troops to the four winds, a rumbling sound began.

At first, you could feel it more than hear it. It started off as a vibration in the boots. It felt like you were space-walking on the hull of a big ship when the engines kick on.

But it wasn't an engine. It was the pounding of a thousand feet, a thousand treads—a thousand hulking monstrosities rushing us from every direction at once.

It was a marvel to behold. I could see a pall of dust, then individual shapes that humped and rolled over the rough ground in waves. Every kind of monster was out there, some familiar, others not.

I saw those bird-like things on two feet. They stood as tall as giraffes and their snouts fired thick beams of radiation at our lines as they came. There were plenty of others, too. Four-legged, rhino-looking things with gun turrets on their backs. Massive rolling tanks with eyes surrounding and guiding muscle-controlled cannons. Their charge was a magnificent sight, really.

We gave them hell, of course. The weaponeers had had time to choose their ground carefully. A hundred belchers lanced out, burning away flesh and melting metal. The enemy fell, flopping and churning their mindless feet like toys that had been knocked over but still clawed at the air.

"Natasha!" Graves shouted. "Launch the rigs! Launch them all! Search and destroy, people. The rest of us will hold them here as long as we can!"

I was in a trench, firing my rifle in bursts. Now and then, I launched a grav-grenade when a big one got close.

I was so into the fight, in fact, that when my vision began to strobe and blue flashes dazzled me, I still didn't get it. I figured maybe one of the troopers next to me had ported out.

But then I faded away, and I understood at last. Natasha had remotely activated my rig, and I'd been transported someplace else.

-50-

When I appeared again, I stumbled and almost fell on my face. I'd been leaning on a trench, firing my weapon at a charging monstrosity.

But all of that was gone. The fight, the trench, the troops around me... I'd been sent across the Skay to the other side of its spherical body. Hopefully, I could give it a gut ache before I was found or died of starvation.

The first thing I noticed was the relative quiet. I'd been hammering away with my rifle, ready to fight to the finish with the approaching horde—and then it wasn't there anymore.

Staggering, I was like a man awakening from a dream. I got my feet under me, and I looked around.

I finally noticed the looming tower behind me. Whatever its function was, the thing was huge. Still, I got the feeling it wasn't as big as the one I'd marched toward long ago, inside the first Skay humanity had ever had the misfortune of meeting.

Stupidly, I wasted a few seconds gawking up at it. I was kind of hoping someone else would pop in—but they didn't.

That made perfect sense, I realized. Natasha had many more targets than she had scouts, after all. She'd preprogrammed the rigs she'd managed to recharge, and they'd all gone off when Graves gave his order. We'd been tossed to the four winds.

Looking up at the massive structure I'd chosen, I realized with cold certainty I'd been an utter fool. What could one man hope to do against such a large target? I looked at my morph-rifle and snorted. It was like trying to take down Mt. Everest with a shovel.

Deciding to make the best of it, I marched toward the structure, which was several hundred meters distant. After all, there was no time like the present to make your last stand.

When I reached the roughly cylindrical tower, it looked kind of like hardened sand. I reversed my rifle and rammed the butt of it into the wall.

To my surprise, my rifle broke through. The stuff was pretty delicate, actually. If I'd had a unit, or at least an 88 artillery piece, I might have managed to do some serious damage.

The material was loose earth, but with a waxy substance shot all through it. Resin? Not really, something much weaker. Almost like dried spit. It was as thin as paper, and it crumbled as I hacked and slashed at it.

I dug quite a hole in a short amount of time—but it was no use. The thing was just too massive, whatever it was. I was a flea biting an elephant.

That gave me an idea. The trick here was to do outsized damage… without killing myself in the process.

Sure, as a final gesture, I'd be glad to self-destruct and make a hole the size of a suburban home in the side of this thing, but I couldn't delude myself. That wouldn't topple the tower. It was just too damned big.

Hiking around the base of it, I found something new: a tunnel in the side. There wasn't any doorway, or much of anything else. Just a tunnel, and a slightly upward graded ramp inside. I walked in like owned the place.

After a dozen steps, the gloom closed over me, and I switched on my suit lights. Something approached. It looked like a termite the size of a forest bear.

I think the worker bee was as surprised as I was. We sized each other up for about a second—then I blew its brains out.

Whistling, I crunched over the mess and kept going. I must have walked a kilometer or more, winding my way deeply into that thing. Fortunately, there were no forks in the road. If there had been, I would surely have gotten lost.

Several more times, I met up with the big termite things. Each time, I dispatched them without hesitation. They were unarmed and seemed to have no idea how to fight.

"STOP!" a voice rang out.

Damn, that was loud! My ear-drums almost split, the volume was so tremendous.

"Uh…" I said. "Who am I talking to? And—lower the volume, would you?"

"YOU ARE A BAD-THING!"

"Dammit," I said, adjusting my helmet. We had ear-plugs that we usually used to connect our suit radios with one another. I used mine as a sound deadener, screwing in the plugs on both sides of my skull until they hurt.

"FAILED-CREATURE! BAD-DESIGN INSECT!"

I got the feeling I was being insulted. At least the roaring voice wasn't hurting my head anymore. It was only annoying with the plugs sunk in all the way—not deafening. I kept walking forward, found two more termites dudes, and shot them down.

"You want to talk, Skay?" I asked.

"YOU MUST STOP. YOU ARE A BAD-THING. YOU—"

"And you'd better shut up, or I'm going to kill you. Thousands more human troops know about this spot now. We'll swarm you, and we'll take you down. It's all part of the plan."

I was bullshitting hard, like I rarely do. I had no troops, and they had no idea I was here. Hell, the rig I was wearing was probably going to kill me sooner or later.

But the enemy Skay didn't know that. Apparently, it was kind of ticked off about my efforts at destroying this holy tower in its core. That made me want to do all the damage I could.

I walked on. The Skay didn't talk to me for a time—but when it did, it had quieted down some.

"Is this voice more pleasing?" it asked me in a feminine tone.

I found that change surprising. "Yes," I admitted. "That's much better. Now, what seems to be the problem?"

"You are not allowed here. You are a failed-thing. A mistake. A cull among the herd that has somehow escaped its rightful fate."

"Huh, that's real interesting."

I met up with another termite, and he died like the rest.

"You aren't stopping. You must self-execute. I demand that you do so."

"Nope," I said, marching onward. "Sorry. You don't have that authority here."

"But you are humans. You bow to the Imperial authority of the Galactics."

"That's right, we do. But you're not the proper owner of Province 921. The Mogwa are."

"Untrue. We have claimed this region. We will not be denied."

I stopped—taking a deep breath. "I tell you what, Mr. Skay, sir. If you can produce Governor Sateekas of the Mogwa, and he tells me to stand down, I'll do it right now."

"Sateekas is aboard his flagship."

I nodded, believing the Skay. "Well then, I guess—"

"I'll put you in contact with Sateekas. He will order you to obey me."

That halted my big boots at last. My mouth sagged open. "Really?"

"Yes, bad-thing. Open the channel request blinking on your prosthetic device."

I looked down at my tapper. Sure as shit, it *was* blinking with an incoming call. Shrugging, I opened the channel.

"Uh... hello?"

The image on the tiny screen strobed, but it grew clear after several seconds. "This is Grand Admiral Sateekas," the Mogwa said. "Who am I speaking with?"

Sateekas didn't look all that good. He was, in fact, kind of messed-up. Behind him, over his many tangled limbs, I saw a hanging pall of smoke.

"This is Centurion James McGill, sir!" I said proudly. "I've got this Skay by the balls, Sateekas. Do I have your permission to squeeze the juice out of him?"

Sateekas blinked. He peered. "By all that's unholy... it *is* the McGill. Of every face of every human I've ever encountered, there's only one that I might safely say I recognize—and it's you, creature."

"Thank you, sir. I'd know you anywhere as well."

"Slave-love..." Sateekas said. "Too bad it is too late for us, and for you. My fleet has been broken. Our ships lay scattered and burning in space. We have lost this battle, faithful McGill..."

Blinking once, then twice, it was my turn to feel cold shock overcome me.

Could it be true? Had the Skay truly won the tremendous battle that had surely gone on outside this great hull?

The mere thought of it made my skin crawl. We'd traded in our old, harsh, cruel masters for new ones.

Unfortunately, the Skay were cold, alien machines. In all likelihood, they would be worse than the Mogwa.

-51-

While I stood in that tunnel, stunned by the revelation that the fleet battle outside the Skay's hull had gone badly, another termite-looking dude came scuttling close.

I shot him. It was reflex, really. I didn't even think about it.

"BAD-CREATURE!" boomed the Skay. "You continue to rebel, despite your master's admission of defeat? Truly, you are an unreliable, honorless smear of excrement!"

For some reason, I got the idea that the Skay didn't like it when I shot creatures in this tunnel. That got me to thinking, and it soon got my boots trudging again. I strode forward, kicking the dead termite-thing out of my way.

"Sorry about that," I said. "I'm real, real sorry. That bug-thing just popped out of nowhere and startled me. I'm a combat-creature, you see, and my instincts are to kill anything that looks wrong to me."

"A feral disease. An infestation of malignancy..." The Skay seemed to be lamenting his fate at having been infected by humans.

Infection—it was an accurate analogy. The giant Skay inner-world was like a being, and we were like an invasive disease. We'd gotten in by jumping into his mouth, and now we had metastasized, firing individual troops all over the interior to do whatever harm they could. Maybe, just maybe, if

297

we did enough damage we could send him into system-shock and the damned thing would die.

"Uh…" I said, thinking out loud as I marched more quickly. I was moving at a trot now. If this zone was important, if this mountain of waxy sand was a critical organ, surely the Skay's antibody creatures couldn't be far behind me.

"Mr. Skay, Grand Admiral Sateekas," I started. "Just so I'm clear on things, how did the battle go?"

"You're curiosity is pointless, human disease-creature," the Skay complained.

But Sateekas answered me pridefully. "The Mogwa fleet has been defeated, and many ships have been lost," he said. "But two of the three Skay ships have been lost as well, McGill. It was a glorious day. Too bad you missed most of it."

"Only one Skay left, huh?" I asked.

"You describe the situation accurately," Sateekas said in a bitter tone. "The final Skay, the smallest of the three, was held back from the initial conflict. It chased after your ship, *Legate*. That worm Turov managed to wriggle away, going into warp. The Skay gave up the chase, because we'd taken the opportunity to launch our attack, seeing that the enemy was out of position."

"I see…"

"This is immaterial prattle!" the Skay interrupted. "There is no cause for this cretinous slave to be furnished with a full battle-report! You, Sateekas, will order your beasts to stand-down. They are crawling within my subsystems, causing injury. If you do not order them to halt their depredations, I will crush the remaining Mogwa ships that lie broken before me!"

Sateekas' eyes narrowed. He was a wily old tactician, I had to give him that. We'd always had a grudging respect for one another, despite being on different sides of several conflicts.

I could tell his radar had lit up. He'd realized the Skay was panicking about whatever I was doing, and that might give him an edge—or at least a chance for revenge.

"McGill-creature," Sateekas said in a grave tone. "I hereby—"

At this point, I wasn't sure whether Sateekas was about to order me to stand-down, or to press on and destroy whatever I could. Either way, I didn't like it.

You see, I'd already decided I wasn't going to stop. If Sateekas gave me the order to do so, that meant the Skay would have an excuse to destroy helpless Mogwa. On the other hand, if Sateekas ordered me to press the attack, the Skay was going to berserk and kill them all anyway.

The only way I could see out of the situation was with a little old-fashioned sleight-of-hand. McGill-style chicanery, if you will.

Accordingly, I reached out my hand and muted my tapper. Then I began banging on it and cursing loudly. "Damn this thing!" I shouted. "This human tech breaks down at the worst possible moments. Sateekas, sir? Could you repeat that? I didn't get it, sir."

Of course, I saw Sateekas flapping his gums, but I heard nothing.

"Sorry! Not getting audio now. I'll tell you what, you try calling me back. This connection was thready at best from the beginning. We'll start fresh."

"You will do no such thing, failed-beast!" the Skay complained. "The transmission was made. You have—"

"I have nothing. Patch the next call through to me, so I can talk to my master."

"I am your new master. I have conquered Province 921 in fair battle. The claim will hold up in any Imperial court of adjudication. Therefore, I—"

"Sheesh!" I shouted. "What's with all the tech failures these days? Do you Skay know how to build a proper translation box or not? All I'm hearing from you now is squeaks and farting noises."

I was in the zone of pure fabrication at this point. But even I, with my magnificent skills in such situations, knew that I was living on borrowed time. Any minute now, the Skay would catch on to the fact I was full of shit and stalling in every way possible. At that point, he'd wipe out the Mogwa ships in a rage and run me down with his freakish defense-creatures.

Already, in fact, I thought I could hear something coming up the tunnel behind me. It wasn't the whispery sound of scuttling termites, either. It was more like the churning of larger, more purposeful feet. Something *big*, something *angry*, was on my tail.

Picking up the pace, I started to run. My boots tore holes in the papery tunnel floor, but I didn't care. I didn't even bother to pause when I ran into more termite-things. I killed them mid-stride and kept running.

My tapper was buzzing and chirping on my arm, but I ignored it. None of it mattered now. Sateekas was dead, or he wasn't. Either way, I was committed.

The trouble was I didn't exactly know how I could do something nasty to this giant machine. I wanted to. Really, I did. But how?

Then I reached the end of the ramp, and I almost stumbled. In front of me, space had opened up. An open abyss yawned wide.

It was dark, and when I say dark, I mean it was like opening your eyes at the bottom of an unlit coal mine. The only sources of light I could detect came from my suit, my tapper, and a distant hazy glow from above.

Looking up, I thought I saw some kind of opening. It was slate gray, where everything else was pitch black. A circular opening, very distant, up very far above me.

Could that be the top of the mound? And the space around me—it felt big. Like I was at a cave mouth that opened onto a cliff. I could feel, rather than see, the abyss that lay before me. The lack of sound bouncing back in my direction was a clue as to the size of the place. It was hot and very dark.

Flipping up my visor, I caught a blast of hot, dry air. It gushed up into my face, rising and drying the sweat from my skin. It was as if I'd opened an oven and peered inside.

Thinking back about my run, I realized I'd been inside the walls of this cylindrical shape all along. Spiraling around this central void that formed a vast empty chamber in the middle.

What could I have found? A chimney? That's what it seemed like. The mysterious structure was a smokestack the size of a mountain.

Maybe I was inside a cooling tower. A subsystem designed to bleed heat out of something else far below. I wasn't sure about the details—there was no way to be certain, no way to know the truth.

I heard a distinct rustling behind me. It was purposeful, deliberate movement. There was more than one creature coming, I could tell that now. There was an entire pack of them on my tail. They'd followed me up that long, long winding tunnel. Soon, they'd either push me into the abyss, or they'd kill me where I stood.

There was one more thing that Natasha and the other techs had rigged-up while we'd prepared to teleport all over the inside of the Skay. It wasn't anything fancy, just a final gift to present to the Skay, should any of us live long enough to find something worth destroying.

I only had one move left. I fooled with my rig, trying to turn the self-destruct back on.

It was a desperate play, but there wasn't anywhere else to go now. I was at a dead end, and fighting back into the tunnel wasn't going to help.

Holding two buttons down at once for five seconds, I did a factory-reset on the device. That should make it reboot and start the count-down again. Unfortunately, it had to go through a booting process. All these years, and computers still took their sweet time to start functioning.

When the first monster showed up, I unloaded on it with my morph-rifle. The thing fell in a tangled heap. The second one—I took him out too.

But there were more. Too many more, and they came in groups of two or three. After about a minute of desperate battle, during which I shouted and cursed myself hoarse, they managed to push me over the edge.

Falling... I was falling with the creatures. We were tearing at one another, pointlessly struggling as we fell together into that abyss I'd climbed above. I didn't know how long I had until I hit bottom, but I figured it couldn't be more than a few seconds.

I don't remember what happened at the end. Maybe I smashed into the bottom and died. Maybe the rig finally rebooted, realized it was overdue to self-destruct and blew me apart.

Whatever happened, my engrams of the event are lost forever.

-52-

Coming back to life again struck me as something of a surprise. I'd kind of counted myself as permed this time around—but I'd thought wrong.

Even weirder, my hazy mind was able to recall the talk with the Skay, the rush up the tunnels inside of that strange, papery cylinder, and even the part where I fell at the end. I was at a loss to explain it, but there it was. I'd undeniably been revived with memories up to the point of my most recent demise.

"What's his score?"

"Eight-point-five."

"Good. I would have taken a seven. There's no time for a reroll now—call in our aggrieved party."

"Will do."

Groggy, I tried to peer at the bio people, but they didn't look familiar. When you woke up after a revive, it was kind of like being a baby again for those first few minutes. My senses barely worked, and I felt kind of dazed.

Sure, I knew I was aboard a ship on somebody's Blue Deck—but it could have been anyone's ship. At least the bio people were regular humans, not near-humans, or Claver-clones or Rigellian bears. They were normal folks.

That didn't mean I was in the clear. I'd recently disobeyed my legion officers by not blowing up when the teleport-rig timers were supposed to go off. I'd also pretty much flipped-off two sets of Galactics—the Skay and the Mogwa.

When a man like me has gone out on a limb like this one, well, it was best to play it as carefully as you could. Just in case I was in trouble, I played opossum. I laid there and mumbled incoherently. Sometimes in the past, seemingly good people had revived me with bad intentions. I didn't recognize these voices, or the environment—so I pretended I was helpless.

Finally, as the bio people prodded me and asked dumb questions about my apparent lack of capacity—another individual arrived. I knew his voice in an instant.

I'd been expecting someone special. Maybe Graves, or Turov—or even Armel, or Winslade. But the individual who came to loom over me was more threatening than any of these, and more familiar.

"James?" asked a deep male voice.

The voice was just a little wrong. I knew it, of course, but I didn't hear it quite this way most of the time.

"McGill?" I asked, opening my eyes and sitting up.

There I was. Looming over me was my own twin—and he was a tall one.

I'd always known that about myself, but it was different seeing yourself in person. For a tall guy, you just get used to looking down on everyone else. When you meet someone who is actually your size or larger, it's kind of threatening. Kind of a shock.

The bio people pulled away from the two of us. They'd been getting out the defibrillator and the mind-probe machine—but none of those would be necessary.

James McGill—the other guy, the one who was fully dressed and wearing all his gear—he grinned at them.

"He was playing you," he said. "That's what I would have done. McGill—me, I mean—when you revive one of us, it's kind of like one of those movie scenes where the science folks unwittingly wake up a monster. What always happens in those movies, huh? Why, the monster plays it cool. He seems dead or helpless—until he makes his move."

McGill turned back to me, and he was still grinning. "Isn't that right, James?"

304

"Sure is," I admitted. "Uh... can anyone tell me what the hell is going on?"

The second James pointed a thick finger at me. "We were hoping you could shed some light," he said.

That finger was as thick as a flashlight. *Damn*, I had big hands. No wonder people flinched a little when I reached for them. It was no longer a mystery as to why they called me a gorilla all the time, either.

"Uh..." I said. "How much do you remember, brother of mine?" I asked.

McGill shook his head. "Nope. I asked first. Right now, I'm the legit McGill. I'm for-reals, you're a mistake."

I got it then. I'd figured it all out at last. There could only be one James McGill in existence—God knew that one of us was enough. We weren't like Clavers. We didn't want to make some kind of perverse clone army. It would never have worked, anyway, as we could never have all gotten along.

That meant one of us had to die. Either this fine-looking older McGill, who had been reported dead and then revived fair and square—or naked-assed, bewildered me.

"Can I take a shower first, to wake up some?" I asked.

McGill shook his head. "No stalling. This is kind of important, James. I know you understand."

I sat up then, and everyone stepped back. Getting off the table and stretching, I walked over to the lockers. There were uniforms in there. I felt like putting one on. When a man is buck-naked, sticky and freshly revived, he's always at a disadvantage. If I was going to be judged up against another McGill, well, I was going to do it dressed and geared like he was.

A big hand landed on my shoulder. There was only one fellow in the room with a hand that big. Only one on the whole ship, probably.

I grabbed the hand, pulled and twisted—but he broke free. Most men would have been on the floor, but not another me. He was just as tricky and mean as I was.

He went for a low kick, reaching out to stomp at my feet. That was a good, wicked move. A naked man has many vulnerabilities, but one of the worst is his bare feet.

305

Fortunately, I'd anticipated the move. I straight-armed him, shoving him back. He staggered into the table I'd just been born upon. At that point, his hand fell on the butt of his pistol.

"Gentlemen!" a female voice broke in. It was Turov. She'd arrived, and she looked annoyed. "Back off!"

We both glanced at her. She was our girlfriend, and our superior officer. She didn't look very threatening, standing there all cute and small, but I knew mean things came in such packages.

Glowering, I took a step back. The other McGill took his hand off his gun, and the bio people began to breathe again.

"Two of you…" Galina said, sighing and looking us up and down. "My good fortune is boundless."

"Is this *Legate*, then?" I asked.

She shook her head. "No. *Legate* was destroyed. You're aboard the *U. E. Berlin*, one of our newest battlecruisers. It is Drusus' flagship. They're reviving key people here, such as myself."

That made sense to me. The ship did feel like a United Earth ship, but it wasn't like *Legate*. It wasn't a transport at all, it was a true warship. That meant the engine sounds were more throaty, more powerful. The walls and bulkheads were thicker steel, and every door could be sealed against pressure extremes.

"Okay," I said, looking around with new respect. "What can I tell you?"

"What's the last thing you remember?"

"Falling to my death inside some kind of Skay chimney."

I briefly described my march up into the guts of the ship. I told them about the termite things I shot, and then I finished off with my discussions with Sateekas and the Skay itself.

Turov's finger came up and aimed at the ceiling. "That's the part that's interesting," she said. "You have experiences with both the Mogwa high command and the Skay that we have no other record of."

"You mean he claims to have them," my twin said.

"Uh…" I said. "If you don't mind my asking, I'd like to know how it is that I can recall these things at all."

306

"That's what I want to know," James number two added. Ever since we'd struggled, I'd come to think of him as a copy, a knock-off, a crude facsimile of myself. One look at those dark eyes of his confirmed he was thinking the same thing about me.

Turov sighed. "It makes sense that you can, James. Your memory engrams have been confirmed as authentic, and that's actually the main reason we brought you back. You see, when you had a connection relayed by the Skay to Sateekas, that allowed you—and only you, of all the humans inside that doomed ship—to get your engrams transferred out. No one else was ever in contact."

"I get it. my tapper sensed the connection and downloaded automatically."

"Exactly. Earth fleet ships were in the system and their network saved your recorded mind. We have, therefore, raw video of the transactions between you and Sateekas—but we don't have everything. The packets sent with your engrams were downloaded, but the rest was done using an Imperial code. We want to know what was said—and what you did to that Skay ship."

"Oh, that..." I said, and I felt an urge to invent a tale in which I was the hero. Instead, I told them the truth. This was mostly because I couldn't come up with a good enough lie on a story so complex and detailed.

Naturally, however, I edited out certain details. I didn't mention how Primus Graves was against the move from the start, and how I levered him into it. In my version, I was following orders like a marching cadet.

McGill number two stared at me this whole time, squinting hard. I caught onto the idea that he was there to determine the veracity of my account.

"Well?" Turov asked, turning toward him. "What do you think of his story? Is it accurate?"

"Damnation," he said, "no wonder people are always saying I'm a good liar! To me, he seems pure as driven snow. But it's hard to tell for sure..."

Turov twisted up her lips. She seemed unsatisfied with this response.

I was kind of surprised myself. I figured that James number two would probably shit all over my story in order to make sure I was the one getting permed instead of him. But he didn't do that. He pretty much said nothing.

Thinking it over, I came to the conclusion he liked my edited version. After all, it cast a good light on both of us. In addition to that, it made me believe he thought he was in the clear. That he could expect to keep breathing. I didn't like that part so much, as it meant I had to die.

One immutable rule of the Empire was a legal concept called "the maintenance of the individual" by lawyers and scholars. Essentially, it said that you had to execute copies when they were discovered until there was only one version of any person. To do otherwise was to invite chaos. I supposed that Clone World with its teeming numbers of Clavers proved the point.

"All right," Turov said, turning to me at last. "McGill! Take your shower, suit-up, and move quickly."

"Uh…" I said. "Where are we going?"

"To the brig, where you will await trial."

"I see."

And I did see. They were going to execute me, and they were going to do it right. Under watchful eyes that looked very familiar, I took my shower and dressed. I don't mind telling you that I took my time, soaping up and everything.

"This is taking too damned long," the other me complained. "He's stalling. We have a battle coming."

"It's hours away," Turov said. "Stop whining—he's your own flesh and blood, after all. Have a little respect."

"What battle is that?" I asked, stepping out of the shower and pulling on a fresh uniform.

"The Rigellians are still coming, remember?" Turov said. "The Mogwa fleet was mostly destroyed. It surrendered—but then you blew up the last of the three Skay. Then—"

She stopped talking, because I was whooping and clapping my hands over my head in celebration.

Turov frowned at me and my happy-dance. "What's wrong with you now?"

"I didn't know until right now that the Skay ship *blew up!*" I told her.

"Oh… right. It did. We don't know if you did it personally. We understand that commandos were thrown all over the inside of the big vessel. All of the Skay's defensive units had been rushed to overwhelm you, so they had little defense at the vital organs."

"That's right! That's how you kill a Skay, you get inside, and you tear shit up!"

"All right, all right. Get dressed and start walking."

I did as she commanded, heading for the door in a crisp new uniform. I now looked more like a twin to the other James than ever. That gave me ideas, as I couldn't help but wonder if anyone would notice if I managed to make a switcheroo somehow.

"Uh…" I said, glancing back from the doorway. I couldn't help but notice Turov and McGill number two both had their weapons out, and I had nothing but my bare hands. At least I wasn't naked anymore. I thought about bolting and running down the passageway, but I knew they'd just gun me down, shooting Earth's biggest hero in the back.

"Get going," Turov said. "James, you stay right behind him. I'll bring up the rear."

Marching along, I saw bio people ducking out of the way. They knew the rep Varus legionnaires had, and they'd all heard the rumors about twins being born. It was best for your health to stay clear when we were around with guns drawn.

We took a few turns and went deeper into the warship. The passages were more utilitarian down here in the lower decks. There was a lot more hard metal, and it was poorly ventilated. I was used to a troopship that had more amenities than this battlewagon did.

I was about to remark upon this, in fact, when shots rang out behind me.

When I first heard the gunfire, I figured all that happy-talk about going to the brig was to give me something to think about before the deed was done. Maybe they'd decided to shoot me now and shunt my dead ass out of an airlock down here, with none the wiser.

As God is my witness, I thought I'd been hit for a full second. When you're walking in front of people who have a clear and present reason to kill you, and their guns are out, it's hard not to expect sudden death.

But I was wrong on every count. I turned, grabbing at my own body. There were no holes, no leaking organs. I was untouched.

One of my two guardians, however, couldn't say the same. One was facedown and dead. The other was standing tall.

My mouth fell open, and I gaped, and it wasn't even an act this time.

-53-

"Galina?" I asked. "You shot the other McGill?"

"Yes. Pick up his gun—quickly! There are no cameras here, and I jammed the body-cams just in case... Hurry, get his gun!"

Watching her closely, I stepped forward and picked up poor old McGill's weapon. A quick check told me the weapon was loaded and fully charged. It was primed and ready to go.

"Huh..." I said. "I thought since I was the copy... I mean, I thought this poor boy had the right to—"

"He did," Galina said. "But... let's just say he knew a few things that you don't. You should be happy that I shot the wrong one. Can I count on your silence concerning this detail?"

I thought that over for maybe two seconds, then I nodded and grinned. "You know what? I bet he was a bad grow anyways. He seemed kind of twitchy."

She shook her head. "No. He was revived to answer questions, and he did so poorly. From now on, *you* are the original, not the copy. Don't let anyone know you were the one on the Skay ship. You don't remember that."

"Right... I'll keep that on the down-low."

Some security types arrived about then and Turov calmly explained that a mistake had been corrected. She indicated the dead man on the deck with a hole in his back, and they flipped him over. They did a double-take when they saw my face, and I almost laughed.

"You see?" Turov said. "A mistake was made."

"Clearly so," said the lieutenant leading the group. He was Fleet, and he was bemused. "You Varus types play by your own rules, don't you?"

"That's right," I said loudly. "You'd better not fall asleep on watch around us."

Looking disturbed, the man ordered his lackeys to carry my body and they all hurried away.

"These Fleet boys are getting ideas," I remarked.

"They certainly are. They're becoming more uppity every year."

"I guess it's because they've got big warships like this battlewagon these days. They figure they're important."

Galina nodded. "That definitely has something to do with it. I miss the days when it was all about the legions and nothing else."

Together, we marched up to Gold Deck. I played the quiet gorilla role to the hilt while Drusus and the warship's captain, a man named Barlow, asked Galina questions. Things were going pretty well, but then somebody asked the *wrong* question.

"So, what did you find out?" Captain Barlow asked. "Was it all a waste of time?"

"Completely," Turov said. "He knew nothing. We still have no idea why the Skay ship died. Possibly, our attacks on the outer hull ruptured something inside."

I snorted at that. I couldn't help it.

Drusus had been listening closely. He eyed me for the first time. "Have you got something to add, McGill?"

"Uh… well sir, nothing much—but that Skay ship died *somehow*. Even if we don't have proof, it seems obvious that the commando team did deadly work. I mean, if you send in a sapper, and he dies in a fiery explosion, you have to figure he must have at least lit the fuse, right?"

Drusus nodded slowly, thinking that over.

312

Galina, on the other hand, was giving me her patented death-stare. I ignored this, as I didn't think I was giving too much away.

"Well," Drusus continued, "I guess we'll never know for sure. Perhaps it won't even matter. While the battle between the Mogwa and the Skay is over, with no clear winner, we're about to face Rigel head-on. Let's hope we win a clean victory this time."

He gave us a tight smile, and I hollered liked he'd given us a high school cheer.

"We're gonna whup them good, sir!" I insisted. "You watch."

The bridge crew blinked at this, but they smiled. It's always hard to hate the optimist.

Our warships glided among the broken Mogwa vessels, rendering what aid we could. Some of their ships were patched up to hold air and fuel, and we transferred survivors there for safe-keeping.

A few hours later, we got quite a surprise.

"Praetor?" the battlecruiser's captain called out. "We've got a guest coming aboard."

"A guest?"

"It's Sateekas."

Drusus looked kind of pale. "The grand admiral? He lived?"

"Yes, and he's insisting that he be allowed to come aboard our flagship. He wants to have a word with you personally, sir."

We all looked at Drusus. He was in a tough spot.

Once, years ago, we'd killed a group of Mogwa survivors after a battle had gone sour. We'd flushed them all out the airlock afterward and let them burn up as they reentered normal space. Today, it looked like we might be faced with a similar choice.

On this occasion, however, the situation was tighter. There were Mogwa ships all over local space. Sure, they were in bad shape, but we had to assume someone had a working deep-link. For all we knew, every move we made in this star system was being recorded and relayed back to Mogwa Prime even now.

"What are your orders, Praetor?" Captain Barlow asked.

Drusus hesitated, but only for a few heartbeats. Then, he lifted his chin high. "Bring him aboard. We've got nothing to hide."

Nodding, the captain relayed the order.

We waited after that. About half an hour before the fleet from Rigel was destined to arrive, none other than Sateekas, the Grand Admiral of Battle Fleet 921, stepped aboard our humble flagship.

"Grand Admiral on the bridge!" called out one of the marines.

We all stood at attention.

"All hail the Grand Admiral!" I shouted.

A few people glanced at me, others called out "hail!" but weakly, in my opinion.

Sateekas took it all in stride. He didn't seem to care much what we did or said. He slithered onto the deck with those six churning limbs and made a beeline for the command chair in the middle.

Berlin's captain looked shocked, but he reacted quickly enough. He stepped out of the way, and Sateekas squatted on his chair.

Baleful orbs rotated, scanning us. Sateekas hadn't said a word yet, and he was acting kind of peculiar, even for a Mogwa.

"Welcome aboard my flagship, Grand Admiral," Drusus said. "I'm Praetor Drusus, commander of this fleet and the legions in our holds. To what do we owe the honor of this visit?"

"Honor?" Sateekas' translation box squawked out at last. "You dare speak of honor? Earth's fleet stood idle while my force was destroyed wholesale."

"We were moving steadily toward the enemy. They advanced and struck with great speed. Your ships and theirs fell upon one another before we could reach the battle zone."

"This might be true, but you still hung back after the first two Skay were destroyed. My ships drifted in ruin. We were defeated, and the Skay toyed with our lives. All that time, you did nothing!"

314

Drusus opened his mouth, then closed it again. He was befuddled. I had no doubt at that moment that Sateekas was right. I hadn't witnessed the battle. I hadn't even gotten a proper report on how it all went down—but I knew a guilty man's face when I saw one.

"Not so, Grand Admiral!" I shouted.

Every eye in the place turned toward me. Most of them looked confused, like those of the regular captain and crew. The legion people who knew me, however, looked horrified and sick.

Only one set of eyes brightened. Those belonged to Sateekas himself.

"Ah! The McGill creature! You live again!"

"That's right, sir," I said. "I spoke to you while I killed that last Skay. Earth's ships hung back because they knew they couldn't win against a Skay—but more importantly, they knew they didn't have to."

Several officers moved to shut me up. A few marines even rushed forward, at a signal from Captain Barlow, to perform an arrest. But lucky for them, Sateekas fluttered his limbs.

"Let the McGill speak! I command it!"

The marines and a dozen other people with gritted teeth backed off.

"They don't like to brag, sir," I told Sateekas. "But I have to tell the truth. This matter is too important."

"Brag? Brag about what?" the Mogwa asked.

"About single-handedly destroying that last Skay without losing a single ship," I said, as if surprised he didn't get it. "You see, we didn't want you to feel any... well... embarrassment about your performance in this struggle. We had an unfair advantage, so you shouldn't really compare the efforts of your ships and crews against ours."

The Mogwa blinked, as did plenty of others. A few jaws dropped open, and hands rose halfway to protest—but they didn't dare. They didn't want to blow it.

"Explain yourself more clearly, human," Sateekas said. "And try to do so without insulting the lost heroes that crewed my ill-fated fleet."

315

"Of course, Your Highness. You see, we've tangled with the Skay before. In fact, I've commanded missions inside the body of one of them before—twice before. During those missions, we learned a few things. We studied their artificial organs, their power-sources and so on. The moment this battle began, we struck the nearest of them, inserting a crack commando team. It took a while, but we managed to tear that Skay up something awful."

Sateekas rustled his limbs contemplatively. At last, he seemed to relax a little, and he returned to the commandeered command chair.

"Your tale is incredible, but it fits the facts. I myself spoke with you while your sabotage efforts were in full swing. The Skay was in near panic, and it must have suspected your infection of its interior would turn out to be fatal... But still, why would your fleet hold off? Why would you speak of not shaming thousands of Mogwa heroes?"

"Well, you see, it's like this: We knew our ships couldn't do much against a closed Skay hull—we don't have that kind of tech. Your own fleet only managed to crack two of them. Rather than throw away our ships against an impenetrable target, we stood off and waited for it to die. We had, after all, poisoned that last Skay from the inside. It was only a matter of time until it died."

"Amazing..." Sateekas said. "I find your account believable in every detail, now that I see it in a fresh light. Your tactics were flawless. I must apologize, I was stricken with grief to have a second fleet wiped out while I watched. This war has been fateful and costly..."

Sucking in a deep breath, Drusus pasted on a smile and dared take a step forward. "We offer our humblest condolences for your losses, Grand Admiral. Please know that all of Earth is with you this day. We will never forget the sacrifice made here in this star system for our benefit."

Sateekas shuffled himself around and peered at Drusus. "What are you prattling about? We didn't come out here for your benefit, we did so to defend our rightful territory along the frontier."

316

"Uh…" I said, sensing that Drusus was blowing it already. He had his heart in the right place, but he just didn't understand bloodthirsty aliens the way I did. "What the praetor meant to say, sir, is that he'd liked to express slave-love for you and all your multi-limbed brothers."

Sateekas glanced around irritably. "He should have said so, then. But never mind. We have another critical task at hand. You will assume an aggressive battle-posture and direct your guns to greet the Rigellian ships that are about to reach this system.

The officers looked at one another in shock.

"Grand Admiral?" Drusus asked. "I don't quite understand… are you asking for our help to defeat the fleet from Rigel?"

"No! I never ask anything from a slave! Your ships are hereby commandeered. You are under my command now. Do you animals understand this?"

A few heads nodded. No one looked like they felt too good in the guts.

"Excellent. Now, turn your ships sunward. The enemy will come out near the battlefield. We've studied them, and they like hard and fast attacks. Prepare yourselves! This will be a glorious moment in your pathetic history of holding back and skirting battles. I will allow none of that today!"

-54-

The crew moved toward the warship's controls and the great vessel wheeled about, accelerating on her new course. Despite this seeming obedience, I found myself eyeing my fellow humans critically. I could sense an undercurrent of tension among my fellows. They were whispering, casting meaningful glances. Several had placed a hand on the butt of their pistol.

Sateekas had made one serious error. The Galactics often made this mistake when dealing with humans: they trusted us. They didn't seem to quite get that we weren't like the tame races of aliens who served them with devotion among the Core Worlds. We were barbarians, through and through.

Sensing that something disastrous and possibly fatal was about to happen to the Mogwa, I spoke up again.

"Uh… Grand Admiral, sir? Can I assume this battle will be recorded and transferred to the Core Worlds when it's finished? When we're all basking in glory?"

He glanced at me. "Better still. My surviving ships are transmitting every passing moment of this event live via deep-link. The Mogwa of Trantor already know of your bravery, humans. Rest assured."

At that, hands slid away from weapons all around the bridge. Sateekas had unwittingly prevented his own assassination.

318

Drusus walked up to stand next to me. Without looking at me directly, he spoke in a quiet tone.

"McGill, we owe you a great deal, but please control yourself. Only speak if absolutely necessary. I can't tell you how many officers here have requested—no, *demanded* your removal from this bridge."

"And yet you've kept me here, on duty and watchdogging this Mogwa? Thank you, sir! That's quite a vote of confidence."

"If we live to see the dawn, we'll have to talk further on the topic." He walked away, looking shaken.

"Looking forward to it, sir!" I called after him, deciding to take his words in the best possible light.

Paralyzed into inaction, the crew and the Varus officers on Gold Deck didn't seem to know what to do. The Mogwa ships were crippled, and their leader was alone and vulnerable in our midst.

But that didn't matter. Everything we did now was being broadcast live to the Mogwa homeworld. If we dared move against Sateekas, we'd be labeled traitors and marked for dead by the Mogwa and all their allies.

That was the problem with this kind of war—the civil kind. You just didn't know who would come out on top in the end. That meant throwing our lot in with either side might be tantamount to suicide.

Aw well, there was nothing for it, I guess. It was time to sail into the teeth of the enemy and pray for the best.

On the big forward screens and holotanks, I watched the Rigellians as they began to arrive in the system. They were distant contacts, positioned and sized by gravimetrics, but not identified.

The tonnage kept adding up. That wasn't a strict accounting of their strength, but it did give us some idea. Already, their fleet outweighed ours and the balance kept getting worse as more ships arrived every few seconds.

"Big ships…" Turov said. She'd come to stand near me now as well. "Those bears like big ships. Maybe it's to compensate for their small stature."

"Maybe so, Tribune. I never much liked Squanto and his team—but I respect them. They might be small, but they pack a mean punch."

Speaking of Squanto, a bear looking a lot like my least-favorite rival swirled into existence on the central projection zone. He hung there, bigger than life, looking down at all of us like we were mice.

"That's Squanto himself!" I hissed at Turov.

"Shut up! Get off Gold Deck, McGill!"

She grabbed at my arm and began trying to drag me toward the door. She looked like a kindergartener dragging her daddy. I found this amusing, but I played along, walking with her.

It was already too late.

"The McGill..." hissed the furry figure on the holo projector.

Slowly, Turov and I turned back to face Squanto. Drusus had been saying something about greeting him, and hoping we could keep the peace, but the bear had been ignoring all that hogwash.

His black eyes drilled into me. I realized all of a sudden why Galina had been trying to get me off the bridge. She'd known this moment was coming.

"It is as I suspected," Squanto said, his translating snake-bone looking necklace rattling as he spoke. "The mindless creature sent to us died in agony, and it swore to its dying breath of its innocence. But here now, I see the proof of my convictions. You humans did not truly send us the vilest of your kind, but a copy instead."

I looked down at Turov, frowning. "So you did send another James to Rigel?"

"Of course we did. They offered peace for a single life. Quit complaining—it wasn't really you."

She did, however, look somewhat contrite. She couldn't meet my eyes. We'd laid in bed together a hundred times perhaps, over the years, and this was a pretty big betrayal. I knew that if I'd sent one of her twins out to some alien torture-party, she'd be pissed about it.

"I will not give you the satisfaction of enjoying your joke for another minute," Squanto said. "I will destroy your fleet,

320

your people, your planets… your very bones will be burned to heat our homes at night."

"We had a truce, Squanto," Drusus said. He glanced at me, and I thought he looked a little ashamed—but he kept on talking anyway. "Perhaps we could make this right by—"

"No!" shouted Grand Admiral Sateekas, interrupting all the humans. "I will not hear of it! The McGill owes no blood to this rabble from the frontier. We will fight them here, and we will destroy them utterly!"

My eyes drifted to the tonnage indicators. Rigel's fleet outweighed us by more than three to one. Now, I'm no math-wiz, but I sensed the situation wasn't developing in the best possible way for Earth's fleet.

"Advance!" Sateekas ordered, flopping one nasty limb at the growing swarm of ships on our screens. "Let us destroy them!"

"Um, Grand Admiral?" Drusus asked. "They outweigh us significantly. Perhaps it would be best to withdraw from this encounter and face them at a more opportune moment. After all, this star system is worthless and—"

"No!" Sateekas howled. "I won't hear of it. I'm now assuming ownership of all Earth forces. You are relieved of command, Drusus. For cowardice in the face of the enemy, you're hereby demoted as well. Get away from me!"

Shocked, Drusus stood there with his mouth open. He looked around at the other officers, who were mostly Fleet people.

"Did you not hear me? Get off my bridge!" Sateekas ordered. When Drusus didn't instantly obey, he turned to *Berlin's* crew. "Captain Barlow! Arrest this fool! See to it at once, or I'll have you both executed."

Captain Barlow stepped forward. He drew his pistol and waved it at Drusus. "I'm sorry sir," he said, "but you're under arrest. My marines will escort you to your quarters."

"The brig!" shouted Sateekas. "Put that fop into the brig. And where's the McGill?"

As Drusus was marched off the bridge, I walked up to Sateekas with big friendly grin. "What can I do you for, Grand Admiral?"

"Are you able to conceive of this fleet achieving victory over the barbaric creatures from Rigel?"

"I sure am!" I boasted. "The teddy bears have never been much of a contest."

"Excellent. You're now in charge of all the ships in this star system. You alone among your species have the proper cunning, loyalty and fierceness of spirit to lead."

"Uh…" I said, blinking. "So I'm the admiral now, huh?"

I looked around the bridge, and pretty much everyone who met my gaze appeared to be thinking about vomiting. "All right then. Let's get down to business."

I cracked my knuckles, and we got started.

-55-

Humanity's fate under the Galactics had never been pre-planned. Instead, we'd rolled with the punches from the start. That was largely because the Empire depended on ignorance and fear to keep its countless citizens in line. We never knew exactly what the response would be to anything we did, and thus our alien overlords kept us in the dark, guessing about our future.

For less forceful men, the situation often posed an insurmountable barrier. Unsure as to how the Galactics would respond, they were paralyzed into doing nothing. I suspected this largely had to do with the heinous penalties involved. The Mogwa thought little of us, and they'd happily destroy Earth for the slightest infraction.

I knew we couldn't afford to think like that today. We couldn't be driven by pure chickenry. All thoughts of declaring neutrality, or negotiating ceasefires—all that kind of crap fled from my brain. The sun had set on peaceful resolutions.

Instead, it was time to get on with the business of destroying these mother-effing bears any way we could.

"Captain Barlow?" I asked *Berlin's* top officer. "Are our ships all in formation?"

He looked kind of shocked, but he answered. "Yes... uh... sir. They're in position and standing by."

"Get them underway. Advance at half our maximum speed. I want every Gray Deck on every transport in the fleet—hey… we *do* have transports with legions on them, don't we?"

I turned to Graves, and he nodded stoically. I could tell that he wasn't approving of my command status, even though it had come down direct from Sateekas. That was just too damned bad in my book. Sure, it was against every Earth regulation known to man. But I didn't care, and more importantly, our Mogwa overlord didn't care, either.

Imperial Law had always trumped Hegemony Law, but that usually didn't matter. The two rarely came into conflict. The fact was, year-in and year-out, we didn't hear from the Galactics all that often. They left us alone and stuck to their petty border wars in the Galactic Core.

Not today, however. We'd seen the carnage firsthand, and this battle was going on only a hundred-odd lightyears from home. By putting me in command, Sateekas was wielding the power he'd always had—at least in theory—over Earth and her forces. Of course, none of this was sitting well with the Fleet officers on the bridge, but I figured they were just going to have to get over it.

"How many legions?" I asked Graves.

"Six… *sir*," he responded in a growl.

I ignored his poor attitude and nodded thoughtfully. "That's a pretty good shock-attack, if we do it right. Have them break out short-range weapons, those triple-barreled shotguns we've been experimenting with."

Graves squinted at me. "You think we're going to board the enemy ships? We can't get through their shields at this range."

"Nope. Not yet. We'll fire a big barrage of missiles. Set them to go off a kilometer away from the enemy hulls."

"What good will that do? No shockwaves in space reach that far."

I grinned. "Right, but EMP's do. We'll knock down their shields for a moment and then teleport aboard."

Graves looked down for a few seconds, working his tapper.

"What do you think of this mad plan, Primus?" Turov asked him. "Is McGill full of shit or what?"

"No… I think it could work. But why not just launch T-bombs if we're going this route. Why troops?"

I opened my mouth, realizing I didn't have a good answer. I'd wanted to board them, and I hadn't even thought of using Teleport-bombs.

"Because they'll detect T-bombs," Sateekas said. He'd been listening in, although it hadn't seemed like it. "McGill proves his genius again."

My mouth snapped shut. When you're kind of a dummy, and someone else gives you an out, you glom onto it like a drowning man grabbing for a life-preserver.

Startled by Sateekas, Graves took a step toward the Mogwa. "They can detect bombs but not troops?"

"The Skay have shared tech with Rigel. I know the enemy sensor arrays well. The Rigellian fleet can sense solid metallic objects like bombs coming at them—even if they are teleporting through hyperspace. That's how the Skay that first visited your world was able to stop most of your attacks. Troops are a different matter. If we arm our invaders lightly, they should be able to penetrate."

"And the ships from Rigel don't have hulls made of stardust…" Graves said thoughtfully. "They can't stop us once their shields are down. But the timing will have to be precise. Otherwise, thousands of troops will splat into the enemy warships like so many bugs hitting a windshield."

Most of this conversation came as a surprise to me. I'd wanted to send boarding parties, and I'd come up with the idea of blowing down the shields—but that's where my brain-child ended. The rest of this was coming from someone else.

In the manner of leaders throughout time, I stood back and let the others chatter about the details. I didn't listen much, and I soon became bored. In the end, I knew they'd credit me with the whole scheme anyway, so I didn't bother to absorb it all.

Instead, I walked over to Turov and gave her a smile. "Hey, Galina. This is pretty cool, isn't it?"

"What's cool, McGill?" she said, crossing her arms and narrowing her eyes.

"This is a first, that's what! I outrank you—just for today, I'm sure. But you have to admit this is a unique set of circumstances."

She didn't look impressed, happy, or even thoughtful. She looked kind of annoyed. "I'm not calling you 'sir.' You can forget about that."

"Really? Not even once? It's good for my ego. It might even help me win this battle."

"You'd better ask that god you keep talking to about that. We're going to need all the help we can get."

She stalked off, and I watched her go. She still had it, I must say. She'd been revived recently and freshened up to the youngest copy of her body. She always looked her best after a solid death and revive.

"McGill!" Graves barked.

I turned toward him, realizing he'd been talking to me while I stared at Turov's butt. It wasn't all that uncommon of a situation, so I shrugged it off and nodded to Graves.

"What is it, Primus? Report!"

Graves wanted to grind his teeth. I could tell. I wasn't calling him sir anymore, and it bugged him, it really did, but I figured that was just too damned bad.

"McGill, don't let this situation go to your head. It's temporary, I assure you."

"We're all here living life on a temporary basis, Graves. I'm well-aware of that."

He sighed. "All right. I've been coordinating with the troops on various Gray Decks. The captains of the warships are ready as well."

"Uh… ready for what?"

"For you to give them the signal to attack. The missile barrage, remember? It has to hit before we can back up the strike with teleporters."

"Oh yeah… fire the barrage! All missiles at once, put three or four on every front-line target. Go time!"

Graves turned to *Berlin*'s captain. They nodded to one another. The orders were relayed out to the fleet. As we were on the bridge of the flagship, all other captains followed our lead. Moments later, more than a thousand missiles took flight from hundreds of launch tubes.

The greatest space battle in human history had finally begun.

-56-

Space battles aren't like land battles at all. To me, they're a lot longer and more boring—until the sudden, violent finish that always comes at the end.

In space, you can see your opponent even when they're hours away. There are very few obstacles to hide behind. The Rigellian fleet was visible, approaching, maneuvering, firing missiles and probes at us. Just being able to watch them and know they were coming to kill us was stressful to some people, and it gave affairs like this an element of suspense.

For me, however, this didn't work. I tended to fall asleep if the danger wasn't immediate. As it was, I was jolted awake about an hour after our missiles roared away. There was a little drool on my uniform where my head had lolled forward to touch my chest.

Snorting and stretching with my fists thrown wide, I straightened up in the command chair, looking around and yawning.

All around me were tense, sweating humans. Every few seconds, they checked and rechecked their charts and numbers and colored flight arcs. These indicators ticked along, shifting ever so slightly by a few pixels now and then—like I said: *boring*.

Graves stood over me, and he looked irritated. "McGill, something's happening."

"Yeah...?" I said, sitting up and yawning again. "Have they hit us, or run off?"

"No, nothing like that. But their fleet has split into two forces."

That got me to blink a few times. "Huh? You mean they're trying to flank us?"

"No, they're letting half their fleet fall back, trailing the first wave."

I began scratching my chin. I let that good sensation continue by scratching along, all the way up the side of my cheek until I hit my sideburns around ear-level.

Graves watched this with disgust. Under normal circumstances, I knew he'd kick me or something. But he couldn't pull that now. It was nice to be allowed to wake up more slowly and naturally for once. I'd already figured out why having a high rank was a pretty good racket.

"Let's take a closer look," I said, and techs worked to project the situation on a battle computer in front of me.

I glanced around while they worked on this, and soon I frowned. "Where's Sateekas?"

One of the techs answered me. "While you were... um... thinking, he left the bridge. I think he's doing something down on Blue Deck."

"Huh..." I said, not really liking the sound of that. But then I looked on the bright side: He'd left me in charge and taken off. That was the kind of situation that let old James McGill shine.

"How long until we're within striking distance of their front-line ships?" I asked

"Several hours, sir."

I felt bored all over again, but then I noticed Graves was leaving the bridge—and Turov was already gone. I was surrounded by Fleet pukes, and I didn't really know any of them. There wasn't a friendly eye in sight.

"Hold on!" I called after Graves. "What's happening now?"

"I'm not sure, but I'm getting strange reports from Blue Deck. Apparently, your best pal Sateekas has commandeered all the revival machines."

As he was still walking away, I followed him into the passages.

"Yeah? Wonder what he's doing down there... wait a second, you don't think he's aborting our Varus people and churning out Mogwa, do you?"

"Sounds like a good guess to me. We can't do a damned thing about it, either. All their wrecked ships are beaming home a vid every second or so to Mogwa Prime."

I thought that over for a few seconds. Graves seemed to be in a hurry. He was walking fast, and I had to lengthen my stride a fraction to keep up. "I get it," I said. "Since we've turned on the Skay, we have to stay with the Mogwa. We can't very well get into a fight with two sets of Galactics at once."

"You should be proud. You pretty much started this nightmare single-handedly."

"Aw now, Primus, that's just unfair. I didn't send three giant bowling balls out here from the Core Worlds looking for trouble. I didn't get pissed and order the Mogwa Battle Fleet to come here to challenge them, either. All I did was wreck a lot of stuff."

"That's your forte."

"Yep."

We reached to Blue Deck, which was in the dead center of the big battlecruiser. Graves sucked in a breath to steel himself, and then he brushed past the orderlies and stepped inside. I was right on his heels.

The scene was one of chaos. The bio-people were rushing around, some playing medic to dead and wounded people on the floors. A team of marines surrounded one door, so I walked up to them and peered over their heads. They were guarding a revival chamber.

"Hey Centurion," one of the marines sneered. "Back off."

"I'm not just a Centurion," I said. "Sateekas, Grand Admiral of Battle Fleet 921 made me an admiral today."

The marine didn't look overly impressed. "Yeah, well, he's making a lot of changes. Don't get in his way. We've got orders to shoot down anyone who interferes in the Mogwa's actions."

"Uh…" I said, casting a glance back at the dead and wounded. "Did some of these "Blue Deck types complain or something?"

"That's right. Captain Barlow told us to clear them out of the way, so we did."

I nodded thoughtfully. Things often went like this when the Mogwa came to town. All our usual rules and regulations—even our chain-of-command—went out the window at their slightest whim.

About then Graves caught up to me. He'd been talking to the bio-people. "Is Sateekas in there?" he asked the marines.

"Yes, Primus."

"What's he doing?"

The marines looked furtive. They knew Graves and had respect for him. They held their rifles up to their chests with hands that clenched and unclenched.

In my own mind, I played out a scenario which might let me take out all four of them. I didn't think I could do it—but I was pretty sure I could put down two before they could get their act together. After that, it would be tough…

"We don't know exactly what he's up to," one of them spoke at last in a lowered voice, "but we do know he's hatching out aliens with the revival machines. He aborted every grow they had running and seeded his own."

"I see…" Graves said. "Gentlemen, I need to get in there and talk to that Mogwa. Are you going to shoot me if I try to walk past you?"

The marines looked nervous. They eyed one another. The noncom in charge sighed at last.

"No sir. Not you, sir. We just couldn't. That six-legged spider in there doesn't deserve—"

"Good enough," Graves said. "I thank you for your loyalty to Earth."

So saying, Graves moved forward. The marines grudgingly stepped aside.

Quick and neat as you please, I strode after him in his wake. The marines all glared up at me, but I didn't even make eye-contact. The key to slipping by in most situations is to look like you belong—like Graves meant for me to follow him.

It worked. Graves opened the big sealed door, and I zipped right through before it could swing shut.

About then, he looked over his shoulder in surprise.

"They let you in here?"

I shrugged. "Of course. I am acting admiral, after all."

Graves shook his head and walked off. I followed.

We passed a long line of steamy chambers with revival machines inside. Glancing through the porthole-like windows, I could see cases where the bio-people had been slaughtered. In other rooms, they worked feverishly. I got the feeling Sateekas had been liberally applying his usual buffet of incentives.

In the seventh room, we spotted Sateekas. He was berating a bio-girl who didn't look like she felt too good.

A birth was in progress. I didn't know what it was, but it wasn't human. There were clawed feet inside the birth sac, and the alien had a humanoid shape to it, but it was much smaller than a normal man.

Then I saw the dark, wet, matted fur, and I knew the truth.

"He's reviving a Rigellian!" I shouted.

-57-

My automatic response, when confronted with treachery of any kind, is to strike the perpetrator dead. In most cases, that approach had worked out well for me.

Accordingly, my gun was out the moment I strode into the room, brushing Graves aside. My murderous intent was clear.

Sateekas and the bio-girl looked up, and their eyes widened.

"McGill?" Sateekas said. "What is the meaning of this? I left you in charge on the bridge."

"That you did, sir. But there's no battle at the moment. I came down to see if I could give you some help."

I grinned as I spoke, and I leveled my gun. The barrel wasn't aimed directly at him, however, but rather at the mewling bear cub he was midwifing for.

"Why are you threatening—oh..." he said, breaking off. "Of course. This is your sworn enemy. I'm not surprised that you recognize him. There is no being in the provinces that hates you more than this one."

That made me squint a little. "I do believe... yes, I'm sure of it. Is that Squanto? Is that *really* Squanto?"

"Yes, yes," the Mogwa said impatiently. He scuttled toward me, and I have to tell you honestly, it was all I could do not to shoot him square in the brainpan right then and there.

333

Graves was tugging at my elbow. I knew he was worried I'd do it, despite the fact Sateekas was wearing a jingling load of body-cameras that were obviously broadcasting every second of the action to his fleet. Those vids, in turn, were all flowing uphill to Mogwa Prime.

Still, I wanted to shoot him—but I didn't. I lowered my weapon instead and kept my idiot's grin pasted on my face.

"What is it, Grand Admiral? Did we catch him? Did he die already from our missiles, or something?"

"No, fool," Sateekas said, glancing back over his several humping shoulders toward Squanto. "He's a copy. We authorize and catalog most of the revivals in the Galaxy, and every legal machine reports back its activities with regularity. This allows us to keep backup data on important creatures. You knew that, didn't you?"

My face was as blank as any sheet of paper had been after a timed test in middle school, but I broke out of that after a few seconds.

"Of course I knew that!" I laughed. "Every kid on Earth knows that. They teach us about Mogwa accomplishments every day. Reciting them was like saying my prayers before—"

"Yes, yes," the Mogwa interrupted impatiently. "In any case, we have access to individuals of interest. We can make a copy at will, although the copy will be out of date. Still, this can often yield good results. We can question this wad of meat then dispose of it. For the Mogwa, this method of extracting information is a critical advantage."

"Ah…" I said, blinking and thinking that over. It seemed kind of strange, but the more I considered it, the more powerful it grew in my mind.

If you were at war with another power or even *considering* going to war, interrogating members of the opposing military faction without them ever knowing you'd done so… wow. That would be an impressive advantage.

Now that he was satisfied I wasn't going to shoot Sateekas out of hand, Graves took a step forward. I noted that he also had his pistol out—he must have had it aimed at my back.

That saddened me a bit. I knew without a doubt that he would have fried me if I'd moved to kill Sateekas, no matter how deserving of death the Mogwa was.

"Grand Admiral," Graves said. "Are you using *all* these revival machines to make more copies like—"

Sateekas shushed him. "Don't worry about it. This prisoner shall suffer the same fate as all the others. There will be no evidence, no trace of our actions."

We blinked at him. Was Sateekas really pulling a move? I hadn't seen that side of him before. He was usually blustery and very straightforward. Maybe the loss of yet another fleet under his command had made him meaner.

"Grand Admiral," I said sternly, "we're here to arrest and execute this prisoner."

Squanto looked alarmed. Sateekas looked pleased. I was supporting his act to put pressure on Squanto.

Graves looked at both of us like we were crazy. He shook his head. "All right. I can see you've got this in hand, McGill. I'm going to go check on the other revivals. Don't do anything stupid."

"Hey!" I called after him as he left, "that's disrespectful, Primus. I'm an admiral now, don't forget!"

He waved a disinterested hand over his shoulder at me.

I turned back to the revival scene. Squanto was coming around. In fact, he was squinting at me. He wore restraints, which I thought was a damned good idea. These bears were small, but they packed quite a wallop when you let one loose.

"Beast of the field," Sateekas said to him. "This is your opportunity to confess your crimes. Your fleet lies broken. Your homeworld will soon be extinguished. However, we can still grant you an easy, honorable death."

"You speak nonsense, Galactic," Squanto said through a translator box.

"Ah," Sateekas said. "A bad grow. Clearly, this creature is mentally deficient. A pity, but we should put it down immediately. McGill?"

Without hesitation and with a very real grin, I parked the barrel of my gun in Squanto's fuzzy face.

"Wait... how can I be here? How is it you have revived me?"

Sateekas shook his head. "Your mind is not current," he said. "You flew out here from Rigel, intent on battle with your betters."

"Yes, yes. I recall that."

"What you might not remember is that you were defeated. The battle was glorious—but brief. All your ships were destroyed."

The bear blinked at us. "How is this possible? Only a moment ago I was on my bridge—"

"Ah!" Sateekas said. "I see the problem. We captured your body scan moments before we destroyed your ship. But the mental backup, the engrams must be backdated. You're describing the situation as it was several hours ago. At this point, things have progressed and come to a conclusion. One that didn't go well for your side."

"Prove these claims," Squanto insisted.

The Mogwa made a farting sound with his mouthparts. "You are not in a position to demand anything. We, in fact, have demands to make of you."

"I will not cooperate in any way. I will—gah!"

He broke off as Sateekas applied a nerve-stimulator to his body. The bear fell back, spastically twitching and arching his back. I felt a little sorry for the bastard—just a little.

"There now," Sateekas said. "A small taste of what is to come."

"Such barbarity," Squanto complained. "It will do you no good. I won't—"

He broke off and began performing a new dance. I was left sickened after a few minutes of this. I didn't like Squanto, but he didn't deserve this kind of treatment.

Coming up with a thought, I dared touch one of the Grand Admiral's limbs. He shuffled around and peered up at me. "What is it, McGill?"

"Uh... are we broadcasting all this?" I asked.

"What do you—?"

336

I touched his harness of cameras. "I mean, what if the enemy is picking up your signals, just the way we picked up theirs?"

The Mogwa considered that. "This could be considered a breach of trust," he admitted.

"No shit. It could also serve to make them mad. To improve their morale and make them fight harder."

"Hmm..." Sateekas said. "You're right, McGill. I'll disconnect."

He touched his harness, and the body-cams stopped glowing. I checked with my tapper, and I saw no emanations coming from him.

In the meantime, Squanto had managed to piss some blood. I don't know how he did it. We're all born out of a revival machine with empty bladders.

Heaving a sigh, I drew my pistol and shot Sateekas in the tapper. One of his six limbs dangled and bled.

Then I shot him dead.

-58-

Sometimes, being a man with a conscience was a terrible burden. A more callous individual could have watched Squanto suffer and laughed about it. Maybe someone like Winslade, or Armel, could let the little bear-like monster be tortured to death, then get recycled only to experience it all again. Each clueless, newborn Squanto would relive every moment of agony as if it was a fresh experience.

But I didn't want to be a party to that. I just wasn't that kind of man. After devising a means to stop the abuse, I had to end it. Despite the probable consequences, I'd taken decisive action.

The question was, what now?

Squanto, panting and shivering, sat up slowly on his gurney. He looked down at the carnage on the deck. Then, slowly, he looked up at me.

"You slayed the Mogwa?"

"Yeah…" I admitted.

"Why?"

I struggled to answer, but then I thought I could communicate it in a way he could understand.

"I've been tormented to death and revived over and over myself," I said.

Squanto shrugged. "This explains nothing. Are you claiming to have perfected the technique? Are you planning to use this as a tool to suborn my cooperation? If so—"

"Nah…" I said. "What my experience taught me was to recognize when a creature isn't going to break. I saw that in you—even as I saw it in myself."

Squanto considered. "A compliment of sorts. Unexpected."

I shrugged. "I give credit where credit is due. You lost the battle, just like Sateekas said. Getting you to give away information on where the last of your people might be hiding—well, that's too much to expect."

Squanto blinked. "You imply that much time has passed."

"Only a few months," I said. "After we won the battle at—"

"That's not possible. Right there, I know I am still being deceived. You humans lack the capacity."

I laughed. Long and loud. "Oh, sure, we lack the capacity. That's how we blew up three Skay ships. That's how all these Mogwa vessels lie broken all over the star system, and only the humans are left standing. Didn't any of your people notice this? Didn't you at least suspect we had secret weapons to utilize?"

Squanto looked troubled. He dabbed at his fur where he'd been abused.

"There were… questions," he admitted. "Some thought it odd that the star system was full of broken ships, but only a single human ship had been destroyed."

"Exactly," I told him. "Now, in case you're still doubtful, I'll offer up exhibit B." Here, I pointed at the Mogwa corpse that lay in a slumped heap on the deck between us. "Would I have the balls to kill him if he was still a threat?"

Squanto considered. "It seems irrational. But in my dealings with humans, I've noticed a distinctive… what are you doing?"

Loudly, I reloaded my pistol, despite the fact it still had a full charge. "Finishing things up. Torturing you was a waste of time, but listening to your prattle is even worse."

Slowly, I lifted the gun and pointed it at Squanto.

Now, at this point, the frigging little bear had every reason to believe I would shoot him. He'd just seen me shoot down a Mogwa out of irritation. His eyes, never full of anything but malice, began to look a little desperate.

"Wait," he said. "I can give you information."

"No you can't. We already won. We don't care where you hide your pathetic genetic material and your last younglings. I don't plan to hunt them down and finish them. It's a waste of time. The Mogwa and the Skay are much bigger threats to Earth."

At this point I was way off into the weeds of imagination-land. I was hinting at realities and events that were entirely figments of the fevered McGill mind.

But Squanto didn't know that.

"This is so upsetting," he said. "Can't you at least provide me with some information before I'm executed? It's a tradition with my people to list the crimes of the accused before justice is meted out. Isn't it the same with yours?"

I nodded grudgingly. "Yes, it's the same with Earthmen."

"Well then, tell me what's happened. There has been mention of my homeworld, of—"

"Yeah," I said. "The Clavers rebelled, see. They saw the moment was right, and they struck."

"How is this possible?"

I shrugged. "They're mercenaries. After you lost your fleet, you didn't look viable to them. So, they sold out to Earth. You were using them as guards at your more vital systems, weren't you?"

"Yes, but—"

"Well, they shut down your planetary shield. Just as we were experimenting with doing back on the space station. You remember, that's where you and I most recently met."

Squanto's eyes were sliding back and forth. I knew he was thinking hard, studying the deck.

"This allowed your ships to get to Rigel after destroying our fleet. It is possible—but I need proof."

"What for?" I asked, laughing and playing with my gun. "I'm done with you. This was a totally wasted effort. You don't know anything I'm interested in hearing."

I grabbed one of his feet and dragged him close. Squanto skidded to the edge of his gurney. His feet dangled, and the claws worked at the air.

"I am useful," he insisted. "I know secrets about the Galactics—about the Mogwa and the Skay. Let me tell you of them, and you'll be at an advantage when they come back here for revenge."

I appeared to consider his words disinterestedly. Eventually, after he'd done some more squalling, I let him explain.

"Their stardust hulls *can* be penetrated," he said. "Nearly half our fleet had this capacity."

Blinking a few times and thinking that over, I nodded. "That's why half your fleet hung back when they came to attack, isn't it?" I asked. "The rear group must have had the armor-piercing weapons."

"Exactly. It was predicted that we didn't need to endanger our armor-piercing cruisers. We let them drift to the rear of the formation and separate."

I grinned at him. "Bad tactics to divide your forces."

"The Earth fleet should have been easily defeated by half our fleet. I can't imagine why the battle didn't play out—"

"That's your problem, right there. You Rigel pukes have no imagination."

It was more than just another insult. I actually meant they had no imagination. I think that's what made them gullible to my bullshit. They just weren't used to complex lies that were woven together with partial truths. They were suspicious and mean-spirited, sure. But anyone could bamboozle them if they're good at it—and I was one of the best.

"In any case, there you have it," Squanto said. "We have technology that can be explained and emulated. All you have to do is show me one of our wrecks, maybe one that has the weapons systems largely intact."

"Uh-huh," I said, thinking that over. The truth was, if I hadn't been lying about almost everything I'd told this vicious little bear, his help in working with armor-piercing weapons would be a big bonus.

But as it was, I was running out of time... and so was Squanto.

A rattling came at the sealed door. An eye popped up to peer inside. It was some bio, and she looked angry and baffled. I'd made sure the door was locked after Graves left. She rattled the door again, flipped me off, and left—but I knew she'd be back soon. Then they'd see the mess on the floor named Sateekas, and the game was about over with for James McGill.

"Looks like our time is about up," I told Squanto.

"And what is your evaluation of my proposal, human?"

"Huh? Oh... that's a fine idea, Squanto. But you see, I'm short for time, and our scientists will probably be able to figure your weapons out for themselves now that we know what to look for."

"What? Such duplicity! Why should I have expected anything else from McGill? Perhaps if I explained the basic concepts of a deal: I offered help, and I delivered. You must now honor—"

"Nope. Not good enough." I grabbed his foot again and hauled him off the gurney. He landed on his feet and stood swaying and growling. Despite being only a meter tall, I knew he would have put up a good fight if he hadn't been manacled.

"Honorless barbarian!" he complained. "Lying creature without spirit, without genitalia, without—"

I backed-handed him one, and he snapped at me. Those teeth missed me by a whisker, and the snapping force of his attempted bite gave me an idea.

"Quiet down, bear," I told him sternly. "Listen, maybe you *can* do something useful. How about you become my pet?"

"What?"

"You heard me. I'll give you a collar and a box to sleep in. You sit at my side during parties—but I don't want you to talk too much. That would ruin it. Just let me and my guests pat you on the head now and then. That's sure to impress the ladies."

I wasn't good at reading alien facial expressions, but I'd wager a stack of credits as tall as I was that Squanto didn't like my idea. His black lips curled back and yellowy fangs were revealed.

342

"Maybe you could wear a funny hat," I mused further. "That's it! I'll let you go on living if you agree to wear a collar, a leash, and a funny hat. I'll teach you a few tricks, and you'll have to let the ladies pet your head like this."

Reaching out, I patted him on the head like a dog.

Now, no matter what you may think, my mama didn't raise a fool. I knew I was pissing off old Squanto something fierce— in fact, I was counting on it.

Snap!

He did it, quick and neat as you please. One second I was thumping my palm on his fuzzy skull, right between his rounded high-standing ears, and the next moment two of my fingers were in his mouth. The stumps on my hand showed blood and gray-white bone.

Blam! My pistol, which had been in my other hand, went off. I shot him between the eyes, and he slumped down dead. Gingerly, while cursing up a blue-streak, I dug my loose fingers out of his mouth and moved to the door.

Right about then it opened. Two burly orderlies stared at me, but their angry faces changed to dismay and even a touch of horror at the scene they witnessed.

"He did it..." I said, gasping and holding my bloody, severed fingers as evidence. "That crazy bear—Sateekas should never have revived him. They're strong you know. Real strong. He got hold of a weapon and shot Sateekas. We struggled, and he took my fingers off—but I got my gun back."

With a pain-filled grin, I showed them the pistol and the fingers.

"Either of you boys got a flesh-printer handy?" I asked as they rushed past me to check on Satcckas. "I need to reattach these, pronto."

343

When Graves caught up with me again, I'd almost made it back to the bridge.

"McGill!" he shouted. "Halt!"

I waved some bandaged and cell-bonded fingers at him over my shoulder. "No time for chit-chat, Primus," I said. "I've got a battle to run."

"No you don't, Centurion," he said seriously. Something in his voice made me stop marching along. I turned back slowly to face him.

As I'd expected, he had a gun aimed up at my nostrils.

"Mutiny?" I asked. "Have you forgotten I'm an admiral now?"

Graves shook his head. "No longer. You killed Sateekas, so we're back to Earth ranks and Earth rules again."

I blinked at that. The truth hit me, and I heaved a sigh. "Damn. I kind of liked being brass. It sure didn't last long."

"If you like breathing, you'll start explaining yourself."

"Uh… maybe it would help if you told me what you think you know first."

Graves' eyes were slits. His pistol was aimed at me with a perfectly steady hand. I could tell he wanted to shoot me now and ask questions later, but I kept on grinning and hoping he'd listen a little first.

At last, he lowered his gun with a jerk and a sigh. "I know I left you with a Mogwa Grand Admiral and an enemy prisoner. Ten minutes later, everyone is dead except for you, and your fingers are in some bear's teeth."

"Yeah... that's pretty accurate." I quickly gave him the cock-and-bull story that I'd given the bio-people. He seemed reluctant to buy it.

"But why did you get your gun close enough for him to grab it? And your fingers...?"

"Well..." I said, looking sheepish. "I suggested he should be a pet for us. You know, like a dog or something. Then I demonstrated what petting and head-scratching was all about... and, well, he kind of lost his temper. I had to put him down in the end."

Graves closed his eyes and shook his head. He lowered his gun. "I should have known it would be something goofy like that. Can't you even keep your wits about you while interrogating a prisoner? Now the Mogwa will blame us for Sateekas' death."

"Not if we revive him real quick," I said, explaining about the tapper I'd blasted.

Graves looked alarmed. "You shot his tapper? Just like that?"

"That's right!" I said proudly.

"I'll put in the revive order for Sateekas immediately," Graves said, working his own tapper. "We'll blame it on the bear."

"Rightfully so!"

After he'd dispatched some detailed orders, he looked back at me thoughtfully. "You mentioned something about getting useful information out of Squanto. What information?"

I told him about the two groups of ships, and the capacity of the rear group to penetrate collapsed stardust hulls. That changed his tune in a hurry.

"Come on, Drusus is waiting for us on the bridge. This might change our plans."

"Uh..." I said, but he had taken off and half-ran ahead of me to the bridge. Sure enough Drusus was there. He eyed me sourly upon my arrival.

"McGill… or should I say *Admiral* McGill?"

"No, no, sir," I assured him. "I'm just plain old McGill again. Don't even thank me for getting us through that tough spot. I don't mind going above and beyond the call whenever I can to serve Earth!"

"Above and beyond…" Drusus mused. "Yes, that is an apt description. You killed the Mogwa again, I understand."

There was a chorus of gasps from the bridge crew. Apparently they weren't up-to-date on all the goings-on down on Blue Deck. What really surprised me, however, was that Drusus would bring up my questionable past in this area. He usually tried to cover it up.

"Uh… well sir, there was a mighty unfortunate accident down on Blue Deck. Those bio people made a critical error, endangering Sateekas without cause. But the perpetrator has paid for his sins, let me assure you of that much."

"The next question is: who will pay for yours, McGill?"

I didn't like this line of questioning one bit. Drusus seemed to be in a really bad mood. It was about then, as I puzzled over his responses, that I remembered the circumstances of our last interactions.

Drusus had been arrested, humiliated, and dragged from the bridge. Then I'd been put in his place by Sateekas. Maybe that was the reason he was moody today.

Deciding that a change of topic might defuse the situation, I pointed at the approaching two lines of enemy ships. There sure did seem to be a lot of them—but I ignored that and grinned at Drusus.

"Hey, you know what? I learned why they did that. Why they formed up two lines to attack us, splitting their force."

Drusus frowned. Maybe he'd been about to order me thrown into the brig like he had been. But my statement distracted him enough to get him to listen.

"Why, McGill? Why did they do that?"

I told him in detail how they had weapons in the rear ships that could penetrate the collapsed-matter hulls the Galactics liked to use. He listened closely, but he didn't seem too excited.

"They have tech we've only dreamt of…" he said. "That indicates we're going to be outclassed as well as outnumbered in the coming battle."

"Maybe so… but I've got an idea."

Drusus waved his fingers at me in irritation. "It will have to wait. We're making our final preparations to meet Rigel's fleet head-on."

"But sir—"

"If you want to be part of this battle, McGill, head down to Gray Deck. Suit-up and prepare to board the enemy."

"That's a great idea, sir. That's exactly what I'll do—but make sure our boarders hit the second line of ships. The rear line, sir."

Drusus had pretty much dismissed me in his mind, I could tell. He'd taken a step toward the battle screens and the big holotank, his eyes looking right past me.

"McGill, you had your shot," Graves said. "Come on, we'll head down—"

"Why?" Drusus asked, turning to face me. "Why hit the rear line?"

"Because the bears don't want us to. That's why they let those ships fall back, see? They're protecting them. They consider the front line expendable."

Drusus glanced back at the screens. "I'll consider it. Now, go suit up."

That was it. That was all the reassurance I got. Graves had one gauntlet on my arm, and I let him drag me off the bridge.

-60-

Not twenty minutes later, I found myself ready to launch into the blue again. We all stood on Gray Deck, with our teleport rigs cinched up to our gonads and our weapons loaded. To my happy surprise, we'd been issued high-powered shotguns designed to penetrate Rigellian personal armor suits. Bear armor was very tough, but accelerated blasts of depleted uranium pellets had been tested and approved for the job. You just had to get in close enough to nail one of the little friggers.

"Listen up!" Graves called out. "We're aboard *Berlin*, not *Legate*, but this ship can launch a teleport assault wave the same as any other. 3rd Cohort has been given the honor of participating in this operation from the deck of Earth's flagship."

There was some ragged cheering in the ranks, but I thought it was tepid. We all knew the odds—it was doubtful anyone would survive this attack, whether it was successful or not.

"Frigging suicide," Harris grumbled nearby. "We're nothing but a pack of lemmings running off a cliff!"

I didn't argue with him, partly because he was right, but mostly because I wanted to hear the rest of the briefing.

"There has been a last minute change of plans for this cohort," Graves continued, and I'd swear on a stack of bibles that he cast an evil glance in my direction as he spoke. "We're

348

not going to attack the front-line ships. We're going further. We'll strike the rear rank instead."

"Say what?" Harris demanded. "Has Drusus gone crazy? The missiles with the EMPs won't even hit the rear line! We'll splatter like balloons full of paint!"

"Red paint," Leeson added unhelpfully.

"Shut up," I said. "Both of you."

They shuffled and glared at Graves. At this point, they assumed the brass had ordered this change of plan. I quickly decided not to enlighten them as to the identity of the real culprit.

I, of course, was the mastermind behind this odd change. I wasn't happy about the new plan, however, as Drusus hadn't embraced my thoughts fully. He hadn't altered the course of our missiles to miss the enemy front line, nor had he sent another barrage. He'd just decided to throw my personal cohort—and my loud-mouthed ass, I might add—directly at the rear rank.

Despite all rumors to the contrary, I'm not mentally challenged enough to believe this was all some kind of accident. Drusus had decided that if I wanted to participate in a mad scheme, I was free to do so—as long as I personally led the charge.

Forcing my gloves to hammer against one another, I managed to get my unit to produce a scattered applause that died out quickly.

Leeson sidled up to me. "They're screwing us in particular, aren't they McGill?"

"Seems like it," I admitted.

"Did you get Drusus' daughter pregnant or something?"

"He has a daughter?" I asked with sudden interest.

Leeson rolled his eyes at me and shook his head, but he also shut the hell up. My ruse had worked: he asked no more questions about the origins of this brewing disaster.

"...as a direct result," Graves continued, showing a bunch of green and red contacts approaching each other on the forward bulkhead, "we'll launch last, waiting for the first line of attack to commence in... eight minutes."

349

What followed was the longest eight minutes of my day. The two opposing fleets crept toward one another on the screens, moving one pixel at a time every second or so. At the six minute mark, the enemy fleet fired a wave of missiles at us. The missiles approached—but they exploded way too soon.

"Look at that!" Harris shouted. "They screwed up! Those missiles are nowhere near our ships!"

"They aren't aiming for our ships," Leeson said.

We watched, and it turned out Leeson was right. The missiles created a mass of particles and radiation right in front of our wave of attacking missiles. They couldn't hope to hit our birds directly, as that was hard to do at the kind of speeds we were talking about, but they did manage to take out hundreds of them by creating a field of debris and gasses.

Graves stepped into view again as this development unfolded. "The enemy has just destroyed sixty percent of our missiles at a safe distance from their fleet. Most of them will do no damage. The good news is, we're very close to effective EMP range…"

We watched for about two more tense minutes. At that point, the enemy launched another, even bigger wave of missiles.

"Shit, our birds are never going to make it," Harris complained.

I was clenching my teeth, and squinching my eyes almost shut, I don't mind telling you.

Then, something happened. Bright flashes expanded all along the line.

"Our birds are going off," Graves said calmly. "Yes, that's confirmed. They reached their effective EMP range. A wave of electromagnetic energy should take down the enemy shields momentarily."

A confused but hopeful cheer went up. Then, as the situation clarified, the cheering grew stronger.

"It's confirmed," Graves said, "the frontline shields are down. Our sister ships are launching their teleporters. Victrix, Solstice… even the nine remaining cohorts of Varus. Yes, they're all away. The boarding effort has begun."

"Did you see that?" Harris called out excitedly. "Those damned Fleet pilots are earning their pay today, by damn. They're fancy-boys, every last one of them, but you've got to hand it to the techs when something works right!"

I felt a surge of pride. Even if we were doomed to slam into the forward shields of that second wave of more advanced ships, the Rigellian crews were suffering right now. They had to be.

"Can you imagine the chaos aboard those ships?" Leeson laughed. "Those fuzzy fuckers are eating both barrels on their own bridge, I bet. Wish I was there."

"You will be soon enough," I promised him.

He glanced at me with doubt in his eyes, but he nodded. He was willing to entertain the idea that we'd be successful too—but he didn't really buy it.

That was all I could ask for, as I had no trust at all in the outcome of our cohort's attack. It seemed like a doomed folly to me.

Soon, our ships reached long range, and our cannons began to rock the deck.

"What's wrong with the enemy line?" Harris asked. "They look drunk."

"Must be our men," I said. "They're tearing it up."

Cheering broke out again all around us. It sounded like real cheering now, not the kind men put up when they're trying to build up their confidence.

Enemy cruisers, battleships and destroyers sagged and listed off course. Six of them blew up—then two more crashed into one another.

"It looks like the gambit has paid off," Graves said with his usual lack of passion. "They aren't even firing back."

Our ships began pounding the enemy fleet. It was wonderful to see—and terrible. Because as each ship transformed into a colorful gush of plasma and debris, I knew everyone aboard that vessel had died. Both their men, and ours.

"Heads-up!" Harris shouted, pointing. "Look back there, at the rear line!"

I did look, and for just a split-second, I thought maybe I'd see Squanto and his captains falter. I dared hope that they'd become fearful of our tactics, and they'd turn to run.

But that wasn't what was happening. Instead, they rolled forward, forming a wedge-formation. They still had as many ships as we did, and they weren't running. They were attacking with clear determination.

"Ready-up!" Graves ordered. "Visors down, run down your final checklist. Make sure everything is green, then jump on my command."

We hugged our heavy guns to our breastplates and blinked our eyes hard to clear them. Every visor snapped down. Every ammo pouch was sealed and resealed.

"Shit, shit, shit, shit…" I heard Harris say quietly on officers' chat, his breath blowing over his mic.

Graves lifted his arm, and we all watched, knowing that when it came down again, it would be like the falling of a guillotine blade. We'd all launch in that single instant, come Hell or high water.

"Wait," Graves said, frowning down at his other arm, where his tapper flashed. "I'm getting a stand-down order."

"Praise the Lord," Leeson sighed.

"We're to wait for Drusus' direct order to launch. Standby."

"Shit…" Harris repeated one more time.

Even Adjunct Barton spoke up: "Centurion? Are we going or not?"

"We're going," I assured her. "Stand ready. Don't even blink."

Every ship in Earth's Fleet, having demolished the first line of the enemy, angled its nose upward a little to clear the debris field. We kept our line formation, and we made ready to face the approaching second wave of ships.

Cannons fired on both sides simultaneously this time. We watched as the projectiles, invisible except for the computer-guesswork on the display, approached both fleets. It was hard not to feel your balls crawl up into your guts at moments like this.

If we'd been crewmen, at least we could have been at our battle stations doing something when the moment of truth came. As infantry, we were spam in a can. Victims waiting to learn of their fates.

All of a sudden, a cruiser near *Berlin* blossomed into a brief globe of flame. Then six more of our ships did the same, all along our line.

"They're punching right through our shields," Harris said. "You knew about this, didn't you McGill? That they could penetrate anything with that rear rank of ships? I heard about that—don't think that I didn't hear."

He said this with an accusatory voice, and he eyed me with what could only be called hate. Harris was a serial messenger-shooter.

"At least we put the hurt on before we got stomped," Leeson said. "Our troops did that part right."

I stopped listening to both of them about then. It didn't really matter what a man's last words were, did it? Did anyone ever care afterward?

-61-

Graves, who'd kept his arm high now for several full minutes, finally let that tireless limb fall.

"Go, go, GO!" he roared, and we scrambled to obey, activating our jump-sequences.

All over Gray Deck, a thousand deep blue pulses began. Soon the throbbing lights flared bright. Over and over, rippling with such rapidity that the eye was dazzled, men blinked out.

Then came my turn, and *Berlin* was gone. I was gone.

Teleporting, even over short distances, is essentially an exercise in temporary nonexistence. Oddly, you maintained a sense of consciousness during these jumps. You could *feel* the time and the millions of kilometers passing by at super-light speeds.

The sensation wasn't a pleasant one. It was like being broken down into pixels, then packets, then being transferred over radio waves to another location where you were hastily reassembled.

Staggering a step, I found myself whole again. My eyes, wide as they could be, swept the scene.

I'd half-expected to briefly glimpse a rushing warship that slammed into me. Or, maybe I'd be burnt to a cinder in its hellish exhaust.

To my surprise, neither of these circumstances prevailed. Instead, I stood on a deck of sorts, with my helmet...

I tried to move my head, but I couldn't. Something had me. Something was gripping my helmet.

Cursing and drawing my combat dagger, I slashed above me—and drew a long silvery line in the metal ceiling.

I almost laughed. My helmet had fused with the roof of the compartment I was in. I should have thought of this. I should have ducked low—we all should have.

Rigellians are only about a meter tall. A two-meter high ceiling—my height—was excessive.

Working at the neck, I unsnapped my helmet and pulled my head downward—only to have it stop short.

"Ow!"

My hair was stuck in the ceiling, too. I'd been lucky to escape with my scalp. If I hadn't been crouching a little, with bent knees…

But that didn't matter. I had to get free. I was helpless if any enemy found me now. I steeled myself, then pulled down, hard. My neck muscles and my body's weight did the work. My hair was ripped out—or at least a third of it.

Cursing and bleeding from my scalp, I stood free and looked around with my shotgun at the ready.

The first figured I saw come my way almost got a face-full of pellets—but then I realized it was Leeson.

"Adjunct," I said. "Status report?"

"I don't know shit. We're on radio silence, remember? So as not to give away our positions aboard the enemy vessel?"

He was looking at me funny. I wiped blood from my face, but it trickled into my eyes anyway.

"I'm fine," I said. "My helmet merged up with the roof, that's all."

Leeson laughed. "Didn't your mamma tell you that you were too damned tall?"

"She did, as a matter of fact. Move out."

We left the compartment that some computer algorithm had found for me to land. It was a storeroom, by the looks of it, crammed with equipment.

Walking out into the passage beyond, I had to hunker down more. My head was grazing the roof. Leeson, however, could walk without a problem.

"Take point," I said. "I have to crouch."

He did so, and we gathered troops as we went. We were down on the lower decks of the target ship. I guess the software had favored these less populated regions for a boarding party.

One full unit. That's all I had. The rest of the cohort had been spread out over ten other ships just like this one.

My hundred and twenty-odd men were stacked against the crew of whatever ship we'd invaded. Normally, that would sound like a pretty easy fight—but Rigellians were tough.

After we'd managed to round up about half my unit, the first contact was made. Gunfire exploded in the passages ahead. Smoke rolled along the ceiling.

"Got him!" called an eager voice.

I rushed to the scene. An unarmed sailor had been blown apart by one of our regulars. Putting my hands on the boy, I wanted to murder him for a second—but I relented.

"It's on," I said. "They had to have heard that, or at least their computer must have registered the death. They'll arm themselves and resist. Everyone listen-up: we'll have to rush through the decks. Leeson, you take a platoon and hit engineering. Don't let them scuttle the ship. Harris, you come with me. We have to take the bridge."

"On it, Centurion!" Leeson said, gathering up twenty men and heading down deeper into the ship.

Harris followed me at a trot. He was cursing steadily, but he was down for the fight.

We didn't have to wait long. We reached the first stairway upward and met the enemy head-on as they poured down the steel steps to greet us.

Both sides fired indiscriminately. We were armored, and they weren't. That saved a few lives on our side, but not many. They carried heavy guns capable of punching through armor.

Still, we were better equipped and better-trained. We shot them all, shoved all the dead and wounded aside and rolled up to the next deck.

It was some kind of hold, mostly food-stuffs. We killed a few bears as they scrambled out of the mess hall and advanced. Many of them were unarmed, and they surrendered.

There was an ambush on the next level up. It was the crew quarters, by the look of it. Firing over bunks and closing with us to wrestle, the enemy fought like the animals they resembled. We managed to put them all down, but it cost us more good men.

I didn't like the odds. We kept winning, but we kept losing troops. If they had an organized contingent of marines waiting on the bridge—well, surprise only went so far.

After we cleared two more decks, we finally met up with their professionals. We were only one deck below the bridge, by the guesses of the software in my tapper. A full platoon greeted us there. They ambushed us, and blood was everywhere. In the end, we were in close-quarters with knives. I think if they'd had armored suits, they might have won the day.

But they didn't. I wondered only briefly if Rigel marines weren't given armor, or they hadn't managed to put it on before this battle started.

The last push was to take the bridge. That was a bloody mess. Their captain wouldn't surrender, so we had to kill him. He looked like road-kill once he finally slumped into a brown-furred mess laying in a sticky blood-puddle on his command deck.

After a stunned moment, I realized the fight was over. Every bear was dead or had surrendered. Since there weren't any death-timers on our teleportation harnesses, it was possible we'd get out of this alive. The thought had never occurred to me until now.

"Contact the fleet," I ordered. "Tell them we've taken our ship and not to fire on it."

"Uh…" Harris said, "I don't think that message is getting through, sir."

The enemy screens were still displaying the battle going on outside our hull in space. The two fleets had closed and almost merged. There were many dead vessels on both sides. Radiation, explosions—everything was going on outside in the silence of space, and none of it looked good. I couldn't even tell who was winning, but I knew it was bloody on both sides.

357

Leeson had died in Engineering, but his boys had taken control down there despite the loss of his leadership. Barton had died clearing the cargo holds—but again, the bears had been wiped out. They were only crewmen after all.

Harris and I were the last officers aboard, and our unit had suffered about fifty percent casualties along the way.

"Natasha!" I called out. "Get over here, and get to figuring out these consoles!"

Natasha slid out from under the low-slung table-like console I stood over. She stared up at me. She looked tired and slightly injured—but she could still move and think.

"Centurion?" she answered me. "Um… I'm working on this one right now."

"That's good. What's coming at this ship? Are we under friendly fire?"

"Um…" she said, sitting up and fumbling with her equipment. "I've hacked into the main ops panel, but I'm not sure yet… okay, hold on, I've got something. We've got contacts incoming—probably missiles."

"Told ya," Harris said. He stood nearby, unhelpfully glaring at us with his arms crossed. "Drusus doesn't give a shit if we took this ship. He's going to blow it up anyway, and revive us later on when he feels like it—or maybe never."

I ignored him and focused on Natasha. "Girl, you need to get me a line out of this coms system to our fleet, pronto."

"I hear you, Centurion. I'm doing my best."

"Let her work!" Harris said, seeming to change his tune. He hated dying.

I walked away, and I began haranguing my team. We had every surviving tech working on the ship's controls. So far, all we'd managed to do was kill the engines.

"Hey, Centurion!"

It was Carlos. I almost didn't turn around, but finally, I gave him my attention.

"These bear ships don't matter," he told me. "We can't expect to keep any of them. At best, we'll figure out how to turn her guns on the next ship over."

"You're wrong," I told him. "This ship has armor-piercing weapons. Earth needs that tech."

Carlos shook his head like I was some kind of a dreamer. Maybe I really was one, but I always dreamed big, and once in a while it worked out.

"Sir? I think I've got a solid feed to Turov," Natasha said from the next compartment. "She's not happy, but I'll patch you through."

"She *should* be happy," Carlos huffed. "We busted our humps taking this ship."

I shushed him and took up a microphone-looking thing that had actual, honest-to-God *wires* running into the ship's console. I hadn't seen a com device with a wire attached to it in recent memory.

"Sir?" I said. "This is James McGill, reporting in. We've captured an enemy heavy cruiser, and we—"

"Shut up, McGill," Turov said. "This is very important. Can we safely cancel the missile barrage targeting your ship? Don't bullshit me on this one, do you have full control of that vessel or not?"

"We're all clear here, sir. No need to blow us up."

Knowing my rep for honesty wasn't stellar when it came to coming up with reasons the brass shouldn't kill me, I used the camera pickup to sweep the bridge. There was nothing to be seen other than dead bears and live humans.

"See? We're on the bridge, and we're in command. This ship is important, sir. I think—"

"Your ship does seem to be intact. That's good—I'll redirect the missiles. But James, the *Berlin* is on fire. We're losing hull integrity, and the ship is dying. We've suffered heavy damage. How much space is available on that vessel of yours?"

"Uh…" I said, looking around with big eyes. "She's probably got room for a thousand crew below-decks, easy. But you'd have to hunch, and we've got a lot of prisoners—"

"We'll deal with the prisoners later. I'm jumping to your ship with our command staff. Stand by."

"Uh… but… sir…?"

Turov was gone. I let the com equipment sag in my hands. My jaw sagged low with it.

"What's wrong, McGill?" Carlos asked. "No nookie tonight?"

Moller slammed her heavy hands onto his shoulders, but I didn't even look at them. I was too stunned for that.

-62-

Turov, Graves, Drusus and about sixty others popped into existence aboard our captured ship a few minutes later. As we'd figured, they came in at the same LZ we did—the lower storage decks.

They rushed up to meet us, weapons upraised. They breathed a sigh of relief to see my friendly, weary unit of troops.

"Set up the gateway posts!" Turov shouted. "Bring everyone across, leave only a skeleton crew on *Berlin*!"

Graves moved forward to push past me, but I grabbed his arm at his bicep. "What's going on, sir? Did we win this or lose it?"

"That depends on your perspective," he said. "We've killed more ships than we've lost—but it wasn't cleanly done. All those battlewagons we've been building over the last decade? They're pretty much gone."

My eyes swung toward Drusus. His mouth was a tight, bloodless line. He looked a little pale. He'd presided over bloody battles in the past, and he never seemed to enjoy them.

Finally, after staring at his surroundings for a few minutes, he turned toward me decisively. "McGill? Have your people managed to get navigational control over this ship yet?"

"Maybe weapons, communications and sensors—but not the engines or helm yet."

He nodded, then turned to Turov. "Have *Berlin* send all her techs over next. And our best damage-control personnel from the crew."

"But sir," she said, "those men are trying to keep *Berlin* from blowing up."

"I'm well-aware. Follow your orders."

Drusus turned back to me. "Lead me to the bridge."

I did so, while Turov and Graves stayed down on the lower decks, coordinating the evacuation of *Berlin* onto this nameless vessel.

It was a weird situation. I recalled that in ancient times, when ships were driven over seas by wind, rather than pushed by fusion jets of hot plasma, ships were often captured by boarders. They sometimes would scuttle their prize, or tow it to back to port. On other occasions, they manned the new ship and took her for their own if their original vessel was too damaged or simply smaller.

Pirates, that's what such men had been called. We were like pirates now, but in space rather than riding on the sweet, salty sea.

"Who have you got working on the electronics, McGill?" Drusus asked.

"Specialist Natasha Elkin, sir. She's the best."

"Excellent. Who else is on her team?"

I thought that over. Kivi was dead, as were the other techs. "She's pretty much all I've got, sir. You only sent a single unit at this cruiser, remember?"

He cursed a blue streak, and I got the feeling he did remember.

"All right," he said when he'd paused to rest his mouth. "Here's what we're going to do: we're taking this ship. She's our new flagship. We're turning her guns on the enemy—from the rear."

"Uh... but sir, that will kind of give away the fact that we've taken her. You'll most likely lose your flagship again when the bears figure it out."

"I know that, McGill... but events have progressed. This war isn't going in our favor. Both fleets are heavily damaged, and we've got to win this battle right here, right now."

I stared at him, and I nodded. "Pushing all our chips into the pot, are we? Well, you can count on me, sir."

"I know I can. Take over managing the bridge. I've got to communicate with our other vessels and do what little coordination I can from here."

Techs began to pour in from the lower decks. Turov had gotten her gateway poles set up and put them to work. The best from *Berlin* rushed into the bridge and Natasha taught them the basics. They went to work, some with a bloody arm hanging or a bad leg—it didn't matter. In these situations, troops sprayed nu-skin all over injuries to stop the bleeding and kept on working. There was, after all, no escape when you were on a spacefaring warship in the middle of a battle.

After maybe ten minutes, we managed to get a decent level of control over the ship. None of the captured bears would help us, I had to give them credit for bravery on that point. Moller had loudly threatened them and then executed six, but they hadn't done anything but growl at us.

Finally, Drusus had put a stop to that. He directed Natasha to take risks, and she did. Using some highly educated guesses, she got basic control over the helm, and we swung the big cruiser around.

"I can't aim the gun turrets independently, sir," she said. "But I can tell where they're aiming, and I can fire them. If we use the helm and get lucky..."

"Do it," Drusus said. "Swing slowly, fire at will. Choose the biggest ship the enemy has nearby."

We swung to starboard, and I watched. So far, the bears were too busy fighting the Earth fleet to have paid attention to our cruiser, which had lost power when we invaded and drifted to the rear of their formation.

"One shot," Drusus said. "That's probably all we'll get. Don't miss, Elkin."

"She won't, sir!" I boom loudly. "She's the finest damned—"

"James, please," Natasha said, so I shut up. Her voice was stressed, her face sweating. She didn't need my cheerleading right now.

Suddenly, without any warning, the cannons boomed. *Damn*, they had a kick! Drusus pitched forward, having not braced himself properly. His chin smacked down on the console, which looked like it was made of granite, and I heard an awful cracking sound.

Groaning, he attempted to pick himself up off the deck. I offered a hand, but he brushed me off.

"Did we hit them?" he hissed out.

"Salvo is away. Eight seconds until impact—or nothing."

Eight seconds is a damnably long time to wait when you really, really want something to happen. But in the end, we weren't disappointed.

One of the biggest of the enemy ships caught our fire right in the fantail. It blew up in a series of chained explosions. I wasn't sure if that was the way the weapons worked, or if parts of the enemy vessel had exploded on their own.

Whatever the case, I war-whooped and a dozen others did the same.

Drusus finally tore his eyes away from the scene and he looked at us. He smiled, and blood ran from both corners of his mouth. I think he'd broken some teeth when he'd caught the console with his chin. But for all of that, he was as happy as I'd seen him in recent memory.

"Turn the ship," he said with his bloody, broken mouth. "Do it again, Elkin. Hammer their rear line with armor-piercing rounds."

That was it, I realized. The reason our warheads had smashed through the ship's armor and ran through it like shit through a goose—we'd pierced their vessel cleanly, and they'd angled all their shielding forward to protect themselves from the Earth fleet ahead.

Natasha worked the controls. We swung back the other way with sickening force. This time, Drusus braced himself properly. He had both hands planted on the console, fingers spread wide.

The big ship bucked again, and another deadly salvo sped toward our enemy's flank.

-63-

Our attack on the rear of the enemy fleet broke them. After taking heavy, heavy losses, then getting kicked in the ass, Squanto seemed to think it was best to cut and run.

We watched in amazement as his fleet all went to warp together and flashed away. They left behind about sixty odd Earth ships, most of them damaged, and a lot of drifting debris.

We searched the wreckage for hours, but there were precious few survivors. This local patch of space was so full of radiation and fragments of flying metal, even those who'd gotten away from their ship on lifepods had usually died before they escaped the battle zone.

Taking the opportunity later on the bridge, I shook Drusus' hand and slapped him on the back. He looked startled and bemused.

"We whupped them good, Praetor!" I told him happily.

"That we did, McGill. Unfortunately, it was a pyrrhic victory."

"Huh?"

"Over two thousand years ago, King Pyrrhus defeated the Romans in a great battle. Unfortunately, he lost most of his army doing it. Ever since, they've called such costly conflicts 'pyrrhic victories'."

"Uh-huh… but with all due respect, sir, I have to disagree. We won this fight fair and square. We even managed to capture a few of their best ships."

Drusus nodded, and he paced the deck. He always had been a worrier and an over-thinker. I guess that just came with the territory of being top brass.

"That's all true," Drusus said, still pacing. "But if Rigel, like the Romans, have another hundred ships back home, they'll be able to deploy them and wipe us out. We have to head home immediately, as soon as we can get what's left of the fleet underway."

"Agreed sir, agreed. But look at things from their point of view. What if we had more ships at home? Couldn't we press this advantage and make a stab at their home world, finishing them off? I can guarantee you they're thinking the same thing we are."

Drusus chewed on that. "Yes. You're probably right. But we can't take the chance. We have to head home."

"And so do they."

He smiled briefly, a flickering thing that soon died. "You're right," he said with a sigh. "There's a lot of pressure when your every decision might become Earth's epitaph. They'll probably rush home, just as we're going to do. Both sides will build up again, squatting in our home camps. We'll be back to square one."

"Not so!" I assured him. "We won this one. We surprised them with our strength. Did you know that Squanto figured he didn't even need the second half of his fleet to beat us? He thought he could do it with one hand tied behind his back. We gave him a schooling!"

Drusus looked at me sharply. "How do you know what Squanto was planning?"

"Uh..." I said, thinking of all the shenanigans that had gone on down on Blue Deck, including the most recent and untimely demise of Sateekas. "Just an educated guess... He held back half his ships, and they had the armor-piercing cannons."

He eyed me for a second longer, then dropped his gaze. "Right. Well then, I thank you for your service. You went above and beyond. Your most recent examples of conduct unbecoming an officer are hereby forgiven."

"Hot damn!" I shouted. "*All* of them?"

Again, he gave me that leery eye. At last he sighed and shook his head. "Sure. Why not? Now, get off my new bridge, Centurion. I've seen enough of you for one campaign."

I hustled away, knowing that it was best to get while the getting was good.

* * *

For several long days, we patched and repaired ships. The vessels that were beyond saving we scuttled. Then we took the whole remaining mess into hyperspace, and our battered fleet limped toward home.

We didn't make it all the way there before I was summoned back to the bridge. I got there and found Drusus, white-faced, was gazing up at a projected, super-sized Mogwa.

The worse news was that I knew the Mogwa in question. He was none other than Sateekas, Grand Admiral of Battle Fleet 921. He was using a deep-link all the way from Mogwa Prime to talk to us.

Unfortunately, he looked kind of pissed.

"There's the creature," he said, his malevolent eyes fixing on me. "There's nowhere for you to hide, McGill. It's now time for you and your lying masters to face your fates with dignity."

Upon hearing these fateful words, anyone else I knew would have felt their guts turn to jelly. After all, I was almost certainly guilty of whatever crime he was referring to—and a lot more. But fortunately, I'm built of sterner stuff than most.

"What seems to be the problem, Grand Admiral?" I asked in a spritely tone. "Maybe you need an update, sir. We destroyed the Skay trio and the fleet from Rigel. Were there some other ships in the area we didn't get around to?"

Sateekas ruffled his lobes. "Boasting? You dare so much? True, one of the Skay—the smallest of them, I might add—did succumb to your sabotage. After that, you managed to crash your fleet into Rigel's own with such vigor both were broken like the brittle membrane enclosing a youngling's birth-pod. Other than these two dubious—"

"Grand Admiral," Drusus interrupted. "I think what McGill was trying to say is that we did our best, and our performance exceeded every predicted outcome."

Sateekas glared at Drusus now. "You must refrain from addressing me with that vaunted rank," he said. "I am no longer a grand admiral. I command no ships. I doubt I ever will again."

Right then and there, I knew what was bugging Sateekas. He'd always been a fleet man. A creature that was only happy when commanding a ship in the darkness of deep space. Now however, he'd managed to lose what had to be his third fleet of warships. By all logic, I doubted he'd ever be trusted by the Mogwa High Command to pilot a space-tug.

"Uh…" I said. "That's real sad, sir. Maybe we can help you with that."

Sateekas cocked his head a little. Was he picking up human mannerisms? It could be, as he'd been out here in Province 921 often enough.

"Absurd," he said. "No one back home on Trantor knows what a human is, much less cares for whatever it is you may say while vouching for me."

"Oh… right. That wasn't what I meant, sir. I was suggesting that Earth will rebuild her fleet. And when she does, she might need a grand admiral. You are, after all, in command of this province."

To my right side, Drusus became agitated. It was like he was having a muscle spasm of some kind. I tried not to look at his shocked stares and twitching fingers, because I found that sort of thing distracting under the best of circumstances.

"An intriguing offer…" Sateekas admitted. "I will consider it. However, this isn't the reason I'm calling. I am contacting you to ask about the odd circumstances of my most recent death."

That gave me a little jolt in the brain-pan. I'd almost forgotten that I'd shot him dead before the battle had broken out, what with the excitement of combat and all. Apparently, he wasn't completely in the dark. He knew I had been around, and that the death had been an odd one.

368

"Oh, that!" I said loudly. "Let me explain, sir." I shook my head and laughed.

"What's amusing you, creature?"

"I'm sorry sir, but the whole thing is kind of funny. You see, that little fuzzy bastard Squanto almost got me, too. He took my fingers off with a nasty bite."

I had prepared for this possible moment, and I shared a few photos I'd staged with Squanto and my severed fingers.

Off to my right side, once again, Drusus was putting on some kind of commotion. I wasn't sure what he was carrying on about, but I sure as hell wished he'd cut it out. I needed to concentrate right now.

My lie was getting more and more elaborate. You didn't just play with that kind of thing. You had to work it like a blob of clay on a pottery wheel, shaping and molding it gently until it turned into a vase or something in the end. You couldn't just go and slap it around. If you did, the whole thing was likely to blow up in your face.

"How did the barbarian arm itself?" Sateekas demanded.

"These bears are very resourceful. When you took my gun and aimed it at him, threatening his life, he—"

"Are you saying it was my fault?" Sateekas asked, his voice rising dangerously.

"Not at all, sir. He bit your hand or foot-thing—whatever you call your appendages—and then grabbed the gun from you."

Sateekas squinted at me. "There is some evidence to support this farcical tale. My tapper was damaged during transmission—that's what the forensics indicate."

I felt a tickling line of sweat form under my arms. The Mogwa had some kind of forensics to work on tappers? That was just like these slimy aliens. It figured they had a deciphering scheme that could work on a corpse's last memories like a damaged black box on a crashed plane.

"Uh... that's real good then, sir," I said, keeping up the happy act. "Well, to make a long story short, Squanto bit us both and managed to kill you."

"Why would you make a long story shorter?" Sateekas demanded. "I seek the full truth."

369

"Of course you do, your Highness! Of course! But my intention was to go straight to the most important stuff, and there isn't much more to tell. With great luck, I was able to get the gun back and shoot him before he could do any more evil."

Without speaking, Sateekas examined the bullshit evidence, posed shots and such-like that I presented. The rest of the bridge crew was as silent as the dead while this process went on, no doubt pissing in their pants the whole time.

At last, Sateekas sat back and took a deep breath. "I'm not going to return to 921 for a time," he said. "I'm tired of the darkness, the dying, the humiliation. I—I might retire here on Trantor."

I knew that was a tough choice for failed leaders in Mogwa society. A governor who was an all-powerful ruler on the frontier was a nobody living in a studio apartment on their homeworld. To have Sateekas give up like this... well, I'll tell you it just didn't sit right with me.

"You shouldn't do that, sir," I said. "You should come on back out here and see us again as soon as you've worked out a way to do so. Don't give up on old 921! We've got a lot to offer."

Sateekas seemed unmoved, but flattered. "Your slave-love is uplifting, but it is an ineffective motivator in this case. The matter is closed."

"Thank you, sir!" I did a bow, and I did it poorly. By the time I looked back up, the screen was dark.

Standing proud, I strutted over toward Drusus. He looked a little worse for the wear.

"How'd you like that, sir?" I asked.

"I would vomit if I could," he said. "But my stomach is as hard as a stone."

He proceeded to complain and dress me down for all my assumptions and misstatements. I nodded and looked contrite throughout the tirade, pretending to listen and take it all to heart.

When he'd finished, I was tossed off Gold Deck for good. That was just fine with me, as I knew he'd get over his tummy ache eventually.

370

Realizing I was hungry myself, I began a long search for good food and good company. Both proved hard to come by on a captured Rigellian warship, but I did run into the helmsman girl I'd been standing near for hours on *Legate's* bridge. One thing led to another, and I ended up enjoying the voyage home.

-64-

A few weeks later, we returned to the Solar System and slid into orbit over my favorite blue-white world, Earth. I was pretty happy just to see the place hadn't been bombed or anything. There had been some speculation that Squanto might try to beat us back here to serve up some payback.

But he hadn't. I knew why, too. I'd gotten to know the galaxy's most hateful little fuzz-ball pretty well by this time. He didn't like taking chances, especially not when utter defeat could be in the cards. We had, after all, recently destroyed their planetary shielding system. They were vulnerable, and still probably didn't know if we had more ships than we'd deployed at Clone World.

So, he'd been bound by all the laws of logic to run his furry butt home to defend Rigel. That was just fine with me. I'd had about enough fighting and killing for one year.

As we suited up for shore leave, I did my best to straighten my hair and put on a smile. I'd struck out with the ladies aboard the battered Rigellian ship on the way back, so I was looking forward to meeting some fresh faces at the first space station bar I could find.

When they finally docked and the air began to hiss, equalizing pressure between the space station and the ship, I was standing right there in line to disembark. Before I could rush into the open doorway, however, an arm swept into my path.

Darkly, I looked down at the crewman and almost gave him something to remember me by. Then, the hatch puffed open, and a stream of people came aboard.

Now, this wasn't protocol. Usually, when a ship docked with a station, those who wanted off were let out first, then others who wanted to board were allowed to do so. Docking tubes weren't huge, and there usually wasn't enough room for two full streams of people to share it, going in opposite directions.

Wondering who the VIP was that had been given priority to board before we got off the ship, I watched until I saw three faces. The first face I didn't recognize. He was tall, kind of too pretty for a man, and he had one of those tight-lipped expressionless looks that people always carved into statues. The only thing I knew about him was his origins.

"A Rogue Worlder?" I asked aloud.

People glanced at me, giving me up-down appraisals with their eyes. It was considered rude to mention Rogue World as Earth had, after all, blown up their home planet.

I didn't care. I just wanted to know why he was here, and why he was so important he was keeping me from getting off this ship.

Opening my big mouth to voice these complaints, I froze. My lower jaw sagged down as I caught sight of the second person in line coming out of that docking tube.

She was almost as tall as the first man, and she was of the same genetic background. She was Rogue Worlder, a famous scientist, and her name was Floramel.

"Floramel?" I asked aloud.

Her eyes flicked to me in surprise. "James...?" she said. "Please stand aside. We have work to do. You can socialize later."

My eyebrows shot up, and I managed to close my mouth. Socialize? Did that mean what I hoped it meant? Could it be that good old Floramel had started to miss the craziest man in her life?

Then, bringing up the rear of the trio, I spotted another familiar face. She was the biggest shock of them all.

"Etta?" I demanded. "What are you doing up here, girl?"

Etta was my daughter, and I shouldn't have been surprised to see her, as she worked for Floramel—but I *was* surprised. I hadn't yet wrapped my head around the idea she was all grown up and working as an intern at the labs under Central. That was going to take some getting used to.

"Father?" Etta said, almost as surprised as I was. "You came to greet me and welcome me aboard?"

"I sure as hell did!" I said, and I made a big show of sweeping her up in my arms. "Nothing would keep me from greeting my little girl!"

"Father, you're embarrassing me," she whispered in my ear, but I didn't care. "You smell kind of bad, too."

I set her back down on her feet and beamed at her. "Here to figure out this ship, huh? She's got armor-piercing weapons—have you heard about that? They're supposed to be capable of punching through a stardust hull at close range."

"We've heard, James," Floramel said. "That's why we're here. We must learn all we can as quickly as we can."

"Okay, okay," I said, watching the three of them slide by and vanish into the ship. "I'll buy you dinner later on!" I called after the two women.

They both gave me a backwards glance. Etta looked happy. Floramel looked dubious—but she didn't look scornful. That's a subtle variation on most women's faces, one I was more than familiar with. The translation for me was: I had a chance.

Marching down the docking tube, I found the bar I was seeking and made fast work of a six-pack. After all, I'd been cooped up in a space suit for nearly a month I needed some serious rehydration and cooling off.

Later, I bought myself a shower at a booth in the low-gravity zone, and then I ate a fake-steak that was two fingers thick. A voice spoke behind me when I was half-done with it.

"Eating without us, Dad?"

I turned and invited Etta to the table. I was happy to see she'd come along with Floramel in tow. Standing and pulling out two chairs with a flourish, I seated them both and ordered more steaks.

"I know these come out of a can," I said, "but they taste as good as the real thing to me."

"Genetically," Floramel said, "they're indistinguishable."

Resisting my natural urge to roll my eyes at her, we all began swapping stories. They ate when the food came, and I finished my cooling steak at the same time.

That's about when a fourth person showed up and crashed our little party. It was Galina Turov, and she put her hands on her hips. She cut a fine figure standing over all of us like that.

"Galina," I said happily. "Won't you join us?"

Her eyes slid over Etta and landed on Floramel. "I'm not here for happy hour," she said. "You, Floramel. You're wanted on the gunnery deck. They've found something new."

Floramel stood up like her butt was on fire. She was still chewing, too.

Marching away, she snapped her fingers at Etta. I didn't much like that, but my little girl stood up as well.

"I'm sorry Daddy," she said. "I've got to go."

"Uh..." I said. "That's all right. Figure out that gun, and you'll be able to write your own paycheck around here."

They left, and Turov continued to stand over me.

Not being the overly-curious type, I reached out a big hand and swept up the two extra plates of chow. They'd hardly been touched, as these ladies ate like pecking birds.

"When I heard Floramel had come aboard," Turov said, watching me, "I knew where to find her—in your company."

"Uh-huh..." I said, chewing. "You want a plate? This fake stuff is as good as the real thing, and there's never any gristle."

Galina made a face. "I'm not hungry."

"Aw, come on. Don't be jealous. It's not like you wanted any of my attention on this trip—coming out or going back."

She frowned harder. I kind of expected her to leave in a huff, but she didn't.

Now, my brain usually operates slower than the average, but I was catching onto the fact Galina was upset about something.

"Come on," I said. "Have a bite and tell me what's bothering you."

I kicked out a chair, and she reluctantly sat on it. She still wasn't technically at my table, but after a while, she sighed and scooted up. "Give me that," she said when another round of steak arrived. I'd ordered it with my tapper the moment I saw her come in, but I pretended it was for me.

"I'm gonna starve!" I complained.

"As if," she said, rolling her eyes. She began to eat, and her face shifted. "This really isn't bad. Those Rigellian rations were awful."

A few dozen bites and six drinks later, she finally told me what was on her mind.

"You never visited me," she complained.

"Uh... I've been kind of busy, sir. What with all the fighting and dying and stuff."

She flicked her eyes after Floramel. "That kind of stuff?"

I blew out a puff of air. "She wasn't even with us on this mission!"

Galina sighed. "All right," she said. "Forget about all that. I came here because something you did on this campaign has fired the imagination of our great leader, Drusus."

"What's that?"

"You revived Squanto. You questioned him and killed him again."

"That was Sateekas' idea, actually."

She flapped her hand disinterestedly. "Whatever. Drusus has decided we need information. That we're going to do the same thing."

Now, she had my attention at last. I looked up from my three plates of fake-steak and raise my eyebrows. "You're going to make a back-dated copy of Squanto?"

She flattened her lips and shook her head. "Not him... Winslade."

"What? Really? How would that even work?"

"You killed him back aboard *Legate*, remember? We're going to roll him back to just before that confrontation."

"What the hell for?" I asked.

"Intel, of course. We'll tell him there was an incident, and that we suspect your involvement. That we lost his files throughout the campaign, but we've recovered old ones and printed out a new Winslade."

I thought that over. "Why not just print one and beat on him until he talks?"

She shook her head. "Don't you recall how confident he was? How certain he was of our defeat? He knows things, and any copy will be just as ready to die. No, we have to spy on him. We have work with him until he reveals himself."

Thinking that over, I caught on at last. "And I'm supposed to be his watchdog, is that it?"

"Well, you at least have to be involved. You were there when he died. You know what he said. You must not give away the fact he died long before we reached Clone World as a known traitor."

"Uh-huh..." I said, thinking that over. "Okay. I'm in. Two conditions, though."

"What's that?"

"First off, I think we should revive Centurion Leeza and do the same mind-trick to her."

"Leeza? Armel's concubine? I don't think so."

Frowning, I recalled my talk with Leeza before I'd shot her dead. She'd known this moment would come. She'd known that I was her single chance to catch a break and return to our side and leave Armel. She'd given me good intel, and I owed her one. Because of all this, I decided to persist.

"She's a good officer," I said, crossing my arms. "She's better than Winslade, anyway. She indicated to me that she wanted out of Claver's army. If he can accept defectors, can't we?"

Galina looked suspicious. "Did you sleep with her?"

"Never," I said firmly. Seeing right off that she didn't believe me, I appealed to reason. "There never was any time for that, just think about it."

"Okay..." she said, "but we don't have any recent records for her, and..."

377

She broke off as I worked my tapper and transferred the scans I'd gotten from Leeza's tapper the day she died. "I see you've come prepared. What else?"

"Huh?"

"You said there were two conditions. I know that even you can count that high."

"Oh yeah, sure," I said, smiling despite her bad attitude. "The second demand is this: I want you come up to my room tonight for a nightcap."

Turov eyed me like a cat sniffing at a new can of food she wasn't convinced she liked yet. "Are you sure that's what you want?"

"I said as much, didn't I?"

She paused for a time, running her finger over the rim of her wineglass. "All right," she said at last.

With the matter of sleeping arrangements settled, I ate with gusto and tried to keep from grinning too much. My gambit had paid off... or maybe it was the booze. Either way, I was in a pretty good mood.

-65-

A few weeks later, I was demobilized and sent dirt-side. The swamp was stinky the night I got back to Georgia, but I didn't mind. It was home-sweet-home to me.

The only sad thing was that Etta didn't get to come home with me. She was stuck dismantling the advanced weaponry aboard the captured ships. Apparently, she'd become Floramel's sidekick over the last year, even though she was technically just another student. I wasn't sure how I felt about that, but she seemed happy.

I'd always known she'd head off into the sunset someday and leave us behind. It was just the kind of girl she was born to be, I guess.

On the other hand, I'm more of a homebody. After seeing so many worlds and varieties of alien, I was no longer seeking adventure. Often enough, it came to find me.

After a few weeks of easy living, during which Galina visited me twice for some weekend relaxation, I got another kind of visitor entirely.

Mind you, when I first heard the tapping at my door, I assumed it was Galina. Sure, it was midweek and she usually came down in her air car on the weekends, but somehow I expected it was her anyway.

Opening the creaking door of my shack, I wore a pleasant grin of greeting. There was a beer in my hand, and a fan blowing at my back to keep me cool. What more does a man really need, after all?

But when I saw two faces looking back at me, my expression melted into one of confusion and even alarm. The man on the left was familiar enough. A Claver-Prime, the sort I'd recognize anywhere in the galaxy.

Standing at his side was a smaller figure. She was kind of thin and similar in looks to Claver. In fact, she had the hair color and an expression that was... *too* familiar. She wasn't sneering, not exactly, but she looked like she knew what was going on, and that she figured I didn't. I got the feeling that fact amused her somehow.

"Good evening McGill," Claver said. "We're sorry to disturb you on this lovely, hotter-than-hog-sweat Georgia night. I hope you don't mind if we ask for a moment of your time?"

He was being polite—unusually polite for Claver. I don't mind telling you that I was in a state of near-shock to find him at my door. We'd just fought a war on opposite sides, and I'd killed thousands of his brothers.

"Uh..." I said, still slack-jawed and baffled. I wasn't sure if I should draw a gun on them or not, but as they were in a peaceful mood, I decided to hold off on that kind of thing.

The woman turned to Claver and smirked with half her mouth. "You're right. He is kind of slow on the uptake."

"As dumb as hog's fat," Claver agreed. "But he's reasonable, if you stay on good terms with him."

"But we're not on good terms!" I blurted out. "Hell, Claver. You're shit-off crazy to come knocking on my door tonight. I just killed thousands of your brothers. What possible reason could you have for—?"

"Hey, Bigfoot," the woman said. "Listen up for a second, and I'll explain."

She aimed a finger at Claver, while I glowered and lowered my head in anger. She was talking down to me just the way Claver always did.

"This man is Claver-X," she said. "The *different* Claver. You remember him, right? This guy is the one that the rest of the Claver-Primes want to kill. He didn't fight against you on

380

this last campaign. In fact, he's the one who took you to Dark World and showed you what the enemy was building there. Does that ring any bells?"

I blinked once, then twice… then a third time.

At long last, I got it. I got it all. It was as if a river of knowledge had been injected into my sagging brain. Wisdom, light and clarity of thought struck through my surprised, beer-fogged mind.

It was my turn to point at her. "You're Claver's sister-clone! Abigail!"

She smiled. That smile was kind of nice. Kind of happy. I got the feeling she didn't get recognized and greeted with enthusiasm too often.

"That's right," she said. "I heard a rumor, McGill. I've been told that when you heard my broadcast cries for help over the radio you wouldn't give up until you found me."

I nodded, remembering the day. "Too bad I was too late."

"You were years too late," she said, "but at least you tried—not like my brothers. They left me there to rot." Here, she backhanded Claver's chest.

He didn't react, he just watched the two of us and let us talk.

"A damned shame," I said. "Now, maybe you can tell me what you two are doing here on my doorstep tonight?"

Abigail looked up at me again. Her head tilted, and I kind of thought she might have decided she liked me. That wasn't really a surprise. For some reason, throughout my benighted life, cute, smart-ass women had always been attracted to me. This was doubly-true if they were evil—and I was pretty sure Abigail qualified in that department.

Deciding there wasn't going to be a shootout, I invited them inside. I found two fresh beer bottles and put them on the table. Abigail sat gingerly on my stained couch, looking a little concerned about it.

"Don't worry about the couch," I said. "Those stains won't bite. I've sprinkled lots of nanites on them, mind you, but there are some things even they can't clean up."

"That's encouraging."

Claver-X cleared his throat, and we gave him our attention. "We're here because things have changed," he told me, sipping the beer I'd given him.

"How do you mean?"

"There's a civil war on. You know about that, I hope."

"Sure do. The Mogwa and the Skay are fighting over succession to the Emperor's throne, right?"

He nodded. "That's part of it. But things are worse than that. The war has widened, and it now includes most of the Galactic races. The central disagreement is over ascendancy—and bigotry."

"Uh..." I said, unsure what he was talking about. "How so?"

"You've met the Skay, I know you have. Do they seem intellectually competent to you?"

"Are they smart? They sure are. No toaster here on Earth can compare."

He nodded. "They *are* intelligent. Artificially intelligent, certainly, but still sentient. In the past, they had to fight a war or two just to get recognized by the other Galactics."

"I didn't know about that."

"No, of course not. Very little of importance is taught in Earth's schools these days... Let me give you the quick version: the Galactics who were organic in nature originally fought to keep the machine intelligences out of the Empire entirely. After the machine races proved they were strong enough to compete, the organic traditionalists relented and brought them into the club. They accepted the Skay, but they didn't really like them, if you get my drift."

I nodded. The conflict was easy to visualize. If robots on Earth ever got smart, lots of people would prefer to put them down rather than give them tax IDs and voter registration forms. Frankly, I'd probably be one of the chief objectors to robot citizenship.

"Well, the Galactics eventually let the Skay into the club. A few more similar types joined up, and soon the Empire was something like thirty percent machine-brained and seventy percent fleshed—but it doesn't matter. What broke the treaty between these two factions was succession."

"The toasters wanted the throne?" I demanded. "That's insane!"

The clones both glanced at each other. "He's a traditionalist," Abigail said. "We should have expected it."

Claver-X nodded. "Anyway, the meat-type Galactics decided they weren't going to serve a machine Emperor. Not the least of their concerns was the fact that the appointment was for life—and these machines could live forever."

"Okay," I said. "This is all very interesting, but I don't see why you two came all the way out here to meet me and talk about it."

"McGill..." Abigail said, "X here—by the way, I think that's a great name you've coined for him—he told me that you would listen to us. That you, out of all the people on Earth, would give us a few minutes to explain."

"Well... I like to give people a chance. It doesn't always work out, but that's my policy."

"Yes," she continued, "so here's our message: recent events have put Earth in a bad position. The civil war is hot, hotter than ever, and you're on the map now. This province is seen as a battleground between the Mogwa and the Skay. And that's just the beginning, we fear."

She looked at her brother again, and I had to wonder if they had a private thing going on. I hoped not. It gave me the willies just thinking about it.

Originally, the Clavers had sworn off women and offspring on their home planet to keep from splitting apart and fighting about who got what. As long as everyone was a type of Claver, all just clones, it was easy to agree on a goal.

But one day a different clone had been born—this guy right here, Claver-X. He was nicer than most, and he liked women to the point where he broke the contract. He'd made himself a female out of his own DNA—he'd made Abigail.

I didn't know how she'd been revived after I'd found her skeleton years ago. But somehow, Claver-X had managed the trick. Or maybe she was a new copy, grown like the first one from one of his own cells.

Again, I suppressed a shudder. I don't like to be the prejudiced type, but clones who were fooling with their own genetics kind of spooked me.

"What can I do about something going on at the Galactic Core?" I asked. "What can any Earthman do?"

They looked at me again, speculatively. "There might be some things we can do," Abigail said. "But you'll have to get us inside. We need to talk to the important people."

"Uh... you mean like Turov?"

They laughed.

"Not that witch," Claver-X said. "She'd boil us both in oil for fun then revive us and hand us over to whoever paid the most."

I couldn't argue about that. I had feelings for Galina, but I didn't let them fog over the fact that she had certain flaws in her personality.

"Well..." I said, thinking hard. "I might be able to get you to Drusus, but I don't know how much he wants to listen to you."

The two of them smiled. In each case, it was a thin-lipped, cold thing. The same smile on two people at once.

"Drusus will do," Claver-X said. He stood up and made as if to leave.

Abigail frowned at both of us. "Is this a bargain? A deal struck?"

"I guess so," I said.

"But what does McGill want out of it?" she asked. "I don't want some kind of nonspecific favor hanging over me forever."

I understood right away what her problem was. She'd grown up with Clavers, and since they were all merchants, they didn't understand anything other than horse-trading.

Claver-X shook his head. "McGill just wants to do what's best for Earth. Isn't that right, boy?"

"Yep," I agreed. "I don't need any extra credit, or nothing. I can see the problem, and I can see how you might know things that could help. Getting that information into Central could help us all."

Abigail squinted at me. I could tell she didn't know what to make of this overgrown country boy in his shack.

384

She shrugged after a few seconds of scrutiny. Then she stood up, and she offered me her hand. I took her small hand into mine, and we shook. While we touched, she gave me that smile again. The one with a sparkle in the eye.

Her tiny hand squeezed mine twice. It was a small thing, but it was an undeniable signal.

Trying not to let on, I grinned like an idiot and nodded my head. At last, they walked out of the place.

After they were gone, I sat on my couch and gave myself a shake. I felt like I'd dreamed the whole damned thing.

That night, I drank a lot of beer and thought about the future. Winslade and Leeza were coming back to live among us. That was going to be hard to take.

But the thing that occupied my mind at first was closer to home—I could still feel that strange girl's hand in mine, giving me a suggestive squeeze.

Abigail had Claver's tricky mind, disguised in the body of a woman. I could already tell she was going to be a world of trouble. I could almost forgive the rest of the Clavers for having voted her conniving butt off their planet years ago.

Sleep didn't come easily that night. I left my window open, and I could see the stars out there. There was no moon, and in the country darkness, the heavens were a river of light.

To the ancients, our galaxy was a dimly glowing cloud seen on the blackest nights. They didn't know they were looking at billions of suns—but I did.

Out there, inconceivably far away, great fleets were storming worlds like mine. The Galactics were killing billions of sentient aliens, scorching planets, and feverishly building more warships.

Only a starman like me knew this truth. Only my kind looked up at the night sky with dread. We humans were on the fringe of the fringe, living like ants on an island in a vast sea— but we were vulnerable. Just about anyone could come along and stomp us down forever.

The way I figured it, the battle at Clone World had bought us some time. Rigel, the Skay and even the Mogwa couldn't be happy with having lost fleets here. With any luck, they wouldn't want to come back again anytime soon.

I dared to hope our relatively peaceful existence in Province 921 would continue... at least for a few more years.

Books by B. V. Larson:

UNDYING MERCENARIES
Steel World
Dust World
Tech World
Machine World
Death World
Home World
Rogue World
Blood World
Dark World
Storm World
Armor World
Clone World

REBEL FLEET SERIES
Rebel Fleet
Orion Fleet
Alpha Fleet
Earth Fleet

Visit BVLarson.com for more information.

Printed in Great Britain
by Amazon

64995075R00234